Maria Nathusius

Joachim v. Kamern

Diary of a poor young lady

Maria Nathusius

Joachim v. Kamern
Diary of a poor young lady

ISBN/EAN: 9783744795623

Printed in Europe, USA, Canada, Australia, Japan

Cover: Foto ©Andreas Hilbeck / pixelio.de

More available books at **www.hansebooks.com**

COLLECTION

OF

GERMAN AUTHORS.

VOL. 12.

JOACHIM V. KAMERN; DIARY OF A POOR YOUNG LADY.

BY

MARIA NATHUSIUS.

IN ONE VOLUME.

CONTENTS.

JOACHIM VON KAMERN

BY

MARIA NATHUSIUS.

JOACHIM VON KAMERN.

The October sun was shining, bright and warm, on the richly tinted vine: its light fell through the windows of the garden parlour, and was playing on the floor. In the back-ground of the room was reposing a sleeper, very still in his deep peace; in his pale hands he held a myrtle-wreath; on the white cold pillows lay Monthly roses and mignonette and other late children of the autumn.

"No child weeps by his coffin," said Klaus softly, "no sister, no brother either; he is so utterly, utterly lonely." Klaus was standing with Elizabeth his wife at the door of the ante-room; both were faithful servants of the departed. "Now all is over," said Elizabeth with a gentle voice, "The Lord has now received him, and if his life were lonely, it is over, and he is blessed." A carriage drove quickly over the loose sand of the castle-court-yard. "There she comes," said Elizabeth eagerly, and her lips trembled. "She? Really?" asked Klaus. Light, quick steps hastened through the hall, the parlour door was opened, a lady entered, slender and pale, with light hair, dressed all in black. She saw the sleeper, her hands clasped convulsively, she went nearer, laid her cheek on the cold pillow, caressed both the hands, and wept bitterly. "Here I am," she

1*

said softly. Much sorrow lay in the words, — and
without consolation.

Elizabeth, who had withdrawn with Klaus, came
back after a while; she who had been so composed
could not help weeping too, as she gave a letter to the
disconsolate one. His love and kindness reached
beyond his death; he had felt before-hand how hard it
would be to look so anxiously on a dumb mouth and
on closed eyes, without an answer to so many questions, and without consolation in such deep sorrow.
Now the answer was there, and there were words of
comfort.

DEAR THERESA.

You are very dear to my heart; once to the heart
weak with all the pangs of youth, now to the heart
strong in the Lord. Do you weep? Ah yes, when you
think of my sorrows, you will weep, and that is comforting to me at my departure. Look back on your
life; it was bright, gay and deceptive; yes deceptive,
for when seen closely they were only husks of the
heavy servitude which you have undergone. Those
were sorrows to me because I loved you so much. If
you weep now, you will be homesick for the dear
Father's house. Come now — I am going home, and
I long that you should follow me. Here I have given
you up, given you up to the Lord for guidance; that
He may some day give you to me again. And what
have I of consequence to say to you? Go now on to
the road which leads upwards; that is love the Lord
Jesus Christ, love Him so truly with your whole heart,
and your whole soul, that He will love you still more
in return. Oh if you did but know how blessed it is

to love the Lord! What is the world? Not worth a thought, compared with this blessedness. Blessed in spite of every woe; blessed in great loneliness. If I look back on my life, it was hard, very hard; and yet so very lovely, so rich, already a foretaste of heaven. And, if it is any consolation to you, then hear, that my heart still loves you with pangs of love; that I feel lonely, and would gladly have pressed your hand at my departure; and yet nothing fails me of a joyful confidence that the sufferings of all this time are not worthy to be compared with the glory which shall be revealed in us. Weep not for my earthly sorrow. Comfort yourself with my heavenly joy.

And one thing more! If you can spare sorrow to my darling, — do it. You know whom I mean. Yet as the Lord wills. If you wish to hear of my life, Elizabeth has the key of my writing-table: if you shrink from it, she shall burn the papers. O dear Theresa, if I could but spare you sorrows! I can not; but the Lord can, He will. Thou dear Saviour, I pray Thee lead her, be with her with rich grace and love, strength and happiness. Amen.

On the evening of the same day, the dead man was buried. Many followed, and many wept sincere tears. The nearest relations and heirs followed also — three men of different ages, all three dressed in deep mourning. When the mourners had left the church-yard, and the Sexton had closed the vault, one of the three in crape remained behind. He went up and down under the old lindens which stood between the church and the parsonage, and seemed as though he could not tear himself away.

The last beams of the evening sun had vanished from the slate roof of the church tower, stars were appearing in the clear sky. "Yes, they are above and not here," said the young man in his heart, "and now farewell thou dear home, thou dear parsonage, thou church-yard and you gloomy, shady trees. You guard for me my dear sleepers; I go; but your image I take with me in my heart, and everywhere Heaven is over me."

Comforted he left the peaceful church-yard, and went down the lime-avenue to the castle.

"There comes our dear young master Joachim," said Klaus to Elizabeth, who both were sitting in their room.

Klaus talkative about the departed; Elizabeth quiet and thoughtful.

"See now, Elizabeth," continued Klaus, "how like he looks to our late dear master; he looked just like that when he came back from the University, and he has just his temperament, and his mind, and his first name — a pity that he is not a Kamern." "May the Lord prosper him," said Elizabeth sadly. "Amen!" added Klaus and the young man of whom they had just been speaking came in. All three held out the hand in silence. Then the young man said calmly, "I am come to say farewell to you, I am going away to-day." "Away?" asked Klaus and Elizabeth in astonishment. "It is better I should go away soon enough of myself than that they should send me away," answered the interrogated one with a smile. "You? sent away?" exclaimed Klaus violently. "You belong here. Who wishes to send you away?" "Be still, Klaus," said the young man gently. "You know where I belong; my uncle's love has assigned me a lovely place; thither I go and will think of him in gratitude and love. My home here and you all remain dear to my heart. Now let me go to-day, it is moonlight and my mother is expecting me."

"Hear me," interposed Elizabeth again very quietly. "The Count of Olshausen is upstairs with his young gentleman and Madame Theresa and Annie too; tea is just sent up, and you'll go to them as is becoming; be friendly. The gentle-folks must go back to Olshausen; remain here to-day, to-morrow you can go. In a week the will will be opened; then you will come again." "I will go up," said Joachim laughing, "and also be friendly if that is permitted me, but then I must go away to-day because my mother is expecting me." He thereupon bade Klaus to look after his horse, and went up. He did not remain long upstairs, and when, after a friendly leave of the two trusty people, he rode to the gate, Klaus said, "Cousin Alfred cannot have been very friendly. Now God's will be done, but I should like to know what will become of the matter, and what of us and of our troop of children." Elizabeth again had nothing to say to his talkative speech, but Klaus thought he could read from her face that she knew more than he did. She also and not he was appointed to keep all keys and all possession of the house, till the opening of the will. No seal was put on it, and neither the Count of Olshausen nor Joachim Frederic the two nearest male relations of the deceased had anything to say.

Collected Letters and Papers for the Life of Joachim von Kamern.

4th August 1822.

DEAR MOTHER.

I thought of travelling from here, if the Lord will on the 12th, to Luttensen by sea, from thence we could perform the journey in one day with our riding horses. Klaus has been very dissatisfied with this plan since yesterday. He has had a bad dream. The brave youth, though he has studied here for three years with me, is his aunt's foster-son still. In the hope of soon talking to you I have no inclination to write much. Yesterday Landhorst gave me a farewell feast. My heart was very heavy. I part unwillingly from my friends, and yet I am glad to go. One door shuts, another opens; I know the Lord is leading me, my life lies in His hand, and has long been opened before Him. Dear mother, I shall so enjoy living again with you in my dear Kamern; learning from you how I may be faithful in that which the Lord has committed to me. May He help me!

My friend Joseph is not coming with me now; he wishes first to pass his examination, — say that to the dear people at the parsonage. I cannot understand why Joseph cannot reconcile himself to Netty: he always maintains that she cannot forget that she is a noble maiden. She has shown it plainly enough in marrying his brother. I am very fond of Netty and am pleased that she is my aunt, though I do not reckon this marriage a very great proof of her magnanimity. She was no longer young; to stand alone in life is hard, and our dear parson is the most splendid man that she would ever have got. What is my god-child doing? I hope the young fellow can at last talk plainly; only tell him that if he cannot say Uncle Joachim I will bring him no soldiers. Good-bye, dear mother! God protect you and bring us joyfully to each other.

Your faithful son,

JOACHIM.

Enclosure from Klaus to his Aunt.

HIGHLY ESTEEMED AUNT.

According to our reckoning we should be in Kamern again in a week. Would to God we were there! My master wishes to make a piece of the way by sea, but I have had a bad dream, that our ship was wrecked at Olshausen. Do not wonder that the sea is not concerned in it. You know how it is in dreams; it was quite natural. I came happily out of it, but my master perished. See to it, Aunt, whether my Lady cannot fix that we travel by land. Now as God wills; my master is perfectly right, by land or water we are constantly in His hand. I wish to tell you one thing more, I have a moustache. Do not think that I have fancied it; it is natural at my age, and it has grown very much lately. You will also be very much pleased, for I believe that I look much more like my father. That your Elizabeth is with the Lady up there at Olshausen surprizes me; it may be a good school but will not last long, and in your place I would not have let her go up there. Now I commend you to God, dear Aunt, and remain in all esteem and love   Your nephew

KLAUS RIEDERN.

Castle Kamern, 15th August 1822.

DEAR JOSEPH,

In spite of Klaus's evil forebodings, by the Lord's help, we are happily arrived. The reception was, as I had feared, very solemn. Flowers, wreaths and speeches. The old choir-master had practised with the children the hymn "Jesus go before." I do not know why this made such a peculiar impression on me. Though it is not a cheerful reception-song, I thought it beautifully chosen by the old man. In the fulness of happiness and of joy, we should still hear the voice "Rejoice as if you rejoiced not." I sang the hymn in joyful confidence. "Jesus, order Thou my path all my life long." In the evening your people were here, Netty quite like the clergyman's wife. I do not know what you desire in her, to me beside the clever, lively Christian she seems almost too simple, but little Joachim is a great credit to her. He can scarcely speak yet, but he brings out his gibberish with great boldness, and will have you understand him. He has teazed valiantly for the lead soldiers, but with small success. Onnon Ochenanim, said he, and wanted the soldiers with a good right, for he generally puts me off with Onnon Ochen. My mother told me that I had just as much difficulty in learning to speak, and we are both of us very much like our late grandfather. When you see Netty with the child, you will be won by her, in spite of all your dismay. I do not know what the Burger-people always expect to find in the nobles, but I think they are often deceived. But I have not gone on with my narrative in order. Our voyage then was prosperous, very beautiful and splendid; I could plainly see how beautiful my northern home is.

Southern colours may be wanting, but how magnificent the sea is, such deep violet, such light blue, so varied and glittering, bordered with silver, and strewn with stars.

The waves proudly bore the ship along. I stood on the deck to meet the breeze, it was as if my breast must breathe as strongly, and heave boldly, like the element beneath me.

We landed on the green shore of Luttensen and trotted away briskly through beech-woods, meadows and harvest-fields. When we came towards evening to Olshausen, I noticed a certain restlessness in the good Klaus. He asked me whether I should not like to pay a visit to my aunt; I replied I wished to make the first visit with my mother. He knows very well that my longing for it is not great. After some time he said again his aunt had written to him that Miss Theresa was back from Switzerland, and had grown quite tall. I replied she must be old enough for it. At last a light dawned on me, — the good youth wished to see Cousin Elizabeth here. I proposed to him to stay here with the horses, and I would go on foot through the park to Kamern — a good half hour's walk. Yet he did not wish that.

Before the park I got down, in order to go along the somewhat shorter and charming foot-path by the lake. When I came to the trellis-work which separates the flower-garden from the park, I stood still in curiosity. Cousin Theresa is really grown tall — a slender Blonde with the same child-like face: she was playing with a young doe, hid herself behind groups of flowers and then spoke patois to it. I had hidden myself behind the thick junipers, and looked through the trellis, as it were into a fabulous world. I thought

there must be the same loveliness here in the hearts
of men as in the scene before me. But I thought
again dost thou know how it is with the hearts
of men here, and how it will be? The Lord leads us
wonderfully, and makes us all happy with His grace.
I know not how long I had sat behind the juniper, I
was lost in deep thought. Then with very happy
thoughts I went along the foot-path by the lake. The
setting sun shone on the hills and on the tops of the
beeches; long dark shadows lay on the bright green
of the little meadows by the shore. Swans made silver
furrows in the crimson water, and a gentle evening
breeze stirred the high reeds beside me. Hallelujah!
Praise ye the Lord, ye heavens. Praise Him in the
height. Praise Him all His angels. Praise Him all
His host. Praise Him sun and moon. Praise Him all
ye stars of light; mountains and all hills, fruitful trees
and all cedars; beasts and all cattle, creeping things
and fowls of the air. Kings of the earth and all
people; Princes and judges of the earth: young men
and maidens, old men and children should praise the
name of the Lord, for His name alone is high. His
praise reacheth to the earth and heaven. To be able
to sing this is a blessed thing. — I could not help
thinking again of the lovely apparition behind the
trellis. Theresa would not join in the Psalm. She
has been brought up quite differently, in opposition to
the word of God. In early youth she learned to laugh
at the inhabitants of Kamern castle. She will not
have unlearned it by her education in Switzerland.
But I am very glad to have made her acquaintance in
this way, and I can not help wondering at the childishness in her appearance. I have always had a certain

sympathy for this child, who stands to me almost as near as a sister. My father was so fond of both his sisters, they were so near his heart; Aunt at Olshausen still more than Netty. His vivacious and somewhat stormy nature was perhaps not adapted to gain her heart, especially when my uncle always stood between them. Uncle put off the blame chiefly on my mother, so that the two sisters-in-law never became intimate. You know how my mother now with all her love and gentleness, tries to become more intimate with her relations, but has very little success. My aunt is indeed good-natured and friendly when she is with my mother, but her interests in life are too different, and my uncle holds high the banner of the world, and every one who lives with him must do homage to it, and every one who is opposed to him is despised and ridiculed without reserve. My mother proposed to me to-day to make a visit up there. I know not why, I have no inclination for it. I feel as though I must first consider how I shall stand with my relations. Shall I follow your advice or do as is pleasant to me? It will very likely stop short at the latter.

For some time I should like to live quietly with my mother: rest would do me good after the busy days of leave-taking. You ask exactly what my plans are? I have very little to tell you. I mean always to have a great deal to do, and then do not know where to begin. I have already settled in and entered upon my rooms; now I wish to begin with dear Kamern and its inhabitants. I think by and bye the Lord will show me my work. I must send you greetings from Christian, Netty, and your nephew Joachim, and also from Klaus. The good youth has been obliged to give up his moustache. Aunt Braunsen saw in it a sign of a worldly disposition, and when Cousin Elizabeth assured him that she thought his beard did not become him, he willingly gave it up. Farewell, dear friend, the Lord be with you and with

Your friend

JOACHIM.

Letter from Theresa to her school friend in Lausanne. (Not sent.)

Olshausen, 20th August 1822.

I would have written to you long ago if I had known what.

All your dreams about my brilliant life here, about dissipations and adventures are nothing. One day passes as monotonously and tediously as another. I do not say tediously for me, but in your sense. I must confess to you in confidence that I have found out again here all my old pursuits. I put in the ponies, feed the dogs, help the maid make butter and cheese, and eat the people's lard-dumplings. My nature which had become refined with you, must again become accustomed to our rough northern fare: only think! I got a red nose by it; mamma was beside herself and we could make no visits for six days. Visits? You will say, that must be delightful. You are mistaken. That is at present the most tedious part of my life.

Before dinner when mamma does not trouble herself about me, I entertain myself very well in my own way: afterwards the intercourse with the interesting neighbourhood goes on. We have visited them all,

and the return visits have begun, but I assure you it
is no beautiful matter. I could describe much to you,
but I know you desire other things and I know nothing about them. It is nicest at Windfort: there is
a house full of children there. I had a good game
with them last Sunday. The two eldest boys are
twelve and fourteen. We speak such beautiful patois
together, — very different from your conversation. We
played also at robbers and gens d'armes. I defended
an old early French entrenchment in an apple orchard;
I threw unripe apples and attacked the whole army of
children. — One thing I got again. I thought my nose
would have got another shape, it burned like fire, and
mamma was very angry. We have been once to my
aunt's at Kamern. She also came here again. I do
not know why, but always when I am with her I get
on wonderfully. Her eyes are so beautiful and kind:
when I look into them it is as if they attracted me,
and as if I should like to follow. I am resolved never
to make a jest of her. The daughter of her former
lady's maid is my new maid, not altogether such an
abigail as would stand in your estimation.

Fun and pleasure, she does not understand. — She
only pleased mamma, because servants now in the
world are too wicked. She hopes that behind her
pietism at least a tolerable servant is hidden. "She
does not steal," says mamma, "is not too idle, and not
giddy." That she sits by herself every evening, and
every Sunday when it is possible runs off to Cousin
Christian to the church, we must excuse. She naturally tells me much of my aunt; I must confess I
like to hear such accounts. When Cousin Joachim
has made his first visit here, I shall go for once with

Elizabeth to the church, — of course secretly while
mamma is at breakfast and making her toilette.
With Aunt Netty and her pastor, intercourse is broken
off because of the marriage. Cousin Joachim has been
at home a week, and has not been here, and so I cannot go first to Kamern. He would think perhaps that
we are more eager to see him than he to see us.
Papa and mamma are very angry with him; they expected he would scarcely breathe in Kamern, before
he would be on his way here. He has, as papa said
lately, taken quite another tone in these last years.
You must know, my dear child, that Cousin Joachim,
in spite of his youth, is a complete pietist, but, except
that, very loveable. With him your assertion does not
hold good, that it is only people who have done harm
in the world, who embrace pietism at last, in order to
cheat the devil.

Cousin Joachim has always been very discreet.
Elizabeth maintains that he was something quite extraordinary at the University. I should like you to be
with him; I must say I am afraid of him. I must tell
you too as a joke that I have seen Joachim already.
I was playing with my doe's house in the garden,
when he went through by the trellis, and hid himself
behind the bushes. Afterwards I saw him go along
by the lake. I think it was very wrong that he did
not come forward. But as I have said, when he has
been here, I shall go with Elizabeth to church, and
shall also visit Aunt Netty. Remember me to our
Lady Philosopher. I shall write to her next time; this
time I know of nothing to say, but then I hope to have
heard Pastor Frederic's preaching. He is very famous
in this neighbourhood. I like him very much except

that I am very much afraid of him. In September brother Alfred is coming. He has holydays and is coming for more of a visit. I am delighted at it. I have thought a long time, but know of nothing else to say to you. I have a little grey-hound which I feed and am bringing up. I am sewing him a bed too, because it will soon be cold.

Letter from Hortense to Theresa.

Vervenay, 24th August 1822.

MY DEAR FRIEND,

I am now settled into my new home, and the school is happily behind me. Aunt and cousins treat me very kindly, that is to say like a poor orphan. That will all come right. In the winter we are going to Geneva. I maintain what man wishes to do, he can do. I will make my future for myself. Your future, you dear German child, I see already before my eyes. I have permitted myself to draw the following sketch for you — the ideal of a North-German lady. She feeds the cattle, eats lard-dumplings and yellow pease, and will soon belong to the dear neighbourhood. Rely on me, if you live for the winter in such a residence, you will not escape your fate. Your mamma must then have the prudence to choose me as your companion. I would bring life into your world there, and be afraid neither of Cousin Joachim nor of Cousin Pastor. You are not yet quite educated, my child; you are still the little northern prodigy, as Professor Moller says. He was telling lately as a great joke, how he had advised you, at your first lesson on the piano, always to keep the piano free from dust, and how he had caught you the next time, hard at work scouring it, with your sponge fastened to a stick, you were going bravely up and down among the strings. At his just reproaches you made such significant gestures, that he found it necessary to adopt another tone. But, dear child, I must tell you, that I am very curious to see how you are getting on. Pray, invite me. The detestable Lady Philosopher will have written you a long letter of warning, but you are sensible enough to know what a fanatic she is. I love virtue too, and only wish to do you credit as a friend, but what is madness, is madness; she was talking lately of the devil, of good and bad angels; I was your bad angel to lead you astray, but her prayers should defend you. What madness! In your place I would not answer her. She will soon be sent away from the school, because Miss Amelia notices already what a dangerous influence she exercises on childish hearts. Many hang to her like burs; go up to her room with her, to pray and sing. Then she praises the Germans, and makes out the French to be bad. Once for all, dear Theresa, I believe I should be very useful to you, especially if you remain in the country for the winter; so do invite me. I find it very tedious in the world, it is of no use, something must be done. Write soon. I need not assure you how much I love you.

Your

HORTENSE.

From a former Governess of Theresa.

Lausanne, 18th August 1822.

DEAR THERESA,

Your things are packed. I put these lines in with them. I seem as though it were my duty still from a distance to care for you. You are very dear to my heart, and my prayers are very heart-felt wishes for blessings on you. Once more I repeat my parting words — do not correspond with Hortense, do not be fettered by her. In a week I shall leave Lausanne. I am going for the present to my friend in Berne, but long very much for Germany. If you hear of a suitable place, think of me. But it must be a house where I could without hindrance bring up the children in the faith — especially where they do not look only for instruction, but for education also. You know too that French is not my native language. Now, farewell, the Lord preserve you, and take your heart wholly into His gracious keeping.

In faithful love

Your

SOPHIE SOMMER.

Answer.

Olshausen, 29th August 1822.

DEAR SOPHIE,

I am heartily glad: I had written to Hortense, but had not finished the letter. I bless the cup of coffee which fell over it so that I had laid it aside. It is very hard to me to write anything to her. But I am still more glad that I have a place for you. The brother of Herr von Hagen at Windfort, is looking out for some one to educate his children. That will be a house for you. He a good old fellow as is said of him here; she, delicate; with four children, she has need of help. I have pretty much settled the matter with him and naturally spoke provincial German as we like to do here. You must learn it too. He said, "If you

2*

can give me your word that the young person is a
little bit simple, I will take her." I assured him of
that. That you can sometimes give long lectures I did
not tell him. Pardon me, dear Sophie! for all that, I
love you very much. When you are once at Frondorf
I will write you long letters. I have not time yet for
a diary. Now answer quickly. You are to have a
hundred thalers, and your travelling expenses, and to
be here at Michaelmas. Excuse my bad writing and
the blots. Mamma has sent for me. My aunt from
Kamern is here.

Your

THERESA.

Joachim to Joseph.

Kamern, 6th September 1822

DEAR JOSEPH,

I will allow you to scold if you on the other hand
allow me to do what I like. Only give up wishing to
make me any thing else than that for which I am
designed by nature. You laugh at this nature, but it
has its merits in spite of your zeal. I lately listened
to a conversation of the old coachman and Klaus.
The old man said, "I don't know, Klaus, you are a
clever fellow, and a brave fellow, and have been
away for three years, but you cannot get yourself so
much respected by people." Klaus answered, "We
shall see about that some day." "See some day!
what does not happen, does not happen," said the
old man, shrugging his shoulders. And he is right;
only he should not tease the poor youth to such unnecessary exertions. What is his failing then or what
is wanting in him? What he does not reap of honour

with the multitude, he reaps in love among his friends. And so let me also poor youth alone. The Lord has divided His gifts differently; to whom He has given little, from him He will require little; and He prospers the simple-hearted.

Christian seems to observe the matter. He is silent and sighs, but I am very glad at heart. Yet I am active in my way, that is I am thinking, seeing and hearing.

I cannot send away the steward before I understand how to fill his place. I cannot make proper changes among the people, before I know them closely; therefore it seems as though the old course would go on here: but only have patience. Comfort Christian if he opens out his heart to you, and also make him less exacting on me. He is very zealous and impatient. Netty lamented to me that he entertained the thought of leaving Kamern, because the heart of his flock was closed against him. I must now help with all my might, and put my hand to it. Besides I call that rashly spoken. The Lord alone knows the hearts of men, and knows the time to open them. We should only be his faithful and humble fellow-labourers, and not desire to see what we have done; the Lord sees it, that is enough. Yesterday Christian accompanied me when the old Städing fetched me to show me his new improvements in the forest. On the way there the old man began his lamentation, — that is first, he praised himself, his industry, his pains, three times he had had these same places planted, he had improved the ground, had it watered — every thing in vain! The ground was in some places too hard, in others too marshy; sometimes there was a great deal of rain, sometimes it

was too dry, then came the worm, and ate the roots of
the young plants; in short the old man, in huntsman's
fashion, not in the gentlest way, spoke out his dissatisfaction at the ill-success of his work. Christian
saw the opportunity for a lecture of reproof. He showed
him that he must leave a share and the responsibility
with the Lord, he had only to prepare the land and
to sow, to wait, to tend; the Lord has the best part to
do, and we must quietly and patiently acquiesce in
what He does. Our Pastor is speaking from experience,
I added; He too must often work on hard ground, and
often sow and plant in vain; — as it is said "patient
in tribulation, and rejoicing in hope." Above all things
do not mourn over the weather, dear Städing, that has
been so ever since Adam, and is wisely ordered by the
Lord. You see how the earth is full of the goodness
of the Lord, quite beyond your desert. If your improvements give you trouble, you are in your right
place. It says, "In the sweat of thy brow, shalt thou
eat bread." Christian became silent; I think he had
taken these words to himself, and it can do him no
harm. I must tell you in confidence that I intend to
begin the reformation in Kamern so much desired by
Christian, quite quietly with himself. After I had let
the forester go, I walked a long time with Christian.
His state of mind did me good, he did not say so
much to me. Now I am sitting in my room by the
open window; the rain is falling warmly and softly.
I close my eyes; it is as though heaven's blessing would
fall also on me, and would refresh and bless. There
is nothing more beautiful than to be quite still, to have
nothing, and to be able to give nothing, but to receive,
ever to receive. I do not understand how people can

be so busy with outward affairs, I have so much to do
with my own eternal happiness; and I feel then as if
the dear Lord could manage His kingdom without me,
though I would do everything for love of Him, — yes,
everything that I can. And now, dear people, have
patience with me.

About a week ago we were at Olshausen, where it
looks as gay and cheerful as possible. The world is
there playing its game with the utmost importance; —
the more folly, the more importance is given to it.
The devil is a knave, he knows how to make a fool of
his world. When we got there they had just finished
dinner. I found Theresa at billiards with the gentlemen. Cousin Alfred has brought some friends with
him from his Rhine journey, — a young Styrian Count
Stadlein is the most distinguished of them. Rose was
very school-girl-like, but, as it seems to me, quite an
unconscious child. In this circle, alas! she will soon
get conscious. The young people were rather foolish.
Uncle appeared infected with it, but with him everything is studied. I soon felt uncomfortable in this
noisy company. Theresa appeared to me constantly
more unlovely. I asked her whether she would not
accompany me to the ladies, my mother would be so
pleased to see her. In a moment she laid down the
cue, and hastened before me. In the ante-room I told
her casually that I did not like to see her there in the
gentlemen's room, I thought she would be better with
the ladies. I said it rather seriously but still playfully, you will give me the credit of not having been
rude. Theresa looked at me for a moment but answered nothing, but I was rejoiced that when shortly
after the young gentlemen pressed her to come back

into the billiard-room, she decidedly refused and remained sitting with my mother with her sewing. I
was now as amiable as possible, so that my rude words
might be forgotten. When I saw her sitting so seriously
and so lovingly with my mother, I was almost sorry
for my words. I asked her, at parting, whether she
was not angry with her ill-behaved cousin? She shook
her head. She has many good qualities, the Lord will
help her, and I have a good confidence that she will
not, like so many who resemble her, perish in the whirlpool of the world. A week ago we were invited to a
larger party. My mother has never excluded herself
from these family meetings, and I could not do so,
but besides this time I felt a great anxiety about the
foolish young men.

Towards evening preparations were made for a
dance, for tableaux, and for proverbs, as that was the
order of the day, I was a looker-on; and the young
people tried to lay hands on me. I placed myself
forthwith in position, the thing was amusing. "I wish
to enjoy life as long as I am young," said Count
Stadlein. "Not only as long as I am young," I replied
to him; "I wish to enjoy it also when I am old." He
looked at me with some astonishment. "But why do
you exclude yourself from the dance?" "That is too
dull a pleasure for me," I replied. "If I dance I must
be merry too, and sing, and jump. I only do it with
children. This silent and solemn flying around and
complimenting each other, has something gloomy in it
to me. I could not join in it." Some young people
made harmless jokes on this head, but Count Stadlein
said bitterly, "That is a matter of taste, indeed. I
thought you considered it a sin, and should like to

have heard your explanation about it." "Certainly I do consider it a sin when it does not happen in the way of which I was speaking, and when it is one of the many impresses of the godless world, — of the world which lives without God. But, sir, why are you here?" asked a young pert voice. I could not help laughing; he was quite right, but I controlled myself and answered with affected gravity, that I did not come for my own sake, but because I thought by my proximity to give pleasure to the company. No one ventured to reply anything to this dignified speech. Thereupon I invited them very cordially, as this was not the place for such conversations, to a sober cigar parliament at Kamern, there also to discuss in a becoming way the subject of the godless world — how she can sing merrily and prettily, and what is the end of her song. Many of the young men cheerfully and readily consented. One said I was a very peculiar sort of hypocrite, and he should wish to make a closer acquaintance with me. Count Stadlein, however, is mightily stern, and as far as possible hostile to me. Alfred said lately to me, half in earnest, half in joke, that my character was too exciting for Count Stadlein. So matters stand at Olshausen. I am afraid they will stand, and not get any farther. If this account has not interested you, I am sorry for it; I will now hastily tell you of my dear Kamern and its inhabitants. Of Christian I wrote to you at the beginning of the letter, and he has also lately written to you himself. Netty is an admirable pastor's wife, and grows more and more in my estimation. She visits the poor and sick in the village, is quiet and cheerful over it, and is loved by young and old. It almost seems to me that she fills her position

better than Christian, he has learned too much, and is
a self-absorbed professor. He must throw a great deal
over-board, to become our good pastor at Kamern. I
am beginning the reformation, as I said, with him.
Netty is in league with me. We understand each
other without words. My mother agrees with us, yet,
to balance parties, she sometimes holds with Christian.
She has also a great power over him. Now that it
becomes almost autumnal, we have already spent
splendid evenings by lamp-light in the garden-parlour.
I say we, and forgot the chief person — the little
Joachim. That wise and sensible people may be un-
wise parents has often happened in the world; and I
must confess to you that Christian and Netty's mode
of education is their weak side; but I must add in
their excuse, that the boy is an uncommon character.
Even my mother who (as she is in everything) is a
model educator, (pray, don't apply that to me) seems
weak when opposed to him. I will not speak of myself. I feel a kind of elective-affinity for the boy, and
believe, what older people assert, that he is a copy of
me on a small scale. To Klaus's disgust I have not
ridden the brown for a fortnight because Joachim the
second maintains the horse is nasty, — it has such
great bones and one slips so on it. I lift the little
man almost every day on to my horse, because it
pleases him so very much.

Now I have still to tell of myself and Klaus. Of
myself that I am a diligent economist. I rise at five.
Do you ask how that is possible? I tell you that is
the brave Klaus's affair. He has orders to get me out
of bed by five. At first he could not succeed. I
reproached him. He assured me he always thought I

was awake, as I talked to him. You know I can carry on a simple conversation even in sleep. I gave him to understand that he must talk to me in a more interesting way than hitherto. One morning (the heat had disturbed me in the night) Klaus suddenly called with a loud voice, "Master think of something!" "Of what?" asked I, half asleep. "Yes, think of something," thundered he again. "Of what?" "Why think it is possible it will soon snow." I could not help laughing heartily, and was awake in a moment. "Was not that interesting?" asked Klaus. "Highly interesting," said I, "you must always make it so." I woke more quickly the next morning, for the good Klaus made use of the same wit, because as he thought one could not so suddenly think of anything new. Besides nothing else was needed, for when he, in a morning with faithful zeal, made it snow, my risible muscles were set in motion, and now habit has conquered. So I get up at five o'clock. I roam over field and forest, and with true pleasure when sometimes I forget all money considerations.

Yesterday I sat a long time under "the seven brothers." You know the isolated, beautiful beeches on the Hagenberg. Autumn has not yet tinged the leaves. The lake lay wreathed with green at my feet — on the left Olshausen, on the right Kamern, in the far distance a streak of silver — the sea. This is the only point where we have a distant view; for the eye, and for the longing of the heart, there is often a necessity to be unbounded. A shepherd stood near me leaning on his staff — he also was looking into the distance. That is a delightful calling and would have been very suitable for me. I thought, we should see who would do it best. I looked; he was standing immoveable, and I closed my eyes or opened them, and watched how white cloudlets were passing lightly over the blue sky. When the sun began to set, and the old sexton at Kamern was ringing the evening-bell, the shepherd set himself in motion with his flock, and I followed him. I am now always in a frame of mind full of happy youthful enjoyment. I am afraid of every distraction, lest I should disturb this frame of mind; my lonely wanderings give me many such contemplative hours. Yet they come to me also in the house, in the presence of my dear mother. Now she has confided to me the office of leading the family worship. I entered upon it with trembling, but it gives me great joy even in the preparation for it. We are now reading the Old Testament, so that we may begin Advent with our dear Lord Jesus Christ. The Old Testament has never so taken hold of me, and touched me as this time. I feel again anew, that the Lord God, through His Holy Spirit, can constantly disclose more and more of the Bible; one veil falls off after another, the light constantly becomes brighter. Great is the compassion and long-suffering of God! how He pardoned his people Israel from time to time, how He followed him, how He led him by love and by severity. His salvation lay so near his heart, that He sent His only-begotten Son as a redemption for many, that all who believe in Him might not perish but have everlasting life. Why should I not be joyful in soul in spite of all the burden of sin, and the misery of sin. Our life is a conflict, spent in falling and rising again and falling again; but faith and love and comfort are also there, and the Lord Jesus Himself is there. What we could not do He has already done for us, and before us is the goal of our longing and striving, eternal in peace, and joy, and blessedness. Therefore, as we have sung to-day,

> Onward, onward go!
> Zion, walk thou in the light,
> Trim thy lamp and make it bright;
> Let thy love no coldness know;
> For the living waters wait,
> Strive to pass the narrow gate,
> Onward, onward go!

> Suffer and endure!
> Zion, suffer without fear
> Sorrow, anguish, taunt, and jeer,
> Faithful till death end the strife;
> Look unto the crown of life,
> If thou feel sin's serpent sting,
> Still rejoice in suffering.

> Press thou on, press on!
> Zion, press toward thy God,
> Do not with the dead remain;
> Strengthened with the life divine,
> Like green branches on the vine,
> For illusion strength obtain.
> Press thou on!

> Still hold on, hold on!
> Zion, hold thou fast thy faith,
> Thee let no man luke-warm find:
> Up! the treasure hangs in sight;
> Up! forsake the things behind;
> In the latest, sorest fight,
> Zion! still hold on.

And now God be with you, dear Joseph. Look upon this letter as something methodical. I cannot, as you do, sit down quickly and throw off a few lines. I am not fond of writing, and when I am at it I do not like to do anything else. If you go to Berlin you might come through here.

Your faithful

JOACHIM.

Letter from Theresa.
(Not sent.)

Olshausen, 12th October 1822.

DEAR SOPHIE,

Do not be uneasy about my not being well. It is nothing but the old story — the favourite lard-dumplings.

Yesterday I had almost made a vow never again to eat them; I was so vexed that I was obliged to stay here. Yet to-day I feel very much pleased with my evening.

It will certainly give you pleasure, so you shall hear about it. Yesterday morning I was told to go to mamma.

The box with the ball-dress was come, I was very curious, and mamma, in her eagerness about the dress, did not look at her little daughter. When at last she hands over to me the light silver-spangled stuff, and, highly satisfied, is stroking the hair back from my forehead she cries out in terror: "But, Theresa, what if the matter?"

Yes, I looked horrible, not only on the lips but further towards the nose, I had hateful bright spots. The dress was packed up, my sentence was spoken. It was to remain at home! Mamma was vexed; Alfred still more so. Count Stadlein's partner for the country-dance was missing. I shed tears; not on that account, but I did wish to go and, you may doubt it, dear

Sophie, but I wished very much to see and to talk to you again. When they were all gone I was standing alone by the window in the twilight. I could not set to anything for vexation.

All at once I thought of going a walk and called Elizabeth. She came, but with her cloak on. She had leave to visit her mother for the evening. "I will go with you to Kamern and visit Aunt Netty," cried I with delight. I would hear nothing said against it: it was full moon, fine weather, — no obstacle. Elizabeth grows dearer to me every day; if she were not my lady's maid, I might be still more friendly with her. We went along the foot-path by the lake; the moon was shining through the bright trees, and on Elizabeth's quiet face; my feet rustled in the leaves, — shadows were dancing on the sedge. Elizabeth was so quiet and only said yes and no; but then she sang so softly and with such a touching voice that I could have wept. "Now all the woods are sleeping" as the hymn says. It is very long but I should like to hear it again, and I should like to learn it. We got so quickly to Kamern but I did not trust myself to Aunt Netty, I was afraid of her husband. I went to Elizabeth's mother, Mrs. Braunsen's, who was so long lady's maid to Aunt Anna, and who lives in the church-yard corner, — a little house very small and quite alone behind the parsonage garden. A little light was glimmering through the dark lime-trees, and it was burning in a little room in which I should already like to live.

Mrs. Braunsen was very polite, and so refined and amiable that I could not help thinking all the time os Aunt Anna. I begged she would do as though I were not there. Elizabeth brought tea, — brown bread and

butter set out on a white cloth, and I felt as though I
were with people of rank. Mrs. Braunsen said grace,
I gladly joined in, but just as if I were in a dream
I liked to listen to all she said. When Elizabeth was
taking out the tea and her mother was helping her, I
looked through the window in to the bright moonlight and on to the church-yard with the church. I
went out that Elizabeth might be alone with her
mother. They thought I wished to go to Netty, but it
was far pleasanter out there. 1 was not at all afraid:
I could not help looking at the stars and thinking
what would become of me. I went from the church-
yard into the lime-avenue and the garden. The castle
lay so quiet and so bright, and two golden rays of
light fell upon the grass-plot from the garden parlour.
I went across softly and looked in. I thought all the
time I was dreaming. Aunt was sitting on the sofa
and Joachim was in the arm-chair reading aloud. I
sat down softly on the low window-sill, and heard his
voice plainly. I could not help looking at them both.
I don't know why. I prayed too that the dear Lord
would make me happy. I forgot too that I was sitting
there. Joachim suddenly got up and walked to the
window. I was very much frightened and squeezed
myself quite beneath the window-sill! I only saw his
hand which he laid on the rail. It seemed as though
he stretched it out to me to help me. I thought "Now
if thou couldst grasp it, and say Joachim. Don't be
angry with me and help me to become good and reli-
gious, and, dear Aunt, I love you so very much." I
could not help crying very much; it was fortunate that
he went from the window: I stood up and slipped
away, but when I was obliged to go through the gloomy

shade I was so afraid. I looked back to the bright light, I turned round, I wished to go to the aunt because I got more and more afraid, but was ashamed, and hastened very quickly through the avenue, over the church-yard, towards the little light. I know not how I looked. Elizabeth and her mother were terrified when I came in, but I was so joyful at heart. I never experienced such an evening. Mrs. Braunsen accompanied us part of the way. When we went by the lake, Elizabeth could not help singing the hymn again, and I thought of the garden-parlour, and the little house in the church-yard-corner, and I was sorrowful when I got to Olshausen again. — I feel *ennui* at Olshausen. To-day at breakfast Alfred and Count Stadlein were vexed that I was so melancholy, and said — dancing was tedious and great companies too.

Count Stadlein, who is very cunning, seems already to have a suspicion whether I did not do something strange yesterday; he looked at me so piercingly with his black eyes. First mamma was angry that I could talk so rudely and foolishly, and when I cried, she said I was ill and therefore excited and nervous.

I went to my room as I was obliged, and lay down on the sofa, but not for long. I wished to go for a walk alone, and to rustle my feet in the leaves. I stood under the seven brothers. The sky was cloudy. Kamern with the dark lime-trees and the pointed spire was in mist, but I looked through the mist and at last I went back. I was not down to dinner — the sick diet here was beautiful. I made plans with Elizabeth. I wish so much to learn to sing hymns, and have begun with the hymn of yesterday. Then I wish to be industrious with her, and to sew for the mission.

I do not know whether it is a good thing to sew for the blacks, but Aunt Anna does it and Mrs. Braunsen.

Mamma must not hear of it: she would be very angry, and Alfred would tease me. I made lately, for a lottery, a rose-coloured silk glove case. They laughed at me and asked what the Hottentots could do with it. I have not given it up but will sew in secret with Elizabeth. Working with the maid no longer gives me any pleasure. It is often so horribly cold out there. Now I have written away the afternoon; the moon is shining again, and I am singing all alone "Now all the woods are sleeping."

DEAR SOPHIE,

I had written you a long letter but I can not send it, it is too marvellous; I will burn it. I promise you henceforth to keep a journal. Writing to-day has given me much pleasure. I shall also have a good deal of time now.

You have been to Kamern lately and not come to us. I am sorry for it. I should have been so glad to talk to you. I quite believe the people there have pleased you. Could you not send me some pretty books to read? Think of it! Papa wishes to go with us for a longer time to Berlin. I should so much rather stay here. I know of nothing else to tell you to-day: I hope you will be at the birthday at Windfort, then I will tell you a great deal. My love to all the children. I will send the promised doll to little Mary by the Doctor. Your

THERESA.

Joachim to Joseph.

Kamern, 5th December 1822.

DEAR JOSEPH,

Autumn has shaken all the leaves from the trees; the view from my window is very extensive, I see almost to Olshausen, at least the lake glimmers through the bare twigs. Christian's light also sends a greeting through the lime-trees; mine greets him in return. When his goes out, it is a warning to me to go to rest, and thus we exchange a good-night. We have now celebrated the first Advent. It is a beautiful thing that the Church celebrates her most splendid feasts at a time of year when, withdrawn from the visible, we can live for a far fairer and more blessed world. We sing our Hosanna to meet the King. "Praised be He who cometh in the name of the Lord —Hosanna in the highest." I learn more and more that, with a simple well-ordered outward calling, life thrives best in the quiet of loneliness. I feel happy here, and everything externally is ordered according to my wish. What indeed is happiness or unhappiness? If we have the Lord, we have the advantage over the world, and our rich and our barren times consist in having Him more or less. Now during Advent we shall meet once a week with Christian and Netty to sing and read — the servants also are by turns to take part in it. It has happened twice already, and yesterday another festivity combined with it which is certainly worth the pains that you should enjoy it with us. To Joachim the second (who when his obstinate stern Uncle Joseph comes will yet take his heart by storm) to this young fellow, was announced that in the

3 *

coming season Master Rupert would come as precursor
of the Holy Christ, and that he would throw beautiful
things into the room for all good children.

Joachim has done his utmost to show his goodness; no one doubted it, but many of my young friends
in the courtyard also counted themselves among these
good children. Yesterday in the twilight the little
company appeared: they were assembled in the ante-
room, and Joachim as the smallest but bravest served
and kept order. When I was just on the point of
putting on the fur cloak, and of taking the sack with
the apples, and nuts and sweet-meats into my hand, a
carriage drove up — Aunt from Olshausen and Rose.
Aunt comes oftener now: I fear from *ennui*: she is
pretty much cut off from the rest of the neighbourhood by bad roads. Yet it is pleasant to us. Uncle
has been for a long time at Berlin, but just in his absence mother can get on best with aunt. She has
also met Netty and Christian here, and yesterday
especially the two sisters appeared to me like they did
of old. Theresa was highly delighted when she heard
the object of the youthful assembly, she declared she
would belong to the children to-day and profit by
Master Rupert.

I asked whether she was a good child too? She
did not take the joke as I had intended it, and turned
away gravely. I was sorry for that. I tried to make
up for it. And she is so easy to appease; she was
soon merry again, and the centre of the delighted company — that is she brought a wonderful animation into
it, talked patois with the children, as though she could
speak nothing else: she danced with them and sang,
and Joachim the second was astonished, and in aston-

ishment gave his sceptre to the ambitious intruder. I
listened a long time at the crack of the door. Then I
played my part (I hope well); the children in spite of
timidity hastened to gather round the hideous Giver,
and Theresa ingratiated herself wonderfully with
Joachim when she offered afterwards to share her gifts
with him. The boy seems to make his way even with
the Olshausen ladies. Aunt was in a very good
temper: she invited herself to the Advent feast. My
mother appeared, in honour of the visit, to wish to let
the Advent celebration fall through. I on the con-
trary was delighted at the thoughts of it. The more
joyful and the more sure of our cause we are, the more
magical is the influence on others, and on those who
do not participate. I said at table what our guests
must expect after supper. I praised the time of Advent: I added since they had joined us to-day, they
must sing Hosanna with us to our King; and I was
sure they would enjoy our festival more than we
enjoy those which they give us at Olshausen.
Aunt received these words well. She assured us
she herself loved quiet life more than company,
and on that account had decidedly put off the
Berlin journey. For Rose's sake I should rather have
been there, added she: the girl leads a mad life here,
driving about in the stables and in the village with
Elizabeth, and will never learn what she owes to herself
and her position. Theresa laughed at this accusation
and I allowed myself a few more observations. I do
not doubt that Theresa is in good company with Elizabeth, and better than with the gentlemen in the billiard-room, and Theresa gave striking evidence of it
that evening. When our company was assembled

after supper Christian gave a short discourse on the time of Advent. He shortly explained the Gospel of Sunday. Afterwards "O how shall I receive Thee" was sung — the first hymn. When I handed Theresa a hymn book, she said I know the hymn by heart, and so she said at the second which we sang. That astonished Christian, and he asked her, half in jest, whether she had learned the hymns at Lausanne. "O no," answered she abruptly, "I learn them now in my mad life as mamma calls it. Aunt Emma took pleasure in the singing of her daughter, and with others asked her to sing a hymn alone. Theresa's voice is insignificant but clear and child-like. She sang some verses from "Now all the woods are sleeping." A hymn never touched me so much as the last verse but one.

"My Jesus, stay Thou by me
And let no foe come nigh me
Safe sheltered by Thy wing."

I stood near her, and fervently commended this feeble creature to the heart of the Lord. You see I am a regular mystic; I believe that the offering of such a prayer must act immediately and marvellously on the one for whom we pray, and more than the most eloquent words of our lips. If it be so, the power of this my prayer will help to open this heart to the Lord, to touch the lips that they may cry Hosanna to Him. Yes I confidently believe it.

Dear Joseph! have you your own thoughts about what I am writing? I have my thoughts too, and the Lord grant they may be His thoughts. Amen. And now help me to pray. Oh if we could be more still, and pray more constantly, we should make more progress than with our much talking and doing. So may the Lord help us all.

Your friend

JOACHIM.

Theresa to Sophie.

Olshausen, 15th December 1822.

DEAR SOPHIE,

I am living a splendid life and enjoy myself and I have had a feast which you might celebrate with your children. It is not my discovery. I learned it at Kamern, and had a most pleasant time there, mamma too: — she stayed so long that the moonlight was over, and cousin Joachim was obliged to go before us on horseback with a lantern to light us. Mamma is on very good terms now with the Kamern people. She says they lead a sensible and happy life there, and that it was not a bad thing of Netty that she accepted the Pastor. He is amiable, and what he is now he will be when she is older. Mamma is angry now with Papa that he went to Berlin; and Papa is angry that she would not go with him, and wishes to stay till the spring. We get on quite merrily here. You know the sport of Master Rupert.

Last Sunday they were all invited from Kamern — Christian and Netty and little Joachim too. With Elizabeth I had made a little sky-blue dress for him which suits him very well. I had invited many of the farm people as well and got ginger-bread and apples, and Cousin Joachim was obliged to act Master Rupert because he is so tall and looks so formidable. The servant held a board with green bushes and lights over his head, which was a true cap of light, and so he stood in the half-open door and flung his gifts into the dusky room, and on to the frightened children. They were all the merrier afterwards: little Joachim made especial fun for us. Dear Sophie, I want to tell you that I cannot sew for the mission now, and I have not begun the diary. Christmas makes me a great deal to do. I am making a great many presents with Elizabeth. We are also invited to Kamern: you are to come too with all the children and to all, *all* I wish to give something. Dear love. The Doctor wants to go and takes this note with him. Your

THERESA.

Sophie to Theresa.

DEAR ROSE,

Only work and employ yourself well. Never think that all work is unnecessary for you, and that, by the renunciation of a wish for luxury, you can have all done for money. Work is such a great blessing for yourself, and not to be paid for by money: and in order to free yourself from the depressing thoughts of the uselessness of your work, do more works of love whether for the mission, or for your poor or for your friends.

My children are devoted to you with great affection. Little Mary would do anything for Aunt Rose. We are very much delighted at the thoughts of meeting at Kamern, and we are also eagerly practising the Christmas hymns. I have still a great deal to do and because I have so many claims by day am obliged to call in the help of the night.

God be with you, dear Theresa. Your

SOPHIE.

Joachim to Joseph.

Kamern, 14th January 1823.

DEAR JOSEPH,

The lovely Christmas days are over. I am delighted that you have enjoyed them with us, and have lived in our dear circle. But I have more knowledge of human nature, dear Joseph, than you and Christian. You good lively people! It is beautiful that you have so soon overcome old prejudices, but I fear you have taken up new ones. I fear — for I might do so — you were right this time. I cannot share your rapture about Theresa. You laugh. Theresa is very lovely, but a shaking reed. Uncle has got his way that she shall go with Aunt to Berlin. Can you think that she will stand firm there. Count Stadlein is said to be very rich and is a far more agreeable son-in-law to my uncle than I am; and for Theresa I am surely not more attractive than a young man of the world. You see, dear Joseph, how weak I am, my heart has become foolish. Should I ever forget that marriages are made in heaven. The fields of snow are so bright and the blue sky and the sunshine. I have run through field and forest in order to out-run my folly, but, dear Joseph, you will at once see how it is with me. My thoughts belong to her; her image has placed itself in my soul, I love her dearly, yes, dearly. I am anxious about it. I have wept like a child and was never more happy than in those tears. Is it the Lord's will? Oh I am afraid of this happiness. I am afraid of my weak heart. The world is so beautiful; the place of my home is so beautiful but only with her. I am so happy, but only with her. I make plans — she is in them. I lie down — I think of her. I wake, and think of her. My heart has no rest: it is touched with sorrow; but this sorrow causes me no pain. Oh Joseph, pray for me, pray for my weak heart, and for my happiness. The star of evening is there appearing in the bright sky, clear and still: — it will always shine again in like purity till it sees me again at peace. Time passes away, unrest passes away — the Lord knows when and how. Shall I send you this evidence of my weakness? No one here has the least idea that the man in me is become a fool. I walk about with great repose — with great dignity. I never said such sensible things as now. I disputed with Christian how a Christian must love: — the true-hearted man defends my folly.

Netty enjoyed to hear him talk. I believe women do love to see a man weak in this way. She is angry with me about my cold-heartedness. And the cold-hearted quiet man when he is alone, weeps like a child. Write to me, Joseph, give me a lecture; see whether you can do it more seriously than I do myself: — dear fellow, do this friendly service to me. I say no one guesses the state of my heart; perhaps, though, my mother may, and she ought to know least of all. I believe her only weakness is anxiety about my happiness. Oh, she would have more sympathy with my folly than I have myself. God be with you.

Your

JOACHIM.

Letter from Theresa to Frau von Kamern.

Berlin, 18th January 1823.

DEAR AUNT,

My promised letter will, perhaps, be too long for you. I am so eager to write. You must also keep your promise and write a great deal about Kamern. We have now been in this great city for two days. We live "under the Lindens" — a broad street and a chief street. The driving and walking and riding is incalculable. Our house on the other hand is not extraordinary. Alfred says, papa has been stingy. Our own carpets, table-covers and furniture, give some appearance to the matter. Besides papa is very formal; I am quite frightened at it, and he has already said to me in confidence that I am a regular peasant-girl. Papa has not brought a carriage with him. Count Stadlein lives with us in one house. His carriage is at our service; I believe that is why the count boards with us. We have a joint establishment. On the very first morning a hair-dresser came to mamma and me. The creature tormented me horribly for two hours. I paid him out well, and I was so pleased that at going away, he said to mamma that he would never dress the young lady's hair again. First he cut long pig-tails from my back hair, then he frizzed innumerable little locks with a curling iron, and then towered them up one on another — two high mountains on my fore-head. He called this "Coiffure à la neige." Quite right, for with the spring these snow-mountains will thaw away in Olshausen. Papa brought me besides a white satin hat, around its brim adapted to these tower-ing locks, twined moss-roses and vine-branches. Alfred

declares that papa chose this with a meaning — "with
roses one should think of the grapes." Dear aunt, in
their hateful worldly sense I detest that, but I thought
of you, and what you said to me about youth. With
those thoughts I put on the remarkable hat, and made
some visits. In the evening we were at the theatre.
I believe the theatre will give me the most pleasure. I
saw the enchanting flutes and thought I was enchanted
myself. One thing more. This evening I had my
first riding lesson in the riding-school. Papa and
Alfred and Count Stadlein looked on. I was very
brave, but I know the horses here have no foolish
tricks. Only tell little Joachie that if I came to Kamern
I could ride better than he. Oh, dear Aunt! I like
much better to be at home than here. I hope we shall
not stay here long. Mamma has a very bad nervous
headache to-day. That has freed me from a terrible
dinner. I had already, with Elizabeth's help, built up
the snow-mountains on my forehead, and papa had
furnished me with infinite rules for behaviour. All in
vain! I am sitting with Elizabeth in our little back
room, and am writing to my dear aunt.

Besides I am beginning to amuse myself on my
own account with Elizabeth. At tea-time every necessary was again wanting; since no larder exists here
we resolved to go and buy. I hastily frizzed myself
à la Olshausen, put on my travelling-hood and went
with Elizabeth into a sausage-shop. The sausages
there were arranged like wreaths, and hams between
and smoked goose-breasts. We bought some of all
and, in another shop, butter, cheese and sardines. We
were very much pleased with this store, and I begin
to find it quite pleasant in my little back room. To-

morrow is Sunday, so before the others make their appearance, I shall go with Elizabeth to church. I hope also mamma will be so poorly that I need not go into company. Now, farewell, dear Aunt, I earnestly beg you, write to me soon again. Give my love to Joachim, and little Joachie, Netty and Christian. Please, send Elizabeth's letter by Klaus.

Your

Loving niece
THERESA VON OLSHAUSEN.

Joachim to Joseph.

Kamern, 20th February 1823.

DEAR JOSEPH,

Your lecture is not very striking, dear Joseph. Do not think that my present state of mind is the result of it. The heart is a desponding and sorrowful thing; if it fears conflict, if it is anxious, it may timidly fly. When the danger is over it gains wonderful courage. Now listen how here in Kamern, in spite of winter, it is spring. Early on Monday I stood wondering at the window. Forest and park gleamed in the silver light of spring, against the rosy morning sky; a wreath of stars adorned every twig, every flower-stalk, every blade of grass. It drove me out earlier than usual, a gun over my shoulder to give some appearance of an object to these vagaries. I went along the path by the lake. I forgot myself, and stood lost in the beauty of the scene. The clear frozen surface of the water encircled by beeches and birches and slender reeds; in the back ground Castle Olshausen with the park all berimed with silver, and a light blue and rosy mist over them. Suddenly two figures came out of Olshausen Park; they were undoubtedly Rose and Elizabeth. When Rose saw me she beckoned with her pocket-handkerchief, and hastened impetuously nearer. The more she hastened, the more I slackened my pace. My fool tries to fortify himself as well as he can. Elizabeth left us in order to go to her mother. I lead Rose through the park. She was very talkative and very merry; her joy of heart was to be read in her bright eyes, and though I walked beside her in a very dignified way, my heart leaped in equal bounds with hers. Aunt became so nervous at Berlin, that the physician at last ordered her home. Mother invited Rose to stay the day with us; she stayed. Towards evening I took her home. But the next day the physician brought her back to us himself. Aunt's illness had become nervous fever, and as several people at Olshausen lie ill of it, his advice is, that Rose should stay some weeks here. Thus it is spring at Kamern. I feel as if I were in a dream when I sit in a room and hear her light steps on the corridor, and hear her chattering with dogs and cats, or see how eagerly she lessens mother's little household affairs, and then again sits quietly by her, and listens attentively to serious conversations. Dear Joseph, good fortune gives spirit — perhaps a haughty spirit. The world never appeared so fair to me, men so loveable, Heaven so near. Is that youthful delight? and the delight of love? To be joyful, sorrowful, thoughtful. I was thoughtful, the star of evening was appearing in the sky. Mountaineers were playing below in the meadow — the sounds touched my heart with longing and joy. I walked on to the corridor. Rose was sitting on the first step. She wished

to rise, she is often so shy with me. I have once begun to play the somewhat serious stern cousin, and do
not know how to begin anything else. I sat down by
her. I wished to be small and lowly beside her. We
sat at first silently by each other. I gave her my
hand and asked whether she liked to be with us? She
nodded and at the same time looked at me so lovingly,
that I could not help being strong and saying no
foolish things. I remained silent, covered my eyes
with my hand until the tones had died away and Rose
went to my mother. I conclude for to-day. The
Lord be with you and with us all. All is well at the
parsonage. Little Joachie is our daily companion.
Of Klaus I can tell you that he is very merry. It is
very pretty when such young people are in the house,
he said this morning with delight. Elizabeth is with
Rose. I might learn from him many a tender attention to these young people — amongst others he daily
rides for some hours like a lady to train the brown, so
that Rose may satisfy her love of riding here.

I heartily greet you.

Your

JOACHIM.

Diary of Theresa.

Kamern, 21st February 1823.

At last I will begin a diary. I had not time in
Berlin. Four days here are already passed in such a
way that when I lie down in the evening, I can scarcely
wait till I get up early in the morning. Yet two
mornings I have overslept myself and could not go to
prayers. This morning I hurried very much and dressed

properly, for aunt does not like a young girl to appear
in the morning in négligée. I was standing timidly
at the door of the room, it felt very strange, I heard
Joachim's voice — "We will begin." Then I opened
the door quickly. Aunt was sitting in the arm-chair;
Joachim at the table, the servants nearer the door.
I sat down by aunt; Joachim read so quietly, not at
all a clergyman's tone. I could not help looking at
him all the time and listening to him. To-day he was
much kinder to me; if I could only tell him that I am
so fond of hearing him, but he is always so grave
with me, and then he is so tall that when I stand by
him I scarcely reach to his shoulder. After breakfast I go with aunt into the household. She has a
certain apron and cap for it, puts on gloves and takes
the basket of keys. I dressed myself just the same
because I think it so pretty. We enquired about
dinner for the parlour, and the servants gave out what
was necessary from the larder; then I sorted fruit.
The very little spots in fine apples I cut out and laid
among the peels; fruit is scarce this year. Apples
with great spots I gave to the cook. She is to make
fried apples of them to-night. Aunt praised my sort-
ing. Afterwards I sewed industriously with aunt.
Joachim kept us waiting for dinner. He was the
whole morning among the household. After dinner I
stayed in the library and played the piano. Joachim
sat on the sofa and went to sleep over it; I was so
glad he did, because he had the tooth-ache. I got up
quite softly, and placed myself with a book in the
window. Aunt called us to coffee. We were very
happy. Towards evening we went a walk and I with
aunt to see a sick woman. Oh! how beautifully and

comfortingly aunt can speak. I wish I could! but I am afraid of sickness and very much of death. In the twilight I practised my old hymns alone. I had almost forgotten them in Berlin; now I have written this, and soon Netty and Christian will come and eat fried apples with us and then there will be a lecture. We are now in passion-week. I like to hear it and can say nothing more but that when a day is gone, I am so pleased to look back upon it.

February 22d.

To-day I was with aunt earlier than the servants. Aunt kissed me kindly on the forehead, and asked whether it gave me pleasure to solemnize the morning thus with them? I bent over to her and could. not help crying. Joachim had gone to the window; he surely does not believe it. I said in a low voice to aunt, "Dear Aunt, if you forsake me, I shall not become pious. I do not know how to begin anything alone." Aunt said she loved me very much and would never forsake me, but my best support must be the Lord above. I do not rightly understand it, but I believe it. Elizabeth is so happy. She is not afraid of death; she says earth first appears truly beautiful to us when we learn to trust in Heaven. I should like to learn to trust in Heaven.

Febr. 25th. The days here pass so quickly and I have very much to do. Little Joachim has the influenza. I must amuse him. Joachim also plays with him. I like to be at the parsonage. I am no longer afraid of Christian, and Netty is always kind and friendly. She goes to see mamma too and is not afraid of the infection. Mamma is still very ill, but not dangerously. To-day I practised the hymn, "A Lamb has borne our guilt." It is so touching, I could not help crying, and do not know why.

March 2nd.

Yesterday I was with Elizabeth at Mrs. Braunsen's. We drank tea there again, and it was very nice. She read to us and we sang together. Aunt and Netty went to see mamma. I quite deceived Joachim. He thought I was gone home. At last he heard where I was and fetched me. He was angry that I had locked up the larder-keys, he was obliged to eat of the servants' food. That made me very sorry. I cannot tell whether he is only angry in joke. To-day I had asked aunt what was his favourite food. "He has none," she said, but before he ordered for himself on his birthday, vermicelli-pudding and hip-sauce. I ordered it in the kitchen and gave out everything for it, and when it came on table he noticed it, and said, I wished to make up to him for yesterday. He thanked me very kindly, and said the dish had never tasted so nice to him. After dinner I sang. He sat with aunt on the sofa.

March, 8th. The spring sunshine is already warm. I went to-day to the house-keeper, and fetched a quantity of fresh eggs, and carried a basketful to little Joachie. I also sat on the grass-plot with my grey-hound and sunned myself. Oh! how I do enjoy the spring, and how beautiful it is here. I should like to be here at Easter.

March, 16th. One day passes like another. I have not much to write. The day before yesterday Sophie was here with all the children. Joachie was also here with them. I went quite into a passion once, but aunt and Joachim were not angry about it. Joachim has promised me that in a few days he will ride out with me.

March, 20th. It was very delightful to-day. I sat with aunt in the twilight. She told me of the Lord Jesus, of His teaching and of faith in Him. She repeated to me very beautiful words about Him from John and Luke. I did not know all that before. When Netty came I went to my room and read it. "Behold what love the Father has shown us, that we should be called the children of God! Therefore the world knows you not because it knows Him not. For all that is in the world is not of the Father but of the world. The world passes away with its pleasure, but he who doeth the will of God abideth for ever." Oh! He abideth for ever. I should like also not to taste of death. I should like, when all here is over, to be eternally happy above with all whom I hold dear. I read in the 6th chapter of Luke. The will of God is to be plainly seen therein; I believe I understand now. "Blessed are ye if men hate you, and separate you from their company, and reproach you, and cast out your name as evil for the sake of the Son of man." In Olshausen they live in the world, and despise aunt because they will not hear the will of God, and like to live differently. They scorn and despise a faith which they do not know and understand. But I see and feel that this faith makes one far happier; that they are happier here than in Olshausen, and if I do not know and understand much, I can yet love the Lord Jesus, and pray to Him that He may ever open my heart more and more to faith. And I can learn

His will if I read the Bible. And if I once know His will I must do it, or else I should be very unhappy: even if I should possess all the fortune of the world, without it, I should always think of death with fear and therefore have no joy in life. We must all die, I see that, and all have the consciousness of another life — the bad fear; — the good rejoice. This life is so short and its pleasure only illusion, and it is so beautiful and happy to live here for Heaven. I will say all that to papa, if he wishes to compel me to the old life. I will consider still more all that I wish to say to him; and if he is wiser than I am, and I do not know what to answer, I will say to him that it does not matter to me whether folly or prudence, but I should feel happier if I lived according to God's will than if I lived with the world. Oh! I am afraid of papa — he is so wise, and can do as if he were the only one who is right.

March, 22nd. Because in those days I was very serious, aunt asked me whether I was melancholy. Then she spoke about cheerfulness and sorrowfulness and seriousness. But she need not have done so. I see it in herself and in Christian and Netty and Joachim. We drove to Mardorf to-day. I enjoyed myself again very much, but I was not so wild. I believe that that is not pretty. I shall be seventeen in May.

March, 26th. To-day it was really too beautiful. I have had a ride and a long way to the Seven Brothers. Because the horse was not quite to be trusted, Joachim led it by the bridle. There I got off. We tied the horse to a beech-tree. The sun shone so warmly on the grass and the moss. Joachim showed me the little moss-forests, how they shoot from the earth towards the warm spring air; how every flower is different, and equally delicate and full of art. So nature now begins to unfold more and more of her beauty, and, if we are attentive, we shall see the same wonders in the smallest as in the great. Oh! how sweetly the birds sang, and the lake glittered in the sun. I reminded Joachim of the winter-day, how beautiful the lake was then, but more beautiful still to-day. And I was able to be very confidential with him to-day, and related to him my evening-walk by the lake with Elizabeth, and how I was alone in the garden, and looked through the window and should so like to have come in. And then he said — I don't know what! I was very happy that I was sitting by him. I felt as though I had nothing to fear, and that he believed what I said to him. The sun went down. We rode home and I was quiet this evening. I am often rather quiet than merry.

Joachim to Joseph.

Kamern, March 29th 1823.

DEAR JOSEPH,

I did not write to you of our delightful, quiet life because there was nothing special to tell about it. I feel constantly more certain that it is the Lord's will for me to bear Theresa on my heart. Will this issue in joy or sorrow? that is in His hands. Struggles will now arise, but Theresa's heart is mine and I am very happy.

Since Wednesday she has been at Olshausen again. Uncle came quite unexpectedly with Count Stadlein and Alfred to fetch her. He was thankful for our having received Rose, and so polite over it that there

was no escape from him. Count Stadlein was silent
and on the watch. I have no doubt that he is in love
with Rose. I feel uncomfortable in his presence, he
appears to me like the evil one. Rose makes me sad.
I should so like to be always at her side, but — yet I
have a strong confidence that she will stand firm.
Uncle invited mother and me on Maundy-Thursday.
I have brought a house full of young people with me,
said he laughing, and as there is no pleasure in the
country yet, I must amuse them in-doors. I asked
him in what the pleasure would consist? "Oh!" said he
evasively, "that is not my concern. I only bring the
young people together, give them room enough, provide
food and drink, open the piano, and their youthful
enjoyment will do the rest." I asked him seriously:
"Have you remembered, dear Uncle, that we are in
passion-week?" "That is my responsibility, dear
Joachim," answered he lightly. "Opinions about such
things are divided, and you know ours do not agree."
"Well," answered I very quietly, "but permit us not
to come this week. On Good-Friday I go to Holy
Communion with all my household; to-morrow morning
to confession, and the Saturday we also spend quietly;
but on the first day of Easter we could come to you."
Uncle made some courteous reply, and took his leave.
Rose took a warm leave of mother. She said she
should come early to-morrow with Elizabeth to church.
Rose was at church Thursday and Friday. Alfred
was with her, but she went alone to the Holy Communion. Oh, Joseph, I have stood with her before
the table of the Lord. He will make me strong in all
my weakness. To-day felt hard to me at first; I felt
lonely; I wandered to our dear hill, and along the

footh-path by the lake. I saw the company walking
in the park; I heard them laugh; Rose was with them,
but surely not her heart. Dear Joseph! I was very
happy when I wandered back. I considered whether
it is easier to be a Christian in happiness or unhappiness? I think in happiness. I have made a vow to
the Lord. My heart desires so very much to be happy;
and what does it desire? Not money and property,
not honour and renown; it desires the one whom my
soul so dearly loves: — I would tread one path with
her. I would bear joy' and sorrow with her. The
star of evening is shining again, and looks on my
restless heart, — it will also behold my peace. All,
all will pass away; life is nothing, so utterly nothing;
but the future is vast, eternity shall be our inheritance.
If I could only hold that fast as the helm in this
troublous sea of life! Good-night, dear Joseph, to-
morrow is the day of our Lord's resurrection; my heart
rejoices that He is risen, that He is living, that He is
my Lord and Saviour; in this joy shall it be strong,
very strong, and celebrate a very joyous Easter-feast.

Tuesday after Easter, April 1st.

The manuscript shall come to an end at last. You
shall have enough this time. Your complaints over
my silence shall be turned into sighs over my tedious-
ness. You shall spend the Easter-day with me for
once, and see at the same time that Christian has no
reason for his fears. I snubbed him pretty severely
lately. He thought that from love to Rose, I should
go with the world as much as I could justify. He at-
tributed it to my loving and considerate nature: yet I
understand he may use as a reason for it "want of

strength of purpose" and so on. I bade him leave me
in peace and to my own conscience. If I never do
great deeds I will love the Lord and do what this love
impels me to do. I will be faithful in the little; I
will acknowledge Him before men, and praise Him
and exalt Him openly. Yes, that I will do in His
strength, which is mighty in the weak. Christian
must not require me to do it in his way; he must
leave me to my own way. Now he has given me the
very amiable promise to leave me to the Lord, and we
are very good friends. The first day of the festival
was a very bright spring-day, a true Easter-day.
Long before church I walked up and down in the
garden-parlour. I heard the bells ringing for the third
time, and looked far up into the blue sky. I then
conducted my dear mother to the church; the servants
followed us in holyday clothes. Christian preached on
the resurrection. As he followed the mighty impulse
of the spring, new and fresh life arose in his whole
being: the congregation was so attentive: surely Christian had prayed to the Lord before he went into the
pulpit. We all felt his power. After the service I
stood in the church-yard and looked at the Kamern
people who are very dear to me. No! it is not so bad
as Christian thinks: I looked there into many a peaceful face, into many a bright eye. Oh I feel such "a
rush of love" towards them. I reproached myself that
I had not got nearer to them, but, with the Lord's
help, I will become a faithful Landlord, take care of
their spiritual and bodily weal, so that I may give an
account to the Lord some day of my stewardship, and
may bring to Him many faithful souls, and say to
Him, Lord here are we whom Thou hadst appointed

to go on the pilgrimage together; — here are those whom Thou hast placed under my protection. — A troop of children looked smilingly at me — they were my friends of the winter. I shook hands with them — the little girls courtesied, the boys took off their caps and the mothers were delighted at our friendship. I have not troubled myself about them for the last few weeks. I have constantly gone thoughtlessly through the yard — but it shall be different. Klaus went, beaming with joy, with Elizabeth and Mrs. Braunsen to the little house in the church-yard corner. You faithful people will be happy yet; only have a little patience. After all the church-goers had dispersed, I went into the parsonage. I found Christian and Netty in the garden, they were standing before a peach-tree in blossom, they wished to count the buds in order to calculate the crop. I helped them, but it did not succeed. Afterwards I hid a basket full of painted eggs for little Joachie.

The boy has come too short lately; he was doubly affectionate and grateful for the time that I bestowed upon him. That was Easter morning, dear Joseph. Then we drove to Olshausen. It was strange to my mind to be suddenly in a company where nothing is to be observed of Easter. A great part of the neighbourhood was assembled with holyday clothes and cheerful faces. But how was it in their hearts? Silence! dear Joseph, I cannot enter into it when faithful Christians complain so much of the scorn, the mockery, and the contempt of the world and, so to say, make a martyrdom of their faith. It affects me in quite a different way — it is elevating to me: I feel a joyfulness and a gladness, to set against this

trash and this misery: so that I must be on my guard,
that in my own great happiness, I am not forgetful of
others as brethren. My mother knows me in this respect, and in my joyful Easter mood, foreboded danger
for the company: and as she always expresses herself
in few words she said, "Dear Joachim! nothing agrees
better with great joyfulness and confidence, than
humility and quietness. With joyfulness and confidence, and with humility and quietness, a Christian
should enter into worldly company." I could see
that very well, but it could put no fetters on my
overjoy.

I mixed at once with the young people, and acted
as if I belonged to them. To entertain half a dozen
young girls, and to take the conversation out of the
mouth of as many young men is not difficult. Cousin
Alfred attempted to introduce me to the people as "the
serious cousin," and so far things go on very satis-
factorily in my presence. To introduce some originality
into the conversation, and to bring it out of its old
ruts is necessary in such company. They consider my
openness as irony. I can express my meaning to them
in that way, and if it comes naturally to be serious,
that certainly happens too.

Uncle gave me a place near a young lady of the
neighbourhood, the most beautiful and clever, according to the universal opinion; it was considered perhaps a place of honour. Rose with two high mountains
of hair on her white forehead, sat at Count Stadlein's
side, obliquely opposite to us, so we were divided in
conversation. A more shallow superficialness than in
such a clever lady can scarcely be thought of. She
appeared to wish to impress me and went thoroughly

into it, but, with some skilful evolutions, I got the conversation again on my side. I represented to her a young lady according to my ideal, and that of a sensible man. Pious and humble, not vain, either in dress or in conversation, industrious, demure, charitable, loving and gentle; in everything — the foundation for a quiet loving wife. My clever neighbour with great adroitness, drew for me the ideal of a young man, and I must say it was a true German knightly youth, adorned with all the virtues. "Whence is it," said she, "that there are not more of such ideal characters?" I answered "because the fear of God is wanting." She looked at me with a puzzled look, but I wished to show that I was in earnest and went into the thick of the fire. I described a man without the fear of God — how he remains unreliable, childish, and empty in all his relations, what airs he can give himself.

She interrupted me after a short time and said with great self-complacency — "I know your views upon that, and do not share them. Besides so-called pious people are very much inclined to consider godless, people who are not like themselves, but they do not know what we cherish in the heart." "By their fruits ye shall know them," was my reply. "No," said she eagerly, "what fills our heart is often too high and sacred for us to bring it into the market of life. I reverence our religion also. It is noble and lofty; but always to apply its teachings to common life, and to carry them out, is impossible. Circumstances are often too weighty, the demands of our vocation too distracting: a fanatic often does not see it, but every quiet practical man sees it." Those near us had, by degrees, turned their attention to our conversation. Rose and Count Stadlein

too, though silently. The discourse of my wise young
lady gained great applause on all sides; her views
were repeated in different forms. When the storm was
over the fanatic began again. "You think thus; you
recognize the sublimity of our religion, you feel its
sacredness at your heart. When the Lord says 'I am
the Almighty God, I have created you, I support you;
life and death, happiness and unhappiness lie in My
hand' — then recognize that. If He says farther:
'Walk before Me and be perfect' — then will you
grant that He has a right to demand this? It is however too sublime, too holy, you ought not to let it be
seen before the world. Therefore you do not walk as
the Lord requires, but as circumstances and the world
require." My neighbour said proudly: "I am not afraid
of your showing us our inconsistencies: I believe all
here are taking pains to be just and brave." "Yes,"
I answered quietly, "in the sense of the world which
requires little — not in that which the Lord requires.
If the world reverenced His holy word at its heart,
the Ten commandments would surely lie at its heart
as the simplest and most comprehensible part of His
word. How could you call yourselves brave and just
when you daily tread these commandments under foot?
I will not explain in detail how society despises these
commandments, it does not deny it, and even excuses
itself that, from circumstances, it is not able to follow
them. But what would you do with a servant who
speaks thus? — I have a very good master, I owe him
much, I revere him also in my heart, but I must not
let it be seen by my fellow-servants; it is not the
custom amongst us — they do not respect the com-
mands of the master, they scoff at this service and do

what seems good to them, and I must join with them?
You would say that is a foolish and impudent speech,
and would scout the servant and his fellow-servants
from the house. No, a servant who loves his master,
who is not in league with his foes, opposes himself to
them, even if it is the custom of a great community to
follow them." "But our Lord is our dear Father also,"
interposed my neighbour Miss Haineggen again, "Who
makes allowance for His children. We know well we
are not perfect — we all have our faults." I replied, "a
father makes allowance for his children who love him
and who are striving in that love to do his will; and
who, when they fail from weakness, ask their father's
forgiveness. But children who break loose from their
father and say we could not do what he desires —
that might be fit for the old times, but not for us, we
are too wise for it, we must act according to circumstances, we must enjoy our youth, — and such-like
excuses as are heard from disobedient children: for
such children, a wise father will make no allowance —
he will not receive them until they are sorry for their
sins and repent. And so with our Heavenly Father.
He is true and is a strong and jealous God. He will
bring His disobedient and unrepentant children to account. When His grace has given us our time, the
hour of judgment will strike for us all, and then the
empty excuses will be dumb with which the world
alternately comforts itself and brings itself to destruction." They wished to reply to me again, but I here
broke off the conversation. "You are too wise," I
said, "not to see that I am right, but I will judge no
man. Every one may examine himself, how he stands
with his Heavenly Father." Do not imagine, dear

Joseph, that I hope to convert people by such conversations, but by them a stone may be thrown at every
conscience, which would touch it at a seasonable moment,
and if only we, once and again, throw such a stone
into the life of society — the Lord can speed it.   But
it should not be so hard to us to do missionary work
among men of the world. We must only do it in confidence and in the name of the Lord.   For though the
world has intrenched and palisaded itself, as also it
casts around it opinions and mockeries and trifling: —
its bulwarks are mere houses of cards, and its fire
mere glittering sky-rockets: and if one goes bravely
against it, illusion and deceit disappear, and the world
stands there in all its wretchedness.   But especially it
ought not to be hard to us men to lead the young
girls: — they allow themselves so willingly to be ruled
by men, and only take the rule on themselves, because there are so few men, but only foolish young
fellows.

My clever neighbour confessed very naïvely "We
are articles of fashion.   You know the omnipotence of
fashion. We must conform ourselves to it. If your
ideals come into fashion, most girls will direct themselves accordingly; but until men show another taste,
the education of girls will remain the same." I advised
her, since ladies had succeeded so far in the work of
emancipation, to force a better taste on men.   I combined with it a description of a young man of the
world repulsive enough, but my neighbour entered
into it, and even helped where my memory failed, in
a very clever way. I must confess that my description
of a man of the world was entirely founded on Count
Stadlein, but I say to myself now for my com-

fort that I certainly had not the energy to let him observe it.

When our conversation, from the sportive and allegorical, had passed to simple earnest, timidity in speaking of serious things was soon overcome, and every one acted as though there were nothing more on his heart than the fear of God. If however there is much self-deception in such conversations, yet the world and worldly pleasure suffer less thereby: and at the same time one gets glimpses into the hearts of men, and can confidently hope that many a word falls on to good ground. As we were walking in the garden after dinner, Miss Haineggen came up to me again, in order to continue our serious conversation. The thought that a reorganization of men could proceed from women, seemed to have struck her, "but how is it to be begun?" asked she. "Make a beginning," I said to her, "to-day, — this moment. Show that you take no pleasure in follies and worthlessness. Let your own character and employment be something different, and have the courage to acknowledge it before the world. There is not much courage in it, for the world is cowardly. But before you try to make anything of other people, you must be something different yourself. Your own heart must first be filled with the fear of God, the love of God, and the word of God. You must become a humble child of God yourself." "I will follow your advice, and read the Holy Scripture," said she rather condescendingly, but I was delighted at this decision. "But never read," I said, "without praying first. Pray that the Lord would enlighten your heart to understand His sacred mysteries: for they are hidden from the wise of this world, and only revealed to

the children of God. You know what is involved in
being a child of God — you know not what you might
become. No one can teach it you; it will be learned
and experienced. No one is brought to faith by per-
suasion, it is a gift of grace, for which we must pray
and wrestle. Therefore pray and search the Gospel,
and then the Lord will do His part. He says — 'Ask,
and it shall be given you. Believe and you shall be
blessed'" "I will try to convince myself of the truth
of your words," said the young lady and left me. She
certainly was in earnest in what she said.

When afterwards Alfred with his friends reassumed
the old tone of jesting and teasing and frivolity, and
made propositions of pleasure for the rest of the day,
she opposed him, and advised him to try whether to-
day we could not get on without dancing and acting.
Miss Sophie Sommer — the very amiable governess in
the Hagen family, was her ally and we resolved to
pass the evening in music and reading. I read to
them from the life of Anna Lavater — traits of her
youth — the description of her quiet life in the house
of her parents, — and afterwards her engagement to
Lavater. It was a sociable evening: the young girls
sat on foot-stools and seats, several young men also
stayed. Miss Haineggen sang songs from Goethe, and
from Louisa Reichardt. Rose's hymn "Now all the
woods are sleeping" made the conclusion. I do not
know why, I am still often anxious when I think of
Rose. On Friday she took leave of me cheerfully. On
Sunday Count Stadlein was standing by her, and she
gave me her hand in a very embarrassed way. To-
day I stood in a lonely place above the lake. I saw
Olshausen and the park plainly in the moonlight. My

heart was heavy and full of longing. I stood a long time leaning thoughtfully against a birch-tree. Then a gondola appeared below me. I recognized the voices of Alfred and Count Stadlein, and Rose's ringing laugh. Oh how heavy this life became to my weak heart. Yet I know I am foolish, and make myself needless care. Now good-night! pray for me, and for those dear to me.

"Safe folded by Thy wing."

Your
JOACHIM.

Kamern, 3rd May 1823.

DEAR JOSEPH,

I only add a few lines to Christian's letter. I have no time, we are keeping my dear mother's birthday,— I with no joyous heart I can tell you. They are all here from Olshausen. Uncle's politeness can no longer conceal his hostility to me.

In a few days he is going with Rose to Silesia, to fetch his sister, and to go with her to Wiesbaden. Do not think only the parting makes me melancholy. I have a decided feeling that Theresa is being led into the world, — never to return from it. I see through uncle's plans. Aunt confided his mind to me. She wished to warn me and to put me on my guard, but it is not single expressions which annoy him: — my whole character is repulsive to him. He lately said to aunt with extreme violence, that my presence was a burden to him, — a thorn at his heart. She must as far as possible avoid any meeting with us. Why he is here to-day, and why specially kind and attentive to my mother, I know not, but feel that it is ill-will. Rose is depressed and embarrassed. Yet what can I write to you? It is better that you should come. Only say when the carriage shall come.

The dispute with Netty whether you shall stay with me or with her, is not yet decided. I hope she will give in. God be with you.

Your
JOACHIM.

Theresa to Sophie.

Wiesbaden, 20th June 1823.

DEAR SOPHIE,

I have been lying on the sofa and crying all day — I do not know why. My heart is so heavy. I care for nothing, and nothing gives me pleasure. Mamma is lying upstairs. She has a headache, and I have no one with me because I do not know what I want. I thought whether it could be home-sickness, but it is not that. Dear Sophie, I love you very much, and love all at Kamern, but I am not home-sick.

Since I have learned to know the life here, I can be happy neither with you nor at Kamern. Men are different, and tastes are different, but papa is quite right it is no sin to live pleasantly. Why has the dear Lord ordered the world thus? He has made rich people and has made poor people.

The rich people must spend their money. If we do not wear velvet and silk, how can the weavers live and the goldsmiths and all the people? If I were with you I would discuss with you, but I cannot write. Dear Sophie, I am so open with you because I know you will not hate me for it. You once said to me, the more worldly I might be, the more you would pray for me. I love you very much; even if I do not share your fanaticism, I think it very beautiful. People here are generally repulsive — the young girls too. I have no friend here. Do write to me from Kamern. I dare not write to aunt, because I am afraid of being open, but I love her very much. Dear Sophie! never speak of what I confided to you that evening. I am frightened at it. I deceived myself. I am not good enough for him. I should not be happy there: the life is not fit for me. I was very happy there once. Here we live very pleasantly. We have picnics, and water-picnics; and I ride every day with papa and the gentlemen, on the promenade. Count Stadlein has broken in the loveliest horse for me, and papa buys me everything pretty which I see in the shops and wish for. I have already danced a great deal at the Kursaal. Dear Sophie, all that is surely not a sin. I do not do anything wicked, and I will take care not to become so repulsive as the young girls here. They talk so frivolously and tell stories too. One thing I could sincerely write to aunt, that I keep my promise to pray every evening, and if I know nothing else the Lord's prayer, or "Safe folded 'neath Thy wing." Dear Sophie, I do not know why I am so melancholy: the air is very sultry, heavy clouds hang in the sky, thick dust lies on the green, everything looks grey. Papa is walking up and down with Count Stadlein on the terrace, and everybody seems disagreeable to me to-day. Count Stadlein is very amiable, but he is not at all like people with us: to-day I was afraid of him. I have long tried to find out what I should like. I wish it were winter. I would sit at Olshausen, in the housekeeper's room, and roast apples. I would look,

5*

through the window, into the people's room and hear
old Samuel tell the grooms and the maids of the war-
times, and of all that went on here then.   The people
are all so well known to me, and I understand them so
well.   Dear Sophie! write to me soon a very long
letter, but so that papa cannot read it.   He sometimes
breaks open my letters.   But do write even if you are
angry with me, and give my love to all the children
too.   I wished to bring some pretty things for them
with me.

Your

THERESA.

Sophie to Theresa.

Mardorf, 6th July 1823.

DEAR THERESA,
    I am delighted that you still love me, and that
you think people repulsive there, but the day of tears
especially delights me.   May the Lord send you many
such days of tears; it is surely a gift of grace in order
to open your eyes.   As concerns your secret, I will be
silent and, to be as open as you have been, I think he
is too good for you, and I very much wish he could
see it himself; and do not doubt he will, when he hears
about you.   I will not take the trouble to reproach
you; the Lord Himself will take you into His school.
May He do so in right earnest! then you may look
back on your life with sorrow and repentance, and be-
moan with true grief of heart that you ever trifled with
a love, which is worth far more than all the foolish
and hurtful illusions, with which they are now seeking
to amuse you. — Yes, only to amuse, never to satisfy
you; the voice in your conscience will never leave you

at rest; the Lord grant that. I shall tell you about ourselves and Kamern. We are living lovely summer days. We encamp in meadow and forest. The children are exceedingly delighted and Mr. and Mrs. von Hagen are kind enough to promote such expeditions. A few days ago Herr von Kamern was here with his mother and his friend Joseph. The young people were wishing to go to the Rhine and Switzerland. I hope they will not go to Wiesbaden. Frau von Kamern is quiet and melancholy. Her son tries in every way to cheer her; he would succeed best in this if he could convince her that it is not hard to him to forget a certain frivolous maiden, and if he would soon make another choice. If she sees her son happy, she will willingly give up her favourite wish. Pardon me for expressing this so openly. I am convinced you entertain the same thoughts about it, and truth always was dear to you. God grant that it may ever remain so. I conclude for to-day, I feel as though you knew all that I would say to you, and that my love and my prayers for you remain the same. If you write to me again, I should be very much delighted.

In faithful love

Your

SOPHIE SOMMER.

Letter from Theresa to Sophie. (Not sent.)

Wiesbaden, 10th July 1823.

DEAR SOPHIE,

Your letter has made me very melancholy. I am home-sick also, oh, if I knew how to begin. If I could but ask aunt to pardon me! but it is too late. Think of it! I am all but engaged to Count Stadlein. People

speak of me as a fiancée, and I do not know what I
wish. Oh! if I could only be as happy as I used to
be! Here lies a new ball-dress, and a new ornament
too. I have no pleasure in putting it on. I have
been sitting a long time already with the pen in my
hand, but I am too sorrowful for writing. Papa knocks
at the door and drives me to my toilette. I am to be
presented to a princess to-day. Oh, dear Sophie, do
you not believe I shall be happy? Life here is so
beautiful. If I could only forget Kamern. I feel
always a pang at my heart, when I think of it. Oh!
if they had agreed a little better there with papa! if
they had not been too strict! Ah, no! I am not fit
to be there, but it makes me sorry. . . . . .

Joseph to his brother Christian.

Mainz, 16th July 1823.

DEAR CHRISTIAN, ·

I cannot send you the promised letter from Wiesbaden. We were only a few hours in that repulsive
nest, but there was no need of longer time to see how
matters are going, they are worse than I had believed.
Joachim must give up his love. He has long had the
foreboding or rather certainty of his misfortune, but I
believed it was only the fearfulness of a weak heart.
When I wished to calm him yesterday, he said, "I
know certainly that it is the will of the Lord, and that
it must happen. I have loved her too passionately."
"Oh, dear Joachim! the Lord permits us such youthful
love." He so richly adorns the life of His children.

But Joachim persisted in his gloomy decision. We
came in the twilight to Wiesbaden. We heard it was
a dancing evening. We knew where we had to find

our people. We went along, by the high brightly lighted houses of the promenade, to the Kursaal, a place which looks very bright and magnificent. We went into the ante-room and soon saw and heard enough. Joachim soon went away, but I wished to inform myself more closely. As I am quite unknown to the Olshausen gentlemen, I could more easily lose myself among the multitude. Theresa is the queen of society through her beauty and strikingly simple behaviour, so an old gentleman told me; she would be able to make splendid matches if, as is here supposed, she were not the betrothed of Count Stadlein. And Count Stadlein acts as if he already were so. Theresa appears fully in his power. He does not go from her side, and takes upon himself the rights of a protector and guide. Why should I describe details? I have no pleasure in it. It is sickening to me. In short Theresa is taken captive and dazzled by the world — A child which among so many glories has forgotten the loving voice of the mother. It could not be otherwise. The image of the Kursaal in Wiesbaden, the life, the restless activity, the singing and ringing, stand in my heart as a true image of the working of the prince of this world in the soul. I found Joachim in the Kurgarten, going up and down by the pond — his heart is heavy. He has little spirit for Switzerland, would rather go home, yet I hope by the Lord's help he will gain strength from the journey. We travelled here in the night. No one is to know that we have been at Wiesbaden. As we were going home by the Kursaal towards midnight, all was quiet in the dancing-hall. We looked through the windows into the gambling-hall, it was quiet there too; but pale faces were sitting at

the green table, Alfred and Count Stadlein among
them. That is the last disagreeable impression which
I have of both. I will soon write again, I can say
no more to-day.

Your faithful brother
JOSEPH.

Several letters of Joachim von Kamern, which he
wrote to his mother, on the journey to the Rhine and
Switzerland, which he made with his friend Joseph in
the summer of 1823, are here omitted. They are
copious descriptions of travel, under which he sought
to conceal the state of his heart from his anxious
mother. The following is again from

Kamern, 3rd September 1823.

DEAR JOSEPH,
You are quite right. Youthful happiness and youthful pleasure are over, but something better for us remains. My heart can even be hopeful at times. I
say *at times;* when the memory of the spring comes
over it, all its wings become weary. It is incomprehensible that Rose can be betrothed to him. She is
unhappy too, people say. But what of that kind is too
incredible to happen in the world? It is considered
impossible, but yet it happens. Rose was too much
flattered by the world at Wiesbaden. She could not
withstand so many enticements. Yet she has the sword
in her heart, that, perhaps, is the unhappiness of which
people speak. For some days the betrothed pair have
been at Olshausen. I am thinking of congratulating
them. I am peaceful, very peaceful at the thought:
I have fought, but always with a presentiment of victory.

"Is it harder to be a Christian in happiness or un-happiness?" I asked in the spring and thought in happiness; but no, the Lord loves most to be with the most sorrowful. Now I often have such blissful hours as never before, and have never experienced such strengthening answers to prayer as at this time. And so I will heartily pray the Lord that He will make me strong, that He will make me forget earthly sorrow. Oh! in love to Him, my dear faithful Lord, everything is alike to me; sometimes such a feeling of love over-flows me that I could sing aloud — the world lies be-hind me — heaven is won. In such a state of mind I know the Lord will help me to meet the betrothed pair; in such a state of mind I shall approach Count Stadlein and greet him as a cousin. I will speak to Rose of my blessings on her and prayers for her. I will direct her once more to the true Helper, Who may give her strength to withstand the world and to win peace. And then it shall be all at an end, and I will begin to live with the good people at Kamern. It is a year since I came here with like plans; with God's help I will be more faithful now. My mother is re-joiced at my vigour. Her grief at the matter causes me great sorrow, and I conceal from her when my bark is ready to sink. I feel so very much that man's con-solation can do very little for us; it is the strength of the Lord, — the blessed mystery of love to Him, which fills and touches our heart, which makes it young, so that it can mount up like the eagle. Dear Joseph! the time will soon come when my wings shall no more be weary, and then you will have joy in me again. Now for the present have a little patience with me.

I have been a long walk, dear Joseph. I have
been sitting under the beeches, — the country beneath
me lay in an almost summer-haze. I picked a nosegay of scabious and wild pinks for myself, and other
light fresh mountain-flowers. I gazed closely at it,
and found the Lord there, and lifted up my heart full
of love to Him; I lay down on the flowery heath.
Bees were humming around me, gay butterflies were
floating towards the sky. It was very quiet and lonely
around me, and from below, from the lane, sounded
the far-off rattling of a carriage, and the monotonous
gee—gee of the driver. I lay there a long time, I
thought of our summer journey; how the sky is spread
far above the earth, and far above the splendour and
loveliness which the Lord has displayed upon it; of the
shining glaciers; of the quiet meadow-valleys; of the
glorious sea, of all the people who wander over it in
sorrow and joy and pleasure and tribulation. Oh! it
is wonderful, very wonderful; who could ever think it
out — the miracle of our life? No, not think of it.
Reason is too weak. But we can love — love intensely;
love is strong, it comprehends all, soars far above the
earth, penetrates into heaven — rests at the feet of the
Lord. Ah, well! I would gladly have only a little
space at the feet of the Lord — that is blessedness
enough. So my heart this evening is full of peace.
I was still lying under the beech-trees, when I heard
steps in the under-wood. I raised myself up; it was
Rose who stepped from the shade. She started. I
looked at her very calmly. She came suddenly to me,
seized my hand and said weeping, "Joachim, pardon

me. I am very unhappy, but I cannot do otherwise."
"The Lord help you," I answered gravely, "and may
He only always let you feel your unhappiness." Ah,
Joseph, how those cruel words grieved my tender heart
afterwards! I love her still with all the passion of
this weak heart; I would gladly see her happy, but on
that very account, I could not help wishing that she
should feel her misery. I left the place, I heard loud
voices in the wood. Rose was leaning against a beech-
tree, and was covering her face with both hands. Count
Stadlein, Alfred and others came to her. I went without looking round any more. Oh! how far the spring
lies behind me, how full of woe my heart is! Lord
give me peace. Amen, Amen! yes, it shall be so.
There is the star of evening; it will behold my peace.
Farewell, dear Joseph. The Lord be with you and
with

Your poor friend
JOACHIM.

Kamern, 15th September 1823.

Is this a hymn to sing in the choir above, dear
Joseph? An evil wind is blowing up at Olshausen,
and the father of lies does not show himself quite
powerless with us. I have now often been up there
with them; do not think that in my weak wisdom I
went very boldly among them; much is wanting to me
yet. I should like to get higher — higher and not to
see the turmoil at all. I see it; I feel it; I feel myself
in the midst of it; it is often repulsive to my mind.
Whatever the world can devise of pleasure and enjoyment and luxury, is to be experienced at Olshausen.
Uncle is in his place there, he acts host, he arranges,

he talks so wisely, acts so cautiously, is ready for
everyone, that as a conqueror heaven and earth are
subject to him. He makes a jest of every power except
his own wisdom. Count Stadlein is pleased at his
power, because his passion for Rose is still bright and
fiery, and he goes on his way in league with Alfred.
Rose is quiet and embarrassed with me and with mother,
however much Count Stadlein tries to conceal it with
noisy mirth. Oh, Joseph, her appearance touches my
heart! She is still always lovely and child-like; sometimes she tries to be merry and even careless, but yet
it seems only a resource. And aunt? She sighs, but
joins in everything. The splendour which uncle has
suddenly spread around her, and the prospect of seeing
Rose some day splendidly married, consoles her. So
they are going with full sails down the stream of
worldly pleasure. That they have taken Rose in tow
with them, I cannot yet comprehend. I stand on the
bank, and should like to rescue her. I feel as if I
must make a violent effort. I cannot comprehend that
it is the will of the Lord, and yet it is He. I wish
now to turn away my eyes. As I cannot help, I do
not wish to be going along by the side. It depresses
me, it distracts me, I cannot pray, I cannot raise my
thoughts; I have no joy of heart. I cannot live with
the Lord, however much I long for it; and every hour
so spent is a robbery of Him. Dear Joseph, I must
conclude this letter, and yet cannot. I must shake the
dust from my feet — must utter the desolation of my
soul. When they were down here, and twice when
we were up there, I saw Count Stadlein's uncle. Herr
von Lemmen is an old Austrian soldier of very distinguished appearance. Uncle is specially attentive to

him; he is his nephew's guardian, and uncle seeks
eagerly to gain him over. The more solemn and
quiet the old gentleman is, the more eloquent is uncle's
mouth and manner. Beyond the customary forms of
politeness, I had not spoken to the old gentleman, and
felt no desire for it. Yesterday when all was mirth,
and I was standing alone by the table in the window,
the old man came suddenly to me. He took my hand
with both of his, shook it heartily, and said, "Dear
Herr von Kamern, you seem to me the only sensible
man here." I could not help laughing. "It almost
seemed so to me," I said, "but I am very glad to
know of a better." "Well now, my dear," said he
again with eagerness, "learn from me, but teach me
too." He sat down by me, and opened out his mind.
It was ludicrous to me at the moment, for an hour
before uncle had, with great pains, been describing to
me and to some good neighbours, his connection with
Herr von Lemmen, in a very opposite way. Uncle
told of the magnificent and splendid family alliances;
how he used to travel over the estates with Herr von
Lemmen and so on; and the old gentleman showed
me the other side of this picture of life, which is a
truly sorrowful and hateful one, when deprived of the
glitter of illusion. Count Stadlein's father married the
sister of Herr von Lemmen, — a poor but beautiful
and giddy girl. They lived in the world; their life
was foolish, said the old gentleman and at last unhappy
too. His sister came somewhat to her senses, through
the loss of several children. She sought retirement;
poor health made this voluntary retirement into a
necessity. The husband now lived for his pleasure
only, and in the worst way — in great extravagance

and irregularity: — a sudden death put an end to the
matter. The lady's brother became guardian and ad-
ministrator of the estates. He has never succeeded in
bringing them into order; — the disorder is too great.
But that is the least part of it, said he with a sigh.
Herr von Kamern, do you see grey hair on my head?
That young man is the cause of it. He frustrates all
the pains which I have expended on the estates, — he
is a greater spendthrift than his father. Spoiled by
the world and by a weak mother, he is thoroughly
ruined. The lamentation was longer than I can write
here; I could scarcely listen to it. Rose came out of
the bright noisy room next to us, she looked shyly at
us and placed herself in a distant arm-chair. What
the old gentleman had related was only what I had
foreboded: it could not make my heart heavy. But he
obtained from me a promise, not to speak of his communications; I was only to advise him what to do.
He has made the same communications to Uncle Olshausen who seems to pay no attention to them; he
trusts to his administrative talents to order matters
according to his wishes. The old gentleman is now
distrustful even of Rose. I was to tell him the truth.
I did so; I praised Rose, commended her to his heart;
perhaps, I did so too warmly, she sat in such a con-
strained way in the arm-chair. Oh, Joseph, my wings
became weary. The old gentleman left us, I remained
alone; she remained in the arm-chair. I should like
to have prayed, and was so weary and weak; I was
foolish enough to think "there she is, — she is near thee,
thou canst see her; soon she will be far from thee."

Kamern, 22d September 1823.

DEAR JOSEPH,

All is over at last; — they are gone. The old uncle
has sometimes quieted me a little by his friendship.
I saw no one else. We were not at home when they
took leave. Yesterday I felt driven towards the place
once more. I went by the lake. It was a beautiful
autumn day — the wood in autumnal colouring — the
lake peaceful and clear, — bright sunshine above.

I heard loud conversation in the park; it came
nearer; I turned aside to let the loud company get on
before me. I looked after them till they vanished in
the wood — Rose on the arm of the old uncle. Now
it is over; they went away to-day. I have a bad
headache, the sky is cloudy, many leaves have fallen
in the night, a damp mist lies on the bright leaves.
I am very sorrowful; not on account of the earthly
anguish — I know I shall conquer that. No! my
weakness grieves me, I am crushed; when I fold my
hands and look up, I cannot commune with the Lord.
My head gets worse and worse.

Good-bye.

Your

JOACHIM.

Kamern, 4th December 1823.

DEAR JOSEPH,

Weeks have passed in which I could not write to
you; they include a whole life-time to me. I have
become much older and yet so much younger. I have
been very ill but with the Lord's help recovered. To
be really well, and to feel it deeply and thankfully,
one must have been ill — tossed and shaken, as on the

brink of the grave. I thank the Lord for this illness.
When I look back on the past, on my whole life, and
especially on this last year, He has very much to
pardon me. I have much cause to thank Him, to love
Him abundantly. Yet I will not look back, — that is
settled with my dear Lord, — I will look forward. I
begin a new life with this season of Advent — with
this New Year of the Church. For a week I have begun to go out; the air is so mild, the sky so beautiful;
but I do not go my old favourite walks — they have
seen my weakness, my misery, they would make me
sad. The peaceful feeling of reconciliation has not
yet penetrated so deeply; but it will do so, and my
dear home will again belong to me in all its loveliness.
To-day about noon I was walking, as I so often do,
in the yard along by the barns. The sun was warm,
the monotonous beat of the flail sounded so familiar;
I spoke a word with the thrashers or with the children
who play in the straw before the doors. I am glad
now to seek people's company, because I have neglected
them. I am touched that they show such great joy
to-day at my recovery, when I have done so little to
deserve their love. With the Lord's help, I will now
be a kind and fatherly master to them, I will take
some trouble myself about them. One old thrasher
said to me, "the eye of the master sees more than
twenty eyes of bailiffs: and the love of the master does
more than a stern word." I have also great pleasure
now in the household; I am so fond of activity, and
should like to understand everything. The steward is
going at Easter, that I may have no one between me
and the people. Our connection will come to a very
natural end, he is going to Lubbendorf, a little estate

three hours journey from here, which I bought and which he will manage for me. He is to take the inn-keeper's Dora as his wife. I shall often go there; and, in the summer, mother will go, and the people from the parsonage. Lubbendorf is in a lonely situation by the sea; we shall have sea-bathing there. So we are making summer-plans and sit together almost every day in a confidential circle. That my recovery should happen at the time of Advent, at the time of year which is dearest to me, heightens my feeling of health and enjoyment. Besides I have also got a spiritual duty for this season. I am president of our reading-evenings, which we have instituted as a celebration of Advent. Poor Christian has been for some time tor-mented by a violent cough. He is glad to confine himself now to necessary speaking. My office gives me great pleasure. When I return from my quiet walks, I study the Bible and hymn-books and books of devotion, in order to bring together suitable subjects, and to give some inner coherence to our celebration. I enjoy the whole evening, for if we do not have a longer service every evening, we never conclude it without a shorter time of devotion. I mean to con-tinue that, the rest of the year, and for my whole life. What can I do better than build at the kingdom of the Lord? At this time I have even thought I should like to be a pastor and preacher — it is the most beautiful and sacred vocation — to preach the gospel, and so to live it oneself, that because the heart is full, the mouth overflows. Oh! if our heart is so full of rich love, our words must sound lovingly to others; and only the overflowing of our own heart can set other hearts in

motion. I should like, with the Lord's help, to be a
true pastor. I should like often to be alone with myself and the Lord, and to be gathering, constantly
gathering, and only to give when I myself can contain
no more. May not a danger lie in too great zeal, in
always wishing to give and to do? We often tax our
treasures too much in that way, and the words sound
from an empty heart at last, and then we are sorry
that, with the best zeal, and the truest love for the
Lord, we see so few fruits of our labour. Dear Joseph,
I must confess I think it is rather so with our Christian.
His zeal to do something in his calling is great; he
scarcely gives any time to himself. He would like to
serve the Lord with every minute of his life, but he is
easily cast down if he does not see an advance in his
building; and this state of mind hinders its growth.
Pardon me that I, a poor layman, make bold to find
fault with you; the calling may be sacred but difficult
too, who knows how it would be with me? So I will
confine myself humbly to my station and calling, and
only pray for the faithful curates, — pray for the faithful Christian, that the Lord would richly fill his heart
with the sweetness of the gospel; that he, from his own
joyfulness, from his own peace, may fill our hearts
with consolation and joy. I shall not be able to help
encroaching a little on his office. I must be able to
preach a very little sometimes, to feed my flock, which
the Lord has committed to me, in my own house and
farm. Oh! I shall not be able to omit, ever more
distinctly to acknowledge my Lord, to sing more joyfully to Him, to honour and to praise Him.

And I of all Thy loveliness
By day and night will sing,
And of my heart from day to day
A joyful offering bring:
My stream of life to Thee shall pour
And to Thy name for ever-more,
    In thankfulness o'er-flowing,
The mercy Thou hast shown to me,
My theme, while I have breath, shall be
    In thankful memory growing.

And now enough for to-day, my dear Joseph; I already hear little Joachie trotting up the steps. Even our little community is to be called delightful, and I have often felt compassion for those people who could not have the pleasure of being in our company! Joachie has naturally a seat and a voice there, especially in the social part of the evening. When we read he plays with sand on his little table, or something else which my mother has thoughtfully provided. When the sand-man makes his eyes heavy, I take him and put him to bed on the soft corner of the sofa and there, so to speak, he snores his little part. I believe this is not quite the orthodox treatment of children; but Netty is kind enough to yield to circumstances, because she sees the boy is indispensable to us. Without him one chief element would be wanting in our circle, but especially to me. Christian with his vivacity is naturally always the chief person, if Netty with her simple native wit does not get the start of him. My mother is more for hearing than talking; yet there is a power in her silence, the influence of which we all feel.

Few words only are needed from her to open a bright and melodious fountain. I do not exactly know what I do in the company myself, but I often feel a great need of satisfying my favourite inclinations in partnership with little Joachie. Perhaps it is a matter of convenience? But when I can no longer follow Christian's spiritual flights, and my mother's thoughtful reflections, I walk about in the harmless world of childhood. Therefore I am the boy's favourite. He is already standing at my knee and asking what I am writing. "To Uncle Joseph — shall I send your love to him?" Yes and Joachie could go now into the dark room; only it must be a little bit bright. The little rascal! He wishes to say something laudable of himself, but one sees that it is in reality so with the old one. It is often the same with us bigger people. I forgive him that also.

God be with you.

JOACHIM.

Kamern, 25th December 1825.

DEAR JOSEPH,

It is still very early and it is very quiet; the bright moonlight lies on the landscape, on the church, and the lime-trees, and the little parsonage. The bells have been ringing the whole hour from four to five: that is a beautiful custom, the festive peal in the bright moonlight-night. I woke and celebrated Christmas with all my soul. I saw the star shining over little Bethlehem — the angels were singing "Glory to God in the highest — peace on earth and good will to men."

I went with the shepherds into the lowly hut — to the child, Who lay there in the glory of His heavenly dignity. I looked into His bright eyes, — kissed His hands and His feet. My heart is full of joy. The angels could not have announced the message more blissfully than my heart is now filled with it, and would cry to the whole world, "Behold I bring you glad tidings of great joy." I could sing I know not what — quite a new song, much more heavenly and glorious than all songs. The tone of love therein would surely rouse the whole world, rouse it that it should come to the little Child, and should behold in faith this miracle of love.

Oh Love, who hast the clouds of heaven divided,
To my great misery to condescend,
What impulse to the vale of grief has guided
Thee, for my sake, an exile drear to spend?
Oh it is love that gave that wondrous power to Thee;
She, like a mother, looks up on my misery.

So great Thy love! so great the tribulation,
By which for me Thy tender heart was torn;
No miracle too great for my salvation:
Thou for my sake the thorny crown hast worn.
Of love like this no ear has ever heard,
Which clothed in human flesh the everlasting Word.

No sorrow now our hearts from Thee can sever,
Immanuel is with us in our need;
He is my fount of joy both now and ever,
And even grief and death my way shall speed;
The sorrow which may yet betide,
Can never harm me while I still in Christ abide.

And sin itself has suffered condemnation,
And since His death it can condemn no more;
What matter now the fires of temptation,
If Christ the precious blood and water pour?
Immanuel can its rising power repel;
He will not leave the soul — He loves it far too well.

With life eternal, He is still providing
Glory and wealth and rapture from above;
I am with Him, and He with me abiding,
In which I trace the working of His love.
Now I am satisfied, my heart is stilled,
Because with streams of purest love my soul is filled.

I have made a vow to-day. I will sing a song of love to the Lord — not a new one. I poor simpleton have a clumsy tongue: — no, my whole life shall be this song; love shall shine from my eyes, shall speak from my whole being. To Him, to that lovely Child, to the great Saviour, to the mighty King, my life belongs. He will grant me a child-like spirit — a king-like spirit. Yes, I will regard myself highly and as a king: — all that belongs to this poor world here is beneath my dignity; earthly joys are for me a mere play of shadows: the world's honour and renown mere childishness; the cares of the earth too small, and to bear them is not fit for me: their grief, their woe, their pangs, at the highest, only wet my feet like waves upon the sea-shore. I only share all with my King — His joy, His honour and renown are mine: — mine are also His pangs — His anxiety for my soul's salvation, His tears in Gethsemane, His death-agony on the cross. What is life here? With the Lord Jesus Christ, it is joy, peace, blessedness.

It is fleeting, it is short, the days fly away, the forms around our path of life, which quickly change, may disturb and distract us, may take rest and oneness from our life: but our gaze goes on before: we have only the one Heavenly Image before our eyes. It sheds such a bright peaceful light over our path, that the gay entanglement around us flies away, like an image of the mist. What is life without the Lord Jesus Christ? Nothing! worse than nothing — it is death.

Behind every pleasure and joy, — death is beckoning; behind the highest honours, — death is standing; behind riches and enjoyment of every kind — death is

threatening: so it goes on from one day to another
speedily and swiftly to the end; and when thus a
worldly life has distracted and befooled us, fettered the
soul and paralysed it, death appears to it like an
image of terror, until struggling, it becomes his prey.
"Pause and bethink yourselves!" I would cry to the
world. I would suddenly put a lock before the stream.
Look around you! see your misery! Oh such pictures
as these do not belong to the joy of Christmas, dear
Joseph, and besides they do not suit my weak powers.
I would rather be a preacher of life, than a preacher
of death. I should like to speak only of love, and to
animate hearts with the wonder-working power of love.
Yes rejoice, rejoice you weak children, you poor sin-
ners, the Saviour is born, and "Glory be to God in
the highest, peace on earth and goodwill to men."
Amen. This shall be my early Christmas greeting. I
have arranged everything for morning worship; but all
is still quiet in the house. I can still talk to you.
Last year you were with us, and our house was very
lively. This year it is quieter; only Aunt Emma is
here. Uncle is staying with Alfred, and Theresa at
Vienna for the winter. Aunt is very weak, suffers
from nervous headache, and is obliged almost every
week to sit, for two days, in a dark room; and in the
outward darkness light is dawning in her soul. Elizabeth is her faithful nurse.

Yes, aunt comes nearer and nearer to us; and
yesterday, with joy and emotion took part in our
festival. But who else took a very joyful part? who
but dear little Joachie! When it was dark yesterday
evening I took him in my arms, wrapped him warmly
in my cloak, and so went to the churchyard, over the

crisp snow. Then the little angels sang from the
tower. Our choir-master has not trained his choir in
the best possible way, but it sounds so beautiful coming down from the bright starry sky; and my little
Joachie looked devoutly up with folded hands. I am
very fond of the boy. When he raises his dark lashes,
and looks at me with his bright starry eyes, when he
strokes the hair from his forehead, and holds my head
with both hands, he is irresistible, and it goes to my
heart, and I think the Lord has given this child to be
near thee, that it should in part belong to thee. Yes,
I will help to bring up Joachie. To spoil him, you
say laughing! Oh no, I will discover the true wisdom.
Now I am only beginning to sing before him my
favourite song. I did so yesterday, under the lighted
Christmas-tree and beside the beloved manger. There
were a number of children and widows at the festival,
as well as Joachie. We sang; I read the gospel; and
when the strangers were gone I played with the boy;
and when he had played till he was tired I put him
warmly to bed, in the corner of the sofa. Poor Christian still suffers very much with his cough; besides the
many festival services are a toil to him. Netty is
anxious about him; she tried also to find a substitute,
but there is no clerical student to be found in the
whole country, to whom Christian could give up his
place in the pulpit. Klaus has just been in and
brought me my cool refreshing morning draught. He
wished me a joyful and happy festival. Yes, Klaus, I
said, the joy must extend to the next festival, and so
from one Christmas to another, and that I wish for
you also. I asked him what present the holy Jesus
had given to him? You have given me the best present, he

said. I gave him the permission to marry Elizabeth at Easter. I have raised his wages, and he is to live in the gardener's house. There was great rejoicing yesterday at the little house in the churchyard corner. He told me of the things which he had got there; but a little chest with a drawer, which Elizabeth gave him, especially delighted him. Elizabeth and her mother are both richly endowed by the Lord. Klaus also belongs to Him, but less is entrusted to him, and so less will be required. Now my mother's bell is ringing, and the house becoming more lively. At noon the Hagens are coming from Mardorf. The excellent governess is paving the way for the Lord there also. We have spent happy days there and here with each other. We try to be very sociable here in Kamern, and not without success.

The Hagen house is a great favourite of mine because of the many children. In the first place I am still very fond of play, and secondly Joachie must have intercourse with children. We often let him be with the village children, but with them he feels himself like a king and an autocrat. With the Hagen children he learns to be compliant; the little girls especially give him much need of it. We also often see Miss Haineggen there. She is very intimate with Sophie Sommer. Sophie hopes she will turn to the Lord, and if, with her spirit and her activity, she takes pains to serve the Lord, as she has hitherto served the world, she might become a real help in the vineyard of the Lord.

And now enough for to-day. I wish you a joyful and happy festival with all my heart.

JOACHIM.

Kamern, 20th February 1824.

DEAR JOSEPH,

Consider Netty's proposal seriously. I say Netty's:
Christian's wish is the same, but he does not venture
to express it so decidedly. The doctor absolutely
orders rest for the summer, and why take a strange
curate, when you stand so near us? Your consideration
of giving up your place now, and of being obliged at
Michaelmas to look out for a new one, I place with the
consideration that at Michaelmas Joachic will be in
his fifth year, and that you can help me in the laudable
work of teaching him, by and by, his A B C. Besides
our old choir-master would be glad to give up his
flock to you for the winter, and you could make yourself sufficiently useful. So a year would be provided
for, and the Lord would provide afterwards.

Netty is anxious about Christian; his cough sounds
bad, but the physician says that his lungs are sound.
Christian is exhausted, and nervously excited and
fatigued. With the Lord's help, summer rest, and sea
air, will make him strong again. Otherwise we enjoy
our quiet life. I enjoy very much that with the dear
people at Kamern. There is great danger to me in
the desire to undertake Christian's duty, but I do it
carefully and modestly. I very often visit the school,
especially at the singing-times: the children learn my
favourite hymns — indeed singing is my heart's delight. On Sunday morning they serenaded me, and in
return I had a sweet roll made for each of them for
Shrove-tuesday. To gain children's hearts is not
hard, and children become grown-up people, as the
proverb says. If I can not get on with the old, I will
set my hope on the young. Twice the people from

the farm have had permission to take part in our evening prayers. Many a one of our young choir is to be found there, and there are scarcely enough books for the assembly. Klaus takes great interest in my spiritual duties, as landlord and master of the house; and does what he has to do in it with great zeal. His heart was sorely depressed last time. Elizabeth, who has been here since Christmas, to see about her trousseau, was desired by Aunt Emma as her companion to Vienna. Theresa's wedding is to be there the beginning of March. Aunt would only undertake the journey on condition that Elizabeth accompanies her, and Theresa begged for Elizabeth's presence, as a special wedding-treat. Klaus could not be reconciled to it. "Vienna is a long way off," he said, one has never been there in one's life; besides the people are Catholics: who knows what sort of an establishment it is.

We ought not to let Elizabeth go. At last I advised aunt to take him with her as a male escort: so all is arranged; and next week they will start on their journey.

Klaus says, "Vienna is a long way off," dear Joseph, yes, indeed, Vienna is a long way off; from me too very far, and that is well. I have always cause to pray "Lord, lead me not into temptation." Who knows the hidden corners of his own heart? I commend you to God, dear Joseph.

I end with the beginning of my letter. Consider the matter about Christian; but I do not doubt of your consent.

Your

JOACHIM.

Letter from Klaus Riedern to his Master.

As Elizabeth is writing to her mother, I cannot omit to put in a few poor words to my dear master. I cannot say that they do not respect me; I do not have much to do with the people, who do not even rightly understand German, and do not know how to speak any good Pomeranian. Elizabeth too does not trouble herself much about the women; they are, as may be said, uneducated and trifle, and play the bag-pipe all day. Our lady got well through the journey, and has had her first headaches here. We celebrated the wedding yesterday; the evening before, there was much singing and music — but nothing for us. I sat with Elizabeth, and took a young groom with me, who seems respectable. Elizabeth read us a sermon and then we sang. One is obliged here to be on one's guard. When Miss Theresa yesterday was in her bride's dress, I peeped through the door. She looked like an angel.

When she saw me, I could not help coming into the room. The tears stuck so in the dear young lady's throat, that she could not speak. Mistress embraced her, and said, dear Rose, I did not think that you would come into such a strange land. The young lady gave me her hand and said, "Klaus, I don't forget my home." I thought I must say something to cheer up the two ladies. Dear Miss, I said it is best with us; and there is nothing to compare with our yellow beans and breasts of geese. There is some substance in them: and so I said something at which they could not help laughing heartily. The young Count disturbed us in our merriment, he is always going about like the foul fiend. In the evening I had a confidential conversation with the old uncle, who is quite on our side. "The outlay goes a little too far," I said. He assented to that, and praised my master at Kamern as the most sensible man.

Why should the husband have carriages and horses and the wife carriages and horses too? said I; they have them in one place, and I would rather go with my wife than go alone; and disunion comes of separation: and they have not got trusty servants: before their face it is "What do you please?" and "Your noble grace" and, behind their back, curses and abuse. I said that will not do; Miss Theresa is a good child of the country. Elizabeth too said to her yesterday, (because she was so melancholy) "if your new friends here dance and caper for you, your old friends in Kamern will pray for you, and we will see who can do it best, and who can hold out the longest." Herr von Olshausen is in great excitement about the festivities, and has himself called count.

This evening there is a party at the house of the young pair; to-morrow a ball at the aunt's, then at a cousin's and so on. When we have gone on a little while in this way we shall begin our return journey. Our lady would rather go to-day than to-morrow if it were not for the parting.

Till noon she is always alone with Miss Theresa. But "a week at the most" she said. I end this letter with the prayer that the Lord may faithfully keep my dear kind master, and bring us happily to each other again and remain most obediently Your faithful

KLAUS RIEDERN.

Kamern, 15th March 1824.

DEAR JOSEPH,

There greet you

Your faithful brother Joachim,

Your dear sister Netty,

Your dear nephew Joachie,

the honourable lady at the castle of Kamern,

and

Your very devoted friend Joachim.

Only come. Our hearts and arms are open to you.
It is still stormy and rough without, and yet you
would be warm with us. It is delightful that you are
coming a fortnight earlier. You will have a taste of
our winter life. This winter is dear to me. I do not
like to part with it, and I am not sorry that spring
keeps us waiting so long. Fix when we shall send to
fetch you from the post-office and do not forget to
bring something with you for Joachie — that is the
custom here.

In faithful love

Your

JOACHIM.

A page by Joachim.

(Written Good-friday 1824 towards evening during bell-ringing.)

A thousand times, oh Lord, I bless Thee
For ceaseless love which Thou hast shown;
My sins which did the most distress Thee,
Thou, Saviour, didst Thyself atone.
Ah it is well for me to kneel
To bear my Saviour's last appeal;
Or by the cross in dust to lie,
Where, for my soul, He deigned to die.

My Lord and Saviour, Thou art mine, and I am Thine, now, come what will! Thou hast died for me that I, in spite of my sins, may live. This night I had a dream which has impressed itself tenderly and deeply on my soul. I was walking on a mild, bright moonlight night on some lovely meadow-land; — a hill rose before me. I looked up. There hung the crucified Saviour, but so tall and high that He reached to heaven: pale, and still, and gentle, the Figure stood out against the dark blue sky, with the shining stars. I sank down and gazed up, and I was sorrowful, and yet so happy in my mind, and the dream was in my thoughts the whole day, and the same melancholy and the peace.

Joseph preached this morning on the passion, "Truly He bore our sickness, and took our griefs upon Him. The punishment lies on Him, that we may have peace." "O Lord, forgive us our sin," I never prayed it in such full faith — "as we forgive our debtors," I never prayed it with such humiliation. That pale and glorious Figure of my dream is deeply impressed on my mind; it is silent, and yet it speaks so piercingly. Be still! suffer and love. My soul strives after stillness. Oh, silent Jesus! make me like-minded with Thee — as an obedient child — innocent and still. Jesus, now help me, that I may be silent like Thou art. Draw me wholly to Thee; keep me ever more, faithful Saviour. Jesus, let me like Thee, and where Thou art, some day find rest! I felt an impulse to-day to Olshausen. Till now I had avoided seeing uncle and Alfred again; to-day, when my own sense of guilt is so present with me, other guilt withdraws to a distance. To-day stillness, and suffering, and loving, are so easy to my heart. The sky was dull. A thawing wind roared through the bare trees and the reeds by the lake. I went along the lonely path, and found it for once quiet even at Olshausen. Uncle and Alfred both on the sofa with colds and coughs; aunt with them as their loving nurse. Uncle wished to give me a glowing description of the life in Vienna; Alfred added his with great emphasis. I was silent, the old spirit of contradiction and of admonishing did not come over me; Their honr is not yet come, but the Lord can deliver and bless. At last, aunt turned the conversation. She has been to-day to church and heard Joseph; we talked of what lay on our hearts. The two gentlemen were silent; uncle caught up a newspaper. I left the house and wished him peace. So I have again resumed the acquaintance and it becomes easy to me. I closed my eyes for a time. The Figure of my dream stood before my soul; all whom my heart loves were kneeling at my side, and the figure of Rose so near to me. Oh, Lord! I have undertaken it and I will not let her go — I will not let Thee go unless Thou bless her. Surely she is prostrate before Thine altar to-day, — even though it is veiled to her eyes. Surely she is seeking Thee, and knows not how to find Thee; oh, Lord, call her, and stretch out Thy hand to her. Hold the cords of love firmly to her heart. Amen. The day is ending — "It is finished."

Now "it is finished", I will lie
Upon Christ's burial stone to rest;
With angels meeting in the sky,
Like Jacob once, in slumber blest.
"'Tis finished," by that word now life is given:
And open stands the glorious "gate of heaven."

Joseph to Joachim.

Kamern, 20th June 1824.

DEAR JOACHIM,

It seems very strange to me to be writing to you from Kamern — that I am here without you. The people consider me very much as your substitute. They come with many questions, often very strange ones, to me. I conceal my ignorance, while I refer the questioner to Saturday and to your return. I beseech you earnestly — do not leave me in the lurch. I have nothing else to tell you. Your uncle was here with Alfred. They start to-morrow for their journey to Italy, and meet the Stadleins in the neighbourhood of Naples. In September they will be together at Olshausen. God bless you.

Your faithful

JOSEPH.

Lubbendorf, 21st June 1824.

DEAR JOSEPH,

I am not coming on Saturday. After mature deliberation, I must make myself invisible to the dear people of Kamern for some time; for once I must here in tranquillity look over and consider my zeal and my activity; whether I have enough to meet the necessary expenses of the building I have begun; that it may not be said, "this man began to build and cannot finish it." The life of a dreamer and collector is sometimes necessary to my nature. Early in the morning, I walk with Joachie to the shore. I lie there, I listen to the murmur of the waves, I watch the gathering clouds and the distant sails. Joachie looks for shells

or stones, or dreams with me. We understand each
other. On Sunday afternoon we expect you here.
Lubbendorf is indescribably lovely. Our days pass
quietly away. One does not trouble himself about the
others. We are only together when we like. Christian
is well, but if I had been he, I would not have taken
any books with me except such as are for daily food.
Netty is inspired with youthful romance. My mother
takes a heart-felt pleasure in our enjoyment. Yesterday we made plans for a journey — Christian, Netty
and I; we wish in the autumn to go to the Rhine.

Miss Haineggen and her aunt, who both live near
here, have called upon us; the old lady is very affectionate. I believe this intercourse will be very accept-
able to the ladies in their seclusion here. We have
no society besides; my friend is an old fisherman, who
in his character bears much resemblance to Mrs.
Braunsen. He is very decided and sings, "I have
found the bottom, which for ever holds my anchor."
He is a happy man, and it does me good to hear the
Lord Jesus preached from such a simple mouth. I go
with him sometimes on to the hill. It is something
glorious on these sunny golden days. The unbounded
view over the expanse of water, the freshness and
clearness, the peace. Valentine then sometimes forgets
his trade, and relates his experiences and inward con-
templations. A simple calling and quiet contemplative
life is a blessing. I see more and more how we must
simplify our outer life. It is only a useless thing and
useless activity, but yet we would willingly hold fast
many a thing and give it a heavenly appearance. One
thing is needful, and only one; one thing is blessed,
and only one. To hold the Lord Jesus dear, and to

give evidence of this love, — that is life. But the
Lord will have us altogether; not only for an hour
here and there. Our love must pour forth to Him
like a rich spring of water, it must be powerful enough
to carry away with it everything which comes in its
way; and it must be clear and pure, so that all may
thirst, who see such fresh springs. Good night, dear
Joseph! The Lord bless your service to-morrow evening. Pray with your whole soul, give up everything
for it. Touch their hearts with such freshness of love.
Be yourself so richly refreshed and filled, that others
may desire your riches. I sat till late with old Valentine on the edge of a heath. He related to me about
the death of his last child — a son who had lost his
life while skating in the winter. Valentine has now
to support five grand-children. His daughter-in-law
helps him faithfully. "You see, Master," (thus he
finished his discourse) "the sea is broad, and full, and
deep, and the heaven above us is very high, and the
stars which shine there are countless, but the Lord
and His wonderful world above, and our salvation,
and eternity, are still more so. And it matters not
whether I am a poor fisherman, or whether I am a king,
and whether I live happy days or unhappy days: if I
love the Lord and live with Him here, my little drop
will flow into the great eternity. It is not worth while
to raise a lamentation — life is too small and too short;
I would rather sing praise and thanks. Death cannot
make an end of that — that will go on again above."
When he had ceased speaking we sat a while and
watched the sparkling of the stars, in the sky and on
the sea, and how the waves were edged with the silver,
and one after another rolled in and wetted the clear

7*

sand with foam. Now I am sitting at the open window,
and am listening to the murmur from the distance.
And now once more good night. Remember me to
all my faithful people. I will tell you in confidence,
I cannot hold out long without them. Good as is my
resolution to rest and to do nothing at all, yet again
I feel a strong impulse upon me. Bachmann and the
inn-keeper's Dora are sitting with their people in the
room below, and are reading evening-prayers, and
Valentine is just beginning his evening-hymn with the
children. It sounds afar through the still summer
night. Thus we seek rest in His name.

> Now awake my Saviour dear,
> Wake Thou in the peaceful night,
> Guard us ever by Thy might,
> With Thy loving smile be near:
> And, while sleeping, let us be
> Ever wakeful, Lord, to Thee.

Sing that with us, dear Joseph.

Lubbendorf, 6th August 1824.

DEAR JOSEPH,
I write to you in great haste. If you should meet
the Hagens to-morrow, tell Sophie Sommer in my
name and in confidence from me, that she must prevent Miss Haineggen and her aunt going to the Rhine
with us. Sophie is judicious and will know how to do
it. As matters now stand, nothing can come from us,
but it would be very oppressive to me. I am certainly
foolish and really something worse. In a week we
hope to be at Kamern again. Christian and Netty
are looking forward to the journey, and I am also for
their sake. Whether I do for myself I know not. I

do not believe that Count Stadlein will be back in August; but our journey remains fixed for September; I will conquer this weakness also.

Your

JOACHIM.

Joachim to his mother.

Magdeburg, 5th September 1824.

My very dear Mother,

The trio are quite well; yet it was with them almost as with Peter in a foreign land, who had no bad mind, at every cross-road, to turn back. Christian said, "I am well, thank God, I know not why I travel." "I am a poor giddy mother," said Netty, "I leave my dear little Joachie alone, only for the sake of pleasure." And I could not help asking why I leave my good people at Kamern? Yet I have been the bravest, and given courage to my companions. In reality I thought the journey would be a great refreshment and enjoyment to them. So I brought them happily to Berlin. There is nothing however to be done with a confirmed country-woman like Netty. First, she stood still, we could scarcely move her from the place, sometimes she was quite quiet, and after dinner the first day, she began to cry bitterly. "What kind of a place is this? So many people — so much bustle. We do not know the people; we do not speak to them. I am home-sick for Kamern, I cannot bear being here." I tried to persuade her to go to the Grand Opera; the five days fixed for Berlin must be spent. Netty earnestly protested, and Christian and I in reality quite agreed with her, and also agreed with her that Berlin is really no place of pleasure for Kamern people. "If Berlin does

not please us, I said with bold resolution, to please
whom need we stay here?" Netty sprang up and embraced me. "Dear Joachim, you have always been my
sensible nephew," said she; "we will go on early to-
morrow." "Early to-morrow?" asked I. "It is such
a beautiful evening, what prevents us from leaving the
hot, dusty city?" We all three laughed heartily for
joy, ordered the horses and drove to Potsdam. By
this stroke we had gained four days. Yet listen
further, dear Mother. This morning we started early
from Potsdam, and came on here in good time. Magdeburg may have beauties for its natives, but for foreigners
it appears to me that it has none except the cathedral.
We alighted at a tolerable inn near the cathedral-
square, and went straight to the cathedral. It is a
magnificent building. The evening-sun had enwoven
it with gold, children were playing in the large quiet
square, and even Netty seemed to feel satisfied, and in
a mood for travelling. After we had viewed the church
without and within, we went up one of the towers in
order to enjoy the view. The country is very flat and
there is little to see, but the sun was casting its last
beams on the broad stream of the Elbe, which goes
winding through the green plains; it was a bright
peaceful evening scene. "What mountain is that?"
asked Netty and pointed to a violet range of hills at
some distance. "That is the Brocken with the Harz-
mountain," answered the guide. "The Brocken," said
Christian playfully, "yes, there it is; that is where I
was when I was a student; we might go there instead
of the Rhine." Netty caught at these thoughts with
loud rejoicing, "for," said she, "the mountain cannot
be far from here." "To-morrow about this time you

will be up," said the guide. So, dear Mother, the Peter-
like company is to travel towards the Brocken instead
of towards the Rhine; because it has such a great
longing for home, and would like to return — the
sooner the better. Magdeburg has from this resolution
become a favourite residence with us. Netty especially
thinks it extraordinarily beautiful here. When we
came from the tower, she had a talk with the children
at play, and tried all their faces which was the most
like our Joachie. Then we drank tea and had an
intimate hour together. Now, dear Mother, dear love
from us all. We beg you to read our letters to Joachie,
to the young man. I will just add that our agreement
stands to go the last two stages with our own horses.
The Lord be with you, and with us all.

Your

JOACHIM.

Ilsenburg, 7th September 1824.

DEAR MOTHER,

We went in happy hour to the Brocken — on the
way up, the evening and morning were magnificent.
We looked far on to the world, and I maintain that
since we have been here in the mountains, Netty has
forgotten her boy. Her eyes are constantly tearful
with emotion. Christian laughs at her enthusiasm, but
he carries it to a more serious point, — he is incessantly making poems. Fancy them both, Netty with
a wreath of heather in her hair, resting on the bank
of a roaring mountain torrent, but Christian, in the
midst of it, sitting on a mossy stone, his tablets in his
hand, writing or meditating, looking up at the high
masses of rock. The poems are really very beautiful.

I do not understand how any one can make such, but
I enjoy myself very much. I look sometimes into the
clear mountain water, as, over the bright brown bottom,
a crimson-spotted trout is passing, or as the ants and
chafers are enjoying the rosy forests of heather. Here
a bird hops on the broad palm-like fern, dark green
fir-trees, tall and luxuriantly grown, wave their fine
branches in the blue air, and the golden sunshine;
they cast deep cool shadows over piled up blocks of
rock, which, clothed with a thick covering of moss
always moist, out-glisten and out-shine the richest velvet.
From the green covering, rises a family of red taper-
like flowers, which seem to vie with the fir-trees, and
in order to accomplish it the sooner, have placed themselves on the tip of a piece of rock. There is the
coolness and the loneliness of the forest. A perpetual
gentle murmur goes through the forest, silver brooklets
suddenly appear between the blocks of rock, or murmur
unseen under the covering of green. Yes, dear Mother,
I am very much pleased with it. We know the forest-
life at home, but not the mountain-life. Pleasure and
sounds are different here, and the higher you go the
more refreshing and beautiful it is. When in the
valley below we began to ascend, we did not like it at
all, and Netty feared we had trusted too much to her.
"What are you thinking of," she said, "I am not used
to climbing, and cannot hold out for a quarter of an
hour." When we assured her the further and higher
up the easier it would become, she shook her head in-
credulously and fretfully. But it was with her, as
with all pilgrims who are going upwards, her sighing
ceased, her powers increased instead of decreasing,
and, with merriment and joy, she went from rock to

rock, till we stood on the top with the broad view out over the world; — yes, out over the world, although one is so distant. We see and hear nothing of the tumult, of the broken and chequered pictures of life; — it lies before us in softened colouring, blown upon by the peace of heaven, which up here envelopes us, and fills our souls. Now may the Lord keep our hearts high, so that it may be with us in the midst of the world, as on the lonely invigorating mountain height. Dear precious Mother! we are soon coming to you. The Harz is only small. In from four to five days, we can visit the chief points. We shall then have enjoyed enough beauty, and would all three much rather be at home. Thus this day week the 14th of September, we wish to have the horses according to agreement. My love to Joseph and Joachie. Tell the boy that he must order Frederic to feed the horses. We have brought so much with us from our journey, that otherwise the poor creatures could not draw us.

The Lord grant us a happy meeting.

In faithful love

Your

JOACHIM.

On my 25th birthday, 10th October 1824.

"My thoughts are not as your thoughts and your ways are not my ways," saith the Lord. I have just applied these words to myself, and they have a deep significance to the heart. We might go the ways of the Lord, but we go them not; we might have the thoughts of the Lord, but we have them not; that is the old want which makes us sorrowful, and places us by the abyss of death. But we must taste of death before we can see life. We must sow in tears, before we reap in joy. Thou, dear Lord, forgive my sin, and clothe me with Thy grace. May that be my birthday motto! Is then to-day different from other days? The words suit any day, but it is well sometimes to stand still on the road of life, and to take time for earnest consideration. Such a halting place a birthday may be. A year ago to-day I was very ill — the Lord delivered me; He is the Lord who delivers from death, so He is in a two-fold sense, — not only from death of the body. Am I then sorrowful to-day? Oh, no, very cheerful and comfortable. If my sins make me sorrowful, my Redeemer makes me glad again. Where sin is mighty, grace is mightier still. Oh, dear faithful Saviour, I am so happy because Thou lovest me, and I may love Thee. I would so gladly do something for love of Thee. What then? I know of nothing, except to love Thee more and more, and ever to sing more loudly of this love, and more and more in quietness to cherish it. Amen. In conclusion I have just opened upon, "What shall I do to be saved? Believe on the Lord Jesus Christ, and Thou shalt be saved and thy house." With the saying of Isaiah I will look back — they shall be words of warning for the past; with these words, I will go forward, they shall be the true guide to me, to walk in the ways of the Lord; with them I will pray for the Holy Spirit, who shall fill me with thoughts of God. Amen.

Christmas-day, 1824.

Little Joachie awaked me from sleep. His sweet childish voice was singing, "From heaven above I come to you." Oh, Lord, grant that he may be always eloquent in praising Thy name, and singing to Thee. My choir of singers are just raising their voices. Oh, Lord, I thank Thee also for the love of these children; I thank Thee for the beautiful festival of Christmas. I have rejoiced with the joyful; the room here was almost too small to hold young and old. Oh, I will give, give what I have, with full hands. It is Christmas, the Lord is born. Behold, I declare to you great joy.

> To-day He opens wide the door
> To lovely Paradise;
> The Angel bars the way no more,
> To God be all the praise,
> Honour, and thanks and praise!

Kamern, Sunday after Easter, 1825.

I am truly sorry that I cannot be at your induction, dear Joseph, but the physician orders me to keep entirely to my room. Greet your kind patron, Herr von Hagen, heartily from me, and also Miss Sophie. On Easter-day I was at Olshausen, in company with Emma Haineggen. Last year I was so also. Everything has become different since then, but she has become different also, that rejoices me. She hopes often to be able to be your hearer. She will also come to your induction. And now, God be with you, dear Joseph. It is a beautiful time when the larks sing, the violets are out, and the blackbirds warble, and very much in unison with entering on an office. May spring enter with you, into your dear flock at Mardorf. May the Lord bless His word from your mouth, and animate lifeless hearts. That is the prayer of your friend. The Lord bless you richly; — the Lord bless you with the rich power of prayer, — hearty, sincere, earnest prayer — prayers which cease not to wrestle in faith. Those are the weapons with which we must fight; whereby we draw the Lord Himself with us into the conflict, and where He fights for us, we have prevailed. Amen! so may the Lord prepare us all.

Kamern, 28th May 1825.

I have got out again for the first time to-day, and can I hope accept the kind wish of your patron. I seem to have a great gift as god-father. At Easter I stood god-father for little Klaus Riedern; and in my parish there is not a child born, but I must be its godfather. But I am willing, and it is a beautiful office. Perhaps it will be with me as with my late greatuncle, who was unmarried, and who so often stood godfather, that he was called in the whole province godfather Kamern. He did not perform his duty externally alone, but as it is regarded by the church, — he had the welfare of his god-children's souls in view, and spent a great part of the year in going from cousin to cousin, and from house to house, in order to see the children. Before the Lord, he will surely have taken the rank of a faithful father of a family. But the firstborn among my god-children will always be Joachie. Announce him to Mrs. Hagen as an unbidden guest at the christening-feast. Or only through Miss Sophie, I hope he will be welcome to the nursery.

God be with you.

Your

JOACHIM.

Kamern, 12th June 1825.

What Thou blessest, oh Lord, is eternally blessed. He who finds a wife, finds a good thing, and obtains a blessing from the Lord.

Dear Joseph. We must agree that you are going with resolution towards the completion of your parsonage, and you have besides our full consent. Dear Sophie has been appointed by the Lord for a clergyman's wife just as she was a most excellent governess. And once more may the richest blessing of the Lord be on you and on your bride. I read your letter with great emotion. It must be so when two hearts are attuned to each other, but your hopes and wishes for me are in vain. The Lord has enriched my life enough, I can say "Lord, I am not worthy of all Thy mercy and truth" and I know not how I might have borne such a fortune. The matter is at an end; my earthly love is laid to rest — to rest in my heart; there it lies still, and does not disturb my peace. But it exists and remains my own, and is a treasure in my heart. Even my seeing Theresa again did not disturb my peace. To her as the woman of the world this love does not belong. . . The world has set its impress on her bright child-like features. But only be still, thou faithful love, and have patience: the world assaults, but the Lord will triumph. Now she has a new vocation — surely a means of restraining her, and I was certain that the ties to us were not severed. She wrote a warm letter to my mother a week ago, and invited her to be god-mother to her little girl. The child too is to be named Anna like my mother, and my mother responded with great pleasure to Rose's request. She

also sent a message to me. I answered her greeting
with a word of blessing for little Anna. So the matter
is at an end, and yet ever the same, dear Joseph, but
do not trouble yourself about my fortunes. What is
good-fortune or misfortune? I asked in my youth.
To have more or less of the Lord Jesus, is good-fortune or misfortune. And have I not many earthly
joys? — your being near and your love among them.
The love of my mother is so inventive in brightening
my life, if she could only reconcile herself to my des-
tiny. I beg you to do all you can for me in that way.
And so forward with the help of the Lord! In a fortnight I am going with my mother to Lübbendorf, —
only for a few weeks, but I enjoy myself very much
by the sea-side. We take little Joachie with us and
Christian will come for a few days with Netty. Shall
we not meet before Sunday?

Dear love

JOACHIM.

Three years later.

10th October 1828.

To-day it is time once more to stand still. Do I
do so less joyously than I did once? I am sometimes
lonely in spirit, but that is the will of the Lord. There
is a change in these last three years; they have passed
monotonously, and I scarcely noticed it, and yet there
has been a change. Joseph is living happily with his
wife, his child, his parish, and the cheerful family of
the squire: his time is filled up, he has no longer any
need to live with me. That is very natural, but I am
sorry for myself, but perhaps it will be different again.

Christian — poor Christian is ill; his sick body has clouded his mind, anxiety about his health takes up his time: he may not sing, he scarcely dares to speak. Netty shares his anxiety, and his silence. Netty begged me with tears to keep for her the little house in the churchyard corner, to live in when she is a widow. — Oh the Lord can still help. Mrs. Braunsen, since the summer, has found a still quieter retreat — she rests in peace; Elizabeth cannot get over the loss. My dear precious mother also appears different to me; a slight touch of melancholy goes through her whole being. She has renounced the happiness of her later days, the house will remain lonely. — I cannot help her. My dear, precious mother! I love her dearly, she is the good-fortune and the joy of my earthly days; if I could be the same to her, we could both wander on to heaven in joy and peace.

If the way is lonely, the Lord will all the more be with us. So grant it Lord. Winter is coming with its festival; we will yet celebrate it, it will see me young and cheerful, and my cheerfulness will make my mother's heart cheerful too. Joachie brought me this morning a wreath of monthly-roses; my choir awaked me, oh that I might respond from the bottom of my heart.

> Rise, my soul, and praise thy Maker's merit,
> From thy heart, the joyful tribute raise,
> All my bones, my body, soul, and spirit
> Sing, oh sing, the joyful notes of praise!
> Prepare! and now thy time and powers employ,
> In honouring my God, with hymns of holy joy.
>
> Father, Thy truth seeks nothing but pure blessing,
> Which to the sinful race of man is given;
> Mercy unmerited, my life possessing,
> I feel around me like the air of heaven;

What time of need my God did ever prove,
Able to turn away Thy faithful love?

Nothing had touched Thy heart but mere compassion,
   When Thou didst bring Thy creature to the Light;
For Christ's dear sake Thou hast my soul accepted
   Before the world had dawned upon my sight.
Thou, like a mother, in the days gone by,
Hast borne me on Thine arm unceasingly.

Now from my very heart I would adore Thee,
   God, who to-day embracest me anew;
Let my desire ever be before Thee,
   Unwavering, let me to Thy love be true.
Until, with bliss, Thou bring me safe at last,
Where all the perils of the world are past.

Amen! Amen! I would not cease to praise the Lord. Lord! only be Thou again my loving master, and pardon Thy feeble child. I will be very, very glad of heart, because Thou art my faithful Lord.

18th February 1829.

Dear Joachim is nine years old to-day. Snowdrops are out in the garden, — larks soar in the soft air. My mother has adorned the birthday table with little silver bells: they have no inclination now for such things at the parsonage. Poor dear boy! the spring is coming, but will not bring health to your father.

7th May 1829.

I went with Joachim into the church. While the first hymn was beginning, my thoughts were with our assistant minister, that the Lord might make his weak faith strong, and give ardour to his luke-warm nature. I was absorbed, and did not observe that someone had entered our pew. A slender woman was sitting by

Joachim, bent in prayer. It is spring without; everything is in bloom and in song, recollections of spring came to me — I could but lay my hand on my heart. It was Rose herself, but her features are become paler and more refined. She gave me her hand with a very melancholy look. Lord, Thou seest my heart; my earthly life lies there in deep peace, but I will not let Thee go, unless Thou bless her. I am sure that Thou art continually spinning cords of love, to draw her to Thee: more sure than ever to-day, and that gives me new strength. When we came out of the church the nurse-maid came to meet us with little Anna. I bent down to the child and kissed it on the forehead. "Who is that?" asked Theresa. "Uncle Joachim," answered Anna, rather shyly. We now went in silence through the lime-avenue, and through the garden. Joachim and Anna had taken up the conversation for us. Before my mother's door, Rose stayed behind. — I led the child in "Who is that?" asked I. "Little Rose," cried my mother joyfully. "Alias Annie, but just Rose's face when a child." Rose greeted my mother with great emotion. "I have not been here for a long time, but I do not belong here," added she sadly. Mother remained calm and quiet, and was only ruffled on the surface. Theresa was to tell of her life at Petersburg, her cheeks gained more colour, melancholy seemed driven away. "My husband has now removed to Paris," she said in conclusion, "we are going and Anna is to stay here." Anna here? asked my mother in surprise. "My husband wishes it," answered Theresa much embarrassed. "The child too will be happier here, and it would not suit my arrangements to be a mother to Annie," she added bitterly, "and I would

rather know the child is with my mother than in the
hands of a bonne." We were all silent. "And I
would commend her to you also, dear Aunt," said she
with faltering voice. Mother bent towards her, Rose
wept; but I was playing with the children. Poor
thing! she is in the arms of the world, but she has
the sword in her heart. You will not escape from the
Lord: the Lord is spinning His cords of love, slowly
but surely.

12th May 1829.

We were at Olshausen. Aunt is happy in the possession of her daughter and grand-daughter. — Uncle
in a very ill temper. Count Stadlein fell out with him,
went off in a hurry, and will meet Theresa at Wiesbaden. I have scarcely spoken to her, but my mother
has availed herself of the old privileges of love, and
has spoken seriously and confidentially to her. "I
cannot do otherwise," said Theresa. "I am bound to
this life; and am not unhappy either," added she with
hesitation.

Sophie also wished to be intimate with her again,
but to her she was reserved, almost ungracious. So
she begins Germany again with Wiesbaden, — then
Paris! It became easy to me to-day to be grave and
cold to her. I also said good-bye to her, though she
was going to stay some days; I did not put off my
business journey on that account. What can I do
there? She is going her own way. Only you will
not escape the Lord. — The Lord spins slowly but
surely.

Letter from Theresa.

Wiesbaden, 8th June 1829.

DEAR SOPHIE,

I cannot rest; I must write to you. Forget our last meeting; yes, forget the last years: think that I am Theresa who is playing with the children. Oh, that it were so!

When I think of my home, my heart is ready to break. I often shut myself in, and weep and weep till my strength is gone, and I fall asleep. My husband thinks it is ill temper, he calls me foolish, and leads me into new pleasures.

You would not believe how I am obliged to live. One day goes restlessly like another, always with a crowd not one of whom loves me. When I come home, in the evening, tired and weary, I resolve not to go into company another day, yet what can I do at home alone? I feel lonely, and I go again. Dear Sophie, write to me. I long so very much to hear from home. Speak to aunt at Kamern — but no, it is all over; hearts there are dead to me, and it must be so.

The last evening at Olshausen, I had an impulse to go out of the house. I went the way towards Kamern. The trees were in blossom, but it was cold: there was a heavy dew on the grass. At the highway I came out of the forest; in the twilight a carriage drove quickly by me, it was Joachim. I knew that he was returning from a journey, he was hastening to his mother; I saw them both sitting so cosily in the garden-parlour. "Take me with you," I gently whispered, "I wish to open my heart to her, perhaps she would be able to give me advice."

The carriage vanished, I was alone. I seated myself on the stump of a tree, a herd of deer came out of the forest, the creatures looked at me in wonder, and then leaped joyfully over the path. You are happy, I thought, your home is here; but I am thrust out, I am lonely and quite forsaken. I sat there till the dew had drenched my clothes, then I went back; all within me was still and dead. With such a dumb dead heart, they sent me away, and I have left my child there, because my very heart is dead. Dear Sophie, I am reluctant to send the letter, but it shall go. It is a cry of anguish from my heart: perhaps you will hear it with compassion, perhaps you will have some advice to give me, at least you will pardon me if I grieve you. Can my aunt forgive me? Farewell! kiss my Anna and write soon to

Your

THERESA.

28th July 1829.

To-day we have laid dear Christian to his rest. He died happily; the more his bodily powers decreased, the more unfettered his soul became. Oh! the Lord is strong in the weak. To see that on a death-bed is a great comfort, both for life and for one's own death. I sat for a long time with Joachim under the beeches, he is an orphan now, but he shall yet have a father. I have taken him warmly to my heart. We repeated the last sayings of his late dear father; Joachim wept at them till he was exhausted. As we were still sitting in silence side by side, came little Anna with her maid:

she was very merry, but stopped short when she found her play-fellow in tears.

She picked flowers and laid them silently and tenderly on his lap, to comfort him. He soon smiled and dried his tears. On our way home we laid the flowers on the new-made grave.

.   10th October 1829.

To-day I am thirty years old. That seems to me almost old. But what is an old man? A Christian should always be old enough to die any day, and always young and fresh enough, to wander farther and to work while it is day. I also feel young and fresh; and when my dear household sang "Praise the Lord — the mighty King of glory;" I sang with them with hearty voice, and was able to thank them all. Joachim wrote me a Latin congratulation. I believe the boy learns more than I do, he is not so dreamy, and besides he is a lively and resolute youth. Since he has been here in the house with Netty, he acts as though the house belonged to him. We must be very much on our guard that he does not get spoiled. "Too many cooks spoil the broth."

I have begged Netty and mother to leave the education of the boy to the tutor and to me. Much remonstrance for particular failings does not do. Her love and her prayer might work on him together with us, and the Lord would give His blessing: — He must do the best part. But I have the joyful confidence that we shall live to have pleasure in the boy. Already he is a fountain of joy in our house. We are obliged to be young with him; he brings in life and merriment and all the youngsters of the village as well. To-day

he is holding a great review with the boys in the
castle-garden, in honour of my birthday; afterwards
they are to be treated, and my mother has had plenty
of cakes baked. "She is kinder to the boys than she
used to be to me," said Netty.

Yesterday he rode to Olshausen on the goat, to invite Aunt Emma and Annie. Uncle is in Berlin on
account of a liver complaint, so Annie rules the house
up there. Her grandmother goes on with the little
girl just as my ladies here do with Joachim, and is
already in trouble that Annie is to go to her mother
again at Easter. Annie has arranged to be fetched by
Joachim in the goat-carriage. Aunt Emma will consent without hesitation. So we all enjoy ourselves, to
celebrate the day.

For me, it is always an important division in the
year. With it I take leave of the very beautiful but
dissipating season of summer, and enter the quiet
winter which is so dear to me. I intend to be very
industrious — to live much with my good people at
Kamern. It is a pity that the parsonage is lost to us.
He is a good faithful man; I am not sorry for his
election, but his wife I should not have chosen — that
is his choice. May the Lord strengthen him. May
He strengthen us all and be with us all.

Kamern, 8th December 1829.

Thine eyes on us, oh Saviour, bend,
With help, Thy holy Spirit send,
To rule our hearts, from day to day,
And lead us in truth's heavenly way.

DEAR JOSEPH,

You frighten me, but I hope it is only Sophie's
fancy. I know certainly that I have never given Emma

von Haineggen occasion to believe that; if she does, I am sorry for it; but I think Sophie, after the manner of ladies, wishes to make a match. Dear Joseph, you describe everything charmingly and beautifully. I know too what I owe to myself and to my dear mother; but it must not be compulsion. My heart is too much at rest in her presence, and a marriage of reason would be something wrong in me. I say to you, but to you alone, my heart is employed in a strange fashion. If Theresa were dead, if she were with the Lord, and snatched from my care, perhaps I might again love and be happy, though not with the beating heart of youth. But I have undertaken it, I must bear Theresa on my soul, and I am happy in it. Let me go, I tell you, on my lonely and wonderful path. I am happy in it. And now, do everything to suppress such troublesome gossip. Talk incidentally to Emma about the eccentric Joachim. I should not wish our intercourse to be disturbed; my mother likes it so much. With the Lord's help, we will keep a merry Christmas. I had a pretty present for Emma too, and hope to see the matter arranged, and still to be able to give it. And now God be with you!

JOACHIM.

Four years later.

It is a desolate day. The snow is whirling, the wind is roaring, it might undermine my peace. Oh no: my earthly love is laid aside, an angel of peace keeps watch over it. My life has passed quietly and monotonously — monotonously, and yet in action. I have been cheerful — I have owed that to the Lord: I have been sorrowful, — the Lord has comforted me: I have been lonely, — the Lord has not forsaken me. My domestic state is ordered for this life: so and not otherwise the Lord has willed it. We were sitting in the afternoon around the coffee-table, Joachim was giving us different hints for his birthday, we were laughing merrily together and had heard no one come. Aunt Emma came in, in a great bustle, and Theresa and Annie followed her. Theresa, still paler and with more refined features, greeted us in rather an embarrassed way. That a strange silence was observed at their sudden coming also confused us. The children too must needs add to it. Annie, the very image of her mother now grown slender, overcame her bashfulness, through Theresa's interposition, and made friends with Joachim. She only spoke German awkwardly and involuntarily French in between. Poor Joachim was bewildered. At last he said wickedly, "Annie, why do you speak so foolishly? Leave off! Girls with us speak German." "Your girls are only peasant girls," answered Annie pertly, "and I am a Countess Stadlein." Joachim turned rudely from her and went into the ante-room. Aunt laughed at her grand-daughter. Theresa took the child and followed Joachim. Now aunt's full heart overflowed, and Theresa's fate, which was not unknown to us, was again communicated with many tears. Weak mother, now you are sorry; why did you not take warning? Now the misery is greater than the pleasure, her heart is empty and wearied, distractions and change in external life will no longer help her over the time. It now comes out that she has never loved him. Poor young thing she was violently hurried into it: longing after home after the old times, consumes her heart. Through the open door I saw

Theresa sitting in the ante-room; the children were again quietly playing near her. She was looking, with sad and weary eye, at the falling snow, and it seemed to me as though tears were rolling down her cheeks. Do not be so hard towards her or so cold, said my aunt; she loves you more than all of us: Your lost love torments her and remorse torments her. I was obliged at these words to cover my eyes, my heart became perturbed.

There is still the old love which abides there, and my heart is very weak. She was appointed for thee, and thou shouldst not have let her go so easily, spoke a foolish voice; — her tears are thy fault, go and comfort her, stand beside her like a strong shelter, show her for once that thy heart is by no means so hard and cold to her. When I took my hand from my brow, my mother and my aunt were looking strangely at me. She is still young, she must get a divorce, said aunt in great excitement; she must forget this time of her life, and we must all forget it. Then a shudder went through my soul. The weakness was over. I looked earnestly at the women: "What God hath joined together man must not put asunder." "Rose's misery lies somewhere else than in this marriage." "Joachim, you do not know what this marriage is," said my aunt; "he lives a riotous life, she will soon have only to wait on an invalid." "We should rather see her at the sickbed of her husband, than in the tumult of the world," replied I. "How loveless you are towards her," said my aunt weeping, "and she came here entirely in the hope of hearing counsel and comfort from your brotherly sympathy." Then I felt a warm thrill through my heart, and I knew what I had to do. "*I* loveless?" I said

to my aunt, "surely not, let me go and I will give her
my loving brotherly counsel. I will comfort her with
a comfort which can heal all wounds." Aunt would not
let me go. "Rose expected something different," she said
bitterly. "You are breaking her heart with your words."
Oh if her old heart were broken, her old misery would
be broken with it; and a new happy heart would bring
her happiness and peace. I could not be held back.
I went to Theresa and gave her counsel and comfort,
with warm and happy heart. They were the old
words which I had often said to her before. I spoke
to her of the love of our divine Redeemer, how it could
make us richer and happier than all the fortune of the
world; how we with Him had conquered the world,
and all the misery of the world also. But we could
only love Him with a new heart, — the old one must
be broken in penitence and repentance. At these words
Rose gave me her hand. "Repentance?" sobbed she.
Poor Theresa, the world has dazzled you and given
you a bitter cross instead of pleasure; now take your
cross, and lay it at the feet of the Lord; — the Lord
who says "Come unto Me all ye that labour and are
heavy laden, and I will refresh you." Is the cross
heavy at first? in the light of His grace, it becomes
illumined and light and easy: and at last we esteem it
no cross but as a gift of grace, because it led us to
the Lord, — to the blessed Lord, Who makes us
blessed. Oh dear Rose, may the Lord strengthen you,
and happiness or unhappiness will then lie in your
hand. The Lord has knocked anew at the door of
your heart. Strive earnestly that when God's grace is
leading and turning you, your spirit may truly un-
burden itself of the burden which weighs upon it. —

Wrestle with prayer and crying: persevere in it ardently, let no time seem too long for it, even if it were night and day. I opened the piano and sang with Joachim "Now all the woods are sleeping." With that hymn the Lord had first knocked at her heart.

At the eighth verse my soul wrestled for her

* "My Jesus, stay Thou by me,
And let no foe come nigh me,
Safe sheltered by Thy wing;
But would the foe alarm me,
Oh let him never harm me,
But still Thine angels round me sing!"

The day is over. Rose is at Olshausen; her heart is restless, and struggling after peace. And I? Man had almost caused me heartache again, but the Lord is my help now and ever. The world is so willing to tempt us, she paints in such heavenly colours what is so earthly; she would call pure what is so defiled. But Thou, Lord, care for me! The world shall offer me nothing wherein I cannot possess Thee undisturbed. I will walk farther on my lonely way, if I only have Thee. To Thee, my life belongs; to Thee, I surrender my love. Oh! take it with all its pangs. Forbid me pangs and earthly love, and comfort me instead with Thy love.

Grant that nothing in my soul,
But Thy love a place may own:
Grant that I Thy love may choose,
As my treasure and my crown.
Thrust all out and all remove,
Which my soul from Thee would sever,
And prevent its drawing ever
All its courage from Thy love.

* Translation from Lyra Germanica.

The nearer the foe, the more we must pray and watch. But it is the Lord Who sends him that we may be stirred up from sleep, that we may become warm-hearted again. Dear Lord, I love Thee better than long ago. I feel like a weak child needing love; take me under Thy wings. I do not wish to look around me, nor before me, only at Thee; and so, through whatever the world has to bring before me, Lord, do Thou take my soul.

I was at Olshausen. It looks sad there. Uncle has more pain than ever; he fears that it is an internal disease. He looks yellow, and is discontented with all the world. Now it is his children who make him unhappy. Theresa did not understand how to treat her husband; he maintains she might have led and ruled him more; he would have liked it. But she went indifferently on her own way, and he fretfully on his. Vexation made Count Stadlein a spendthrift. She is guilty of it all, and will at last fall with her child as a burden on her parents. Alfred has given up his diplomatic career; he wishes to be a country gentleman, and is preparing himself with wife and children for Olshausen. Alfred married a wife without property. It was hoped that he would make a career through her family. It did not succeed. "Alfred has not stuff enough for it," as uncle says. So everything has failed. Uncle must take in the sails which once bore him so proudly along. But above all sickness and pain bow him down. Lonely hours by his couch of pain, have given me his confidence, yet I may not speak of the Man Who heals all sickness, and takes all sorrows upon him. I have learned too to be silent. I only speak with the Lord, and the Lord still speaks in His own words.

> Oh Lamb of God, Who art our Lord indeed,
> Receive the prayer which rises from our need:
> Have pity on us all.

18th February.

The curtain has fallen; the puppet-show is over, for truly so it is. Count Stadlein came to fetch his wife away, he was courteously attentive to her; people go on as if everything were in order, the surface as smooth as a mirror, the world knows how to put on a polish. So a party was given, the neighbourhood assembled. My pale uncle acts the host, and attempts to smile. Theresa was animated; with rosy cheeks and lively eyes she led the conversation. Aunt cool towards me and friendly with her son-in-law, seeks to deceive herself and the world. There is nothing else for it. Theresa must go away again. Her father forcibly urges her, evil rumours must be silenced, a good face must be put upon a bad game. I shudder when I think of it. Such funereal deceitful doings, such a pale glimmer over deep sorrow, compulsory smiling over mute woe. But so it is in the world, so it is with all who give themselves up to her. I was standing alone by the window in the cabinet. I was looking at the stars, and higher — "Oh, Lamb of God Who art our Lord indeed, Receive the prayer which rises from our need: Have pity on us all."

I heard steps, I looked round, Theresa came shyly

to me. Annie and Joachie came with her. "Annie
will not forget us," said Joachim gayly, "she will
write me a letter, if she puts gibberish in it, it won't
matter." "I would rather stay at Olshausen," said
Annie. Theresa sorrowfully laid her hand on the
child's brow. It seemed as though I must speak once
more to Theresa, yet I was silent; my words will not
make her strong. I played with the children, Count
Stadlein disturbed us, he was very unkind to Joachie,
so that Annie cried. Now they are all gone. Uncle,
paler than ever, complains bitterly of his pain. Aunt's
coldness towards me has changed into bewilderment at
my equanimity. We shall soon be again in the old
rut with our quiet life. Here we are so already; it is
not quite so yet with my inner life, but it will be so
soon, — very soon. To-day we kept Joachie's twelfth
birthday; as usual, the young people of the village
took part in it. I led the party and their games, although it was not easy to me. Klaus had his fifth
child baptized to celebrate the day. I stand godfather
for the third time; it is alternately with my mother,
but we are glad to do it from love of Elizabeth. She
belongs to our family circle, although generally as an
invisible member; only she looks in with her quiet
self-possession, whenever it is needful. She is nurse
of the sick, helper in our household at festivals, and
our house is always in communication with the little
house in the churchyard corner; Joachie lives with
Klaus and Elizabeth, as I used to with Mrs. Braunsen
and her late husband. There holes get mended, there
the glue-pot is kept warm, and books are fastened together, and Joachim when there is necessity educates
the troop of children better than Papa Klaus. Yes,

so it is all in good order, and I the centre of a circle which I can make happy. I have very much for which to thank the Lord and shall soon be quite peaceful again. I have got over Joseph's removal. One accustoms oneself very soon to anything. One compensation we have from it, that Emma von Haineggen, since her aunt's death, is entirely with Frau von Hagen, and often here. Yesterday she had a cap on for the first time; that pleased me, she looks much older. I laughed about it, and said to her we will both do all honour to our honourable condition of bachelor and old maid. She entered very innocently into the joke. I know her heart is now at rest. Her society gives me pleasure, and I am selfish enough to hope that she may not be married, and may remain in our circle.

That the parsonage here is nothing for us, becomes more and more clear. Yesterday I wished to go with my mother. On the first Sunday in Lent the pastor's wife had quarrelled with the housekeeper about some eggs. Mother could not get over it. I went to him alone. He is almost too reverential; that oppresses me. I esteem him very highly, but can never say so to him; that would sound as if we took a mutual pleasure in strewing incense on each other. He is a quiet man and yet active, loving and zealous, one sees no extraordinary manifestation of it, but observes it in everything. If only his domestic cross were less heavy! If I could but work on the wife. But Netty and mother must be gentler with her, and not be so exclusive. It is true, Netty is quite in the wrong with her. I will speak to her about it; and Elizabeth too might be different. Lord help us! Watch faithfully over our dear Kamern!

* "Abide with us in faithful love,
Our God and Saviour be,
Thy help at need oh let us prove
And keep us true to Thee."

——— ———

Two years later.

Easter 1835.

Joachim has been taken to the gymnasium; now
he is gone, we do not understand why we have done
it. "He is to be nothing more than a country gentleman," says my mother, he might have stayed with
us. His doting mother Netty is gone with him. She
might have stayed with mother. Klaus is indignant
about it. The pastor's wife wishes to hold the young
gentleman under her apron; but if a young fellow
goes to schools and the University he must have free-
dom; he strokes his moustache, and thinks of his
University years. "But, Klaus," I replied, "our Joachim
would not allow himself to be tied to apron strings;
think how he kept us all tied to apron strings here."
"That is true," smiled Klaus, "he is a thundering
young gent, — a pity that he is not a Kamern."
Joachim is loved by great and small. I do not know
how great and small will do without him. His absence
is a great shock to my outer life. Netty also being
gone, I am quite alone with my mother. Shall I let
Elizabeth and her children live in the wing? the house
seems to me so lonely. Mother has of late years become much more quiet. I could be anxious; I am
rather melancholy to-day. But it must be so. The
Lord comes and gives us a new warning. The more
lonely we are here, the more we are driven to Him.

He knows well that we are happiest in His love. Oh, Lord! I come. I will lay my weary heart in Thine; sometimes it seems as though it must have an earthly companion to share its loving and hoping, suffering and rejoicing, but only *sometimes;* and it will become more and more seldom. If I had not already often experienced it, I might be sad, but I was never more happy, than when formerly I was very sad. I never felt richer, than when I supposed that I must suffer want. Therefore bless the Lord oh my soul! bless Him beforehand! I will sing to the Lord all my life long, and praise my God as long as I have my being. Now I have begun to give praise, I would not cease, but would praise and praise anew. Who can fathom it? The Lord came to poor humanity, to love us, to redeem us, and to make us happy. What is the world? What are our days on earth, compared to this eternal blessedness? Lord, here I am Thine; — fill me wholly, and then, oh Lord, receive my soul. Amen.

Three years later.

16th May 1838 (on the day of my dear mother's death).

    "Oh Friend of souls, how well is me,
      Whene'er Thy love my spirit calms!
    From sorrow's dungeon forth I flee,
      And hide me in Thy sheltering arms.
The night of weeping flies away
Before the heart-reviving ray
Of love, that beams from out Thy breast;
Here is my heaven on earth begun;
Who were not joyful had he won
In Thee, oh God, his joy and rest!"

Joachim the first to Joachim the second.

Kamern, 10th August 1838.

I am sorry that I cannot tread in the footsteps of my late dear mother, with your favourite long descriptions of home. You know I am not fond of writing. I am out of practice, I would rather come myself. I have committed to Klaus the younger to inform you about the family; Elizabeth will add about the village. I must just mention to your mother, how I get on with the clergyman's wife; not in order to praise myself, no: just to show your mother, that she is wrong when she says, "my character is not fitted to work on hers." It is not a question of character. We must bring the Lord Jesus into our character, and a heart full of love. Yes, dear Netty, I must scold you, and wish to prepare you to be very friendly towards our clergyman's lady, when you are here.

There is no one left at Olshausen. Alfred is expected with his family. Aunt writes the bath has not suited uncle. He is to go to Berlin to be nearer his physicians. It is feared that his strength is nearly gone. Joseph has written that he wishes to meet you here in the holydays. He wishes to stay some weeks here, with wife and children. Elizabeth is already considering how she can best take in all the guests. Since midsummer you know she has lived in the side wing. I am well satisfied with it. She has to lead the whole household, and I sometimes hear voices and footsteps in the great house. Only I think the children are far naughtier than you were in your youth. Yesterday I could not find one of my many canes; — they had fetched them out of my room in order to ride in the meadow, and had carried them all away. You would have brought me some back. Yet the pleasures which I have from the children are greater than the disturbances. Little Maudlin is especially dear to me. Write to me when the holydays come near. Will you not come by water? I should prefer it, and then I could send for you from Luttensen.

God be with you!

Your

JOACHIM VON KAMERN.

The same to the same.

Kamern, 20th August 1838.

Many thanks for your love, but it cannot be so. The first lonely winter will indeed be hard to me, but I have prepared myself for it. All will go well. I am a very weak man. Your love and your presence would spoil me. I dread the separation and any new change. We will leave it according to the old agreement. You shall continue at your studies till Easter, and then shall begin your economical career as proprietor of Lubbendorf, on your own little property. Bachmann with his Dora shall stay a year with you. Now too you are coming for a holyday visit. Life is always rich and lovely; — we have so much for which to thank the Lord. I have the autumn before me, when my house will be cheerful, and contain many dear people. Then comes winter with its festival. For the first time, I shall celebrate it alone; but the Lord knows what He is doing, He will know how to celebrate it with me.

At Easter, you will be near me again, and we

9 *

shall be good neighbours. Dear Joachim, I love you dearly. The Lord bless you, my dear son, my dear brother and friend.

Your

JOACHIM VON KAMERN.

10th October 1838.

I do not deserve so much love. I wish also to live more with the good people of Kamern. The reading-evenings were rather burdensome to me last season; they ought to give me pleasure. My little choir consists almost entirely of my godchildren. I particularly wish to celebrate Advent with them, and to give them nice presents at Christmas. The infant-school in the church-yard corner was touching, but very ludicrous too, and I was obliged to control my laughter. Old Christabel with her sceptre is peculiar, and so are her theories about the education of children; yet I could say nothing against it, and the clergyman's wife is excellent there. The lectures which I give to the children she takes very well; it gets on better and better. But Klaus and Elizabeth and their children concert together to make my heart soft, — Elizabeth in her thoughtful way that nothing should be wanting on my birthday-table. But Maudlin played the best trick. During the lively celebration, she had quietly emptied my wafer box, and stuck all the wafers on the sofa and carpet. Elizabeth was shocked, but I would not suffer the child to be punished. She thought she was doing such a splendid thing, and her little brother Andrew thought so too. So one celebration has driven away the other; I am not come to myself yet. But Cousin Alfred did not seem satisfied, especially that my choir had their table with us in the parlour. I thought that the best part of the dinner. They sang such splendid songs between every course: — without that I should not have patiently seen Elizabeth's many courses brought on. Now I am almost weary with so much exertion, but yet I can thank Thee, Thou dear Lord — thank Thee for all Thy mercy and faithfulness; and Lord, help me still! I wish to be truly Thine, to depend for ever on Thy grace; and thou, dear Mother, up above, perhaps thou, in Thy blissful dream, wilt have some sense that it is going well with thy Joachim.

Kamern, 24th February 1839.

DEAR JOACHIM,

Uncle wants me. Aunt writes pressingly. I will start to-day. Address your next letter to Berlin. At Olshausen all three children have the scarlet-fever. William and Frederic are out of danger. Alfred and his wife are anxious about the little one. Julia has lost all composure; for four nights I have sat up there, simply on the condition that she should sleep, but she has not done it yet. To-day I send Elizabeth instead of myself.

Dear love to your mother.

Your

JOACHIM VON KAMERN.

Berlin, 4th March 1839.

To whom will you flee for help? Human help is of no use. Ah, Lord, our misdeeds have deserved it, but yet help for Thy name's sake. How terrible it is when a man is struggling with death; yes, struggles, stands up against it, and will not go forward for fear and horror. That is the world's extremity of death. Oh, thou wicked world! thou who recompensest thy children with such an end, where is thy wisdom, thy pleasure, joy and honour? All gone! terror only remains and the pang; there remains death. I have summoned Alfred, if need were I could command him; here is his place at the death-bed of his father. I have urged him to kneel down. Behold here the extremity of death, and there is no other help than from above. Julia is still softened and touched by the loss of her child. Alfred's heart also. Aunt Emma has long ago learned to raise her hands in prayer. We knelt by the bed and prayed to the Lord. Oh, we poor human creatures! we would willingly preach a man into salvation and yet cannot; our words fly off like foam from the rock of an unbelieving heart. But, Lord, Thou canst do it. One gracious look from Thee, and the heart is softened. Oh, have mercy; help, Lord, give us the faith which removes mountains, and which can' also enlighten dark hearts.

Berlin, 8th March 1839.

DEAR JOACHIM,
Uncle expired to-day. The Lord has been very gracious. May he be happy with Him. I travel back to Kamern to-day. I should be very glad to see you there soon, I feel exhausted, and have a great longing for you. We will keep Passion-week together; and at the dear and joyful feast of Easter, you shall settle into your new home. God be with you.
    Your
        JOACHIM VON KAMERN.

20th June 1839.

Theresa is here. She shows a joyful face to the world, — only to the world — not to her mother — not to me. To-day was a quiet Sunday, — the sky cloudy. I remained after church alone in the church-yard. I stood a long time under the lime-trees before the grave. My heart was anxious, and full of melancholy; the world was sorrowful to me, I longed to depart and to be with Christ, — everything, everything over, and my weak heart at rest. I heard footsteps. It was Theresa. She seemed at first irresolute whether to come nearer, but she came. She gave me her hand. "Joachim," she said gently, and then tears choked her voice. I was strong and was able to subdue my grief. We are so far on our way now, both so young and yet already old. She laid a bunch of roses on the edge of the grave. "I loved her very much," said Theresa gently, "and, Joachim, she has also forgiven me." We stood in silence before the grave, — our hearts full of longing after peace. Yes, Lord, so far she has come, help her to attain it. Anna came from the little house in the church-yard corner. We went to meet her, she is a lovely child. It gives me great pleasure that she is to stay here next winter and here to be evangelically confirmed. Theresa is set upon it, and aunt Emma supports her. Anna is amiable, a clear head full of power and sweetness, it almost seems to me as though my mother's spirit were in her — perhaps her blessing as a god-mother, and the blessing of the Lord. He wishes already in youth to make up to the child what her parents must lack. I am enjoying myself very much at Lubbendorf. Aunt Emma and Anna are go-

ing with me; Theresa goes back to Nice, her husband
hopes to gather new strength there; he is, like all consumptive people, full of enjoyment of life, and sanguine
hopes. Anna likes so much to stay here. The Lord
help me to be something to the child! She attaches
herself to me with touching affection. For the winter
she has asked for a little room in the house in the
church-yard corner; there she wishes to help old
Christabel, and to keep me company. Aunt wishes to
get Emma von Haineggen for the winter as a governess and companion for Anna. That would be pleasant
to me, but Emma is very much in request. We scarcely
see her in our circles, unless there is some urgent
necessity in a household. She must above all counsel
and help her, and is very faithful. It would be very
desirable for little Anna; therefore, I will myself ask
Emma about this service of love.

14th August 1839.

We are spending golden days here at Lubbendorf.
One thing vexed me: that Joachim quarrelled so with
Annie. Her faults lie more in habit and education.
She cannot suddenly be a fisher-maiden at Lubbendorf.
But the youth is obstinate, and has had a great disposition towards imperiousness from his youth; he does
not understand how to go on with such a delicate
maiden. To-day I got rather angry, and said to him
if Annie was so disagreeable to him, we would leave
Lubbendorf. He came up to me, pressed my hand and
did not say a word, but a bright tear ran down on his
young beard. It went very much to my heart. I recalled my hard words, and comforted him, and begged
him very kindly to be more amiable to Annie, and

also represented to him that the child, if she is often, in his presence, capricious and irritable, has shown herself at the bottom very kind to him. She decks his room with flowers for him; takes care when he comes in from the fields, or from any other business, about his favourite refreshments; and, more than all, quietly seeks to read something from his eyes. To-day I think I have convinced him of his fault. He cheerfully promised amendment, and at evening prayers I observed by his softened frame of mind, and the choice of his text that he sincerely means it. The Lord possesses the heart of my dear Joachim. How it moves me when I see him perform his spiritual duty as master of the house! Netty wished to give it over to me during my stay here, but I am his guest and he must remain the master to his people and domestics. I know too from experience what a blessing such spiritual service exercises on ourselves in early youth. Now, dear Lord, help him on; help us all on. The days here are so beautiful, so peaceful, and if my spirit has no great power of soaring, it has patience for waiting. A Christian learns by experience not to be too joyful or confident in time of strength, and not to be faint-hearted in weakness; for the Lord sends such trials to his faithful ones. Oh, dear Lord, I wait patiently till Thou come nearer to me again, and shalt make me again richer in Thy grace. I am still Thy beloved child. Amen.

(Three years later.)

18th February 1842.

Klaus and Elizabeth are right. It would be tempting the Lord to travel to Lubbendorf in such weather;

the roads are lost, the snow is driving; I cannot see
the church nor the lime-trees. I feel to-day like an
impatient child. I should like to keep his birthday
with my Joachim; loneliness is burdensome to me to-
day. How the wind howls in the chimney, and how
quiet and large the house is, and my heart so empty!
I am become weak, very weak. I do not see the sun
through the drifting snow, my heart is weary and cannot
raise itself. Have I not already lived through lonely days
and lonely years? At dinner to-day I only tasted food
from love to Elizabeth; it was so quiet around me, and
alas so silent in my heart. Elizabeth asked if we
could not invite the clergyman. I can have no one
here, I am too miserable. I have even put off Maudlin's
visit. So I sit with the pen in my hand, because I
have not strength to seek consolation and want to spend
the time. Oh, my dear mother, thou art looking so
kindly at me, shall I soon come to thee? I am still
young; may still live a long time. Dear faithful Lord,
Thou hast so often helped me. Help me also to-day.

> "Oh Friend of souls, how well is me
> Whene'er Thy love my spirit calms
> From sorrow's dungeon forth I flee
> And hide me in Thy sheltering arms."

Oh, I should like it well, oh Lord! Lord.

19th February.

Thou art my faithful Lord. I may come. — Then
why should I sorrow. If I still have Christ who will
take Him from me? who will rob me of heaven, which
the Son of God has already bestowed on my faith?
Lord! my Shepherd, fountain of all joys, Thou art
mine; I am Thine, no man can separate us. I am

Thine, because Thou hast given up Thy life, and Thy blood for my good. Thou art mine, because I embrace Thee, and do not let Thee go, oh! my light, out of my heart. Oh, let me, let me go where Thou mayst embrace me, and I Thee. Lord, I thank Thee that already light arises in my soul. —

20th February.

Lord, I love Thee dearly and am very happy. What was it? The veil has fallen off, I possess Thee again. I am very weak; without Thy strength, I am nothing, nothing at all, oh, abide with me! I was in the garden, the sun shining brightly. I picked some snow-drops, they are now before me, their tiny bells ring in the spring; oh, that they might do so also for my soul! Dear Lord, I am Thine, Thou art mine; no man can separate us, and should it appear so, I cling to Thy grace — I am Thy child — Thou canst not let me go.

Easter 1842.

* "In the bonds of death He lay,
 Who for our offence was slain,
 But the Lord is risen to-day,
 Christ hath brought us life again,
Wherefore let us all rejoice,
Singing loud with cheerful voice.
 Hallelujah!"

Kamern, 20th May 1842.

DEAR JOSEPH,
 You desire to hear from us again; that rejoices me much — very much and you shall have a long letter for it. But why do you speak so very sentimentally

of the past pleasure of youth, and of old age? I feel
nothing of it. Dear Joseph, take care that your
children do not get an old papa before their time.
A Christian has the privilege of being always young
and cheerful. If at times it is torn from him, he must
quickly ask it again from the Lord. I know all about
such times of weakness, and my life abounds in them,
but I have always found that it was designed to make
my faith more joyful, and the grace of God more
abundant within me; and that my life became thereby
enriched with greater joyfulness of heart. Dear Joseph,
you must come to me with your family this summer,
and go with me to Lubbendorf. Joachim has had a
little wing built for the bathing visitors; you must in-
augurate it with me, and learn from me to forget your
age. Am I high-minded? Oh no; but I sometimes
feel the sure foundation so sure within me, that I cannot help being a little bold. But now at last to the
subject — you wish to hear how things are looking
with us. On Thursday I sat under my beeches, and
looked down on my own little bit of land. The May
is in full beauty and flower, and I think I have never
seen it so beautiful. My dear Kamern is still very
dear to me; it lay far below me enwreathed with white-
blossomed trees and golden oaks; and, on the left,
Olshausen also attired in white and with fresh green,
and the lake clear as a mirror, and birches and beeches
in May green, and the blue sky above me so tender
and bright, and the air so soft and yet fresh, and the
birds so joyful, and the bees so busy. I felt youthful,
there was an impression that something special would
happen. Attend, dear Joseph. My thoughts and
memories were youthful. Theresa's image mingled

with them in youthful beauty, loveableness, and love to me. She might have been mine, I thought, if I had been more confident. I thought my foes stronger than they were. I ought in all quietness and love to have had more confidence against the world, more courage and boldness. I ought not to have suffered my own to be torn from me. Poor fool that I was! Yet I thought further I could not have done it, and it was to be, and my quiet life is surely best for me, and my home is beautiful; and such a May-day wondrously beautiful, and a little longing and melancholy belong to it, and no longer make me mournful. In my enthusiastic mood I could not help looking at the glory of the spring, and sat there a long time. Then I heard footsteps on the path from Olshausen, — a young girl in a white dress and large straw-hat, with blue ribbons, came out from the beech-green. "Uncle Joachim!" she cried eagerly, and hastened to me. It was Annie. I knew that something special would happen to-day. "We are there!" she said joyfully. "We are no longer subjects of the Emperor, we shall either live in the old wing at grandmamma's, or our compact holds good about the house in the church-yard corner." I had been obliged to promise her when she was here last, if she really wished it, to sell her the church-corner house. She wished to live there with Emma Haineggen (who has become a great friend of hers and of Theresa's), and there to endeavour in every way to serve the Lord. Now she told me with emotion of the life at Nice, of her father's death, it is very nearly a year since he died. Like all consumptive people, he would not believe in death until his strength suddenly failed. Alfred set off immediately in order by Theresa's wish

to settle affairs. It was then so bad that the old uncle
who had taken matters into his own hand, had spoken
decidedly of a bankruptcy; after a year's computation
the result is, as Anna very innocently related, that
they are no longer "subjects of the Emperor;" and,
after covering their debts, only a small sum remained.
Anna tells me so earnestly, and sincerely of her desire
to be here, that I willingly believe it. She is become
far more beautiful in the last two years, very much
like her mother, only Theresa was gentler and more
tender, and her eyes brighter. Anna's eyes are dark-
blue, with long dark lashes; her voice has a deep tone,
and on her brow dwells strength of will, or even defiance. I must be careful that I do not get henpecked.
We both have a talent for it. Theresa is a quiet pale
widow. Oh, Joseph, how it pained my heart to see
her; it was as if I must sorrow with her, as though I
ought not to feel young and cheerful by her side; and
yet I felt in my heart and senses the loveliness of the
May. Towards evening came Joachim. I was afraid
it would be with Anna as it was before, but they were
very courteous to each other. I shall advise Joachim
to be on his guard; the maiden is no longer easily
pleased. I observed that they bear much resemblance
in character to each other; therefore they agree so
badly, and I have a difficult position; I love them both
very much. Joachim stayed here. To-day we were
together at Olshausen. Aunt is anxious about Theresa.
We must cheer her up and divert her; she is so silent,
often sits for hours together absorbed in thought, in
the afternoon too she wandered out alone. But there
is nothing to be done. She has been diverted enough
in her life-time; repose is now natural and necessary

too. The Lord must help her. Anna brought us back through the park. She seems very happy here. I only fear one thing. Alfred will very much disturb her in her plans. His life is cold and empty, and if he had the talents of his father, he would still live differently. Fortunately also Julia counter-balances him. She strives to have a Christian household, though not thoroughly warmed with Christianity within. To-day it came to a quarrel between Alfred and Anna. He wishes to make something distinguished of her. "She is a Countess Stadlein," he says; "she inherited the name from her father, she has money enough from her mother, to enter respectably on the world." He tries to stir up her pride especially by raillery. Yesterday he was telling about Theresa's young life and inclinations, that she had never learned to comprehend her position, that in her powers of usefulness she might rival the best dairy-maid, and "the taste of my dear niece, the Countess Stadlein, appears very much in goose-breasts and dumplings, and to incline very much to the below-stairs in house and company." Anna rose at these words, I believe almost angry, but with great adroitness, she called in the help of pleasantry. She said she wished to be treated like a grown-up young lady, that she knew perfectly what beseemed her position, and also knew exactly her duties towards those below stairs. She had lived long enough in the *haute volée*, and prized the cleverness of a good dairy-maid, or that of old Christabel in the church corner, more highly than the arts of the great world. "That is my view," she said, "and now I throw you down the gauntlet, that I will defend this view — only speak earnestly, uncle." Julia quickly interposed. She feels deeply

Alfred's deficiency in intellectual matters, she also knew that Anna had an ally in me. When we were in the garden afterwards, I warned Anna to be more careful not to offend them. "Oh, dear Uncle," she answered eagerly, "compliance is not always right. One must be decided with Uncle Alfred, he only has courage with a cowardly foe." I could not help laughing, nor Joachim either. The girl is right. Besides, I am afraid, she finds in Joachim a too active-minded companion, compared with Alfred. When we three cousins are together I am always obliged to deaden the fire. I have now been walking for a long time with Joachim up and down before the castle, that is to say each one alone. The moonlight is so beautiful, and all over the blooming world; the nightingales are singing. When I looked at the moon I could not help thinking of Theresa's pale face, but the more I looked up the more brightly and peacefully she looked down on me.

> * "My Jesus, stay Thou by me,
> And let no foe come nigh me,
>   Safe sheltered by Thy wing;
> But would the foe alarm me,
> O let him never harm me,
>   But still Thine angels round me sing!"

And now, dear Joseph, you know how things are looking with us, come yourself and live with us. Answer soon and that you accept my invitation. Joachim sends you a pressing invitation and joins in love with me.

God be with you!

Your

JOACHIM.

Kamern, 18th June 1842.

DEAR JOSEPH,

Delightful that you are coming! and Sophie must take up no anxieties, but bring all the children and servants with her. Elizabeth is delighted to be active again. She wished especially on account of the height of the season which has opened here, to be able to introduce novelties in the house; especially in one room, there was to be new furniture. She values the good reputation of Castle Kamern. I too would willingly have put my hand in my pocket; but Anna strictly forbade it. She does not wish to miss one stool from its accustomed place. Joachim agreed with her, and so we old people have acquiesced.

Elizabeth says, "Countess Anna is right, it is unnecessary, Castle Kamern has no need of embellishment;" and I am delighted that she thinks nothing of outward show, and was, for once, more sensible than old Elizabeth. Thus things stand here, dear Joseph. You see who has the management, but we stand quietly by, and so will you too. Anna is now with great inventiveness providing for the pleasure of your children. Netty, in order fully to enjoy you, wishes to be here for a fortnight, and then we shall settle down by the sea-side. Anna was very sorry not to be able to be here entirely for the fortnight, but we must be careful; the grandmother and Alfred begin to be jealous. I have great pleasure in her company, and Theresa appears to favour it. I have already often met her kindly approval, when Anna is standing by me and acting as though my affection to her were her right. Theresa is getting to take more part in things now. Annie says she enjoys herself especially at Lubbendorf.

Theresa and Annie and the grandmother will go with
us.   And now may the Lord lead you safely!

You will find the carriage at the desired place.

Your faithful
JOACHIM.

Of the beautiful summer-time in Lubbendorf, 1842,
recorded for possible lonely days in winter, and as a
remembrancer that the Lord gives me good days, and
more cheerful than gloomy times, and that I should
not be rebellious or unthankful.

15th July.

We had morning service together for the first time.
The sun was in the clear blue sky; so shall Christ be
the Sun of our days — the Lord of our life.   Amen.

We breakfasted in the honey-suckle bower, the
reddish blossoms rested against such pure blue; the
bed of roses and lilies just by, was also wonderfully
beautiful.   We used the early part of the morning for
going to the shore.   We sat down on the cliff, above
the fishing huts.   Joseph's children were playing on
the beach below; the great boys were rocking themselves in a boat, the little ones looking for shells; their
merry voices sounded up to us.   I thought of the time
when I was young, and when Joachim used to play
down there.   Now he is standing beside me a bearded
youth, but closer to my heart year by year.   May the
Lord take him ever nearer to His heart.   Our party
was very lively.

From a full heart we sang,

* "Day-spring of Eternity!
 Dawn on us this morning-tide.
Light from Light's exhaustless sea,
 Now no more Thy radiance hide,
But dispel with glorious might
  All our night.

Scattered by Thy cheering ray,
 Are the clouds which wrapped us all;
Which have darkened all our day,
 Since our father Adam's fall:
Yet, Lord, in Thy glorious light
  All is bright.

Let the morning dew of love
 On our sleeping conscience rain;
Gentle comfort from above
 Flow through life's long parchèd plain;
Water daily us Thy flock
  From the rock.

Let the glow of love destroy
 Cold obedience faintly given;
Wake our hearts to strength and joy
 With the flushing eastern heaven,
Let us truly rise ere yet
  Life hath set.

To yon world be Thou our light,
 O Thou glorious Sun of grace;
Lead us through the tearful night,
 To yon fair and blessed place,
Where to joy that never dies
  We shall rise."

Now the sea is murmuring through the quiet night. The day was tranquil as the evening, and passed away. No cloudlet troubled the heaven above us or the heaven within us.

          18th July.

Joseph's children hung on my arms, and on my coat-tails. Joseph does not understand it. "My dear fellow," I said to him, "do not be so stern, not too

     10*

solemn!" We have pretty many roguish tricks together,
and bring life into the company. I am glad that I
have not forgotten the way. Joachim has been quiet
for some time; he ought to be a more lively host. But
again it is a good thing that he leaves us alone; every
one lives according to his pleasure. Anna on the con-
trary plays with us children. I am glad of it, I was
afraid she was getting too sensible. To-day we have
carried the last load of hay, crowned with a wreath of
roses. I am leading quite a lounging life — my old
weakness. I might be classed now with the young
steward, who had to give his father an account of his
life in his apprenticeship. He says that he generally
spends the forenoon and till the coffee-hour in eating,
and drinking, reading, and walking, and repose; "the
rest of the time I have to myself." The time which
I have to myself, I often spend with old Valentine,
walking on the hill. Valentine at seventy-nine, can
no longer cast the net; his grandsons attend to that;
but his mind is bright enough to look back over his
life, and to look up to the Lord of all fishermen — the
Fisher of our souls. I was rowing with him to-day in
the starlight; as we came back, Joachim and Anna
with Joseph's boys were singing quite low, and in
subdued evening tones, an evening-hymn; it was borne
to us by the water, and we both joined in.

23rd July.

In spite of the rain, announced by the weather wise,
and desired by every one, we made up our party to
the high forest lodge. I gave over the young people
to Joseph and Sophie, they went on foot. I drove
with Aunt Emma, Netty and Theresa. Theresa was

more lively than ever, her cheeks had a rosy flush; she had that child-like and innocent expression which touches my heart. She was more lovely and more beautiful to-day than her daughter, and there was something shining through it by which I could imagine, how she will appear to us some day as a glorified angel.

Theresa, I believe, now understands my love, she has a sense of it, in spite of my distance, her soul is open, and my soul sings thanks and praise to the Lord for it.

We were sitting before the forest lodge, under the embowering beech-trees. Theresa and Anna were making garlands with the children. The blue sky became more misty, scattered clouds rose at noon, and sometimes there was a sound of distant thunder. We wished to set off home, but the old forester assured us that no shower was to be expected till late in the evening or till night. We liked so much to stay. We all so much enjoyed the solitude of forest and sea. But the sky became grey, single drops fell, a light breeze moved the beech-leaves. Sea-birds restlessly gathered round the watch-tower by the sea.

Our old ladies wished to go quickly home. Joseph also advised it, but we young people, (I sincerely reckon myself among them), were in favour of staying. In the first place we could not get home dry, and a storm up on the hill would be magnificent. We stayed: and dispersed ourselves according to pleasure, in order to watch the approaching storm. I stood alone, on a jut of rock over a little bay. The clouds towered up very dark blue, they rolled nearer and nearer. The sky became deep violet; the waves foamed restlessly in portentous whiteness. Single gusts of wind rushed in, and roaring, drove the water into the bay, and on to the rocks, the thunder was rolling constantly in the distance; the air was sultry, the earth thirsty. I thought, as it is here in nature, so it is also with men. The sunshine of prosperity is delightful, and shines cheerily over life; but our heart is weak, it becomes dry and weary with it; until Heaven shakes it with His tempests, and the rain of grace and blessing follows the storms of misfortune; whereby it rises refreshed to growth and increase, and feels better, nnder the tranquil cloudy sky, than in the dazzling beams of the sun.

Suddenly the thunder rolled quite near me, a whirlwind arose, it lashed the beech-twigs one against another, and the sea rose in angry tumult. I hastened my retreat. By the watch-tower, however, Joachim and Anna were standing much at their ease. Anna's hair was floating in the wind. Joachim had placed himself protectingly at her side. Now they followed my call. I know not what strange thoughts came to me for the first time. Anna and Joachim are, with great resemblance, also very different: to my sorrow, they still bicker much too often, but that often shows only the desire for a more perfect mutual understanding.

It would not be impossible — and for me it would be the crown of all the benefits the Lord has shown me in my life. I could not help constantly watching them both, and entered so deeply into it that I felt quite young again. The Lord often works in His own wondrous way. He could bring it about; and thereby dissolve every bitterness in my fate and Theresa's.

Only one thing surprises me, that others have not made the same observation. I will not betray it; the world, by untimely talk, often destroys such tender buds. We found the company already in the parlour and anxious about us. But Joachim, — I observed it, put on a disguise, and did not trouble himself there about Anna. The storm of thunder and lightning became heavy, we had the full benefit of it.

But it was growing late; the elder ladies were anxious about our return home, when the storm had gone to a distance it rained incessantly from a grey unvarying sky.

In spite of so little prospect of it, Anna prophesied that we should go home in bright sunshine. She was laughed at, but she kept to it. Netty entertained us meantime with the old forester's bread and butter, and sausage, and beautiful straw-berries. We stood by the open windows, and drank in the refreshing scent. The rain rustled lightly on the beech-leaves; and on the green grass-plot below us, was feeding the forester's old fox, and quietly letting it rain on his fur. The young people envied him this enjoyment. All at once late in the evening a ball of fire broke forth under the dark ridge of clouds. He threw his beams over the glittering green; they flew farther and farther, — a golden light flamed forth far over land and sea. No one knows who began it, but, as of one accord, there sounded loudly from our heart: "Praise the Lord — the mighty King of glory." When this was sung, we prepared for our journey home. Sophie took my place in the carriage, I went with the others. Anna had the triumph of our beginning our return, with the last beams of the

sun; they did not reach far, but our songs reached till
we got home.

And now dear Lord, I thank thee for the beautiful
day; how, many lonely days in winter it must counter-
balance.

I have called to mind the text, I will refresh the
weary souls and satisfy the heavy laden souls. Oh! dear
Lord, Thou hast ever done so.

28th July.

Old Valentine has had a dream, the dream lives in
my soul, I cannot forget it. I wished to call the old
man for a row. I found him alone before the hut, his
people were at work, he bade me stay with him, he
was too weak to row. Then he related to me the
dream. "Master I never had such a vivid dream," said
he — "a dream does but seem;" but it may often also
be a prophetic glimpse. I was going up all alone, the
sea was as clear as a mirror, the sun was bright above.
I rowed and rowed. I cast out the net, but could not
get it ready, and thought at last you are foolish to
trouble yourself; it is no longer work for you, you must
rest and pray. When I was laying the net aside, and
looking round me the country appeared quite unknown
to me; and I saw, in the far far twilight, our shore,
our Lubbendorf, my huts and my grandsons. Then I
was so afraid, and I thought why have you rowed so
far? and how anxious those at home will be about you.
Great longing for home seized me. I wished to turn
the boat, but a mighty current bore me to the strange
shore. When I could just see the shore, I felt great
joy in my heart: for my dear kind master stands there,
and calls and beckons. 'Fear not, Valentine,' you

said, 'I am come before you, and I never wish to go back, and you will never wish to go back either.' I got up out of the boat, and stepped on to the land, and was dazzled and quite happy with the beauty. Heavenly glory was around us, and heavenly peace. 'Now,' you said, 'I must first put up a signal for my people, who have remained behind,' and we went up into a mountain, and you opened a great banner half snow-white and half purple. — We are washed from our sins in the blood of the Lamb; if they always have the signal before their eyes, they will some day come to us. We saw our shore now quite in the far distance — a female form dressed in black was kneeling there, and stretching her arms towards us. 'She will follow me first,' you said joyfully. But now we saw our young master and some other people, up there on the height, stick up just such a signal over the hut, and you said 'Now it is all right, Valentine, they have understood me, now we will go on.' Then the dream was over, but still when awake I saw everything plainly, and plainly heard your words."

Valentine's dream has strangely affected me. One often dreams wonderful stuff, but sometimes there is a mysterious power in a dream. Valentine is seventy-nine; that he will soon cross over to the other land, I have often thought; but that I might go before him, never seriously came into my mind. We think of death, think also it is possible thou mayst die young, it may perhaps be very soon; but yet our thoughts are not in earnest. Life — dear, accustomed, daily life, obliterates every deeper impression. Therefore, Joachim, it is well thou shouldst be affected by the dream earnestly to think of heaven, to set in order thy house and thy soul. If it is only

a dream, if it is no prophecy, it may be a serious remembrancer.　Ah, Joachim will have nothing of prophecy; he is young and healthy, life looks so lovely to
him now.　Now Lord, what I cannot do Thou canst.
I pray Thee for a happy death; — whether it comes
soon or comes late. Thou canst make easy what seems
hard to us.　Am I then afraid?　No.　I am like a
child free from care, and lay myself on my Saviour's
breast, and am comforted.

2d August.

I would willingly employ myself with thoughts of
death, but I cannot sing

> "Though the night of death be fraught
> Still with many an anxious thought."

I have never been more full of joy and peace than
now; it is as though there could be no death for me.
Can that be the true foreboding of death?　Should I
slumber away like a child who is put to bed and sung
to sleep by its mother?　Dear Lord, let it be so.　I do
not fear death, I have given myself to Thee, the white
and red banner is my symbol.

> My Saviour's blood and righteousness,
> That is my robe and costly dress;
> And, clothed in these my soul shall be,
> When Thou shalt call me home to Thee.

4th August.

In a fortnight the festive time here will be over.
We speculate enormously in order to make the most of
it and we could not but have a glorious and delightful
time here.

There often passes a light over Anna and Joachim's
features, which makes my heart young; Theresa's looks

too rest kindly on Joachim. Could she see anything?
Surely my observations do not deceive me, and they
also conceal nothing from me, they do not think me
dangerous. To-day they looked together for four-
leaved clover on the grass-plot. Joachim was very
unskilful, but Anna gave him some, and he looked so
happily at the leaf, as though he were now at the goal
of his wishes.

5th August.

There must have been wonderful doings at the
tower of Babel; I could clearly fancy it to-day, it was
just like it here. Julia and Alfred came with the
cousins from the Marches.

Netty used to stay there when she was young; she
saw the young people grow up, and has always been
rather intimate with them. Netty took me aside. "I
beg you, dear Joachim, be rather condescending to-
day: the cousins think your kindness and mildness are
stupidity: you injure a good cause thereby. You must
learn to make an impression." I could not help laughing, but I said, "on your responsibility I will do it: only
tell me when it is enough." Then the confusion began.
The greetings took place and we sat down to table in
the garden-parlour. The cousins with heads almost
between their shoulders, and half closed eyes, lisped in
a low voice: Joachim von Kamern did his utmost to
make an impression on them. Joseph and Sophie
looked on in astonishment, and when I, true to the
character which had been enjoined upon me, implicated
myself in a dispute with the cousins, Joseph suddenly
broke out into a loud laugh. I was obliged to control
myself that I did not join in, and Sophie's imperious

looks recalled Joseph's composure. Joachim the second
was in the plot; he beamed with distinguished courtesy,
before which the artificialness of even Alfred and the
cousins must come to nothing.   Anna played the part
natural to her in the presence of Alfred and Julia, she
was cold and monosyllabic.

Netty put on her most homely behaviour; she acted
towards Alfred and his guests, exactly as if she had
only lately arranged their ties for dancing.   Theresa
was silent, and sometimes looked anxiously at Julia.
Aunt Emma was uncommonly lively and amiable, and
seemed to wish to put a crust of sugar over everything.   She often talked meantime such disconnected
and senseless stuff, that I could not help wondering at
the politeness of the cousins, between whom she sat
and who assented to everything.   So dinner passed off
tolerably.   After dinner Alfred and Julia had a secret
conference with Aunt Emma and Theresa, which ex-
ercised a strange influence on the general temper.
When we were sitting at coffee in the bower, Aunt
Emma said, with some embarrassment, and in a low
voice, "Dear Joachim, Alfred and Julia wish very
much that we should go back now."   "That I can
easily believe," said I laughing, "but we wish very
much that you should stay."   "We have been here a
long time," she continued, "and I especially am longing for home."   "I am sorry for that, but it depends on
whether Theresa and Anna are also longing to go," I
replied.   "We will stay here," said Theresa, with unexpected resolution.   "Well then the matter is simple:
every one has his liberty here," I said playfully, "if
you wish, dear Aunt, to go home we will not be offended, and Theresa and Anna can stay as has been

proposed." General silence followed this verdict and
strange faces. I found myself the rest of the day in a
thorough misunderstanding. Only the cousins remained
unchanged, from Aunt Emma to Joachim, quite a
change of character came over them. Could Alfred
and Julia have been offended that we have not invited
them here as well? It is possible, but why were they
so unfriendly to Joseph and Sophie at Kamern? They
must be punished. And our life here would have
been a tower of Babel from the beginning, if we had
had them here. What a miserable joyless day it has
been! another proof what society is, when the spirit of
God is absent.

6th August.

Do the storms blow from hence? Now, Joachim
von Kamern, you will know not to give yourself airs
only for joke. Stations are by God's grace differently
arranged, and I have a small one, or rather no small
pride in my station, but God makes no rule without
exception. He arranges circumstances so that the form
is necessarily broken and a new path must be trodden.
There!

Netty rings her hands, her motherly heart over-
flows, — Joachim loves Anna. Alfred and Julia and
Aunt Emma are enraged at it. Aunt Emma has
spoken to Netty "like a sister," as she called it. A
Countess Stadlein can never be a wife for Frederic,
family discords and every kind of misfortune must follow such a step! — The ground of family discords lies
somewhere else. The family is said to be proud of
Joachim, and besides he is our Cousin German, and
looks like a true Kamern. There!

Was that why Alfred was so friendly with him yesterday? an incomprehensible point to me in yesterday's confusion. Must we think that the storm only proceeds from the grandmother? detestable hypocrisy! I will show that I can have a will of my own. May the Lord strengthen me to persevere in my anger. I will set my house in order in such a way that Alfred shall wonder. There!

9th August.

Joachim is very much cast down. I will not comfort him too hastily. He must struggle through alone and obtain by conflict that for which his soul longs. Anna must help him; both may show that their love has no need of my help, then I shall be satisfied and will do what I will. I have persuaded Netty to be quiet. We will do nothing, nothing at all, and will wait to see what position the hostile party will take. Aunt Emma has remained perhaps to keep watch. I have not been able yet to ask Theresa's opinion. Sophie and Joseph are preparing for their departure. There is nothing more to be done — the glory of our days is passed.

14th August.

I was walking alone in the garden, Annie came to me. She spoke of the parting, and said, she should feel unhappy at Olshausen, and should feel great weariness if she did not think of some special occupation for herself. She laid before me a well-considered plan. An Infant-school is not needed; either the women do not go to work, or if they go, there are grandmothers or elder brothers and sisters. But a sewing-school is needed; the mothers themselves do not understand sewing and knitting, they could not teach their daughters. Annie wishes to sew for the mission with the grownup girls, and for the widows and orphans of the village, with the little ones. "But money is required for all that," said Annie. "You know, dear Uncle," she continued, after a pause, and very much embarrassed, "when I am twenty-one, I shall be of age, and come in for a little property, it is but little but I shall have some hundred thalers interest from it. I beg you till then to lend me a hundred thalers a year. I will be sure to repay them." I was obliged to recollect myself in order gravely; to ask her, whether she had spoken about it to her guardian. "Uncle Alfred has flatly refused me," answered Anna eagerly; "they were useless things; Olshausen had done very well without them hitherto, and could do longer." — I asked whether she had asked him kindly about it. "That is of no use," replied she quickly. "Emma Haineggen has already disputed with him the whole winter about it, when she was at Olshausen; he does not wish it, at least he will give nothing to it, and what we have already done in that way, we have been obliged to do secretly with Julia's help."

I then gave Anna to understand she should devote her time more to her mother than to other things, but for that also she was prepared. "It is just on my mother's account that I do it, she longs for such employment and will give all the necessary money for it, but I would rather give my own money." The wish was not unreasonable. I thought the matter over and made her another proposition which pleased her well. "Of the house in the church-yard corner I have afterwards

disposed differently, but for the present you can hold
your school there, and arrange according to your judgment. I give you also a sum with which you can
freely manage and conduct it." "Splendid!" cried Anna,
"then I will go with mamma to the little house; there
we shall be free and we shall see Castle Kamern glimmering through the trees, and it is not so far to the
beeches as it is from Olshausen." I was obliged to
cheek her delight, and to try to convince her that she
could only take the management of the little house
and of her property, but must stay with her mother at
her grandmother's. She reconciled herself to it, and
then with great vivacity joined in the Olshausen
plans.

Joachim came to us. He seemed to wonder at
Anna's merriment. She told him of my present, and
added, I am so merry only on that account. At these
words there was something peculiar in the tone of her
voice and in her looks: in his place, I should have
read a great deal in it. Perhaps he did so. Oh, I am
not afraid for my two dear children.

16th August.

No, I am not afraid. The faithful Lord will lead
them. With Him, they entered upon it, with Him,
they will proceed: that is the chief thing; everything
else will order and arrange itself. To-morrow we shall
go away. I was going once more to the shore, when,
as I came out of the little wood, I found Joachim and
Anna who were standing under the weeping birch. I
came up to them. The evening sky was very beautiful, many little cloudlets bordered with gold, the sea
also shone, the shore, the huts, the green forest and

the faces of both the dear ones shone still more beautifully. I felt that they were at the goal: they did not conceal it from me, they shared their happiness and sorrow with me, and laughed and wept like children. I have laid a promise upon them, to be silent for the present. I have my motives for it. Joachim did not agree to it, but he may consent. Anna says I am happy enough, and will willingly keep it to myself as a secret. Later we fetched Netty and Theresa to the shore; they also know nothing. Women are not fitted to arrange complicated affairs; besides Theresa has always been the dependant child, and how childish and helpless she looked to me to-day! The star of evening was in the clear sky, we looked far up into it. I could talk very happily of heaven, an ardent longing possessed me. It is well indeed that we do not know how beautiful it is there, or we might not be willing to stay here below. The greatest happiness here is mingled with sorrow and unrest; it is only an uncertain good, our heart can only possess it with fear and trembling, death is the last bitter accessory of earth. Oh, we were miserable indeed, if we had not the Lord Jesus already here. While as yet we cannot enjoy with Him the blessedness above, He brings it down to us: with Him every earthly fortune is an eternal inheritance; with Him every unrest becomes peace; with Him death is no death: for all which we have in Him here, we take with us to eternal life, if we are happy in Him here. I thought of Valentine's dream, I was in the land of glory, and Theresa was stretching her arms towards the cross of the Lamb.

Oh Lord, let our hope, our longing rest on Thee alone; Lord, help us from the power of Satan and of

death. Oh Lord, I could not be happy without all
those whom my heart loves; and now give faith, that
blessed mystery which only springs from grace.   Oh
Lord, I will not let Thee go unless Thou bless us. We
sat on: the sea gave forth a gentle yet mighty murmur,
silver stars were playing over it — the reflection of the
star-bespangled sky.   We sang together

> Christ, my soul's repose!
> Who Thy equal knows?
> Chief among ten thousand cherished;
> Life of those who else had perished;
> Light from Thee arose,
> Christ, my soul's repose!
>
> That I might be freed
> From my every need,
> Thou, the Life, of death hast tasted,
> And to hide my sins hast hasted,
> Me, from all my need,
> Unto God to lead.
>
> Thou, the light divine!
> Ere time was didst shine:
> And, as our Redeemer given,
> Veiled in flesh the light of heaven
> Which is ever Thine;
> Thou the light divine!
>
> Draw me close to Thee,
> That Thy love may be
> In my soul all dross refining;
> That I may, on Thee reclining,
> From my load be free:
> Draw me close to Thee.
>
> When death is at hand
> Thou wilt near me stand:
> Through the vale of death beside me,
> Thou wilt on to glory guide me:
> That I there may stand,
> Lord, at Thy right hand.

So farewell, dear Lubbendorf, those were days of peace, — very beautiful days.

———

Kamern, 18th September 1842.

DEAR JOSEPH,

I have lately had much to do, and labours which are unpleasant to me. Legal advisers and packets of papers have been in and out. Now all is arranged. It is a comfortable feeling to know your earthly house in order. You wish to hear of Anna and Joachim. You shall soon know, the matter is as you foresaw. I do not share your fears, much will happen against it; they will be against it, but we shall be for it and there will be Another Who will be for it; and so in spirit I see the matter accomplished. Alfred and Julia have persuaded Aunt Emma and Theresa to go with them to their cousins in the Marches. Anna wished to protest, but I have laid upon her for this time to be very acquiescent with her grandmother and uncle. Joachim also sensibly agreed with me, so she willingly consented. Alfred finds himself in the unpleasant position of all men of the world when they speculate; he is in constant suspense. He has an indescribable repugnance to Joachim. Aunt Emma shares it, but both seek to hide it from me. Alfred especially believes that he thoroughly deceives me. A cousin who is heir to an estate is alas for him a man of no small importance. Joachim does not desire money and property: this conviction is a comfort to me; that Anna loves him, loves him just as he is, and for what he is, makes me at rest about my necessary arrangements. I would not throw temptations and snares in

11*

their way. But what are money and property? how
can they be a temptation? Are they not a greater
responsibility and an anxiety on the path of life?
Would that all men were as convinced of it as I am.
I see your Sophie smile at these words! "He may
well speak, he knows nothing of earthly cares," she
will say. O dear clergyman's wife, only confess! you
have often hitherto made yourself needlessly anxious,
and have unjustifiably restricted the jurisdiction of the
Lord.

We must pray, "Give us this day our daily bread;"
in the command to pray, we have also the Father's
promise, and a truly believing child has no earthly
cares. But what do you understand by our daily
bread? Examine yourselves. — I have the courage to
advise you to still greater contentedness, and to less
pretensions and vanity with the children. And now
I have said all. Pardon me! my old desire of preaching comes on. I have not given up my promised
autumnal visit, only I wish to keep my birthday here.
Theresa and Anna will be back then. You are right.
Through Theresa and Anna's presence, my life will
assume quite another form. I am very thankful to the
Lord that He has put an end to the loneliness of my
days. I am a weak man in want of sympathy and
loving company. I had many a heavy hour in the
last lonely winter. Anna will bring life into our silent
rooms. She has already quite settled into my mother's
chamber. Elizabeth is very happy at it. "The spirit
of the dear departed lady has come back to us again
in her," she says. Dear Joseph, it is better that I
should conclude now. I am weary and unstrung.
The day before yesterday, the attorney was here for

the last time. Yesterday I made a round in the house with Elizabeth, looked at her request into chests and cup-boards. I am tired with it and the lonely autumn days which I have before me are dear to me. The sun shines so warmly here into the garden-parlour; so long as chimney-fires suffice, I shall stay here; it is so lovely and beautiful here. I step out of the door into the grapery, and see how the sun is ripening the bunches of grapes, and the gnats play and dance before me. Then I shut my eyes and think of nothing, and let myself be warmed and brightened by the sunshine of the dear Lord. But the Lord be with you and your whole house.

Faithfully

Your

JOACHIM VON KAMERN.

27th September.

I have a constant heaviness in my head, yet I do not feel unwell; no, very well, and quiet and happy. I enjoy the bright warm autumn days. It is as though nature wished, before her death, to shew herself in all her beauty and to insinuate herself into our hearts. I walked in the sunshine; the dahlias and asters shone in the gayest colours, the green turf is more beautiful than in summer. Sometimes a golden leaf floats down from the birch-trees; beeches and oaks and lime-trees are blown by the autumnal breeze; the blue sky stretches above in deepest blue. It is so silent, I hear my footsteps on the soft sandy ground, hear the trumpeting of the gnats, and the chirping of a robin in the elder. Sometimes Maudlin comes creeping in with her little brothers and sisters, and plays quite gently with them.

They lay golden leaves upon the garden seat, and rosy
apples and other small autumnal fruits upon them,
ornamented with gay petals of flowers. I enjoy myself at their table, and am helpful to them in gathering
the fruits and flowers. To-day I gave them bunches
of grapes as a finish, then I sat in the niche of the
vine, and watched their quiet play. Good children
look like angels, I felt as if I were in heaven. I
struck up my hymn which for several days has touched
my heart and Maudlin, who knows many hymns, joined
softly in — Yes.

> * "Oh Love, Who formedst me to wear
> The image of Thy Godhead here;
> Who soughtest me with tender care
> Through all my wanderings wild and drear;
> Oh Love, I give myself to Thee,
> Thine ever, only Thine to be.
>
> Oh Love, Who lovest me for aye,
> Who for my soul dost ever plead;
> O Love, Who didst my ransom pay,
> Whose power sufficeth in my stead,
> Oh Love, I give myself to Thee,
> Thine ever, only Thine to be.
>
> Oh Love, Who once shalt bid me rise
> From out this dying life of ours;
> Oh Love, Who once above yon skies
> Shalt set me in the fadeless bowers:
> Oh Love, I give myself to Thee,
> Thine ever, only Thine to be."
>   Amen, Amen.

These are the last written words of the late Joachim
von Kamern. From the 27th of September till the
4th of October, he attended to his affairs as usual.
He visited the children at the singing-school, in the

house in the church-yard corner. On Friday, the 30th
of September, he held evening service with the men of
the village. Sunday, the 2nd October, he was at
church for the last time. In the afternoon he talked
with the pastor about a kind of Sunday-school, or at
least Sunday occupation for young men. He wished
to know them pleasantly employed on a Sunday, and
in that way to keep them from sinful desecration of
the Sabbath. He also with the pastor arranged the
library of the village, and gave him a commission for
new purchases of books. Monday, Tuesday, and
Wednesday, Klaus and Elizabeth were thoughtful
about his state of health; they were very much struck
with his condition. They often found him sitting on
the sofa with his eyes open; when they spoke to him,
he gazed at them, and only answered after a long
time. Elizabeth urgently begged him to leave the
garden-parlour, and to take to his room, but he would
not break away from it. The days were still so warm
and beautiful, and he could here enjoy them in their
freshness. In those days he would not have Maudlin
out of his sight, and she employed herself either in the
sunny grapery or by the fire, and received a commission from Elizabeth always to keep up the fire. Yet
on Thursday Elizabeth was so anxious about her
master, that she urgently begged to be allowed to send
for a physician, and for young Master Joachim. He
smiled at her anxiety, and said he had never felt so
well as now, that he was only weary and exhausted,
and his head rather heavy, but quite without pain.
He wished therefore to spend just these few days undisturbed and in rest, in order to recover and to be
able to be quite well, and cheerfully to keep his birth-

day in the coming week. He playfully asked Elizabeth
meantime to be getting ready the bill of fare for the
festive day, and in the afternoon played very sweetly
and kindly with Maudlin in the niche of the vine.
On Friday morning he got up very late, and Klaus
observed that his master could scarcely totter to the
sofa in the garden-parlour. Klaus asked anxiously
how he was, and received as an answer that his head
ached to-day. Elizabeth urgently begged that her
master would go to bed again; he made no objection,
only he begged to be allowed to rest here a little
while; he was afraid of returning to his bed-room just
then. Klaus covered him with a silken quilt, and the
room was pleasantly warm. Then the sick man slept.
But Klaus and Elizabeth sent for the physician and
to Lubbendorf. Towards two o'clock Herr von Kamern
awoke. Maudlin was to put a glass of flowers nearer
to him; he enjoyed them and said, "I must gather myself some fresh ones to-morrow." After some minutes
he folded his hands and said softly,

> * "My Jesus, stay Thou by me,
>   And let no foe come nigh me,
>   Safe sheltered by Thy wing;
>   But would the foe alarm me,
>   Oh let him never harm me,
>   But still Thine angels round me sing!"

He then turned to Elizabeth and desired writing
materials. "Elizabeth," he said, "I sometimes feel so
strange, not afraid, but I might die soon, and I wish
to write a few words." With great vigour he sat up,
and wrote one letter for Theresa, and another for
Joachim. Elizabeth was not to give the letter to
Joachim, till after the opening of the will. Elizabeth

was also obliged to receive many directions. When she heard him speak so clearly again, and write so eagerly, her anxiety vanished. She thought his thoughts of death were only the result of late times, in which he had been so active in settling his affairs, in case of his death; and that it had recurred to him in feverish sleep. The sick man closed his eyes and slept again. Elizabeth often looked at him; she would rather have had him in bed, but she would now no farther disturb him with entreaties, because she was expecting the physician every minute. But the physician did not come. Elizabeth became uneasy again. His breathing seemed to her irregular. She went out to call Klaus. As they both entered the room, the last beams of the sun broke forth over the dark church-roof and over the sleeper. He lay there very peacefully and with no deathly pallor, but he had already passed away.

The consternation was indescribable. No one would believe it. Household and court-yard were in commotion, one after another crept to the peaceful couch; anxiously they laid their ear on the quiet face; they crept out again, wringing their hands. The physician, who came about dusk, pronounced that a nervous attack had put an end to life. But Joachim also came. He anxiously and tremblingly laid his ear on the pale quiet features; he too stood, wringing his hands, beside the corpse. The horror of death seized him. "Oh! thou dear one, dost thou not hear my voice? Can not thy mouth comfort me? Can not thy eyes look at me with their old affection? Is not thy hand ready to caress me?" No answer! dumb and still lies the dead; everything is over, vain is every hope — every lamentation. In speechless grief Joachim stayed the night by the sleeper. Elizabeth and Klaus looked in by turns, and seated themselves in the distant niche of the window. But when the morning dawned they came, followed by their tribe of children; all knelt down; Elizabeth struck up a hymn, "Rejoice, rejoice, my soul." Klaus and the children joined in. They sang several verses. Joachim had come to the window; the reflection of the rosy dawn was on the lime-trees; he looked higher and higher. His consternation was over. The Lord came into his poor heavily-afflicted heart; Joachim was able to sing the last verse with them and to weep. His Saviour said he is not dead, he is living; and thou wilt see him again; rejoice in his blessedness, cheerfully resign his mortal frame which was only a hindrance to his blessedness. Joachim was able to pray, to pray ever more happily, to look upwards ever more confidingly, he could seek above, the one whom he bewailed, and find him there. Yes, there above he lives, there he loves. We must all press on, oh! Lord, to Thee and to Thy bliss. The next day passed in sad preparations for the funeral. Elizabeth acted with great circumspection in the matter. She had also caused a messenger to be sent on the first evening to the Olshausen relations. Joachim rode to Lubbendorf in order to talk to his mother, who was ill in bed and could not come to Kamern. He came back on the afternoon of the funeral, and found Alfred and Julia and Theresa and Anna there. We know how Theresa had wept alone by the coffin, how she had read the farewell words.

She was now the richest of all in consolations. She had read the writings and journals bequeathed to her. She knew herself beloved by him, to whom she had scarcely dared to look up. This consciousness brought some reconciliation to a life of disappointment and deprivation. He must die, in order to be her own; now she might confidently go the way which leads to him; now she could do everything, everything from love to him. His death and his love made her strong and steadfast. "If you can spare sorrow to my darling, do it." These his words burned in her heart; when this darling, after the funeral, came, by Elizabeth's advice and wish, to take leave of his Olshausen relations, she tried to comfort him.

Alfred had been during the day peculiarly distant and cold towards him, and Joachim had, not without reason, felt a reluctance to go up. In his grief and his melancholy he feared that through the death of his friend and protector, the bond with Anna would be severed. He had only seen Theresa and Anna to-day in the presence of others, indeed, he almost avoided a closer meeting in order to put off the certainty of his fears.

Julia and Alfred in great excitement saw him enter the family circle, and readily consented, when, in a short time he prepared for his departure. Anna had been considering till now how she must comport herself towards Joachim, in her uncle's presence. She now considered no longer, and followed her impulse. Seriously, but with the full expression of her love, she held out her hand to him. "We may come to Lubbendorf?" said she. "Certainly," answered he; his lips quivered, and he was obliged to control himself, to be master of his feelings. But Theresa was overpowered by her emotion. She went up to Joachim, embraced him weeping, and said gently, "We are coming; re-

ceive us!" That was too much for Joachim, he kissed
Theresa's hand, turned quickly towards the door,
hastened down the steps, and rode away.

Mother and daughter remained, weeping in each
other's arms. Julia and Alfred, though secretly enraged, did not venture to interrupt this scene.

———

The same evening the family were sitting together
at Olshausen. Anna and Theresa, too much occupied
with themselves and their own feelings, did not observe
the excitement of the others. Alfred had informed his
mother of the incident at Kamern, and with his wonted
inconsiderate haste demanded of her to speak seriously
and decidedly to Theresa this very day. Julia cleverly
contrived that Anna should leave the room. Alfred
hoped with the help of Julia and his mother, to get
the reins of Theresa's obstinacy completely into his
hands. They were scarcely alone when he asked,
with bitter and sneering tone, exactly what the scene
with Joachim might mean? Theresa looked at him
earnestly, and then said with a gentle voice, "Lay
aside that tone, dear Alfred. He whom we have buried
to-day, did not speak thus. Let us live together in his
spirit. What have you against Joachim? Anna loves
him with her whole soul, and it will be the comfort of
my life to be able to call him my son." "There, did
you hear that, Mother?" interposed Alfred with great
vehemence. "Theresa," cried his mother at the same
time, "Will you in your foolish weakness make your
child unhappy?" "Unhappy?" said Theresa smiling,
"you will not deceive me about happiness or unhappi-

ness. Oh, lay aside such foolish ideas! Alfred, you
know it was on that sofa, that you painted my happiness in glowing colours. Have you such a happiness
in your mind for Anna?" All were silent. The
mother looked down thoughtfully. It was as though
a veil fell from her eyes; the life of her unhappy
daughter lay unveiled before her, and her own pangs
of remorse burned again in her heart. Alfred was so
surprised at the attitude of Theresa, and at the turn
of the conversation, that he was struck dumb. Theresa
continued; she spoke of her miserable life, of all the
illusions and deprivations, but then, with great joyfulness of her hopes for the future. "And now let us
not embitter life," said she, entreatingly, "let us live
in love with one another." "Dear Mother," she said
turning to her, "you are old, what can the world offer
you? what could make you happier than if your
children and grandchildren are gathered around you
in peace and love? Rejoice in Anna's happiness,
love Joachim as a son, he thoroughly deserves it."
At these words she knelt before her mother, whose
tender heart was conquered long before. "You are
right, Theresa," said she weeping, "Anna shall be
happier than you were." "Come, Alfred, come, Julia,"
said Theresa, turning to her brother and sister: "let
us forget the past, and begin a new life; let us live as
Joachim has lived; let us, on the same ground, renounce
the world and love the Divine Saviour. Oh, I wish
to love Him, I wish to retrieve what I have lost, and
to love you heartily." Alfred was now embarrassed;
the nothingness and emptiness of his life was uneasily
felt during this scene, and yet he had not strength to
gainsay. Julia on the other hand was really touched

by the power of the truth, which spoke from the simple manner and language of Theresa. There was a current of good feeling in her to which she willingly yielded when she had once discerned it. She took Alfred by the hand, led him to his mother and sister, and showed that she was ready for anything. She also called in Anna to whom it was hard to understand the change which had taken place.

"The prayer of the righteous man availeth much." It was surely the blessing of the departed, which here brought their hearts together. Anna received from her grandmother consent to their union, and new assurances of maternal love and fidelity. Theresa was very happy. "We bring this as a birthday present to the beloved one above," said she. To-day is the 10th of October. She spoke also of the written legacy of the departed — of his letters and diaries. She had found in succession his youthful letters to Joseph, which he had had given back to him when Joseph left the neighbourhood. She proposed, at a convenient time, to read them to the others, to real edification and consolation.

The next morning Theresa and Anna went to Lubbendorf; it was a dull heavy day, the first after the smiling days of autumn. Joachim was standing at the window, thoughtfully and hopefully, when the longingly expected and yet unexpected ones, came. He received them with joy; with joy he heard the mind of his relations; he was too happy not to hope the best of Alfred. Joachim and Anna could but humble themselves before the Lord, that they had not hitherto attained the right spirit of love towards their relations. Netty also felt a bitter taste of repentance;

it drove them all to Olshausen, in order as Theresa said to forget the past, and to begin a new life. The grandmother and Julia met them with open heart. Alfred was merely polite and could not conceal a certain constraint. He could and would give no place near him to this Joachim, to whom he felt himself inferior in external and mental gifts, and upon whom he had looked from his youth with dislike.

A week after, the will of the deceased was opened. Since Lubbendorf was already given to Joachim, Alfred had little doubt that he as eldest and contemporary cousin should inherit Kamern, and his only fears were that he should have to pay something considerable for it,· to the other relations. He was mistaken. The darling of the departed got Kamern; the beloved Kamern must not be in unconsecrated hands. But considerable sums of money were reserved for Alfred and Theresa, — the result of the long and economical management of the lonely testator.

Also for Klaus and Elizabeth, and for many others, thoughtful provision was made. To Emma von Haineggen fell the little house in the church-yard corner, and just enough with it for her to finish her days there, independent on others.

But what especially surprised and delighted all, except Alfred, was, that Joachim Frederic also inherited the name of the departed, — he was his adopted son. He now stood as a second Joachim von Kamern, and as a true resemblance of him in the family circle. But he was almost amazed at all that; he looked anxiously at Alfred thinking that it must strike at his heart and at his friendly intentions.

Alfred struggled with his agitation, remained cool

and courteous, said, "I expected nothing else, it had long been planned," and left Kamern shortly after the opening of the will. Julia also was obliged to follow him. Joachim and Anna felt that the proximity of their uncle was laid upon them by the Lord as an exercise in humility and love. Their hearts were quite prepared for it, for they were very happy. "I am not worthy of so much goodness," said Joachim, "but with his name, his spirit also shall govern me, and his blessing shall be my best inheritance." When the transactions of the day were over, and the family found themselves together in the chamber of the departed, Joachim proposed, as master of the house, to hold the first evening prayers there with them. Seldom was prayer more fervent, or hymns more heartily sung, than here. Klaus and Elizabeth who had had a request from their new master, to see in him their old master and to love him, took the nearest places to the family, as they also had the nearest places in their hearts. At the conclusion Joachim read the words, which his father had written to him on his death-bed.

MY DEAR SON JOACHIM,

What more have I to say to you? little, and yet all important. Believe on the Lord Jesus Christ, so will you be happy and your house; yes, build an altar to the Lord in your house, and love Him with all your soul. A house in which the Lord does not dwell, is not a house at all. A man whom the Lord does not confess, is a poor fellow. You will be a true master of the house, if you are a servant of Christ. Once more, let Castle Kamern shine a light in the darkness; place high upon it the cross of the Lord Jesus; stand beneath it armed with heroic courage, and with child-like lowliness. May the Lord make my two dear children strong in the power of His might. The Lord bless you and keep you: the Lord make His face to shine upon you and be gracious to you: the Lord lift up His countenance kindly upon you, and give you His peace. Amen.

"Amen," said Theresa and added softly,

> * "My Jesus, stay Thou by me,
> And let no foe come nigh me,
> Safe sheltered by Thy wing;
> But would the foe alarm me,
> Oh let him never harm me,
> But still Thine angels round me sing!"

Yes, so it must be. Theresa, the calm pale widow, looked ever deeper into the heaven of the Lord, and His peace shone more and more sweetly, in her bright child-like eyes. Theresa's thoughts found a home above, and dear Kamern was to be an earthly home for her still. She could take the favourite walks, when the trees are in blossom, and the dew heavy on the grass, and the deer hastens joyfully by to its home in the forest, she feels herself not deserted, and not alone. She is going the same way; through the twilight are shining the bright lights of the home which is dearest to her heart; she lives in the rooms which were dear to her in her youth. She plays her songs at the piano. She looks thoughtfully towards the sofa though no one is sitting there, and listening to her playing; or she listens whether her aunt's bunch of keys is not jingling in the ante-room. Oh no, that time is over. Theresa does not look back with tears upon the past; in the happiness of her children, she enjoys the present, and looks with longing into the future, and is sure of a happy reunion; yes, sure, for she wrestles with the Lord and says, "I will not let Thee go unless Thou bless me."

END OF JOACHIM VON KAMERN.

DIARY OF A POOR YOUNG LADY.

PRINTED FOR THE AMUSEMENT AND INSTRUCTION OF YOUNG GIRLS.

BY

MARIA NATHUSIUS.

12*

DIARY OF A POOR YOUNG LADY.

"DEAR child," said my aunt to me to-day, "never pride yourself on being a Fräulein von Plettenhaus, but never forget it either!" Trinchen, from the corner where she was sewing, cleared her throat. Aunt cast a stern look at her and continued "Your late grandfather was prime minister, and if your late father —" "had not married an angel," burst in Trinchen. "Miss Katharine, be silent!" said my aunt. Trinchen knew what "Miss Katharine" meant, and contented herself with a few sighs. Good creature! The loftier aunt is, and the more she puffs herself up, the more Trinchen bends and complies, until suddenly her tongue is ready to split, and she speaks with words of fire. How aunt's greatness vanishes then, her words blow away like mist before the pure sunbeams. I was thinking about it and did not hear what my aunt said. She grew angry and very solemn. "Rank and station are God's ordering. The rose must bloom for Him as a rose; the daisy as a daisy. It would ill become the rose to lower itself to the soil of the meadow, and the daisy will try in vain to shine forth as a rose." Aunt spoke thus and more. When she became silent, Trinchen sang softly.

Thou art the Shepherd good,
Thy flock Thou wilt not leave:
Lord Jesus, grant I this
May from my heart believe.
Oh let me hear Thy voice,
That I aroused may be,
As an obedient lamb,
To follow after Thee.

Oh Lord, I know Thy voice,
Of strangers hear I none,
Who care not for my soul
But only seek their own:
The hireling in my need
Will never by me stand;
So I obey Thy voice,
And love my Shepherd's hand.

Oh that I might on Thee
From hour to hour rely;
And look to Thee alone
My heart to satisfy.
Oh let me now be still,
Henceforth from care be freed,
Because my Shepherd knows
His tender creature's need.

At these last words tears ran down aunt's cheeks.
She took up her handkerchief; her fingers were so stiff
that she could scarcely reach the tears. I knelt down
before her and could not help crying, and Trinchen
quickly left the room. Poor Aunt! Sorrows torment
her day and night. Amongst the rest anxiety about
my future. I do not know what she wishes to make
of me. Oh dear Lord, be a faithful Shepherd to her
too: take her many sorrows and her anxieties from
her; give faith to her heart. "Oh let it now be still,
henceforth from care be freed, because our Shepherd
knows, what all His creatures need."

I was up early and stood at the open window; the air so mild, and fragrance, and dew, and spring, beneath me. Everything was still quiet, only Jacob was standing below in the garden, on the fresh-turned brown mould. I ran to help him; his back has seemed to me for some time very stiff, and the spade heavy in his hand, even if it does not fare with him as with aunt. Jacob was unwilling to accept my help; he looked up at the window. She was still asleep, and it is no sin if I help him: I was obliged as a child to dig up my garden, now I may dig a larger piece. But he would not suffer it till I had put on my gloves and my great hat. That was fun! I dug twice as briskly as Jacob; blackbirds and finches were singing the while in the elder-bush, and the larks high in the air, and light cloudlets were floating in the sky. The violets looked dark from the fresh green, and the forget-me-not light blue and rosy in the glittering dew. But we have seen the chestnut tree above us growing: First the thick brown buds shone against the deep blue sky; it was as though we heard the capsules bursting, and five golden leaflets stretched towards the warm sunshine. I said to Jacob "If I only knew why Trinchen is more melancholy now than in the winter. I do not know what to do for enjoyment! Can it be more beautiful anywhere than here?" Jacob shook his head mournfully. "Our house is not too large nor too small," he continued, "it lies on a hill, and yet it is no great climb. Up there there is shade and the beech forest, and here before us meadows and sunshine. It is lonesome here; one only hears the humming of gnats and bees, but yet one can see the chimneys smoking in the village, and can hear the watchman singing in the night."

"It is just so," said Jacob interrupting me. "We are only too much attached to this little piece of land, but our money is melting away, dear young lady, and the garden grows no larger: and, dear child, you constantly require more." "Have we anxieties about a livelihood?" I stammered out in terror. "Yes," continued Jacob, "the old lady must not know it. My opinion now is this." — "Jacob!" called Trinchen, from the kitchen window. He wiped his mouth and was silent, but I shall hear about it yet.

8th April.

I was sitting with aunt at the open window: it was dusk, the star of evening was in the bright sky; the moon was rising full and golden above the delicate tracery of the beech-trees; the voices of children sounded from the village. I felt — I do not know how! I could not rest in the room. I should like to go out into the spring evening, to shout with the children, or to sit alone under the beech-tree, and to look at the star of evening. Aunt was silent at first. Then she said, "You get like Trinchen." "I am glad of that," I replied. But aunt looked sorrowful and it occurred to me how some time ago she had said, Trinchen had never got beyond the beauty of a waiting-maid. Waking and sleeping aunt dreams of her past, of her life at the court. She was admired and celebrated, — all is over. She would like to see in me a second Louisa von Plettenhaus. She has so long been educating me for it. "Do not move so quickly," she says, or, "do not always say what you think," or,

"do not wish always to be setting about something."
Now after she had looked at me thoughtfully for some
time, she said in quite a low voice, "that would be
the only deliverance." I saw she was only thinking
aloud. She has done that for some time, especially
when she has had a great deal of pain in the day, and
is weary and low-spirited. "Dear Lulu!" she then
said aloud "folded her hands, and looked towards
heaven. I wish and pray now only that you should
become a court-lady." I kissed her hand. Oh, that
love to me did not cause her so much anxiety. And
why is she anxious? I am so satisfied; I want nothing,
nothing more than to live as I live now. I only want
one thing, — to give old Jacob a new livery. I did
not tell her that. Trinchen had told me only yesterday
that her only prayer was that I might not become a
court-lady, and might not fall into the hands of my
uncle the court-marshal. So they both pray for me;
what will the dear Lord do?

9th April.

Such beautiful spring days do not let one rest in
the house. Trinchen laments over my waste of time,
yet I rise early. Trinchen had some ironing to do to-
day: Jacob was planting potatoes. I helped him put
the pieces into the holes. "We are sowing now," he
said sighing, "but who knows how it will look at
harvest." "The sky will be above us as it is now, and
the dear Lord too," I answered. The old man will
vex me presently with his sighs. He wiped his mouth
with his hand, a sign that he wishes to be silent. I
was almost sorry for it. It would have been a good
opportunity now to enquire into his secret. But the

morning was too beautiful, and I too merry. I went to fetch food for the goat. Above by the white-thorn hedge, the blue veronicas stood a foot high; I made myself a high blue crown, and the cow took such a fancy to my head-dress, and was so eager after it, that I got almost anxious about my curls.

10th April.

I was very sorrowful yesterday and to-day too. Trinchen asked me whether such a trifling life could please me? But what ought I to do? Aunt assures me I have learned enough to satisfy the highest requirements. I should like sometimes to do a piece of French or English composition, or tapestry work, but I have no paper or wool or canvas. Aunt thinks both useless, and so does Trinchen. What does she desire? I practise two hours every day on the piano, and draw too; and I do not know how to set about anything besides. Aunt maintains that in our station it could not be otherwise. Trinchen shakes her head. Ought I to sew with Trinchen at the shirt-fronts? For whom are they? For some cousin or other: that would not do.

11th April.

I went with my knitting along by the brook. Below on the pasture was Riekchen the goose-herd, with all her company. How eagerly the white stately mammas were talking to each other, and how busily the tender golden goslings were pecking about on the white flowers and green grass. Meantime goose-Riekchen's calling and crying sounded frightful. She complained how troublesome the creatures were. Since

her dog was stolen, she has had to run from one end
to the other. Sometimes they ought not to eat there,
sometimes not to go into the mud: and while she felt
such great anxiety for her goose-children, she did not
take any trouble about her own, who were lying dirty
by the brook. "Why have you not combed your hair
smooth, and why have you not washed yourself?" I
asked the eldest girl. She looked stupidly at me, and
I believe there was to be read upon her face, "Why
should I wash and comb myself?" I was vexed with
the girl, for she let her little sister (who was lying near
her on her back, and who could not get up alone) lie
and cry, and was splashing listlessly with her feet in
the brook. I lifted the little one up, it looked horribly
dirty. I washed its hands and face, and smoothed its
hair, and then it became charming. I made the big-
gest look at herself in the brook and see how shaggy
she looked; she was also to wash herself, and smoothe
her hair, and then to see again how pretty she looked.
She now smiled kindly at me, "Now do you know
why one must wash and comb oneself?" I asked again.
If she had not been shy, she would surely have said,
"Because it looks well." It pleased me, but I must
confess that I was disgusted at the work, and could not
make up my mind to take my pocket-comb for it. The
girl has promised me to wash and comb herself and
her sister to-morrow morning.

12th April.

Yet she has not done it, and looked as bad as yesterday. I gave her a lecture, and also asked Rieke
why she let her children run wilder than the geese.
Rieke made complaint that the children make them-

selves so dirty, and tear the clothes from their bodies, and she had not time enough to tame down their wildness. "The great one might already knit," I said, "she is doing nothing the whole day: and idleness is the beginning of all crimes." "Oh, the girl is too stupid for that," replied Rieke. "She understands nothing in life: there is no commonsense in her. God knows the children are more stupid than brutes. Yes, young lady, the brutes are not stupid: the great one with the black wings knows me, and understands every word." Rieke said more of that kind. I let her speak out and made the children clean and smooth, and to-day used my pocket comb. Then I drew two needles out of my knitting, and made an attempt at knitting with the girl. I believe she would really learn. That would rejoice me only too much. When I came home, aunt was very angry at my long wanderings. Trinchen pleaded for me, "Wandering through meadow and forest is her youthful enjoyment. She has little besides here." Aunt was silent, and gave too a permission for further wanderings. She does it from love to me: she would so gladly offer me more dignified amusements.

18th April.

I have now arranged my school behind the old green-house. Oh it is very pretty. Dora learns to knit, and little Lizzie learns to be polite, and they both learn beautiful verses:

I am but small, my heart is clean,
And none but Christ shall dwell therein.

They have both learned that to-day. I explain to Dora what a clean heart is: that as the hands and the

face could be clean or dirty, so could the heart also.
Before simple children I may speak in my simplicity,
and I know well that the Lord above can give
power to my simplicity.   Oh, if I could but help the
children!

20th April.

My school has grown to six.   Two mothers themselves brought me their children.   Aunt thinks it very
condescending of me; Trinchen praises me.   But I do
not enjoy it on that account alone.   I never felt so well
and happy.   The children were with me two hours,
and besides I sewed at Trinchen's shirt-fronts.   In the
afternoon I practised, drew, helped in the house, and
was quite late in starting on my wanderings.   "Trinchen,"
I said, "the idle life shall cease."   "With God's help,
Amen," answered she.   Aunt went early to bed.
Trinchen sat with me under the beech-tree.   "Dear
Lulu," she said, "until now you have had but little
pleasure in useful employments."   I was silent.   She
was quite right, it never had been pleasant to me to
sit long at a thing.   Aunt says indeed that it is not
necessary for me, and the Bailiff's Adelaide does still
less than I do.   I said this to Trinchen, "Yes, indeed,
it is grievous that most young girls do nothing, that
there are so many young energies to no purpose in the
world.   Only think on what a host of do-nothings the
beautiful sun shines."   I became uneasy at these words:
I was obliged to confess to myself that I am a member
of this host.   "The Lord has given a rich talent to
every young girl," continued Trinchen: "they might
make splendid interest from it, but they bury it deep,
and let the nettles and thorns of vanity and of foolish

and impure thoughts grow exuberantly upon it. The Lord will some day call them to account." Trinchen said more still; I wish to keep it in my heart. She said also that when girls who live in the world and with the world, waste and sleep away their time, like the foolish virgins, that is not to be wondered at: but when girls who know the Lord, and love Him, and might serve Him, imitate the foolish virgins, it is astonishing and very grievous.

Trinchen went on and I could not help crying. What then have I done from love to the Lord? Nothing, nothing at all! I have got up in the morning, and have rejoiced and thought I am alive, I am happy. I have said too I am unworthy of all Thy mercy; but I have done nothing. I have only thought how I could spend the beautiful day most pleasantly, and if it went differently from what I expected, I was peevish and could even be unkind to those who love me. I thank Thee, dear Lord, that Thou hast opened my eyes, and now, give me strength to serve Thee. But how? I woke up in the night, and talked to Trinchen. "How can I lead a different and a useful life?" I asked. "Child, do not be careful about that, the Lord Himself will care for thee. He will send thee a little simple called *must* and *need*."

I did not understand her, but I ought not to talk any more in the night. Trinchen wishes to make me humble, because she is afraid aunt makes me proud; but surely she need not. The story about the dress will lie in her mind: I was very unamiable, but I have resolved that I will be contented with everything which she puts on me.

22nd April.

The spring gets more and more glorious. Everything tends and shoots towards the sunshine: the
plants of green peas stand like rows of soldiers on the
brown earth: bushes and underwood shine in light
silky green, and the buds cannot contain themselves
much longer.

Jacob was dissatisfied about my colony by the old
green-house, but since Lizzie and little David have
chased away the sparrows from his beds of seeds, he
is satisfied, and wishes to reward the children in a
princely way.

26th April.

Sophy Bischop came so late to-day, I asked why?
"I was obliged to take the shirt-fronts to the Steward's,"
was the answer. "What shirt-fronts?" "Those that Miss
Trinchen brought to my mother. So a light has broken
upon me. Everything, everything is clear! Jacob
says, we are anxious about a livelihood. Trinchen
sews for money, aunt is deceived. She would be in
despair if she knew I had sewn at shirt-fronts for the
Steward! And I? Oh I will sew, will work from morning to night, to lessen Trinchen's cares. When the
children were gone, I went to Trinchen to the fire-side.
"How much money do you get for a shirt-front?" I asked
quietly. She got as red as fire, and looked at me in
terror. I felt very proud I knew her secrets, and was
not sorry, no, very glad that I should be henceforth an
important person in the house, for I will earn money,
I will share domestic anxiety, I will be the support of
my aunt, the support of the whole house. Trinchen
could not resist me. I am no longer a child; I must

know everything, I know everything now. Our capital
is spent; the garden cannot support us. Jacob does
his utmost. He sells vegetables and fine fruit and
flowers to the High-warden of the forest; and we, like
other poor people of the village, get wood in payment.
Trinchen sews for money, and has made it possible for
Jacob to serve a cup of chocolate to aunt every morning. With God's help, she shall have it for the future.
I will earn a great deal of money. I will not be a
court-lady. Aunt has written about it to the court-
marshal. Aunt hopes I shall make my fortune there,
and save money from the salary. Trinchen declares a
court-lady would more likely make debts than savings.
She would rather make me a governess in a family in
the country; here I might be sparing and support-aunt.
I have no inclination for that, I will remain here and
work. Poverty shall not trouble me, I am very happy,
it will all go well. If I make two shirt-fronts every
day, I shall earn four groschen. Is not that a great
deal of money? Shall I not also let them knit for
money in the school? Plans intersect each other in my
head.

1st May.

The matter was really sad, but Trinchen and Jacob
followed my example: we heartily enjoyed it. Aunt
announced to us that she wished to pay a visit to the
Bailiff: a certain condescension was very proper from
time to time. Jacob was to get himself ready, with
visiting cards and his newest livery; Trinchen was to
prepare our toilettes. Aunt has forgotten that this
livery was got for my baptism, now nearly eighteen
years ago, and that it was scarcely to be required of

Jacob to shew himself to people in it. But Jacob assured us that he was ready to announce the young
lady, and Trinchen might put just what she liked on
him. I wished to shew myself no less magnanimous,
and surrendered myself entirely to Trinchen's clever
hands. While she made me a large flowered mantilla
from a former dressing-gown of aunt's, and ironed out
the pale red sash as well as the ruffles and pocket
handkerchiefs, brushed aunt's velvet hat, and stuck a
feather from an old cap of aunt's into the hat, I sewed
on Jacob's collar and facings, the remains of a black
silk fancy apron. Aunt looked quite stately in her
lavender-coloured taffeta dress, but I thought myself
strange indeed, when I looked at myself in the glass;
yet I was silent. Trinchen appeared really to rejoice
over me. She stood so long at the garden-gate; until
we were out of sight in the meadows. I must confess
I felt rather oppressed, when we entered the Bailiff's
court-yard. The Bailiff was standing with his Stewards
under the lime tree. His lady and Adelaide were sitting upon the terrace. They had already had dinner
to-day. Aunt generally chooses the times for her visits
when common people are at dinner. Adelaide tittered,
the young gentlemen turned round. I looked somewhat anxiously at Jacob, who however was going behind us quite composed, and at his ease, and now came
with his best manners and received from my aunt her
card, in order to announce us. This was not necessary: the Bailiff came towards us. I saw, before, how
he cast a reproving glance at the young people. He
spoke to aunt of the happiness and honour of seeing
her at his house, and kissed her hand. Two tears
came into my eyes, all embarrassment had vanished. I

felt only gratitude towards the good people. They are courteous and kind, out of compassion: the Bailiff's lady also showed all love and respect to aunt. Aunt talked English with Adelaide; she praised her facility, and found fault with her pronunciation. The Bailiff's lady complained that for the half year in which she had been away from the capital, Adelaide had never had an opportunity of speaking English, and, at the same time, asked whether we girls could not meet sometimes. I was delighted at it, but aunt did not seem inclined. "With pleasure," she said, "if Lulu were not expecting very soon to be summoned to court." "Or to be a governess," I added quickly. I was not in earnest, but, involuntarily, I could not help opposing something to my aunt's proud speech. Aunt gave me a severe look, and we turned the conversation. The Bailiff's lady is a very good-natured woman. She afterwards stuck almost half a breast of veal into Jacob's pocket. It seemed to me very humiliating, and I should certainly eat no meat, if I were to have it given me in that way. But Trinchen says differently. "It is a trial from the Lord to be obliged thus to take alms. We will bend our neck in patience, and yet be very thankful to Him if He sometimes sends such help." Poor aunt! We are afraid she is getting lame in her feet as well as in her hands. I observed that the walk to the Bailiff's was much more difficult to her than formerly.

10th May.

It has rained incessantly for a week. I do not like such weather in the spring; I could be almost melancholy. The children come regularly. We sit in the old green-house. Jacob has nailed up the chinks where the rain would come through. The children are very contented in spite of the bad weather. And I? Dear Lord, I have cause indeed to be contented. There is still something left of the idle life. Trinchen says, "the more you ply your hands the fresher your mind will be." She is right. Yes, I will be contented because it is too sinful, quite without cause, and merely from ennui, to think of being fretful.

11th May.

It is still raining. It does not trouble me. We have learned a beautiful spring song and also we can sing, "Ah, with Thy grace be near us," as a duet for aunt's birthday. In the afternoon I put my drawers in order thoroughly. Trinchen says, "the heart of a girl is in the same state as her drawers." I must confess mine are often in great confusion. But Trinchen is right. Oh, that I could hold my thoughts in check, and discipline my heart with the word of God, and not spare myself where I was wrong.

Who will free me from the thoughts and fancies that now hold me fast?
Keep from idleness, and watch, and guard the portals of thy heart:
No more air built castles cherish, but should still the bitter smart,
And the false vain hope deceive thee, on Thy Lord thy burden cast.
Think He sees from the beginning; clear to Him the future lies;
Therefore no vain hopes will aid thee, take them for a pleasant dream;
When the thronging thoughts beset thee, curb and stem the rising stream:
Counting all the moments wasted, and the sins that thence arise.
Do not spare or save them, grasp God's holy word and pray,
Turn thy heart to heavenly things and earthly thoughts will flee away.

12th May.

The nightingales awaked me. I ran into the garden. Oh, what splendour! The sky so clear, and

13*

ample, and blue; there was a fresh scent of young birch-leaves; hundreds and hundreds of glittering diamonds hung on the dark pines; the foliage of the beeches was green as May, and that of the oaks golden. For a week the rain had thrown a veil over the spring, but beneath it has shot forth into life and unfolded itself; the veil is removed, the miracle is there. 1 stood under the cherry-tree; the silvery twigs floated lightly against the dark blue sky, and the apple-tree above was rosy with its swelling buds. Light, and glitter, and bloom, and exultation dance on the hedges, on the twigs; the birds are singing, the beetles booming, the bees humming. I opened my heart wide, and gazed far up into the blue sky. Dear Lord, oh, that my heart might be a true garden of the Lord; and shoot forth and blossom and aspire towards heaven. I might be sad that I am so poor, so miserable; that nettles and thorns of folly thrive in my heart; but I am so happy to-day. Lord, I love Thee, and I may also sit at Thy feet like a poor helpless child; may gaze far up into Thy blue sky, and may rejoice at Thy wondrous glories.

24th May.

Jacob does not know how to leave off work, everything is shooting and growing over his head. To-day we children hoed the peas for him, and put in the bean-sticks. As a reward every child got an apron full of salad, which has shot up into the air, so that we and the goat together can no longer keep it down. Trinchen has had her headache handkerchief on for two days. She says nothing about it, but we observe it.

Is it possible? I have earned two thalers and sixteen groschen, they are mine. Trinchen looked sorrowful when she gave me the money, but I rumpled her white cap for joy. Then I ran to Jacob. I could not help doing something unusual. I danced a country-dance before him, and he was obliged to sing a favourite song thereto, "When the Prussians marched to Prague." The melody is well suited. He also went on a few bars, so I gave a few skips more. Thereupon I gave Jacob four groschen. With two groschen he was to get coffee-bread, Trinchen's favourite food; with two groschen a packet of Louisiana. He used very seldom to smoke anything else, those are remembrances of better times, but those times shall come again, if I work day and night! Jacob did not wish to take the money. He did not wish to puff it away in that manner, but he was obliged. It is my own money. What shall I do with the rest?

Trinchen had the brown crape handkerchief constantly over her white cap. I knew that quiet hours in the morning are the best remedy. I got up secretly. She would not have allowed me. I made my aunt's chocolate, and the acorn-coffee for us three. I am convinced I made it as well as Trinchen. I wished to sit down to work, but it was still dusk. I had got up too early. Nothing was yet stirring in the house and nothing in the garden; only the nightingales were singing. My eyelids grew more and more heavy; I fell asleep on my seat. Then Trinchen's reproachful words awoke me. She would let me do all kinds of foolish things, but I should not disturb her in the kitchen. Three times too much chocolate had been used, and it was not a bit better for it. It had been, to say the least, a very foolish thought which had driven me from my bed in the night. I was motionless with astonishment and anger, but I controlled myself. I only said sternly, "Miss Katharine!" and left the room. I sat down under the old beech-tree, and could not help crying. It was not Trinchen who spoke with words of fire, it was the troublesome old Adam spoke from her. She thinks that from folly I had a frolic in the night, and had been eating the chocolate too. It is dreadful that a human being can think so badly of me. I could not eat any breakfast. It was like a stopper in my throat. I stayed outside and kept my school. But it is wonderful what I opened on in Bogatzky. "He who willingly endures reproof will become wise, but he who wishes to be unreproved will remain a fool, even though he were a great philosopher." Therefore we must receive the punishment, even if it were not purely that; and there must be no thistles and thorns which would sting any one who touches them. Nothing can be said of us so bad, as not to have some foundation in ourselves; and though we may recognise our weakness ourselves, and strive against it, it is not so earnestly that we should always overcome; but then God comes to our help, with even a harsh reproof from others; for God uses even the faults of others to our advantage. Let us receive all as from Him alone, and strive still more against this very weakness; that we may no longer be a cause of stumbling to our neighbour, and then we shall surely gain the victory and a blessing. But if we are impatient, make use of many excuses, and will allow no blame to rest on ourselves, we make the evil worse and hinder our own improvement, and that of others. Lord, make us better and give us patience.

> For him who flees from suffering,
> It will pursue with doubled sting:
> To those, dear Lord, who may reprove,
> ' Teach us humility and love.

I cannot conquer myself so as to be reconciled to it; Trinchen ought to know me better. *I* eat up poor aunt's chocolate! The stopper in my throat rises higher at such reflections, and I have employed myself all day in thinking what I should do in order to convince Trinchen of her mistake. She has her headache handkerchief on, and looks pale, she feels her mistake; she would like to come near me, but I have avoided it.

13th June.

Yesterday evening I could not get to sleep: there was a sword at my heart, and, when I did get to sleep, I had a wonderful dream. At waking I saw only the words, "Thou shouldst love thy enemies." I have never thought seriously about that, but always thought I was very amiable and easily appeased. Is Trinchen my enemy then? I thought; oh, how hard it is to suffer wrong. I stood up and looked into her chamber. The moon was shining on her pale face; she had her hands folded. I could not help crying. I went back and walked to my window. The full moon was in the sky, and shed its peaceful light over the peaceful world. I looked up at the deep blue, I should like to have drawn down the purity and stillness of the sky into my heart. I prayed, from my very heart, I

prayed; and then the anguish was gone; I was well.
Dear Lord, I am ashamed and grieved that I was not
willing to bear so small a thing; that I had thought
only of myself all day long, and had not the strength
to think of Thee. All uneasiness is over and I knew
too what I had to do. I laid myself down, I slept
peacefully. I got up early, made chocolate and coffee,
and did not go to sleep again. When Trinchen wanted
to get up, I begged her kindly not to do it; she was
ill, and, even if I did not do it well, I wished to attend
to the house-keeping to-day. She looked me in the
face, then took both my hands, kissed them and cried.
I cried with her. Dear Lord, forgive me that I thought
evil of her; she loves me only too much, thinks too
well of me, — more than I deserve. She got up to
morning prayers, and was obliged to lie down again.

20th June.

I feel so anxious as if some misfortune were near.
Trinchen has been lying ill for a week of rheumatic
fever. Since yesterday she is rather better. In the
week I have had to go three times to visit the young
wife of the tailor. She has been lying ill of con-
sumption for twenty-one weeks. Trinchen used often
to go to see her, and strengthened and comforted her.
She asks me every time whether Trinchen is not soon
coming. She said yesterday, the Lord will not let me
die until she is with me again. I am so sorry I am
so foolish, and have nothing to say; at most I can but
read her a chapter in the Bible, or a verse of a hymn.
Yet she enjoys that too, and every time I go in, she
smiles at me. But she is getting constantly weaker,

and I am afraid she will die without having seen Trinchen again.

26th June.

Yesterday evening I was called up again from bed. The eldest little daughter of the tailor's wife stood crying at the door. "Mother is dying; Miss Trinchen must come," said she. Trinchen could not get up, it was impossible, she sent me. "The Lord strengthen you; we can do nothing except through Him," she said. The child had run on before. I stood still first on the hill under the beech-tree. I had never seen any one die. My heart beat violently. And what should I say to the poor thing? I knew of nothing. The stars were shining above me in the clear sky. I knelt down, I looked up, I said the Creed. My heart became fuller and fuller. "Dear Lord, Thou hast come to us from Thy beautiful heaven, from pure love alone. Thy will was to bring us peace. Thou hast died for us, hast sacrificed Thyself for us, that our sin should be taken from us. Thou hast overcome the gates of hell and hast opened heaven to us. Oh dear Lord and Saviour, come now and help a dying woman." I entered the sick room. The mother was lying pale in her bed, father and children stood beside her. "Not Miss Trinchen," said the sick woman in a low voice. "What shall Miss Trinchen do?" I said kindly, "Help me, I must die." "Man could not help you," I said, "our dear Lord and Saviour alone can help you now. We will pray to Him that He will come to us." The sick woman assented. "Come, dear Lord," I said. I felt wonderfully helped, and even the sick woman smiled. I said the Creed, she said it softly after me, her voice constantly grew weaker. I got frightened again. I knelt down, father and children with her; we sang, "Jesus, my confidence." The sick woman looked more and more happy. How it thrilled me to think that He has helped us, may I never forget it! She died during the singing. I wept with the father and children, and presently went away. I sat a long time under the beech-tree; it was quiet, very quiet; the stars were shining. I forgot the present; it seemed as though I gazed far into the future, — as if my life already lay behind me. Happiness and unhappiness seemed to me so unimportant, Trinchen's life of care and tears so rich. I went through the garden, the roses were in bloom, the lime-trees were fragrant. How beautiful and sweet is a rose! Oh, to be happy is also beautiful; if I could but see Trinchen and poor aunt happy.

16th July.

Uncle, the court-marshal, has written such a short hard letter that aunt is quite broken down. Praise God that Trinchen is well again. He calls it folly for aunt to destine me for a court-lady; many young girls in the country, daughters of well-deserving men, aspire after it in vain. He proposes for me a situation as governess with a Frau von Schlichten in Braunsdorf. Trinchen is only grieved on aunt's account. She approves of the matter. To-morrow will be a sorrowful birthday.

17th July.

I laid the wreath of roses round Trinchen's sponge-cake, and my embroidered cap with it. Jacob brought the table bouquet, as he still always calls it; everything was ready to greet aunt on her forty-fifth birthday. I never got up so sad as on this day, and yet it never was more beautiful. The scent of roses and lilies mingled with the lime-blossoms; the tops of the beeches lay soft and round, against the bright morning sky. The children came well washed and combed and in their Sunday clothes. I gave each a bunch of flowers, and took the largest myself. I had as usual on that day put on my white muslin dress, although it is very short. When aunt was sitting in her arm-chair, we set the table before her, and placed ourselves in a half circle, and sang, "Ah, with Thy grace be near us." At first I was very near crying, but Trinchen sang with a clear voice, and I too got on better. Tears ran down aunt's cheeks. I knelt before her and bade her be comforted. She stroked the hair from my brow, looked at me kindly, and said, "Yes, it will go well with you yet!"

20th July.

It becomes very hard to me; yet as my God will! I believe that He will guide me. I am going at Michaelmas. With my salary I can procure things wanting in the household. Jacob and Trinchen will have better days. Aunt is also calmer — she does not call it governess, but *lady-companion.* I am to speak English and French with a daughter of sixteen, and one of seventeen, to draw, and to play the piano, but also to take part in their social life and recreations. I have besides to teach a daughter of twelve years old. The last will give me great pleasure. I am afraid of the great ones, lest they should know more than I do.

Trinchen is indefatigable in looking after my out-
fit; treasures come to light of which I had never known.
My kind aunt has given me her velvet hat; the feather
from the cap is stuck in it; it looks very pretentious.
I work very little now, because Trinchen wishes that
I should have holydays. I go my favourite walks; I
draw the most beautiful points, and paint them. The
little pictures shall adorn my room far away; they are
very pretty. I do not neglect my school. Dora can
vie with me in knitting. The children too are orderly
and clean. Trinchen has promised me to let the
children come to her; Jacob too will take charge of
them, if necessary. They are both so kind; they wish
to make my parting easier. I talk English a great
deal with Adelaide. Aunt is quite pleased with this
practice.

Uncle has written more kindly, and has sent a
complete dress for me. The brown taffeta dress suits
me well; the stuff was so ample, that the frock could
be made long enough. I look half a foot taller in it.
I am delighted with the dress. Trinchen is afraid I
shall be too vain.

The time draws nearer and nearer; my heart grows
heavier and heavier. I have a great deal to do. I
still practise and learn; I am afraid that I do not know
enough. Aunt is often angry about it. But to go
alone to quite strange people! Trinchen says I shall
not walk on such smooth paths there. The best of it
is I do not go alone — no, not alone.

Alone, and yet not quite forsaken,
Whatever loneliness betide;
For in my loneliest hours I waken
To feel my Saviour at my side.
Nothing will henceforth lonely be;
I am with Him, and He with me.

12th September.

My heart is always very full. I do not know what
I shall do; I pack up and get things together. Trinchen
says, I ought not to take all that with me. I should
like to take the whole dear Plettenhaus with me, and
aunt and Trinchen and Jacob too!

16th September.

A morning full of glory and splendour. The
asters shine forth in their gayest colours. The ver-
benas are lying burning red on the green turf, the
geraniums are reflected in the clear pond. And the
forest! — I went along the Herrenstieg; it was so
silent, I heard my own footsteps lightly on the moss.
A wood-pecker was tapping the solid trunks of the
beeches, so that it echoed, aloud as if through a church.
Yes, the beech-trees formed an arch as if for a church,
and it was very solemn in the wood. I picked myself
dewy ivy and fern, and went up on the common, — out
of the deep cool shade, into the bright sunshine. How
resplendent was the broad valley beneath me; on the
left Wenderhof and the meadows, and the bright heights
in warm mist above them; on the right Waldstein on
the mountain; the light fell through the high church-
windows, and the little towers and the tops of the
gables of the church, were in sharp outline on the blue
sky. The shepherd was sitting as usual under the old
grove of beeches, and his flock was feeding on the

slope, and many a white tuft of wool hangs on the rose-bush red with hips. I seated myself on my stone; the gnats were dancing, a great humble-bee hummed before me on a tall thistle; the tinkling of the sheep-bells sound sweetly at intervals "far off and near." I sat a long time lost in thought, and could not part from the scene. Farewell, dear home!

4th October, late in the evening.

My trunk is packed, everything is ready. My limbs and my heart tremble with shivering, and anxiety, and melancholy — I know not what. The rain is falling in torrents. The bailiffs are very kind, they will send me to the train; lately also on Adelaide's birthday they gave me a grey woollen shawl.

They did it so delicately that it was no annoyance to aunt. Kind aunt! Is she sleeping? surely not. Oh, Lord! Thou wilt be gracious to her, for she has loved much; dear Lord, make her strong; give her peace; make me also strong; be my faithful Leader.

> Lord, do Thou precede us
> Whither life may lead us!
> And our souls will not delay,
> Both to trust Thee and obey:
> Lead us by the hand
> To our fatherland.
>
> When hard times are near
> Grant us not to fear:
> And when saddest days assail
> Ne'er our burden to bewail:
> Troubles which may come,
> Shall but lead us home.
>   Amen.

We were obliged to start about five in order to catch the train. The rain was still falling in heavy

showers. I went to aunt's bed-side to take leave.
Jacob stayed in the ante-room, Trinchen stood by us;
we all cried. "Pardon me all the trouble which I have
given you. Thank you for all your pains and labour."
How hard it is to part, when one loves! I shall be
lonely, they will be lonely. "The life will be taken
from our life when you are gone, dear Miss," said
Jacob. And how will it be with me? I leaned back
in the corner of the carriage, and, because I had not
slept at night, I fell asleep. When we were driving
through a swollen forest-brook I woke up; then I heard
rain rustling on the leaves. I felt so cold in my limbs,
and at my heart. When it grew light we left hills
and woodland and came into the flat corn-country.
It had left off raining. The villages here look desolate, — houses only, without trees, and to-day everything washed grey. In such a grey place was the
station where we left our carriage. In the waiting-
room, we found some postillions and peasants. Jacob
watched over me like a chicken, and got me some tea,
but I only drank one cup, and left him the rest. After
some time, carriages drove up; many gentlemen came
in. They appeared to stare at us and whispered
to each other. I grew uneasy. Jacob said, "they
think a princess is travelling incognita; that does not
happen every day." I could not help laughing, but
when the wonderful engine roared away with me, and,
in such violent haste, carried me from Jacob and from
everything which I love in the world, my heart was
ready to break. But I controlled myself. I would
not be weak-hearted. I talked with a lady and enquired too about the stations, so as not to miss the
right one. The staring and whispering did not cease;

some people who when we stopped walked on the plat-
form, always looked inquisitively or laughing into the
carriage. I tried to think what could be so striking
in me, and as the good lady opposite herself, often
looked at me in an embarrassed way, I could not doubt
that I was the object of attention. It might be my
blue plaided dress, Trinchen has lengthened it with a
black satin stripe, and the sleeves too, but it was covered
by the grey shawl. It could only be the hat. It was
fatal to me that Trinchen had stuck the feather in it;
but she covered a shabby place with it. I was to get
out at a "lonely inn." I tried to get over my timidity.
I had my things given me, when even the porters
seemed to laugh at me, I assumed great importance,
as aunt had advised me. That was useful. One of
them even carried my travelling case into the room at
the inn. The carriage was not yet come, the train
roared away. I was utterly alone in the cold inn-
parlour and looked out into the grey, desolate, rainy
world. Then my heart was too full, my mouth quivered—
ready to cry. With God's help I conquered it; "Alone
and yet not quite forsaken."

Only have patience! The Lord is here also in the
strange desolate world; here also He has hearts in
which He dwells. He will also guide thee to those
whom thou canst trust. Oh yes, He will do it, only
have patience! I was undecided whether I should let
them get me some coffee. I was out beyond dinner-
time, but I feared the expense; and eat my bread and
butter. Aunt had supposed that they would receive
me ceremoniously here, would give me refreshment,
and then take me on. I supposed so too. It was the
first disappointment. I fear more will follow. After

some time came a carriage, a nasty dirty basket-chaise; the horses and coachman looked dirty too. I could scarcely believe that it could be the carriage of Frau von Schlichten, but it was; my things were packed in. The coachman directed me to a place on the seat behind. By me, lay a gentleman's old grey cloak: by the coachman, one like it, only lined with Scotch plaid. I asked the coachman whose cloak that was. He replied that the one by him belonged to Herr von Schaffau, the brother of Frau von Schlichten; and the one by me, to Vollberger his servant, and that we should fetch both from the next place. It was very humiliating to me that I was obliged to sit by the servant. My pride rose, but in secret I was glad that aunt was not obliged to see all this. After half an hour we came into a kind of valley; a large village—Grauberg lay on bare sand hills divided at intervals by stone bridges. At the end of the village was the castle. We stopped: about a quarter of an hour passed, and then several gentlemen appeared in the high arched doorway, and among them one old one and one young one in travelling dress. I was surprised that the young one was the master. He is very tall and thin and looks very distinguished, otherwise he did not please me much. He was accompanied to the carriage by two gentlemen: they bowed to me. The two strangers spoke to me of the bad road and of the weather. Herr von Schaffau looked very much vexed for a moment, he did not say a word to me, took the reins out of the coachman's hand, and could scarcely wait till the servant had seated himself by me. I was obliged to get over it, and who knows what will follow? Many of the nobility are said to be very proud and haughty towards their governesses. We had scarcely left the village when it began to rain gently, but soon more and more heavily. Herr von Schaffau put his cloak around his ears, and did not trouble himself about us. I was afraid for my hat. I took it off, put it under the shawl and put a pocket-handkerchief round my head. On this occasion I, for the first time, looked round at my neighbour. How rejoiced I was to look into an old kind face, which reminded me very much of Jacob. He tried to shelter me from the rain, and, especially as he was the first human being who showed me sympathy, it did me good. The road became worse and worse, the wheels almost sank into the ruts, and we could only go at foot pace. When the carriage was once very near upsetting, I screamed. Herr von Schaffau looked round in astonishment. I now controlled myself and was quite resigned. I was frozen, weary, and hungry. I should have been glad even to lie down in the mud. When it was getting dark Vollberger shewed me Braunsdorf. It lies on the same bare range of hills, but here it is planted with fruit-trees. The castle is an old building with two little round towers, and surrounded by high trees. Vollberger told me that it was a park which replaced a most beautiful forest. Meantime the rain had ceased, the clouds parted, and the golden moon was rising over the dark trees; that was a good omen for me. We drove into the castle-yard. One wing of the castle was brilliantly lighted; it looked magnificent, and my courage rose. On alighting I put on my hat again. I saw plainly that Herr von Schaffau looked dissatisfied with that. I will see whether I can take out the feather. He now said a few indifferent words and seemed to compel himself to politeness. I replied very shortly to this. In the lofty entrance-hall Vollberger left us, in order to fetch some one to me. Herr von Schaffau escorted me upstairs. Servants were running hither and thither, and dance-music sounded from the inner rooms. Herr von Schaffau said, and as it seemed to me rather ironically. "Perhaps those are pleasant tones to you?" I could not tell what to answer, for those tones are not so especially pleasant to me. "You are fond of dancing?" he continued. I now said, "I have never danced:" but it occurred to me that I had spoken thoughtlessly, and I added, "at least only alone or with the bailiff's Adelaide." That surely sounded very foolish. Herr von Schaffau made a strange face. A rather sharp-featured light-complexioned girl came hastily and led me to my room, and promised immediately to order me a light and a fire. But she did not come, and I had time to look about me in the room. I perceived that I found myself in one of the towers. Two windows were quite overgrown with ivy, the bright moonlight was falling through the two others. If I had not been tormented with hunger and cold, the solitude and repose in this peculiar and snug little room would have done me great good. My condition was insufferable to me: over there from the brightly lighted windows, I heard the noisy music. I could see too the shadows of dancers sweeping by; everything was lively and amusing: I was forgotten and quite alone. There was a gentle rap at the door. I cried, "come in." A gentleman came in. In the moonlight I recognized the tall form of Herr von Schaffau: he asked for Lucy. "Have you no light?" he said in astonishment. "Not yet," I answered, and

14*

my frame of mind was surely to be read in my tone
of voice. He left me quickly, and, after some time, I
heard loud voices in the corridor. The door was
opened in a bustle, a lady in a heavy silk dress rustled
in, a servant with a chandelier followed her. "It is
as bad as a Turk's family," she said, scoldingly,
"neither light, nor tea, nor anything else." She sent
the servant away, and further expressed her displea-
sure at the uncomfortable condition in which she found
me. I kissed the lady's hand, and asked whom I had
to thank for so much kind sympathy. "I am Aunt
Julia and the sister-in-law of Frau von Schlichten,"
said she, "and as my sister-in-law is accustomed to
trouble herself too little about her child, you will have
more to do with me than with her." She now called
Lucy! — there stands the strange-looking thing again
behind the door. She fetched or rather dragged a
child in, and introduced my pupil to me. I was almost
frightened at the child's ugliness. A thin yellow face
with dark eyebrows almost meeting; eyes as dark
looked from beneath them, gloomily and suspiciously.
The round turned-up nose, and the large delicately
compressed mouth, gave a certain bitterness to the face.
This expression and the words of the aunt instantly
gave me a misgiving that this child was cruelly treated
by her mother. My heart was touched as I bent towards her, and asked whether she would like to be
with me. Lucy turned away, and her aunt excused
her when she left the room again without a word or a
greeting. "It will be your task," she said amongst other
things, (and the sharp voice, the sharp features and
the pointed nose, seemed to me to become softer and
more gentle as she spoke) "it will be your task, to gain

the love of this child. There is something different in her little heart from what appears. Besides my child," and she looked searchingly at me; "you seem to be still very young?" "Eighteen," was my modest answer. "You look still younger, and now do not make much pretension. I have no objection to your carrying yourself upright; that is expected of a governess, but you might bend your head and your eyes a little more: do so at least when you present yourself to my sister-in-law." I felt what she meant, it was the same as if Trinchen had warned me to humility. I will receive it in this way. I thanked her heartily for her good advice; she stroked me on the forehead. "If you will make your toilette quickly, I will help you and will lead you to the company," she said, in a motherly way, but I excused myself to-day, which she quite understood. After a short time tea was brought to me, and by the warm stove I soon felt refreshed and warmed. Now it is midnight. I have been sitting a long time at the window. The moon had passed from the bustling side of the castle to the silent one, it shone upon it with its silvery brilliance, and also on the lofty beautiful trees and the turf of the park. So one day lies behind me: it seems to me a long time. I have experienced much, and much around me is still in obscurity. Oh Lord! give me light. Oh Lord! turn the heart of the child to me; give me strength for my office; give me humility to bear everything which thou layest upon me; let me always bear in mind that everything comes from Thee — nothing from man.

When I awoke the bright sun was shining into the window. I observed that I had overslept myself, but nothing was moving in the castle for a long time. I stood by the open window towards the park-side, and was enchanted with the unusually magnificent view. There is a wide extent of turf, clumps of trees advance or recede, and also on the right extend on to the hills. The sun was shining over the tree tops; it could not be seen whether it was its golden light, or the autumn, which had made them so gorgeous. Beneath my window is blooming a bed of monthly roses; they mingle their scent with that of mignonette. Just by a little bridge leads to a shady walk under maple-trees. I did not hesitate long, I went down in order to look more closely into the face of the brilliant morning. From a pavilion I looked down on the village, and the castle, and the whole country. It is not so monotonous as it appeared to me in the bad weather yesterday; no, it seemed to give me a joyful welcome; only I tremble and do not venture yet to respond to it. Shall I have heavy or cheerful days here? When I returned, the fair Sophy met me in the corridor. "Up so early?" she asked in surprise, "and you have had no breakfast yet?" I replied that I liked to get up early if I did not disturb anyone by it; as I was accustomed to breakfast later. I enquired at the same time the habits and circumstances of the house so far as they concerned me; when I could speak to Frau von Schlichten; whether it was the custom for me to breakfast alone or with the family; and such like things.

Sophy told me more than I wished to hear. The

things which I heard were not calculated to give me courage. Aunt Julia is at the head of the household, she has the rule in everything. Frau von Schlichten does not interest herself in such things. Meantime she takes pains, for the sake of her two daughters, to make her house in every way lively; and understands that admirably. The property, however, really belongs to her brother — Herr von Schaffau, who is on good terms neither with Aunt Julia nor with his sister, and no one understands why he suffers this female establishment here. He has returned within half a year from long travels. At his departure the young ladies were almost children; now he is dissatisfied with them: it is not to be thought of for him to marry Thekla, the eldest daughter; although Frau von Schlichten very much wishes it. He is a severe and stern uncle. It is feared he will not long suffer the ladies here; unless they change for the better. He lives with his people in the back wing of the house, and as the master and mistresses in the castle are at variance, so are the servants also. Vollberger especially is an old spy, a hypocrite and a powerful one too; and as Aunt Julia has all the power in this wing, Vollberger manages everything in that one. There are not in the world two greater antipodes. If the old man never shows his thoughts, one at least knows what they are. But Aunt Julia dissembles her opinion. From that side and especially through Vollberger it happened that the last governess was obliged to leave the house; for he is suspected of telling everything to his master. It really pleased the aunt, for she was too cruel to little Lucy, and she carried on nothing but nonsense with the two elder young ladies; but because

Herr von Schaffau was against her, the aunt held back from being against her, and she was vexed that Herr von Schaffau gained his purpose. In return the aunt has carried her point that you should come, and not an older lady, — the sister of the clergyman here in the place, a very learned lady but a devotee and a simple person, who is not at all fit for the young ladies of the house. So said Sophy and much more. Herr von Schaffau's behaviour is explicable to me, after this; but I find myself in a labyrinth. "If you wish to get on well here, you must hold with Aunt Julia and with us:" this was Sophy's advice. I thought for a moment, and then I said: "Have God before thy eyes and in thy heart;" I will do my duty; and then, whether it shall go well or ill with me, will be as God sees best.

Sophy looked at me and sighed. "You are right after all," said she. "Then are there really no morning prayers in the house?" I asked with faltering voice. "Oh dear no!" replied she, "not on this side at least. I believe the master does something of the kind with his people, and the new Pastor here would like to introduce the new method; but it fares badly with us. Because a fortnight ago he preached so horribly, and Miss Julia said 'mere hints at us,' she has forbidden it; not one of us may go again to church. Now we did not often go," added Sophy, "and if I wish to go to the Holy communion, I do it up in Remkersdorf with my relations." I broke off the conversation; I knew enough for the first time, and enough to think over. But this was only the beginning of the day. I was to experience more. After I had arranged my things in my little room, and had begun to write to aunt, it was almost noon, and Sophy appeared,

as she had promised me, to call me to Frau von
Schlichten, who was at a second breakfast with her
daughters and guests. Some old uncles and young
cousins are here to enjoy partridge-shooting; also there
is no lack of ladies, and every day here, or on the
neighbouring estates, there is some festivity.

The lower storey is very magnificent, carpets and
vases and silk furniture everywhere. I stood timidly
in the ante-room: through the open door, I heard the
clatter of many voices; it is very hard to go alone
among such strangers. Trinchen's words came with
comfort to my soul "If the Lord of all is with you,
you can appear everywhere with comfort: armed with
His weapons, humility and love, you will make your
way through all." Timid as I was, I went courage-
ously in. Miss Julia came to meet me: a silence
arose, they looked at me with curiosity; I was introduced. Frau von Schlichten greeted me with a certain
graciousness, which however did not please me. Then
Thekla and Rosalie came to me. They are both very
beautiful girls, only rather too small as it seems to me.
After they had both said something to me I stood
alone. Aunt Julia sometimes turned to me, and invited
me to eat. I had now an opportunity of seeing and
hearing the people. They were almost all ladies. The
gentlemen were gone shooting. A pretty young man
was called "cousin" by the ladies of the house, and
"Herr von Reinberg" by strangers. He led the conversation; but he appeared to me so foolish, yes, rough,
and common-place, that I wondered how the young
ladies could laugh at his wit. An elder gentleman,
with a large moustache, was still worse: besides he
shewed a certain familiarity with the ladies which was

repulsive to me. Trinchen's descriptions of the world
stood in reality before me. "We spend our years as
a tale that is told." After some time we heard slow
steps in the ante-room. "Uncle Schaffau!" said the
young ladies; and to my astonishment a different tune
was suddenly struck up: only the old gentleman took
a pleasure in remaining the same, but he also was
obliged to adapt himself to the repose and gravity of
Herr von Schaffau. I begged Aunt Julia at her convenience to assign me my employment, and for the
present to allow me to go and look for my Lucy.

She was excessively kind to me, and if I had not
feared that she did it in defiance of Herr von Schaffau,
it would have gone still more to my heart. I found
Lucy quite near my room, in a room which is occupied
by the three sisters. I did all that one does to win
children's hearts, and I observed with joy that she became rather more at her ease. Suddenly she said,
"shall you be as amiable to-morrow as you are to-
day?" I was frightened at the sharp unchild-like tone
in which she spoke. I answered seriously, "With the
Lord's help I hope to become more amiable every
day." "With the Lord's help?" she asked in wonder.
"Do you not understand what that means?" I asked.
"Oh, yes, but" — she shook her head. I went with her
to the window.

"Do you see the high arching sky, the shining sun,
the magnificent trees, the lovely flowers? Cannot He
who has made all that fashion our hearts also as He
wishes?" "Certainly!" said Lucy abruptly. "And I
will ask Him," I continued, "that He will make me
amiable, and that He will give me your heart and
your love." I was much affected at these last words,

I pressed the child in my arms, and a kiss on her lips.. She looked thoughtfully at me, and her dark eyes were tearful and her features did not appear at all ugly to me now, but touching and lovely. We went together into the garden. As the sun was so bright I put on my hat, and took my muslin mantilla instead of the heavy shawl.

Lucy looked wonderingly at me. "What do you look like now?" said she. "Now, what?" I asked rather embarrassed. "Like Donna Petronella in the Preziosa," she replied eagerly and joyfully, as though she had exactly hit upon it. The comparison did not please me. She had before told me of the players who were in the village, and where she had seen Preziosa. Had she read my feelings on my face? She quickly added, "she is very beautiful too." I was ashamed of my sensitiveness, made a joke of the matter, and we went into the garden. We sat in a lovely place under maple-trees. I had made a wreath for Lucy from the very beautiful coloured leaves; then we heard and saw the company from the castle approaching us. They remained standing in the distance. I do not know whether I hear more quickly than other people, it was surely not their intention that I should hear it, but my toilette was the subject of their wit. "She looks just like a princess at the theatre," said Thekla after other observations. "She is a vain foolish person," added Herr von Schaffau. Lucy, anxious and sympathizing, read the impression of these words on my features. I became as red as fire, and involuntarily took off the unfortunate hat. Lucy put the maple-wreath on me, bent towards me and said tenderly, "Don't be sad." I kissed the child's forehead; when

I looked up, Herr von Schaffau was standing before us. He seemed to wonder at our intimacy, and then turned kindly to Lucy. I know not why his harsh judgment made me so miserable. Aunt Julia followed close behind him; she placed herself at my side as if to protect me, yet I felt that her authority could not now prevent an assault from their flashing looks and haughty voices. One elderly maiden-lady came to me and said very kindly, "What a charming hat you have there!" I looked at her just as aunt used to do, when she said, "Miss Katharine!" "Yes, a charming hat!" repeated the old gentleman with the moustache, "but what fashion is it, young lady, it is so unique, so piquant?" I felt such an impulse at my heart; and anger and pride were roused. I drew myself up. "I am sorry not to be able to tell you," I answered quietly, "the study of the fashions has never been interesting to me." They were silent. I saw a visible change on their faces. But the old gentleman continued, "Well said, young lady. I make you my compliments! But mere protestations! On my honour, Would you not have loved to look at the magazine of fashions as well as these ladies?" "I assure you that I see it before me for the first time to-day," I replied, in the same quiet way. "Good gracious!" said the old man, and laughed aloud. But I was near crying. I felt myself so ugly in this fashion, and resolved to let anything befal me rather than to defend myself in this way. I took Lucy by the hand, bowed and left the place. They could not blame me for that. I also plainly heard aunt Julia's scolding voice, and soon came Thekla behind us and asked, with some embarrassment, whether I would not join in a walk. My tears had now really

burst forth. I felt very unhappy. I tried to say no
kindly, and hastened with Lucy to the house. Lucy
now began to speak of her sisters, in a very unchild-
like way. She is really beyond her years. I knew
now what I had to do. It was very difficult to myself, but I tried to excuse those who had hurt my feelings. So I urged on myself to be conciliating, and I
felt that by and bye, the sting in my heart became
loosened. Now I could pray, "Come Holy Ghost and
help me;" now I was able to speak so joyfully of my
Lord and Saviour. I spoke of forgiveness, of the love
of enemies, how He has loved us, and still loves us,
though we turn our hearts too coldly and unlovingly
from Him. I said to her that we would both beseech
the Lord, that He would entirely take possession of
our hearts, so that we could do everything from love
to Him, and even love those who grieve us.

Lucy listened attentively though in astonishment.
When Sophy came to fetch her and to dress her for
dinner, she gave me her hand and looked very kindly
at me. It did my heart good. After some time
Sophy came again to help me also in changing my
dress, and when I showed little pleasure in it, she told
me that my predecessor always dressed in the most
distinguished way. She wished to tell me more about
her and, indeed, only evil things, but I bade her be
silent, because I considered it a sin to listen to such
things; on the other hand, I should be very glad to
hear something good of the inmates of the house.
"Ah, those are only innocent views of the world," said
Sophy, "you will learn something different here." I
was glad now to bring Trinchen's good lessons into
use, and did so to the utmost of my weak powers.

Sophy is an open and good-hearted girl. She saw
how wrong and hateful it is to speak evil of people,
and to listen to such conversations. I said to her that
we would mutually strengthen each other not to fall
into these faults; especially for Lucy's sake, because
the welfare of her soul now rests on ours. She ought
not to hear a loveless word from our mouth, for the
Lord Jesus says, "Whosoever offendeth one of these
little ones, it were better for him that a mill-stone were
hung around his neck, and he cast into the depths of
the sea." Dear Lord! bless these words. Especially
bless them to myself; give me strength for my difficult
but beautiful vocation. Oh, might I but lead this child
to Thee! This endeavour and this hope shall be a
compensation to me for much which I have to dispense
with here. I went into the dining-room with conci-
liatory and generous thoughts; yet they were scarcely
necessary to me. Sophy's pains too about my toilette
were unnecessary; no one took any trouble about me.
I found my place and Lucy's at the end of the table,
two boys sat by us. There was no grace, and I am
ashamed to say I had not the courage to make one for
myself. The boys entertained us very much. The
elder one "cousin Alfred" especially is witty and
agreeable. We forgot the great people, and were contented in our sphere. I was even obliged to caution
my young people because we drew the attention of the
company upon us. Herr von Schaffau's scrutinizing
looks often rested on me, yet he did not appear dissatisfied with our mirth; besides his opinion, his satisfaction or dissatisfaction, shall be indifferent to me;
a man who is unjust and without a conscience in words
and opinions, has no authority with me. So I thought

at table, and in these thoughts found a satisfaction for the injustice that had been done me. But I was soon to have other thoughts. After dinner the young people soon assembled in order to act charades and tableaux. Herr von Tülsen, the old gentleman with the moustache, pressed me very much to take part in them. I thanked him and refused. He asked me the reason. I replied to him that I knew too little of the subject. He went on talking to me. He asked whether I had intentionally chosen such a peculiar style of dress. Trinchen has lengthened and trimmed my white dress with a beautifully embroidered bed-curtain. I see very well that I look different from the ladies here. It distresses me also to be the object of their ridicule, yet it shall not make me unhappy. I answered Herr von Tülsen that from my youth I had been accustomed to see myself strangely dressed, and those around me would be obliged to get accustomed to it, as for the present I could make no change. Herr von Tülsen was very kind about it, said complimentary things in an unblushing manner, so that I was very glad when Herr von Schaffau interrupted this conversation. I went away from them. Great and small were busy with preparations for the representations. I seated myself in a deep bow-window, drew the dark curtains a little forward, and was now alone with the bright moonlight, and the splendid bunch of asters which Sophy had stuck before me. I felt sad at heart. I was homesick. I looked up at the moon and thought how its beams were resting now on the dear Plettenhaus. I closed my eyes, I should have liked to fall asleep, and to forget the strange world around me, and to dream of dear home. Then I heard a noise by me, and saw

Herr von Schaffau at my side. He looked serious and yet kind. I do not know exactly what words he spoke. He asked pardon for having hurt my feelings this morning, and begged me not to mistrust him, and to be quite convinced that he meant well to me. These words touched me, it seemed to me as though *he* had to pardon *me*. He then asked whether I was home-sick and felt sad. I could not deny it. Whether I should get accustomed to the country life? I told him that I had never yet seen a great city. He was surprised, called me happy, and then laughed about it. I could not help telling him of home and felt delighted; though I must confess that his manner inspires me with more fear than confidence. Lucy fetched me to the representations. I saw magnificent things, but undisturbed. It was a matter of great indifference to me, that aunt Julia wished to move me opposite the others; my heart was calm. But it made me melancholy to hear Lucy's comments. Very cleverly, but very bitterly, she spoke out her opinions on the company. I could say nothing in reply. My wisdom was at an end for to-day, and the thought whether I am equal to my office torments me.

7th October.

The bright beautiful Sunday morning chased these thoughts away. I folded my hands, and looked long into the deep blue sky. Lord! teach me the way that I shall go. I opened on the verse, "Therefore saith the Lord he who believeth must not make haste." For trial alone teaches us to pay attention to the word. Yes, Lord, I believe that Thou wilt help me through. I will not neglect to pray to Thee. I was very cheer-

ful. Sophy came in. I should like to have read a
chapter in the Bible with her, but I was afraid of being hasty. I shall not be able to restrain myself long,
and I do not doubt of gaining Lucy and Sophy, dear
Lord, with Thy help. I invited Lucy to accompany
me to church. She assured me her aunt had forbidden
her to go. So I went alone to-day, and, indeed, very
gladly. I was at the church-yard before the bells
began. How quietly the sunshine rested on the graves!
There were lark spurs and yellow marigolds, here and
there in the golden grass. I wandered from stone to
stone, from cross to cross, and made acquaintance with
the quiet company. But also at the same time with
the living in the village. In that house, I read, a
mother is mourned; there a father; and there children.
In quite a fresh-made grave, there rests a widow who
has left five children behind. Poor orphan children!
I wonder whether it is as well with you as it was with
me, and whether you have found as faithful love as I
did? I laid an aster on this unpretending grave, and
thought the while whether there was nothing I could
do from love to these orphan children! At the first
sound of the bells I went into the church; it was so
quiet and clean and light, a true house of God. The
pews are of dark carved oak. The castle-pew is
especially beautiful. But most beautiful of all are the
effigies each side of the altar; on the left, a knight
kneeling, five sons behind him; on the right, the lady
with five daughters. Oh, how beautiful to be a pious
and humble lady! To think what these were, and
how it looks at the castle now! We sang, "The Holy
Ghost we now implore." I joined with my whole
heart in singing it. Yes, He can even come here,

and bring true faith, and the Lord Jesus Christ, and peace. During the singing Herr von Schaffau had come in; I had not observed it. Shortly before the sermon, appeared Fräulein von Ramberg, with much rustling. It is she who thought my hat beautiful, and from love to Herr von Schaffau quarrels daily with aunt Julia, and perhaps also on that account has transgressed the command not to go to church. I was obliged to make a real effort not to give way to foolish distracting thoughts; the sermon helped me.

It was from the gospel of the day S. Luke 14th chapter and 11th verse. He particularly dwelled on the words, "Whosoever exalteth himself shall be abased, and he who humbleth himself shall be exalted." A lowly path does not suit my disposition, and yet I would rather that necessity and compulsion (as Trinchen prophesied for me) should not be the first to bring me into it. Now I wish voluntarily to lay everything at the feet of the Lord. How thankful I am to have found a preacher here. It was what was wanting to us at home. Trinchen's prayers are heard. I shall never be forsaken here. If I am dismayed at the castle, I will go to the little parsonage. Herr von Schaffau stood waiting at the door; but I stayed behind, I did not wish to go with them. At last, when all the people had left the church, I came out; I could scarcely part from the peaceful place. How charmingly church and parsonage stand here on the height! Just behind, on a grassy hill, stand two old lime-trees; and a chestnut avenue leads on into the cherry plantation. I should like to have drawn the picture exactly, but pencil and paper were wanting to me. As I was going towards the foot-path to the parsonage, doubting

whether I could not pay my visit there to-day, the
little swing-door which leads to the garden opened,
and one little child's head after another looked out
and listened. I spoke to them. They came nearer.
I sat down on a grave-stone and soon I had five lovely
children around me, who asked questions, and chattered
very sociably. I heard that papa was busy with his
duties, mamma was in the kitchen, and would quickly
cook the dinner, and that Herr Heber, the tutor, was
there in the garden minding the two smallest little
sisters. I promised soon to visit them, kissed all the
little ones, and went back through the park. Up there
it was a bright quiet Sunday, down here it was desolate
and noisy. The people in the house are very busy;
there is to be dancing again this evening; guests from
the neighbourhood are also expected. There was a
sound of loud laughing and joking from the breakfast-
room. I put off my hat and shawl in the ante-room.
I looked at myself in the lofty mirror, and was delighted; it seemed to me as though I looked like one
of those noble maidens in the church. As aunt never
goes out in the winter, Trinchen made me a dress out
of her black silk cloak; it is rather narrow and scanty,
and the white lace too round the neck, makes it look
mediæval. Herr von Tülsen received me, "Young
lady, you look like a sister of mercy to-day!" "I
wish I were one," I answered, pleasantly. "Ah," said
he, "one may see you are come from church. But
now then! I say to you that if you often hear that
diabolical preacher, it will be dangerous for you." He
then spoke in a very frivolous way of preaching and
divine worship. Most of his young hearers appeared
amused at it, and only looked shyly sometimes towards

15*

Herr von Schaffau, who was standing rather near us, but so engaged in talk that he did not hear this conversation. I looked around me, whether no one would interrupt this blasphemer. Suddenly he said, "You are very silent, young lady." I answered, that I was silent from horror, because I had never before heard anything of the kind. He blushed and that gave me courage. "Do not you think that I am a bad Christian," said he. "You are no Christian at all," said I seriously. He wished to defend himself, said that he was a friend to clever sermons, and beautiful church-music. I was glad that his empty prattle really sounded empty, and made no impression on the listeners. But I had nothing further to do with him, except that when he called our chorales lullabies, I stood up and asked whether I might play and sing to him the one which we sang in church to-day. I put down both pedals to imitate the organ, and played in full chords and sang, "The Holy Ghost we now implore." Oh yes, I felt the power of the Holy Ghost. He himself appeared to be shaking the hearts of the listeners. Chit-chat and laughter were hushed; when I ceased, I saw only faces of astonishment. "Splendid, splendid!" began Herr von Tülsen. I did not listen to him. Rosalie laid her hand on my shoulder, and said, "how beautiful!" Aunt Julia praised me very loud; she did so in order to exalt me in opposition to others. Herr von Tülsen is on her side. He declared, my voice was a five thousand dollar voice; he could wish nothing more than to hear me sing Romeo. He begged me to sing another song. I was almost inclined to follow his request. It gave me pleasure for the moment to be thought something of by these people. Oh, I am very much ashamed. Herr von Schaffau, who had already heard aunt Julia's commendations with a very indifferent countenance, looked searchingly at me. I read in his features, "Is it possible that she is not a vain foolish person?" I felt, indeed, that I was, but no one shall see it now. I refused Herr von Tülsen's request to play the symphony also. I saw the young people were preparing for a walk, and left the room with them and Lucy. Very foolish thoughts, indeed, came into my mind then. Oh, we must certainly be on our guard and pray, "lead us not into temptation." The tempter is very crafty. "Is it wrong to make an appearance conformably with one's position in the world, and to see oneself respected by the world?" thus he spoke. Aunt has made it a sacred duty with me not to lose sight of this; she has assured me that otherwise I should be of no use in my position. It appeared quite true to me, that if I have no authority in the house, I cannot have an influence on my pupils. Oh no! all self-deception is over; the lonely hours have done me good; if only I had not to go into the whirlpool again. Dear Lord, give me a strong heart, give me power to feel Thee constantly near me.

Letter from Lulu to her home.

DEAR AUNT,

I wish to finish the letter to-day and to send it to the post to-morrow so that you may hear from me at last. You would feel at home in my little room. I can only assure you once for all that I have every convenience. That I do my hair myself ought not to trouble you. I do it quickly and well, and even when Sophy afterwards said, she should like to undertake it

when she has more time, I would not suffer it. Now
hear about Sunday. Jacob must hear about it too.
It was grand. I should like for you, dear Aunt, to
have seen Frau von Ramberg in a blue brocade dress,
and golden bird of paradise. Ah, no, I think you
happy in your peaceful world! But tell Trinchen that
Sophy has taken the white feather out of my hat, and
has put a carnation-coloured ribbon in its place. It
was too striking, and it looks less pretentious and yet
very good. The rest of my wardrobe is excellent and
quite sufficient. It would be folly to wish to compete
with the ladies here; they often dress three times a
day! Sophy came on Sunday afternoon to help me
with my dressing. She was almost frightened that I
had nothing of a ball-dress to show; but she was
astonished when I brought out uncle's state-dress. She
stuck white dahlias in my hair and on my bosom,
which looked splendid on the bright golden brown.
So for once I could rustle down the stairs and through
the rooms. Several servants in livery stood in the
ante-room. I afterwards copied one exactly, and sent
him for Jacob, that he may see how the like of him
look. At Christmas I hope I can send him some kind
of livery, but do not tell him that. Besides there is
not one of the servants except Vollberger who is so
well trained and so expert as he is; tell him that, dear
Aunt! When I came to the company I was quite
dazzled by the splendour of the dresses, and by the
appearance of the rooms. The old ladies in brocade
dresses, feathers, and head-dresses; the young ladies in
gauze, and crape, and flowers. There was such a
ceremonious whispering and exchanging of compliments.
The gentlemen with white ties and gloves, walked

lightly over the polished floor; the violins were being
tried in the orchestra. I must confess it produced
quite an impression on my mind; full of awe, I dare
not walk through the drawing-room, and gladly gave
myself into Lucy's protection, who led me over to the
young ladies. Are you anxious, dear Trinchen?
Oh no, the temptation passed over, I did not dance.
Do you know why? I was not asked; at least not
till "the impression" was subdued. I saw how the
old ladies, with their daughters before them, moved
elegantly through the room, and how the daughters
became more and more lively; and how madly they
flew through the room, and then stood all in disarray
before me.

If I could but describe to you the expression with
which they looked down on me, down on me compassionately! it made me proud. I made a vow never to
dance. No, I did not do it on that account, dear
Trinchen! no; I thought of your descriptions of dancing
parties. I felt that in that way they were only on
the broad way. I seemed as if I could see Satan
leading the ranks; that with all the brilliance and
glitter he is laying snares to entangle souls. Dear
Trinchen, at that time you were surely alone in your
little chamber; you were just praying for me, and saying, "lead her not into temptation." I suddenly felt
a wonderful strength within me. I saw no longer any
splendour, I only saw a miserable transitory existence,
and the human beings seemed quite strange to me,
and their insane conduct quite dismal. Herr von
Tülsen now came to ask me. I thanked him and
refused. I wished to leave the drawing-room, but
Lucy begged me to remain till the ice-tarts came. I

remained in my quiet corner, and pushed a flower stand before me in order to be unseen, and gave myself up to my own thoughts; Lucy sat in the other corner of the sofa. The ice-tarts were long in coming. Lucy fell asleep. The dancing-music sounded more and more distant to my ears; my eyelids became heavier and heavier; I also fell asleep. Herr von Tülsen awoke us with his loud laugh. "Pray, how could you go to sleep here?" "Why not?" I answered. "In the midst of the noise?" I felt like one who hears storm and rough weather outside, and who is sitting secure in a warm room. He wished to enquire still farther about my taste for dancing. I evaded him.

Rosalie and some stranger-ladies came to us: their dresses were disarranged by dancing, they looked exhausted: we made room for them on the sofa. If so much splendour could lead me astray at first, I should now have been undeceived. There is nothing more melancholy than a company wearied out with dancing and late hours, especially when one looks at them quite fresh oneself, as I could. I woke up well-satisfied, and only lamented with Lucy that we had slept through the ice-tarts. Herr von Schaffau, who heard this, most kindly promised to get us some the next day. Herr von Tülsen looked at him in astonishment, and turned lightly to Rosalie and me. "Our host is in a good temper to-day," he said ironically, "what can keep him here? He does not generally give us the honour of his company on like occasions." "I can well believe that," said I. "Why so?" "Because he finds it tedious here." "Thank you very much for the compliment," said Herr von Tülsen laughing. I was silent. Perhaps I had been too hasty; but, dear Aunt,

I gained respect by it. Rosalie said I was quite right,
and Herr von Tülsen began to philosophize in a similar
way. But I soon wished them "Good morning!" and
left the room with Lucy. When the sun had reached
its highest, I found my ladies in the breakfast room.
Frau von Schlichten had appointed that the conversation lessons should begin to-day. If the company had
appeared dismal to me in the night, still more dismal
now. The gentlemen had chosen the best part, — they
went shooting: but the ladies, very weary and exhausted, protested against speaking English. Herr von
Tülsen agreed with them: he understands no English.
The conversation turned on the past evening. Thekla
and Miss Ramberg displayed great wit, while they
passed the company in review. I grew angry. Lucy
was hearing everything; she was laughing with them.
I felt that it was now my duty as a governess to step
in. Dear Aunt, you have always doubted of my talent
for it, but Trinchen is right; — "to whom the Lord
gives an office, to him he also gives understanding."
A second time I gained respect for myself. Herr von
Tülsen came to my help. "What do you say to this
malicious criticism?" said he jokingly to me: "do you
not think it horrible?" "I certainly do," I replied
quietly. "Now I am convinced that your lady-friends
are now thinking just as tenderly of you," said he
turning to the young ladies and smiling, "you can
comfort yourselves with that." "Do you think that we
have given them cause?" asked Thekla pointedly.
"That does not matter," replied I; "it depends only on
the want of principle of those who pronounce judgment." "Yes, on the taste for scandal," said Herr von
Tülsen interrupting me: "recollect that the ladies up

there in Grauberg find the time as heavy as you do, and do not wonder if they amuse themselves in the same way." I interrupted him by saying, "You should not make a joke of it; I think the matter too serious." "I leave Fräulein von Ramberg to talk seriously about it," said Herr von Tülsen, "she is fond of the treatment of such subjects. Explain to us if you please the commandment about it." "You make a mistake. *I* am not governess here," said the Fräulein pointedly. So, as I might, I began to speak with some dignity. What is the 8th commandment? "Thou shalt not bear false witness against thy neighbour." What does that mean? "We are to fear and love God in such a way that we do not falsely deceive our neighbour, betray or slander or calumniate, but should excuse him, speak well of him, and turn everything to his advantage." Frau von Schlichten and some elder ladies came in, and interrupted us. It was too flagrant. "The young ones twitter as the old ones sang," whispered Herr von Tülsen.

Thekla and Rosalie laughed. "Will you not repeat the 8th commandment to the mammas too?" asked Thekla. I looked seriously at her, and broke off the conversation. Dearest Aunt, you see that I do not derogate from my dignity, but rather maintain it in the best way, when I am seeking to live worthy of the Lord. Pray for me! Oh what a comfort it is in the midst of this throng to be able to think of you, — of your delightful quiet life and peaceful abode! At Christmas I rejoice in the hope of sending a large box; Jacob must fetch it safely with the cart. God be with you, dearest Aunt. I kiss your hand. The Lord strengthen you with health and peace. I greet

Trinchen, my dear good Trinchen, a thousand times. Does Jacob still take care of my little colony? Does David still get on to the box-tree, or is the box-tree no longer the fashion? Only think! Herr von Schaffau sent a large ice-tart, up into our room for Lucy and me. At the same time I copied Vollberger with the keys in his hand; it is a little picture for Jacob. I wish the tart in his hands could be a real one! A thousand good wishes from

Your dear
Lulu.

One more joke! I must tell you dear Trinchen, but you must not be angry at my foolishness. Fräulein von Ramberg asked me exactly why I did not dance.

You must know she has taken your office of making me humble, but she does it in a different way, and I resent it very much. I replied to her that I had never had the opportunity of having instruction in dancing with my equals. "Whom do you call your equals? if one may ask," said she. I replied, "only families who have two and thirty ancestors to show. My aunt is extremely particular about it, and our first family trouble was that a near relation has lately married a Countess K——." "Two and thirty ancestors, and a Countess K—— a mesalliance?" "Undoubtedly," said I, "not more than a hundred years ago this family lived in a baker's shop!"

10th October.

There is still a buzz in the house. I trouble myself little about it. I found Aunt Julia by the sunny vine-covered wall in the kitchen garden. She was gathering the last sweet grapes. I helped her, and at the same time spoke of Lucy. I begged her earnestly not to let her take so much part in the companies of older people, and also not to take her with them to Grauberg to-day. The aunt looked at me in astonishment "Must the child stay here alone?" "I will stay too," was my reply. The aunt kissed me on the forehead; "That is excellent," said she, and gave me the most beautiful bunch of grapes as a reward. "You are also at liberty sometimes to hunt a hare for us children," said I playfully. "That I certainly will," replied she, "Sophy shall put me a pocket in the left side, and then I can bag it!" The aunt is vehement and rather rough, but yet she pleases me best of all the ladies here. I am sorry that she is so hostile to Herr von Schaffau, and that I am the cause of it. I never saw him otherwise than kind and gentle to her. That he so decidedly goes a different way, is the support and comfort of the house. Must not Aunt Julia feel that? She is otherwise so reasonable and so dissatisfied with Frau von Schlichten, and with the elder daughters. She is so fond of Lucy, — poor neglected Lucy, and sees how his love and anxiety for this child unite with hers. As she said lately to me, I must not take his rudeness to me to heart, and she called him at the same time a devotee and one who was never satisfied. I said I was very sorry to hear that, because Herr von Schaffau was so indulgent to me. I begged her to spare me the miserable feeling of being a cause of discord in the house; and said I should least of all like to see her, whom I had loved so heartily, do an injustice to anyone. I kissed her hand at these words. She felt my sincerity, and kindly kissed my forehead. "I do not mean any harm," said she; "and if he is generous, I wish to be so too. There!" She had on this occasion also given me the permission to take Lucy with me to church, and assured me at the same time that I must not suppose that she had any objection to piety.

15th October.

The day was too beautiful. The mists struggled long with the sun, at last it stood in a clear sky. I also have risen above the mists; all distraction is overcome. Oh how miserable, sad, and empty is the bustle below me. Oh Lord! let me ever feel Thy presence as purely and powerfully as to-day! I prayed for Lucy, for her aunt, for Rosalie. I was very bold. I had the courage to have morning prayers for the first time with Sophy and Lucy. My confidence won their hearts to me. I prayed the Lord's prayer aloud, and read S. Matthew the 5th, and sung with them "Ah with Thy grace be near us." Then I said we should now go comforted to our day's work, but we would pray for one another, that we might be tender-hearted and compassionate, and of a pure heart and peaceable. My emotion was so great that I could scarcely speak; tears ran down Sophy's cheeks. I know well she will not say much, she is very conceited. I began the lessons with Lucy to-day far more cheerfully. I was glad that I was freed from the conversation lessons in the breakfast-room, the ladies and gentlemen wished to take a drive. I am very fond of taking a drive too, but yet they never took me with them: I am fortunate to-day. I came with Lucy out of the door: a great

drosky was standing before it, a little pony chaise
was being led about in the yard. Lucy took the reins,
it was splendid! we drove round in a circle; I believe
I should soon learn to drive. When the ladies and
gentlemen came out of the house, we got quickly down
and ran into the garden. Oh how beautiful the day
was, so peaceful and so bright! I should like to have
followed the flight of my soul. We danced through
the park, and farther still to the hill in the chestnut
avenue. The shining brown chestnuts lay upon the
golden leaves. I felt inclined for play, I stuck little
twigs with red hips and haws on a soft mossy place,
and made a hedge of them. Chestnuts were collected
and divided into companies. There were cows and
calves, and a dog and sheep. Lucy's imagination
quite entered into it. It was a cow-pasture. Then we
got to enchanted princes and princesses, and searched
for stones for grottoes. It was a world of romance.
We sang and skipped and were merry. When Lucy
became more and more intent, and could do without
me, I seated myself in the church-yard just by, to
draw the picture which pleased me so well. It succeeded unexpectedly. I had scarcely put in the blue
sky and the chestnuts in the back-ground, when alas!
Herr von Tülsen disturbed us. He had not gone a
drive with them because of a headache, and assured us
he had been three times in vain through the park, in
order to look for us. Most of the guests are now
gone: the least charming have stayed behind, — Frau
von Ramberg with her daughter, and Herr von Tülsen,
who is particularly repulsive to me. I went with him
to Lucy; he began to make himself merry about us. I
said rather earnestly to him, "Only a child-like mind

would know how to value that, and that he certainly was no longer a child." Then he said some sentimental words; such as "I was mistaken in him," and seated himself very confidentially with us. I was glad that our party just then came along the avenue. The carriages stopped. Ladies and gentlemen got out. Frau von Schlichten looked at me severely, I know not why. Aunt Julia was delighted with our play-ground; Rosalie also;—Thekla only spoke like Herr von Tülsen. Lucy said very impertinently, "Only a child's heart would know how to value that, and she has no heart!" I was secretly ashamed that I had so apt a pupil, and one who knew how to use my words so well, but Thekla went joking on: they had all resolved to go home through the park. The little pony chaise was my ruin. I hinted to Julia whether we could not drive home in it. Herr von Schaffau willingly allowed it, he even drove us himself and sent the coachman on. That was a splendid drive! We did not drive home; no! through the park again, back to the hills, and on and on! Autumn had woven a silken veil over the golden fields, the slanting rays of the sun glittered over them in rainbow hues, and the distance was so misty, and the sky so blue, and the trees so rich in colour. We were very much delighted. Herr von Schaffau also examined my picture, encouraged Lucy to drawing and painting, and promised us both, if we are industrious, his water-colours and beautiful paper. He is very fond of Lucy, and I believe this is the only point on which he agrees with Aunt Julia. Perhaps on that account he bears her harshness. Without her protection the child would be lost in the house. I have never seen Frau von Schlichten act like a mother towards her; her sisters go their own way, and Lucy is really a child of great endowments. She was so witty again in the carriage, but not about other people: she has promised me to be on her guard against that. We laughed to-day at ourselves. I was foolish enough! Herr von Schaffau is very indulgent, and acted as though nothing better was to be desired from us. But at table he threatened me lightly with his finger when we were too exuberant. I became at once rather sensible, and thanked him for the hint. And now farewell, delightful day! I lie down to rest and am thankful — to Thee, dear Lord!

> *   "My Jesus, stay Thou by me,
>   And let no foe come nigh me
> Safe sheltered by Thy wing;
>   But would the foe alarm me,
>   Oh let him never harm me,
> But still Thine angels round me sing."

23rd October.

Trinchen says "the higher you ascend on the mountain the lower you must come down again into the valley." I have been obliged to come down low, very low. The day following the delightful one was gloomy, but I got up as cheerfully and joyfully, had prayers with Sophy and Lucy and then lessons. When I was coming down to the conversation lesson, I believe for the first time with real pleasure, I was called to Frau von Schlichten. She received me in her boudoir with such an icy look that it made my heart shudder. "At your first coming, Miss Plettenhaus," she said, with a sharp voice, and with eyes almost closed, "I was convinced that it was very unsuitable to send you here as a governess. Your aunt has been so foolish as to bring you up as a court-lady, and I cannot employ such an one. Yet I believe you would in time have learned your proper place, and I now only speak of your levity, which does not do in my house."

I was very much frightened at these words: she continued "You know why the last governess was obliged to leave the house?" I shook my head, "Another lie?" said Frau von Schlichten, scornfully. "You have been almost a fortnight with Sophy, and do not know that?" I could not contain myself. I felt a certain indignation rising in my heart. I had never been accustomed to talk to servants of such things, I said, proudly; "I beg you to ask the girl herself." "That is not at all necessary," replied she, coldly. "I am not accustomed to enquire into the gossip of my people. That is only a secondary thing now. Your predecessor in teaching was dismissed on account of her levity. I fear the repetition of like scenes, and with this I warn you. While we are gone a drive, you arrange a rendezvous with Herr von Tülsen, — a beautiful result for the short time of your being here! Poor Lucy appears to have fallen out of the frying pan into the fire!"

My thoughts were distracted. I know not what more she said, except at last that I might now leave her alone. I went to my room. Sophy was already coming to meet me. "What do you say now? Is she not a godless woman?" I looked at her in astonishment. "Oh, I was standing with Betty in the bedroom, and have heard every word." She now talked confused nonsense. I was too powerless to forbid her, but did not hear much. Herr von Tülsen with his riches is to marry Rosalie. Thekla is half betrothed to Cousin Reinberg, who is a poor lieutenant of the guards. Uncle Schaffau is to provide for Thekla, — her mother's favourite; and one thing after another: but it does not concern me, and it seems to me like a confused dream. Lucy fetched me to the conversation lesson. I followed her passively. I turned very red when Herr von Tülsen received me at the door. When I turned away from him, the eyes of Herr von Schaffau met me — as severe as those of his sister. That made me very miserable. Frau von Schlichten sat in our circle for the first time, blamed the pronunciation and expression of my English, and watched me with sharp eyes. Thekla and Fräulein von Ramberg only spoke in unintelligible language, and laughed a great deal. I became more and more uneasy. I felt that I should not be able long to prevent crying, and left the room. Frau von Schlichten followed me, caught me in the ante-room, and said to me, very scornfully: "Do not play the innocent or injured! Disgraceful coquetry! Fie for shame!" If Herr von Schaffau had not come to us, she would perhaps have said more. I hastened away crying; Lucy wished to go with me. I begged her to leave me alone, and went into the garden. That was hitherto the heaviest hour of my life. A thick mist hung on the twigs, everything was grey, and desolate, and blank. I went up and down under the plane trees; the leaves rustled under my feet, the castle looked dismal to me.

Trinchen has often said, "the path of an orphan is hard:" — yes very hard. But the comfort of the orphan, of which she has often told me, I could not now find. The sky was covered with thick clouds; I could only weep. I saw darkness and misery over everything. I find, from Trinchen's letter, that aunt is more infirm this winter; she is longing after me, and I am obliged to earn money here, and eat the bread of sorrow. I heard a rustling behind me. I saw Herr von Schaffau with his hound go under the maples. I felt as though I might tell him my trouble, but no, I could not. I went out of his way. Half way up the hill towards the church, it was very quiet by an elder hedge: only the robins were hopping in the twigs, and singing in subdued notes. They amused me. I looked up at them, as they, with their delicate little heads, and their black little eyes, looked at me. Are they too orphan children? No! they have a Father in heaven, without Him not a sparrow falls from the roof, and "are not ye much more than they?" I wept; but different tears now. Oh, dear Lord, am I then forsaken? No, no. If here they thrust me out, the Lord already knows where I shall go in future. I am comforted, and hope in Him. I have never felt so happy as up there by the lonely hedge, and with the little robins. I forgave Frau von Schlichten, I prayed for her with all my heart for the first time; I prayed for all the souls down there in that silent grey house. I prayed that light and peace might come there. It had become dusk, a little light shone through the mist. It was from the parsonage and seemed kindly to invite me. I could not join the company, there was a longer table; guests from the neighbourhood were expected; I saw how, by and bye, the lights sprung up from the gloomy mass of stone. The little light from the parsonage was more inviting to me. The evening bell was also be-

16*

ginning. It sounded softly through the thick mist. I
went into the parsonage with a heart really relieved.
The whole family was assembled in the living-room.
They were celebrating the evening hour. It was a
lovely picture. The father was sitting at the instru-
ment and appeared to have been singing, three children
were standing by him, the tutor had the two youngest
on his knees, and two older daughters were helping
their mother to draw the stockings from the frames.
The pastor greeted me kindly, he knew me from my
being at church. The children too had not forgotten
me, they were very inoffensive, but the pastor's wife
received me with great politeness. As I had no work-
ing-materials with me I offered to help her. She
used many formalities. The great holes in the stockings seemed to annoy her. She complained, that seven
children made her a great deal of work. She had
never finished with it. I asked to be allowed to darn
the stockings. She said again very politely, that my
delicate hands had probably never handled such coarse
stockings. (Her over-politeness displeased me at first,
but she does not appear badly disposed). The pastor
replied playfully, "Dear child! then you will have the
merit of having taught the young lady." Then she
gave me the needful things, and I eagerly began my
work. That was pleasant. I soon felt quite at home:
the father told stories, the children listened. I was
also to tell one, and meantime I had the pleasure of
seeing the mountain of stockings constantly vanishing
before me, and the pastor's wife also appeared pleased.
When their supper time came I wished to go, but they
begged me to stay. The mother left the room; the
tutor again took the smallest children on his knee; it

was very pretty, but his manner struck me very much.

Carry, the eldest daughter, told me that for a year she had played the piano, and that some time ago on her father's birthday, she had played, "Praise the Lord, the mighty King of glory." I asked her to play it to me. She did so. At first we joined in a low voice, then louder and louder, and the hymn sounded from my heart in full tones. The Lord is indeed so very kind. I felt so happy in this dear quiet house. His spirit breathes there. He will strengthen me in my weakness. The pastor took me home. I begged him to be my real Father Confessor. I said to him, that his sister would have filled my place better. He must therefore stand at my side in my weakness, sympathizing and advising me. He was very kind, promised everything to me, gave me good advice, especially that I should regard the wishes of Herr von Schaffau. He means well. The good of the whole house lies at his heart; it is only through great love and patience that he endures many things in the house with such forbearance. In the few months since he returned from his travels, he has already altered much, and also sent away the dangerous governess from the children. His highest wish is to gain their hearts to the Lord. Aunt Julia is his open foe, Frau von Schlichten his secret one. He does not break with them, in order not to leave an influence over the children to them alone. I had incidentally gathered that from his own words. To hear it touched me very much. *I* desire also to have patience and love in my heart, and not to grow weary in winning hearts, and not to grow weary in praying for myself and for us

all. When we came out of the maple-grove, this side
of the castle lay before us brightly lighted, the music
sounded down to us, the shadows were flying about.
I was glad that I was not obliged to go in. I went
up into my little room in the tower. There in the
stillness, I collected my thoughts, and directed them to
my dear Lord. How every earthly sorrow, every un-
pleasantness becomes nothing at all, when the Lord
stands at our side. The world with her pleasure passes
away, but His will abides for ever. I was able also
heartily to pray for those who are in the din and
tumult down below. I have no fear of Frau von
Schlichten and of all the proud people of rank. No,
I feel love and sympathy. Whatever they may inflict
on me, the Lord can overrule everything for the best.
I am afraid I shall not stay here long, but nevertheless
I shall not be forsaken. I had not long been sitting
thus when I heard aunt Julia's quick steps. She was
astonished at my staying out, and declared I had
caused her anxiety. She did not take it amiss when
I told her how very sad I was, and that I had found
comfort in the pastor's house. She stroked me on the
forehead and said, "The storm seems over; Herr von
Tülsen has not asked after you, he has been very
lively especially with Rosalie. But my sister-in-law
is foolish, the old man will marry neither you nor
Rosalie. Only be careful; such affairs might oftener
arise. You are not exactly suitable for us." I begged
henceforth, directly after dinner, to be allowed to leave
the room with Lucy; that I wished to live up here
with Lucy; Lucy's love, and my duty, and my quiet life
would be better to me than all the gaiety. She looked
rather doubtfully at me. "Good resolutions," she said.

"Yes, resolutions," I said, "but pray for me that I may carry them out, and I have included you also every day in my prayers." I could look her in the face the while quite trustfully, and kissed her hand sincerely and tenderly. "You are an enthusiast," said she, "but if you sincerely mean it, I have nothing against it." A week has since past very industriously and regularly. Frau von Schlichten appears to be convinced of my sincerity. She is kinder again. But Herr von Tülsen is the same insufferable creature, though he scarcely speaks a word to me.

2nd November.

Our house is become quieter. Frau von Ramberg and her daughter and Herr von Tülsen, who went away yesterday, were the last. Herr von Tülsen is expected again at Christmas. The ladies below are worn out and nervous, from ennui, aunt Julia says. Rosalie sits for hours together with her arms folded in her mantilla, while Thekla reads in the Ladies' Popular Cyclopædia or writes letters to the cousin; Frau von Schlichten has a great deal of headache and is out of humour. Lucy and I find it dull downstairs, but up here we live merrily together. The aunt has after great entreaties, committed to us the sugar and coffee-department. I maintained, that if a girl is accustomed early to little practical employments, she learns to enjoy them, and that afterwards it is a treasure for her whole life, and a preservative against ennui. I spoke so sensibly, and so entirely in my own province, that I was quite pleased at it myself. The aunt was obliged to say I was right, so now we are the queens of all the sugar basins. The key of the store-cupboard goes

about with us like a relic, at times there is a breaking,
and grating, and putting in order, aunt Julia praises
our economy. Our design now is upon the dessert and
tea-department, and I do not doubt we shall get it.
Vast plans are connected with that; we wish ourselves
to make the tea-cakes and apple-tarts; our cooking
aprons are already made. Aunt Julia was full of
wonder when she was obliged to give us the linen for
it; poor thing! she does not know what foes she is
generously enriching, and what our intention is with
this linen.

12th November.

Lucy said to me to-day: "Is it not really unjust
that the dear Lord has made me so ugly, and my sisters
so pretty?" I replied to her that it was one of the
world's follies to look upon beauty as a piece of good
fortune, although it has every day before its eyes that
beauty is generally a cause of misfortune. A pure
heart, and to live uprightly in God's sight, on the
other hand, were a far surer way to happiness. I asked
whether I should explain that to her more fully. "No,"
she said, "I know well that Thekla and Rosalie are
not happy. I am already much more so, and know
that I can become more and more so in spite of my
ugliness." "Dear Lucy!" I said, "pray to our dear
Lord that He would give you a pure heart; that He
Himself will enter there; that His gentleness, His love,
His humility, may beam from your eyes, and thus you
will be so beautiful that your beauty will even gain a
mastery over the children of the world, and your happiness will be so great that everything which comes
near you will enjoy the blessing of this happiness." I

told her too of the approaching time of Advent, how we must prepare ourselves to receive the Lord. She nestled close to me and assented. May the Lord bless us.

21st November.

It has been raining and raining the whole week. We have not been out since Monday except that I went once in the rain; even the roads in the park are impassable. The ill-humour downstairs is very great. Frau von Schlichten wishes by all means to go to Berlin. Herr von Schaffau wishes they would try a winter here. He does his utmost to entertain them. He has begun to read Dunallan to them; also I am often obliged to play and sing. I sing as a duet with Lucy, "I am weary, go to rest." Even Frau von Schlichten was pleased with it. Aunt Julia, with great affection, admires everything which Lucy does. But Lucy begins to get proud. She teazes her sisters about their doing nothing, and their ennui, and is in high delight at some pieces of work for Christmas. The little room in the tower often looks like a tailor's shop. Aunt Julia looked for old pieces in all the wardrobes, which have been cut up by us, and twenty children are to have presents at Christmas. We never go down to reading without the great work-basket. Thekla ridicules it, but Rosalie has already often helped us. To-morrow after church we have permission to go to the pastor's. Lucy very much wishes to have some intercourse with Carry and little Mary. She heard with astonishment that Carry already teaches knitting to six little girls. She had heard before of my colony. She wishes to do something similar, but I do not urge her, and think of Trinchen, and how she used to talk about such things.

Saturday, 1st December.

The first snow has fallen, the earth is white; it is also rather cold. Aunt Julia asked anxiously whether I would go out in the garden without a cloak. I became somewhat embarrassed, and said, "I have not one, but I have grown hardy." She lent me a wadded jacket. I was very thankful to her. She asked whether I would take it as a present. I was really very much pleased. "So I need no cloak," said I, "and money." — "Money?" asked the aunt. I suddenly felt confidence enough to communicate my money anxieties to her. It seems from Trinchen's letter that they are in want, and longing for Christmas, and for what I am to send them. I also confessed to aunt Julia that my shoes are very much worn, and I have no money for new ones. She scolded me for not having told her before, and soon came in with fifty thalers. I do not know how I felt. Money is a strange thing. How powerful I had suddenly become! how much I could do! I shut the door in order to consider undisturbed. I do not need a cloak since I have got the jacket, so I could send the twenty thalers to Trinchen; besides I thought that for fifteen thalers, I could get a livery coat for Jacob, and a merino pelisse for Trinchen; only I must first speak to Vollberger as to how much such a coat costs. I ran quickly to him, and as usual he was very ready to do me a service. But how frightened I was when I heard the price of a new coat! I had wished to send something out of the common way for the good Jacob, and so had raised the price; but when I had given up that idea, and we made a second computation of quite coarse cloth, it was still rather much. Vollberger made the proposal to me to take the cloth on credit, and to pay afterwards. I entirely refused that; I should not have felt easy about it, and Trinchen would have seen it in the coat. I went sighing away in order to consider the matter. Kind Vollberger! After some time he came; now, — polite and delicate as he is, he brought it out. He had long ago received a coat as a present from Herr von Schaffau. If I were to have this coat lined with yellow, and provided with new facings it would do splendidly for Jacob. "He, indeed, deserves two new ones if I deserve none!" added he. He esteems Jacob highly on account of his great fidelity and self-sacrifice. In Jacob's modest spirit, I accepted the coat with gratitude. I think of it with rapture when Jacob serves aunt with her chocolate at Christmas! Vollberger will provide me three pounds of chocolate for aunt, also the brown merino for Trinchen. He often goes to the town. I will have my shoes made here; they are twice as dear in the town. Sophy has a cousin who is said to be very clever. So everything is arranged beforehand. I am very happy about it. An express messenger carried money and letter to the post; it will get there just at the first Sunday in Advent. Oh, if I could be there!

Lulu to Trinchen.

DEAR TRINCHEN,

The Lord is very good to your orphan child; I can send you so much money! I have not deserved it, but I will thank Him for it a thousand-fold. This

hour outweighs much longing after you — many tears.
Otherwise I get on well, very well. Advent is coming; glorious season! My heart is overflowing. I
should like to skip, and should like quietly to hear the
little angels sing again. Tell aunt that I live in
affluence, and my situation is entirely to my wish.
Dear Trinchen, are you afraid that it is too well with
me? Ah, no! Only I say nothing of the heavy
hours, but be comforted; the Lord does not leave me
in the deep valley, even if I have fallen into it myself. Be cheerful and celebrate a joyful happy Advent,
think of me! I sing with you,

> * "How shall I meet Thee? How my heart
> Receive her Lord aright?
> Desire of all the earth Thou art!
> My hope, my soul's Delight!
> Kindle the lamp, Thou Lord alone
> Half-dying in my breast,
> And make Thy gracious pleasure known
> How I may greet Thee best?"
>   Amen.

And now good-bye! Give my love to aunt, give
my love to Jacob, write soon and much, do not
pay the postage. With Lucy I myself made the en-
closed vanilla-cakes. It is from your recipe. I am
glad to be able to send some to you dear ones. Aunt
Julia knows it. She also sends her best compliments
to aunt. Think of it! Vollberger is going to send
this letter to the post by a man on horse-back express.

2nd December. First Sunday in Advent.

I rose early. The full moon was in the light blue
sky, and many stars. Oh dear, blessed, sacred time
of Advent, bring me a heart as pure as the pure sky

above me, and fill it with the bright peace of heaven and with quiet joy!

> * "Nought, nought, dear Lord, had power to move
> Thee from Thy rightful place,
> Save that most strange and blessed love,
> Wherewith Thou dost embrace
> This weary world and all her woe,
> Her load of grief and ill,
> And sorrow more than man can know; —
> Thy love is deeper still."

—

We sang that to-day at morning service and said it in our heart too. The pastor said still more. His Advent sermon was very beautiful and powerful. Sophy was very much touched by it; she said to me, she would gladly bring something to the Lord as an Advent gift; she could not bring Him her heart, — that would be too impure; but she would bring him vanity and talkativeness, and passion and envy, and strive that she should be better in those ways at Christmas. But Lucy said to me in a low voice, that she would offer a sacrifice to the Lord, that she should love her mother and sisters and pray for them. I was almost frightened to hear that; that she should call it a *sacrifice*. Yet alas it is true. Dear Lord, help her, and help me, and all of us. This afternoon we have had the twenty orphan children here, and have taken their measure. Three of the children were among them on whose mothers' grave I laid the aster in the autumn. I noticed them particularly. We also practised with them, "From heaven on high I come to you." They are now to come every Sunday, that they may be able to sing under the Christmas-tree at

Christmas. Lucy was very eager. I believe yet that
we shall soon begin a school.

Tuesday, 11th December.

Herr von Schaffau complained to-day of the weak
coffee that he has now to drink. At first, I felt embarrassed, but I soon saw that it was a joke and defended myself as well as I could. Lucy too came to
my help; the matter was peaceably settled. He is
very kind. He has had a large convenient store-cupboard made for us, which stands on our corridor; a
cooking-apron hangs on each side of it, and we are
now often at it for hours together. Trinchen's vanilla-
cakes give special satisfaction. We must make some
every week. Yesterday I heard a secret from Vollberger which crowns all. At Christmas the uncle is
going to contrive a cooking-room for Lucy, — up here,
close by us. Lucy is not to stay in the great kitchen.
I have already founded splendid plans upon it. We
will learn cooking here, while we cook for old sick
people. It is very difficult to me to say nothing about
it to Lucy. I promised that to Vollberger, and he is
as silent as the grave. Vollberger is a brave fellow,
but it is remarkable that when others are there, he acts
as though he did not know me. He said he does not
wish to injure me with the adverse party in the lively
wing by his friendship, and he calls it the wisdom of
the serpent. Can it be on the same account that Herr
von Schaffau is so variable towards me? It often
seems to me that he is satisfied with me, and has
reconciled himself to my being here, but lately in the
presence of aunt Julia and of his sister, he did me
great injustice. I cannot doubt that he means honestly

towards me, and when Vollberger blamed his severity, (accidentally he had also been there to hear it), I was not pleased, and I said to him, "Jacob would never have talked over his master or mistress!"

We had the children here also on Wednesday; otherwise they would not learn the hymns, and besides it gives us great pleasure. Aunt Julia listened to them to-day, she wishes some day to go with us in to the town to buy toys, and all kinds of things for the Christmas-tree. I am delighted about it. I wish to buy also. I have some money left. Oh, I should like to buy a great deal! I should like to give something to everybody, but I should like also to give everybody the blessed joy of Christmas in the heart! Oh, I am very rich. When I sit alone in my room in the twilight, it is as if I could see the lights shining, and hear the little angels singing; and my heart is very full. I know not what I could not do; and yet I can do nothing more than love the Holy Child and worship Him. From pure love He came down to us. Could we then do nothing from love to Him? I spoke about it to the children to-day; — what we could do for love to Him. Rosalie and Thekla looked in, just as I was speaking in that way. They came out of curiosity, and Thekla looked rather scornful. But I did not allow myself to be disturbed. Oh, no! I spoke to them more and more warmly. I told them that people who do not love the Child Jesus are very unhappy, and even if they were rich people, yet they were poor; and even if they were very learned, they were yet very foolish; and if they were very much respected by the world, yet they were only very insignificant; and if they were to give, and have given ever so much, they have yet no true Christmas joy. What the world bestows is only transitory, and there is often more trouble than pleasure in it. But what the Child Jesus bestows always remains the best; — it is peace, and joy, and blessedness. We would now open our hearts to the Child Jesus, and receive Him with His beautiful gifts, and pray Him that He would enter many, many hearts, and bring them joy and blessing.

I do not know whether it was quite proper to speak so, but I could not leave it unspoken. And when Thekla afterwards angrily asked me whether it was right to say such things to village-children, and thereby to give disrespectful hints about persons of rank, I could not be silent. I contradicted her warmly and with emphasis, that I had not spoken at all of persons of rank, that I myself considered them poor and wretched when their days passed emptily and uselessly away, and their life was illusion and folly. She said abruptly that she would be happy in her own way. "No," said I, "you will not be happy. You do not wish to be happy. You do not think of your happiness and of eternity. You are going on the broad way which leads to destruction. Oh, Thekla, you have the knowledge, but the world has ensnared your heart and 'the world passes away and the lust thereof, but he that doeth the will of God abideth for ever.'" The world is a false friend; she offers honour, which to a wise man is ignominy; she offers pleasure, which is only too soon changed into sorrow. Thekla interrupted me. She did not wish to hear anything of that kind. But Rosalie answered, "Why not? that we do not like to hear it, is a sign that we feel it strikes home to us. I like to hear it." That was a great joy to me. I could not help thinking of Trinchen's words. — A great influence is also given to women and maidens; if they would only preach to children and to those like themselves, in all love and humility, but in all confidence, the blessing would be greater than they anticipate. The Lord has perfected praise from the mouth of children. Dear Lord, I beseech Thee for true humility, and for true strength.

When Thekla had left us, Rosalie said she should like to have peace and joy and blessedness in her heart, only she did not know how to begin. I replied that I was too weak myself to shew her the way, only that she should search the Holy Scriptures, with a really humble heart, and read what the Lord Jesus and the Apostles say, and go to church every Sunday; for the pastor knows how to explain the word of God very beautifully. Rosalie replied she had often already attempted to read in the Bible, but it had made her anxious: it was all about eternal destruction and the devil, and as far as regards salvation, according to her opinion, no man could be saved. "Dear Rosalie," said I, "you are in a good road; truly no one could be saved, if our Lord Jesus Christ had not offered Himself for us. Yes, indeed, we might be anxious if His immeasurable love had not taken our sin upon itself. We should truly feel, experience, and believe, this: for this faith we should pray our Lord and Saviour Himself. That is a blessed mystery, a wonderful power, a great joy, a heavenly peace and blessedness. If we pray and pray again, and believe and trust, the Lord will hear us: He cannot leave us, He comes and takes up His abode in our hearts." I said this and more, in the joy of my heart. I thought again of Trinchen: — If the faithful were but themselves more full of faith! but they hold too much aloof from the world, and if they speak of that, which is the dearest to them, and the life of their soul, they do it with such reserve, and so faint-heartedly as if they themselves had no great advantage over the world, and themselves had need of strengthening. We do not yet truly know our Lord, and the power of His strength. But now I will have courage whatever comes. Thou art my Help for evermore.

> * "Nor vex your souls with care nor grieve
> And labour longer thus;
> As though your arm could aught achieve
> And bring Him down to us.
> He comes, He comes, with ready will,
> By pity moved alone,
> To soothe our every grief and ill:
> For all to Him are known."

Now is the time of Advent, — the time of preparation; now we should more than ever invite Him, and open our heart to Him. It seems to me as though I, a poor weak child, could more closely approach the dear and sacred Infant, than the glorified Lord, the Redeemer of the world. Rosalie wishes to go with us to church every Sunday; she also asked when our morning prayers were; but when she heard the early hour, she declared that, on account of her nerves, she could not get up so early, or she should be weary the whole day. Dear Rosalie! I can foresee you will

sacrifice more to the Lord than an hour of sleep! May
He give His blessing. Amen.

13th December.

I said to Vollberger to-day, "we have a plot against
Aunt Julia. You see! we shall get the victory." "Not
yet, Miss!" said Vollberger, cautioning me, "do not set
about anything in that way; you will not give any
pleasure by it to us in the quiet wing; nothing of a
plot!"

I could not help laughing. "Vollberger, we are not
fighting behind her back; all is open and honorable,
and we are not fighting and conquering alone: it is
the Lord above. But aunt Julia will not be able to
help it, she must, on the Holy Evening, sing hymns of
joy for the Christmas matins, and to the Infant Lord
Himself."

"That is all right, I have nothing against it," said
the old man.

14th December.

Yesterday aunt Julia went with Lucy and me to
the town. She was very kind to take me with them.
Thekla had said that if my red velvet hat was to go
to the town in company with aunt's green satin jacket,
she would not be of the party. Rosalie stayed because
of a headache, so we three went alone. We were very
cheerful.

I love the aunt better and better. She also took
"that saucy fellow Vollberger" (as she called him)
with us: he would be useful to us. But he might have
dissolved in his readiness to serve her! They had
wrapped me in a fur; that was very pleasant, for there

17*

was a piercing wind over the fields of snow, and we soon got red noses. In the town I got warm from running and looking about. I had never seen anything like it before. It was fun! from shop to shop. Aunt Julia understands buying splendidly. I had scarcely looked round in a shop and got lost in wonder, when I was obliged to go on. A beautiful cloak was bought for Rosalie, also a dark blue velvet hat. I had to try on both, and must confess I could have made use of both. But only in one way — that of superfluity.

Ah no! Trinchen's letter of reply for the money, warmed me more than the warmest cloak! In short, it is no matter; none at all. Perhaps another winter I can buy myself one. I have bought the merino-dress for Trinchen, it is very pretty. I have bought stocking-yarn for my three orphan children. Sophy wishes to help me to knit. Lilac silk stuff for morning shoes for aunt, and parchment to paint book-marks. That was with my own money; but Herr von Schaffau gave us a good deal more money, and, while aunt was making some calls, we went with Vollberger into a toy-shop and into a ginger-bread shop.

Now we all three looked wonderful as we went through the streets, and many a child looked longingly at us. It very much amused me to see how the children stand before the stalls and shops, and trip through the streets, — curiosity and astonishment and joyous expectation on their faces. Yes, one quiet impulse of expectation, of longing, and of joy, goes through the whole world; only men do not know whence this impulse comes.

We came home rather late. On the way I could

think of nothing but drums, and guns, and dolls; and in my mind arrange and divide them.

I must confess that the splendid tapestry wool, and the beautiful embroidery patterns, which I saw others buying, also employed my thoughts; my Christmas presents seemed to me too mean.

I should like to have put some prettier ones among them, but I quieted myself with Trinchen's warning not to undertake too much, nor to diminish the blessing of Advent by external distracting labours.

I have something for every one; the little pictures are very pretty, especially that for aunt Julia, of Lucy in the nursery. Only for Herr von Schaffau, I have nothing. I maturely considered it, but it would be ridiculous. He draws and paints far more beautifully himself. So that also is settled, and I think only of the presents for the children.

The depôt was in my room. I was with Lucy till eleven o'clock doing them up, arranging them, and putting labels upon them. Aunt Julia and Herr von Schaffau were there at first, but they did not interfere. I had feared that we had bought too many toys and ginger-breads, and now it almost appears as though there would not be enough things for all the children; but Herr von Schaffau has promised us to provide everything necessary. Besides he eat two penn'orth of ginger-bread, and I think that rather much!

Saturday, 15th December.

It is very well that I have not entered on new labours; many unexpected ones arise. The pastor's wife especially takes up some of my time. I am often there and like to be there, and I seem as though I feel a duty in helping a little in the household. The wife is good-hearted, but she does not go the right way to work with her seven children; and if Mr. Heber relieves her from much, there is still no getting through with anything. The children are running about, still, partly in their summer clothes. To-day, I looked up an old dressing-gown of the pastor's, and some of the mother's clothes, in order to make something warm out of them for the children, but it was not sufficient. Mr. Heber bethought him of a very pretty gingham curtain, which hangs over the pegs for dresses in the guest chamber, — really quite useless. We took the good advice, so I hope they will yet be equipped. Poor things! the stipend is too small, their children too many. The pastor naturally wishes on no account to get into debt; so there is often want. I feel as though I must bear all that with them. I feel so at home with them, it reminds me of our own house — always want, but always the dear Lord; yes, the more want, the nearer God is. The dear Lord will also provide Christmas presents for them. Mr. Heber has lately bought some pictures of soldiers. We painted them amongst us, and pasted them with supports behind, and it makes a splendid army for the children.

Lucy has given me some old dolls. Under my hands they have been freshened up; the little girls will be delighted with them. So I have something for each. My pictures form a part of it. I am tolerably forward with my work. In the coming week vanilla-cakes, and all kinds of sweet-meats, are to be made, and the ornaments for the Christmas-tree. The rooms for guests below are being swept and aired. Frau von Schlichten has invited a great many guests, as a substitute for going to Berlin. Herr von Schaffau has not allowed them to go before; but directly after the festival some are to be moved there. Where we shall stay — aunt Julia, Lucy, and I, is undecided.

It will depend on Herr von Schaffau. The aunt told me, that Frau von Schlichten does not wish us to be with him. I do not see the reason of it. The hostility does not seem to me so bad as it was.

16th December.

A beautiful Sunday, rich in enjoyment. When we, in our Sunday dress, were just going to begin morning prayers, Rosalie came in. I held out my hand to her in silence, and at the same time prayed fervently for her. She sang with us "Rise, ye children of the kingdom," and also went with us to church. The pastor spoke more beautifully than ever: it seems so to me every time. He said that in order to receive the Lord, we must prepare not only our heart, but our house also; not only serve the Lord in our heart, but also give strong evidence of it in our daily walk. The sermon was very strengthening to me. I impressed every point deeply on my heart. But not I alone. When we were just going to take our seats at the table, (only we seven, there were no strangers), Herr von Schaffau said, with a firm voice and yet with emotion, "From to-day we will always, before we seat ourselves at table, ask the dear Lord for His blessing." Thereupon he himself said grace. The ladies folded their hands, they were certainly very much astonished. After a pause Herr von Schaffau began to talk, and seemed particularly affable and kindly disposed. We have, indeed, always said grace for ourselves in silence, but it was always with some embarrassment, so that those who did not, must have felt that it was more unseasonable than right. I allowed something to be told me about the family to-day. Vollberger was here late; he is very trusty, and I heard nothing from curiosity, but from true interest. Herr von Schlichten had a little property in the Margraviate, Vollberger told me, and aunt Julia her share in it.

"He managed so badly, that when he died his sister's share was seized too. Herr von Schaffau now took the management, and has been labouring for six years to clear the estate from debt, and to give to his sister an income of her own, however small. Aunt Julia naturally feels chained to her sister-in-law; indeed, she has often said, untenderly enough, that not only what she receives here belongs to her, but that she has a right to demand more. When Herr von Schaffau six years ago took both to live with him, he was younger, and not quite independent of his elder sister; he could not prevent her beginning a similar life here, to what it had been there. On the whole, indeed, things went on in an orderly way here, and that almost a dozen sat with us at our table, did not make us poor," said Vollberger; and whatever dissolute people they were, they had no liberty here; but the treatment of our master was not right. Two years ago, Frau von Schlichten became ill, and was ill a long time, and then the doings ceased of themselves, and Herr von Schaffau afterwards went to England. But I stayed here, and the steward up there, in order to see after his rights; but

'When cats are out, so says the fable,
The mice spring over bench and table;'

and truly the master was scarcely gone, when the

guests made their appearance. Frau von Schlichten wonderfully recovered; the two elder young ladies became ladies all at once, and things went merrily here. The steward would no longer give any oats for the guests' horses; and not always butter and poultry for the guests. I could not witness the goings on of the young ladies and their governess, and wrote to my master. He was there as quick as wind, a year next March. They put quite another face upon it here; but so did our master. Some strange wind must blow in England which had wonderfully strengthened him; all at once he had courage to contend with his sister. He was gentle and amiable indeed, but he carried through his determination. The bad guests were obliged to go, and the servants by degrees; and suddenly the governess too was packed into a carriage, and sent off all in a hurry to the train. Frau von Schlichten is too cunning, she tried to put a good face on a bad game.

"But aunt Julia flamed forth: she called master a pietist, a hypocrite, a miser, and me a dissembler, and tale-bearer. She knows well that master is too generous to turn her out, because she is now as poor as a church-mouse. Early in this year master called hither our new Pastor, whom you know, and know how he agrees with the house here. His sister was to bring our young ladies rather into discipline, but Frau von Schlichten, with her cunning, and aunt Julia, set it aside." I sighed at these words. It is really an oppressive feeling to be the apple of discord in a household. Vollberger guessed my thoughts and continued, "It is different now; you need not be anxious. Lucy's love for you has reconciled master to your youth and inexperience, and has also brought him nearer to aunt Julia: in short, matters stand very well here. But there will be a revolution in the beginning of the year. At Pluggen on the sandy estate, preparations are now being made. It would be a good thing if there in retirement the bread-basket of our merry company should be hung rather higher! Our master is guardian. He can arrange it as he likes. When Thekla was less, Frau von Schlichten thought there was a wife for her brother. Now that she sees which way the wind blows, poor Rosalie at least is to bring her a rich son-in-law. She follows her mother like a lamb, and Herr von Tülsen may be irresistible for many a poor young lady. Do not you think so, Miss?" added he, awaiting my reply. "Herr von Tülsen is very repulsive to me," said I, frankly, "and indeed money could never determine me, to give my hand to a man." "And what could then?" asked he farther. "Oh, he must be much wiser and better than I am myself. I must be able to look up to him like a dependent child, and must strengthen myself with his faith and his love. He might be ever so poor; yes, I should almost prefer that, for I have seen more happiness in poor houses, than in rich ones hitherto. I should willingly take in sewing, and keep a school, and even dig, and plant my garden myself: certainly rather than be obliged to keep myself in my drawing-room, and be obliged to lead such a foolish existence." "I can well believe that," said Vollberger earnestly. "May the Lord give you such a husband." I became very red. I had spoken the words so unconsciously, and now felt how unsuitable it was.

Trinchen would call me a mischievous chatter-box,

and I could be angry with Vollberger, because he
tried so artfully to draw me out. But he means well.
He has already given me many a piece of good advice,
as to what I shall do when the guests come. I shall
not trouble myself about them; in the quiet wing, I
shall keep a happy Christmas with Lucy. When I go
down I shall leave my heart upstairs, and let people
down there slide past me like shadows. But I wish
they were gone again, and I wished they would all go
to Berlin, and would leave us here, and then days of
real industry should follow the days of festivity; — the
cooking-room, the sewing-school, house-keeping; and
then spring, and then working in the garden.

22nd December.

We have had holydays since yesterday. I have
been the whole day in the garden-parlour, the tables
are covered, the things upon them, the tree decorated;
but I have things yet to arrange and to do, and I feel
very solemn and happy in mind in the festive room.
The manger for Lucy is very lovely; the gardener has
made me a charming little garden. I have made a
straw-roof to the stable, and I have painted all the
figures, it is nearly finished. To-day I heard carriages
drive up, dresses rustle, doors bang, the house is in a
bustle, the guests arrived. Oh, how secure I felt, and
how secluded from the world. I have the permission
not to appear at table till Christmas.

I have still a good deal to do at the parsonage; I
wished to go there in the twilight. I walked up and
down beforehand by the quiet elder hedge. To walk
alone is beautiful, especially at such a beautiful time.
After some time I saw a figure coming along the path;

I soon recognized Herr von Tülsen; I also heard him
calling as I hastened very quickly away. The work
at the parsonage does not decrease, it increases; every
time I come, there are new mountains risen out of the
ground, for the Pastor's dear wife. I have advised her
to take no notice of them. The Pastor is of my opinion.
We will celebrate the days in peace; besides to-morrow
is Sunday. The children are scarcely to be restrained.

What a joyous confusion and buzz there is in the
house, and yet a breath of peace too. The Pastor
stands by with bright eyes; when the mountains of his
wife might cast many shadows, he brings light, and
she is so glad to take it.

We sat very industriously till eleven. The pastor
read to us the life of S. Monica; then he brought me
home. It was so lively in the castle, and so quiet at
the parsonage.

24th December.

"Glory to God in the highest, on earth peace and
goodwill to men."

"Shout oh heavens, rejoice oh earth, break forth
into shouting, ye mountains; for the Lord hath comforted His people, and had compassion on their mi-
series."

So it is, no discord can enter into my heart; here
is Christmas; — trouble down below. Guests continued
to come till Christmas Eve. The thawed snow had
made the roads almost impassable. The water overflowed the bridge in the meadow. Herr von Schaffau
rode there himself to prevent accidents.

It almost put us out of humour. He had promised
to go a walk with us. We had, wonderful to say

finished everything soon after three. We had won
the wager, he must really keep his promise. Lucy is
very fond of her uncle. She jumped for joy when she
saw him, a little later, hastening very quickly through
the garden to look for us. We were in the neighbourhood of a pine-grove, ran in, hid ourselves, and when
he was going quickly by, Lucy shook the soft snow
from the twigs, and stopped him. But soon the bells
began to ring; the church shone through the twilight,
and one light after another came up from the village.
We went also, we entered the pew, and aunt Julia
was already there! The silver chandeliers before the
altar were lighted, and the old knights and noble
ladies looked more life-like than ever. We sang the
joyful Christmas hymns; many children's voices sounded
through the others; indeed, it was no disturbance that
quite little voices sweetly lisped among them. Fräulein
von Ramberg, Rosalie and some other ladies, came
later and went with the others. We waited in the
church-yard listening to the bells, till the lights had
all vanished, and then we hastened away. Herr von
Schaffau took aunt Julia and me too. I have never
seen his face look so beaming. He looked happy like
other children. He said to me that he was very much
looking forward to what the Infant Jesus would give
him in the garden-parlour. I was frightened at first,
but I thought he was only joking, for I had nothing
at all for him. Lucy and I quickly put on our white
dresses, and put orange-blossom in our hair. We
wished to go festively dressed to the festival. Then
we hastened and lighted the candles. Rosalie helped
us; indeed, she had really been very industrious in
the sewing. The corner where I had my presents for

Lucy and the others was covered with a cloth. Now we heard little footsteps and whispering; the door was opened; the happy moment was come, which we had so much anticipated, for which we had worked with busy fingers. The little company came in, beaming with joy. We led each to its place, and then we sang, "From heaven on high I come to you," and then, "Oh merry, happy Christmas-time!"

Rosalie and Lucy and I, and Sophy with some of the older children, sang second. It sounded splendid in the lofty room. Then followed the joyous astonishment, and admiration of the beautiful gifts. I was so very much occupied with the children, that I did not notice how the room had filled with the great guests also. Herr von Tülsen's unpleasant voice could have almost disturbed me, but I would not allow myself to be disturbed.

Lucy was delighted with the manger; the transparency, "Glory to God in the highest," shone brightly against the dark plants in pots. Older people also enjoyed themselves, and I distributed my little pictures to the ladies. When the first commotion was over, and I was standing alone by the manger, Herr von Schaffau came to me, "Then have not I got anything?" said he in a low voice. He looked really sorrowful, and at the same time looked so earnestly into my eyes, as if he wished to fathom my heart. Could he think that I have any grudge against him? I should so like to have given him something! He had certainly looked quite through me before I spoke, for a bright, cheerful look passed quickly over his face. When I said to him that, if I might, I would give him something, he answered, "Do paint me the

Plettenhaus," I joyfully promised it. Aunt Julia's loud voice called us to the presents upstairs, and then it first forcibly struck me that surely there would be something there for me; and, with some expectation, I entered the brightly-lighted room. Oh, I got too much! cloak and hat are for me, a dress, pocket-handkerchiefs and gloves and colours and paper, and paint-brushes and beautiful books! I did not know what to say for them all; but the colours and paper, I must confess, pleased me most. Lucy and I again excused ourselves from table. We had more pleasure in busying ourselves among our splendid things. Frau von Schlichten took it very graciously; she just saw that Herr von Tülsen wished to take me in to dinner, and that I thanked him and refused. Vollberger provided us something to eat. We had soon finished, and I chose a very beautiful piece of paper for the Plettenhaus; fetched the little picture out of my room, and began to draw. We were both happy, I can truly say that. Rosalie fetched me after dinner to sing some popular songs to the company.

Herr von Schaffau had strictly forbidden dancing and too noisy amusements, on these festival days. To-day it was music; they had already sung a quartett. I sang too with joyful heart. I felt no vanity. I only saw the joy of Christmas before me. I felt bright and pure within. I embraced all men in my heart, and prayed for humility and gentleness, that I might bear their wrongs, because I am not worthy of all the compassion and faithfulness, which the Lord has shewn me. Surely they read my thoughts; all were kinder. Thekla herself was standing at the piano with Herr von Reinberg, and said, "dear Lulu, you must sing to us oftener." I gave her my hand and said, "How gladly would I fulfil all your wishes." In conclusion I sang,

> Weary now to rest I go,
> Close my eyes on all below:
> Father, let Thine eyes of love
> Watch my slumbers from above.
>
> If I ill have done to-day,
> Father, turn Thine eyes away:
> Grace of Thine, through Christ alone,
> My transgressions shall atone.
>
> To Thy keeping I commend
> Every relative and friend;
> All mankind both great and small:
> Thou, my God, canst keep them all.
>
> To the sick, oh send repose;
> Tearful eyes, in slumber close;
> And the moon in heaven the while,
> O'er the silent world shall smile.

That was my frame of mind. I sang with feeling. When I was putting my beautiful things together, and aunt Julia with Herr von Schaffau and Lucy were standing by me, I could not control myself. I begged aunt Julia with tears that they would all have patience with me; I did so wish I was worthy of so much kindness. Aunt Julia pressed me to her heart, and said tenderly, she wished to replace my distant aunt to me; Lucy leaned against me; Herr von Schaffau had gone to the window. I could not say good night to him, I was sorry for that.

First day of the Christmas festival.

I slept but little. I got up early. I knew that a special pleasure was in store for Lucy. She came earlier than usual. We had our morning prayers. Directly after came Vollberger to see how we were getting on. Sophy was going restlessly about, Lucy wanted breakfast. "There is none to-day!" said Sophy laughing. Lucy had not time to wonder when aunt Julia and Herr von Schaffau led us into the cooking-room. How delightful! A cooking-stove, a baking-oven, and a dutch-oven; — utensils of all kinds. The water was boiling in the kettle. We quickly fetched coffee from the store-cupboard. The aunt and Herr von Schaffau invited themselves to breakfast. The cloth was soon laid — clean and tidy, everything ready. Rosalie was invited too. We heartily enjoyed ourselves, but it was soon over. One guest followed another. Herr von Tülsen came too. We resolutely refused to make more coffee; only Frau von Schlichten, who appeared last, got just one cup. I noticed some excitement in Herr von Tülsen. He asked me in a whisper whether I was always going to absent myself from the company. I replied that to-day I should be at the Christmas-distribution at the parsonage. He bit his lips, suddenly opened my work-box, and pushed a letter in. I was quite in dismay. The thought of Frau von Schlichten, of her suspicion, came over me. I involuntarily looked round at her. She was engaged in conversation, but the serious looks of Herr von Schaffau rested upon me. He had observed us. I could not consider what was to be done. The bells began to ring; the company left my room. Only Lucy stood waiting near me. I put on my hat and cloak, shut the work-box and went with her to church. Thoughts on the letter occupied me. It will be a ground for suspicion, a tempest will arise, they will condemn thee. But I feel so innocent and then I thought, "Nothing untoward will happen; everything will and must be for thy good, and so will the letter. So it cannot make me anxious; it *may* not make me anxious. I was very much comforted. I thought the world is large and there is room for many letters in it, and this one too." When we came out of church the Pastor's dear children surrounded me   They wished to take me with them at once, but I had still something to fetch from home. If I must send the most beautiful sweet-meats to aunt, some little figures in sugar and delicate sweets, must give pleasure at the parsonage. Herr von Schaffau walked by me. I was very much fluttered. The fatal letter! It seemed to me as though he wished to say something, but he remained quiet and grave; quite different from yesterday evening. It made me very sorrowful. Oh, the heart is weak! The bright joy of Christmas was troubled; but the dear Infant Saviour remained still in my heart, and also helped me again. Herr von Tülsen met me on the way home. I could not avoid him. "Have you read my letter?" he asked immediately. "I had not time," I said. "Not time?" said he very bitterly. I got frightened. "I did not think that it was so urgent," I replied, with some embarrassment. He laughed aloud. I got more frightened. But he became quiet and gentle again and offered me his hand, with many wonderful speeches. I shook my head. He said that he could not bear to see me here, that a different position in the world would befit me, and that to free my aunt from her depressing situation, would be a sweet thought to him, that he laid all his riches at my feet, that I should rule like a queen, that

he would follow me with rapture to bring aunt and
Trinchen and Jacob into my kingdom. The last
thought came on me unexpectedly. I looked at him,
breathing deeply. He wished to take my hand. "Lulu,
say yes," said he entreatingly. I was terrified now at
my own thoughts. I felt as though I were being
tempted by Satan. "Go from me, I have nothing to
do with you"—my words carried me away. He still
spoke very eagerly. I wished to go away. At last
he begged me urgently to do as though he had said
nothing at all, that he felt he had been overhasty,
that I was still young; I did not know how to value
a brave heart and manly protection. I should think
otherwise in time; but if the world should abandon
me and thrust me out, then I should remember where
I might seek protection and help. My heart rose high
at these words. Who is my protection and my help?
Thou art my confidence, oh Lord God; Thou art my
help from my youth. "To be poor," I said, "is not
hard; the Lord on high is my Father. He has a large
treasury, He will give me as much as He wills. He
will never leave me; He will never leave my aunt
either. He has constantly covered me with His goodness. I am very rich, but I will worship my God and
serve Him alone." I hastened away. I stood still once
more by the hedge.

Lord, keep me in Thee. I prayed; Christmas
came back again. I went into the lowly stable to the
Infant Saviour. I would willingly have offered crowns
to Him. Oh dear Lord! before Thee all the gold of
the world is only dust; and poor and rich are alike to
Thee. I found Vollberger at the church-yard gate.
"I have been waiting for you here," said he sighing.

18*

"You have been talking a long time with Herr von Tülsen." At that he looked very sad, and I certainly quite amused. "Vollberger, you mean kindly towards me." "God knows it. You are too young yet, the world is alluring." "But God is faithful," I joyfully interposed. "He is my help at all times, — and my dear Father. He takes the first place in my heart. I never feel that more, than if any one else wishes a place in my heart. He who is not reconciled to this dear Lord, may not enter there; to Him I have given my heart. And if *He* is my Guardian, none of you need keep a watch over me." I wished him good night too, because I should not appear down below to-day. Vollberger was satisfied, then he sighed and gave me no farther warning. He gave me a letter from Herr von Schaffau, which I was to present to the Pastor and left me. In the dear parsonage, I soon forgot the perplexity; the world is a wonderful place. I do not wish to be at all proud, for "let him who thinketh he standeth take heed lest he fall;" but I do feel myself high above the world. I was in the garden in the afternoon, in order to fetch more green fir-twigs, and more box; the company from the castle were coming in full dress along the maple avenue, Frau von Ramberg and Frau von Schlichten first. I went out of their way, and let them pass below me. The whole effect had a sort of halo around it. Not for me. I know each one separately in his dissatisfaction, his fruitless endeavour, his emptiness and poverty. A halo shines round the parsonage; wisdom and love rule there. They serve the Lord; He is in the midst of them, with grace, and peace, and joy, and riches. Oh dear ones! The Lord Whom you serve will also

provide for you. And has He not? The mountains
of the Pastor's wife are all removed to-day; the affluence
of Herr von Schaffau has long been a help to the poor
parsonage, and I was not a little proud that the letter
went through my hands. I took a liberty for once,
and fetched whole mountains of cakes from the pantry,
and put them on the tea-table. The children might
for once eat as much as they liked. The Pastor and
Mr. Heber were of my opinion that to-day there was
to be nothing said about sparing or sharing. All
should go topsy-turvy. The children were delighted
and called me their "sugar Lulu," no "cake Lulu."
"Cakes are more beautiful than sugar." So a merry
evening followed the merry giving of the presents.

The Pastor left us in order to prepare for to-morrow's sermon; Mr. Heber and I played with the
children. We led two armies against each other — a
war with peas. I could shoot them much better, and
my party always conquered. Lucy has asked the five
children for to-morrow. She wishes with Carry in the
cooking-room, to cook for us in the evening. It is to
be eaten in my room. The Pastor brought me here!
I am so fond of these walks. I hear many a beautiful
word. Everything is still in motion below. There is
singing going on. The day is now gone. I was
cheerful and enjoyed myself, yet I felt a slight sting
in my heart about it. I have burned the letter.

Does Herr von Schaffau think any ill of me? I am
very sorry about it. Sometimes I feel as though I
could say anything to him, and then again I feel a
deep gulf between us. There is a light shining in his
tower. It is the only bright point in the quiet wing;
I can also see his dark shadow on the window. It is

very miserable to be dependent on the opinion of man. Oh! that I could overcome it. Dear Lord, I am so truly happy and rich in Thy love, in Thy presence, in Thy grace! Give me gentleness, and patience, joyfulness and confidence, towards all men. Let it be to be read in my character, but only as the reflection of my whole soul. Now good-night! I thank Thee, faithful Lord. I am weary, very weary, and lay me down in comfort to rest; let Thine angels watch over us — over us all.

Second day of the Christmas festival.

After much exertion follows depression. I felt it already to-day; slept late, and got almost weary in church. Herr von Tülsen was in church. He walked beside me on the way home. I could not help gaping. Herr von Schaffau took no notice, when I said good morning to him. I was in the breakfast-room. Frau von Schlichten appeared handsomely dressed; I said "good morning" to her and enquired after her health. She was very cold to me, and the others too: even Rosalie was embarrassed. A gentleman came in — a foreign Count; Frau von Schlichten greeted him with unusual politeness.

She presented him to the ladies. I was standing by Rosalie: it was very humiliating. She acted as though I were not there. I rose proudly. I thought, "are these people more than thou?" Then I met the triumphant looks of Herr von Tülsen. He appeared to have observed me, and to have guessed my thoughts. I was ashamed. *Have* I the world so completely beneath me? Ah no! I am very weak. Oh, why does my heart ever move with the restless billows of this life? And yet I feel a firm confidence in my soul, and I shall yet triumph. I resolved to bear the humiliation, to act as though no other position would befit me. I once more talked pleasantly with Rosalie, and when she observed that her mamma was in lively conversation, she returned my friendliness.

She told me that the journey to Berlin was settled for the day after to-morrow; but she wished to stay here, — wished to live with us. Herr von Schaffau interrupted us. He came to us with the stranger and presented him to me. I heard that Count Roden wished to make my acquaintance, because he was a friend of my late father. He also knew my aunt and my late mother. He told me a great deal; I was very much pleased. Dear Aunt! It must have been different then to now. Count Roden is the first, in these fashionable circles, who has been really unconstrained and kindly disposed towards me. He asked me about my home. Every little thing seemed to interest him. Trinchen and Jacob were persons known to him. Although I had a great deal that was sorrowful and mournful to tell, I was quite in a humour for it. Count Roden asked me whether I did not wish to make the acquaintance of my uncle the Court-marshal and his family: he would conduct me to them. He said many flattering things about them. I got embarrassed. Does he not know that I am here as a governess, and not independent? Lucy now came. She begged me earnestly to come; the little guests were there; I must make necessary arrangements. Up here I sat more than an hour lost in thought. I set the children to their work, to their play, but as in a dream. I liked best to sit at the ivied window.

Those were beguiling thoughts, — uncle, — the court, — new friends. Could anything keep me here? No, nothing. Few care for my presence here; to many it is repulsive — indifferent. But would the world there be different and the people? I thought and thought, and considered. No, surely not. There will be friendly and unfriendly ones there, just as here. And had I not done an injustice in thought to many an one already? Oh, it is beautiful here, — the dear parsonage, my room, the garden, the old castle, the kind aunt: and, my dear Lucy, could I part from you? Surely not. The intoxication was over. I was very happy in my kingdom of children. I looked with peaceful heart at the company walking in the garden below me.

I sat down to my new colours and to the Plettenhaus. I was thinking whether Herr von Schaffau would still wish to have it. At that moment the door behind me, opened softly. He himself entered. He should not find me at my work; foolish creature that I was, I put the paper out of sight. He took it out, and said he was glad I had not forgotten my promise. He offered now to shew me how he painted in water-colours. I tried it too. He was very forbearing and patient, and when he rose to leave me, I felt as though I must speak to him, as though I must beg him always to tell me the reason of his dissatisfaction, never to leave me in uncertainty: or to say candidly, if he wished anyone else in my place.

I stood hesitating, and so did he. He saw my thoughts, he looked deeply into my heart, gave me his hand and said, "Dear Lulu, I must certainly ask your pardon, and you are right." That came upon me too much as a surprise. I turned quickly to the

window. Can all the disquiet which I have felt have
been without cause? Herr von Schaffau came silently
to me, and I could reply nothing. The carriages were
bowling again along the road in the park below; Herr
von Tülsen looked up at me. I started back in terror. But Herr von Schaffau left the room without receiving an answer from me. It was very childish of
me. I should have been obliged to go after him, but
the children surrounded me.

I eat and played with the children, and at last
settled the matter. I am to pardon him! And if I did
not meet him very eagerly with it, it may be a warning to him for the future to conquer his humours, and
not to be one day pleasant, and the next unpleasant.
The festival days are now over. I am not satisfied
with myself. I was very much agitated and distracted.
The time was much more delightful in anticipation. I
expected so much from the days. If I had been able
to pray more heartily, I should have been safer. Oh,
if my heart could but be quiet and steadfast. It can!
It shall!

Shadows of evening take,
O'er earth, their darkening way:
Lord Jesus, come and make
Night brighter than the day;
For on Thee to attend
Is sunshine without end.

This day full oft my soul
Hath turned to vanity;
But, written on Thy scroll,
The record is with Thee:
Against myself I bring
A heavy reckoning.

The reckoning is indeed heavy, but Thy grace is strong, and Thy compassion great. I sleep securely, because Thy wings over-shadow me.

27th December.

We had a holyday again to-day. Early in the morning, I wrote to aunt. There was so much about external events, that the letter grew long. I had much that was pleasant to tell. How my completed wardrobe will delight them! I packed up my sweetmeats, Vollberger will take it with him to-morrow to the rail.

I did not go a walk, I painted so as to finish the little picture. I thought perhaps I should be able to give it to Herr von Schaffau before his departure.

At noon Sophy dressed me in the golden brown with orange blossoms. It was for a leave-taking party. The Grauberg family and others came. I went down with a peaceful and firm mind: how utterly different the world looks. Herr von Tülsen, would surely not triumph again: though Frau von Schlichten was so marked in her unkindness towards me, that I was afraid, she was planning to get me out of the house. Lucy looked compassionately and at the same time beseechingly at me. I could kiss her forehead quite cheerfully: she understood me. "To-morrow they are all going away," said she, consolingly. I was very much astonished and embarrassed when Count Roden took me in to dinner. I was obliged to take my place quite high up at the table. Herr von Schaffau was my other neighbour

As he always does now, he said grace aloud before we seated ourselves. I now looked up. Frau von

Schlichten's piercing gaze fell on me. She appeared very angry, and whispered as she sat down to Frau von Ramberg, who made a horrible face. I got frightened. I could not remain here. I begged to be allowed to take my old place near the forsaken Lucy, and wished to go away. Count Roden looked at me with astonishment, but Herr von Schaffau, who, wonderfully enough, always sees through my thoughts, almost commanded me to remain. He looked with one of his smiles towards the ladies, and observed rather loud that Lucy was looking very longingly after me, but she must content herself to-day.

Frau von Schlichten had noticed my movements. She turned red. She had seen my good intention, I was at rest now. Count Roden talked a great deal to me. His character inspired me with more and more confidence. I told him much of home. The remembrance of home life made me lively, and when we rose from table I did not know how the time had passed. After dinner I was annoyed that he mentioned the excellence of Herr von Tülsen and his friendship for me. Herr von Tülsen has told him that it is very dull here: he has laid it on with strong colours. I fear it is at his instigation that Count Roden made me the generous proposition to be for some time at his house, as lady-companion of his daughters: care also should be taken about my aunt. Herr von Tülsen lives in the same little capital. He appears not to have given up his foolish thoughts. I tried as much as possible to talk Count Roden out of his ideas.

I assured him that I would not part from Lucy if they did not send me away. I assured him that I should not feel happy in a court, that I was accustomed to quiet and a lonely life in the country; and very much preferred it. The others had begun to dance. Herr von Tülsen earnestly begged me to dance. Surely he did it to vex Frau von Schlichten, as he found me quite near her. He appears quite to have broken with her, and to have taken up with the Grauberg family. He is going with them to-day.

He begged me at least to stay down-stairs. I replied, that I had promised to be with Lucy every evening, and showed him how she stood waiting for me at the door. Frau von Schlichten now, to my astonishment, said some kind words to me. She was glad at the child's love for me, and could be quite easy to leave Lucy here under my protection. I do not know what is underneath, and will not enquire; it is all right, if she is friendly. Count Roden took a very friendly leave. He will greet my uncle the court-marshal from me. When I asked Herr von Schaffau whether he was going away early, he replied that in any case he should speak to me first

Lucy was a short time in my room. We made plans for the coming quarter. Herr von Schaffau has committed to us the care of the poor in his absence. Vollberger stays here; "as a spy," said aunt Julia in joke: she is no longer afraid of him: Rosalie may not stay. She would like to; but her thoughts will stay behind. We will think of her, and pray for her.

28th December.

Even before prayers came Herr von Schaffau. He asked for aunt Julia. She was not here yet. For the first time he talked long and confidentially with me: it is all right; he is not angry with me; he warned and cheered me with gentle loving words. I am to persevere and go joyfully on my way: if it is necessary, he will take my part. I was very much touched by his kindness. Lucy came in; he drew her gently towards him, and charged her to obey me. "It is not at all necessary," said he laughing, "she is more obedient to you than to me. I might be almost jealous." Lucy tenderly assured him, that she loved him more than before, and aunt Julia too and everybody.

He was her dear uncle, and must not stay away from us so long. "Do you really wish that?" asked he. "I do wish it," replied she, "and Lulu too; don't you?" "Certainly," said I. He saw very well that I sincerely meant it. Aunt Julia now came in and Sophy too; we had not yet had morning prayers. Herr von Schaffau asked, whether he might stay. Aunt Julia too seated herself quietly in the corner of the sofa, — a sign that she wished to stay. I was afraid at first, and felt very weak, but I soon gained courage and joyfulness. All the follies and weaknesses, which have carried my heart hither and thither these last few days, were blown away. I felt a hearty communion with those who were with me, who are so dear and precious to me. I prayed with them and for them, with my whole soul. If we had prayed thus together every morning, it would have been different. I have often misunderstood Herr von Schaffau. In my heart I prayed away every thought with which I had done him injustice: if he had not gone now, I should have borne much from him which I did not understand. After the carriages had rolled away, I went once more into the empty rooms below. I thought over the hours I had lived here. I was obliged to struggle with a melancholy mood. I had many reproaches to make on myself. I had had many vain and foolish thoughts here; had been lazy and dilatory in my vocation. I might have been warmer and more loving towards Thekla, and have taken more trouble about Rosalie. I seated myself in my favourite window. Here I found Herr von Schaffau's gloves and cigar-case. I drew the curtain and fancied that I could hear the noise and buzz of the company. But it was silent and remained silent. Here Vollberger found me. He came to clear away the remains of the breakfast and other things. I gave him his master's things. "Now, dear Miss," said he, "impress once more upon your mind how madly things have gone on here: such things will not happen again. With the old year we will sweep out the old impurity; this two-fold establishment does not answer — either one or the other. Master has done what he could; but the heart of his sister is closed against him. He is now taking her in Berlin into circles which may perhaps have more influence on her than he could; he will find new powers there. I hope, they will not come here again much, and we, as I said, will sweep the old defilement from the rooms here, and may the Lord purify the heart of the sister." I had a good deal more talk with Vollberger, I am very fond of him. It is well that he has stayed with us. This evening aunt Julia drank tea with Lucy and me here in my room. I began to read aloud; aunt Julia soon fell asleep, and snored loudly. She has had a great deal to arrange during the day and has not finished yet.

We have not seen much of the aunt yet. She is still busy in the house. I am glad that we have permission to inhabit the large breakfast-parlour; the splendid piano stands there. Herr von Schaffau wishes that we should have intercourse with the parsonage. Aunt Julia has no objection. She said, for our sakes, she will sometimes entertain the whole swarm of children here. The Pastor's wife can put on her Christmas cap on the occasion; her stateliness will not be unpleasant to the aunt; I will give her some good advice beforehand. In these intermediate days there is not much to be begun, and a tendency to ennui came over me. When I saw the same in Lucy, I conquered my own. I made some calls with Lucy on old people, in order at once to enter upon the duty which Herr von Schaffau has committed to us.

We will not give anything to anyone before we have visited him. Old Sandermann is in want of a woolen gown; that shall be our first work in the New Year. I have seen again to-day how very much people are pleased with such visits.

It pleases them about as much as the gift itself. If only people of rank knew how much comfort they could give to their poor brothers and sisters, by love and sympathy, what interest they could make of the advantages which the Lord has given them through their position in the world! Trinchen has often said that to me. She desires it especially for young ladies. Wives have generally their vocation in children and their household; but the young ladies! Oh, if they were filled with the love of Christ, with gentleness,

humility and sweetness, they could diffuse much blessing in the world; they could lay soft pillows beneath
poverty and sickness, and arouse hearts to think of
the heavenly kingdom. Where poverty and sickness
have loosened the ground, the good seed may be sown,
and the Lord can work much by feeble energies. I
talked in this way with Lucy. She receives it gladly;
she even said to-day, that now she could understand
why the dear Lord had made her ugly, and had not
given her people's love; — that she might love Him
all the more, and not live to the world. I explained
to her that if she loved the Lord with all her heart,
and sought to live piously and with a pure heart before Him, that would be the surest way to gain the
love of everybody. We then sat very snugly in my
room. Lucy finished the day by writing to her uncle;
she promised him a kind of diary.

1st January.

Praise ye the Lord!   His love is great towards us;
Precious it is to praise the King immortal;
Lovely His praise, and sweet to us who listen.
        Praise ye the Lord!

Answer each other with the loud thanksgiving;
Praise Him with harps — our God — the ever-worthy;
For He is mighty, and is strong to save us.
        Praise ye the Lord!

Thank ye the Lord, of all things the Creator!
Fountains of life are in His presence springing,
And, from His heart, upon our souls descending:
        Praise ye the Lord!

Lord Jesus Christ — Thou Son of the most Highest,
Give Thou Thy grace, to all devout believers,
That they may praise Thy name to everlasting:
        Praise ye the Lord!

The sun is shining brightly in the blue sky; the sunbeams glisten on the snow-white earth. In my soul too all is clear, and bright, and sunny. Lord, Thou art my God — Thou art wholly mine. Oh, bountiful Lord! help my poverty; oh Lord, how richly have Thy grace and goodness flowed around me, and how cold and insensible I have remained!

Oh, it shall be different! Oh, take me — take me wholly to Thyself; my prayers shall not cease; and if I grow weary or slothful in it, I will wrestle and strive, till Thou enablest me to pray — till Thou fillest my heart, till Thou makest me strong in the power of Thy might. A new year lies before me, dark — no, not dark; nothing can happen to me but what Thy will has foreseen. Let trouble and conflict come! Thou wilt be near me. Oh, my heart is so comforted, so full of joy, for "I will not let Thee go, unless Thou bless me." Amen.

Lulu to Trinchen.

DEAR TRINCHEN,

Your letter might have made me sorrowful, and aunt's illness anxious. But to-day I have entirely given my heart to the Lord. Confidence and joyfulness shall not fail me. Oh, Trinchen, pray for me, as I do for you. Only be of good cheer, my dear ones, the Lord is a wonderful King. He will lead us, all our life, to His honour, and to our peace. Are you in want again? Speak plainly. I am an almoner, and am not rich myself. I will allow myself to advance something. If you wish I can send you fifty thalers. Is it not wonderful that I, a poor girl, came to such

good people, who are so kind to me. Oh dear Trinchen,
I cannot be thankful enough; but you can also be
thankful for me. Aunt is worse, but do you not yourself say, that she is seeking peace? Is not that a great
mercy?

Those who seek Him, find Him; we will rejoice in
that. Dear Trinchen, write me soon a cheerful letter;
but I wish to know all the trouble which presses upon
you; it is not trouble, if we have faith. Only write
in full faith and confidence, as I have been accustomed
to in you. May the Lord strengthen you!

Your faithful
LULU.

Lulu to her aunt.

My HEARTILY BELOVED AUNT,

If I could but be sitting now by your bed! I
would kiss your hands, I would caress your cheeks, I
would nurse you, so that you should soon be well.
Ah, no! Trinchen is doing that already, and the Lord,
— our dear faithful God, does so most of all. How
quickly will the few weeks pass, and then it will be
spring, and I can visit you dear ones. Till then I will
write you many letters, will chatter as though I were
sitting by you, and beguile your time.

You have my Christmas letters now. You will
have been very much pleased to hear how well I am
getting on. If I did but know how to do more for
you; and I do too! Herewith I send you the green
terneaux, for a soft dress for you, when you get up
again. Your old ones are too thin; do accept it! I
am not in want of anything. My blue dress will last

very well till the spring; and then there will be summer clothing. The solitude suits me. Aunt Julia is very affectionate. Dear aunt, give thanks to the Lord, that He brought me here, and not into a worldly life! Now, for the first time, I can fully recognize that; and should I be ever so poor and lowly, I may serve the Lord Jesus Christ, love worship and obey Him, and so I am happy, — unspeakably happy. May you be convinced of it. May you have no anxiety for me, and may you see for yourself that the world brings no joy and no peace. Oh dear, precious aunt! I am very rich and happy. Hold your Lulu dear, who would gladly spread her hands under your feet.

Tuesday, 8th January.

We had a new pleasure to-day. Carry with her four brothers and sisters, Lucy, and Mr. Heber, and I, went on skates under the Lindenberg. It was head-over-heels with the little ones! Mr. Heber and I had nothing to do but to pick them up, and to comfort them; and yet the little people would not leave off. At last, when their noses got too red, and their hands too stiff, we went in. The pastor's wife refreshed us from the great coffee-pot, and with bread and honey as well. Our appetite was not small. I am here at least an hour every day in order to cut out, to contrive, to consider; I shall soon have got through. I see order in cup-boards and drawers, and everything that is necessary.

The pastor's wife is very thankful; the children love me, and I am very happy in the dear house. Carry helps us in the sewing-school. We had them to-day for the second time; the children are far from skilful — but not so in singing. I gave a singing-lesson too the day before yesterday to the domestics. Sophie wins one after another of them to morning prayers, and they know only a few church hymns.

Wednesday, 16th January.

It was pleasant to-day when we set the silver tea-urn on the fine table-cloth. and sweet-meats and "subtleties" as well. Vollberger ushered the pastor and his lady, Mr. Heber, Carry and little Mary, very respect-fully and ceremoniously into the well-perfumed drawing-room. To my joy the pastor's lady was not embar-rassed, and aunt Julia very sociable. Lucy and I acted hostesses. We had made the cakes, and made the tea. The Pastor entertained us almost entirely. I was very glad that the aunt listened to him with such great attention. She thinks him very clever. But I am sorry that she makes fun of Mr. Heber. Not on his own account, — it is no matter to him, but on her own, and on Lucy's. Her love and respect for her aunt, must become less when she hears that.

I will earnestly beg her not to do it. Mr. Heber is a true man, and that is saying a great deal.

Sunday, 20th January.

Herr von Tülsen is here at church on Sundays; he visits at the parsonage, and sometimes makes a short call on the aunt. I do not trouble myself about him. If he could but be sincere towards himself and towards the Pastor!

Thursday, 24th January.

It has snowed very much in the night. Old

Werder could not come to fetch his dinner. I went there with Sophy towards evening. He is lying in bed; no one is with him. If the cold continues, our supply of wood will not hold out. I spoke to the gardener; he has cut great heaps of dry branches from the trees. I believe we might give away this wood without asking the master.

Monday, 28th January.

The cold becomes more and more severe; we must now cook every day for the poor. Many children too since yesterday have been standing, hungry and frozen, before the castle-kitchen. The old cook gives them leavings, but that is not enough. He would gladly cook for them, but Christine, the kitchen-maid, complains of her work, which is increased by it. At morning prayers to-day I read S. Matthew 25th chapter, verses 31 to 46, where it says, "Come, ye blessed of my Father, inherit the kingdom which is prepared for you, from the foundation of the world. For I was hungry, and ye fed Me, etc. For-as-much as ye have done it to one of the least of these my brethren, ye have done it to Me." But to those who stand on His left hand He says, "For-as-much as ye have not done it to the least of these, ye have not done it to Me. And these will go away into everlasting punishment; but the righteous into life eternal." Christine was there. When the cook afterwards asked her to peel some pails of potatoes for the poor children, she did so willingly. Lucy's eagerness for the cooking-room seemed also to abate. Sophy might very well do it, and cook for the old people; but it should not only make an amusement for Lucy, she ought to do it from compassion, and must make a sacrifice. But I said nothing.

Towards evening when the snow was again falling lightly, I invited her to accompany me to the village. She was afraid of the cold, but she took muff and fur and followed me. We went to see Mrs. Grossen who is ill. She was lying in bed. A little boy was laying a few twigs on the dying embers; the room was very cold. Two little girls were squatting on the ground, the smallest child was with her in bed. "Oh hard winter!" moaned the poor widow. "We have given the last penny for wood, and now we have no bread either." I talked with her. Lucy listened silently.

Afterwards I took her to see old Werder. His stove was quite cold, yet he was contented; his help is the warm dinner, which dear young Miss Lucy cooks for him herself every noon. He prayed for the Lord's blessing on Lucy. Lucy cried; I understood her tears. She felt her indifference. When, on going home, I begged her to visit these two houses herself every day, and see after everything that was necessary, she threw her arms round me, and kissed me. We have made a plan to-day. Aunt Julia, Lucy, and I, and Sophy and Vollberger, have divided ourselves among the sick and needy families, which we must visit. The snow is crisp, there are thick ice-flowers on the windows. We shall have eighteen degrees of cold.

31st January.

Lucy is indefatigable in her visits. She sews also for those under her care, and cooks and cares for them most faithfully. Our pastor says, "to a godly life belong also godly works; to do nothing, and only to wish to be idle, and to look on, the soul cannot endure." How happy I am in this active life! How much fresher my heart is! To be idle and absent is very painful. I have experienced that; and must we not give an account of every hour, of every useless word? Oh, one might be very much disheartened at this thought.

Monday, 4th February.

Aunt Julia and Lucy are both obliged to keep their rooms; they both have hoarse coughs. I have undertaken their sick visiting. An icy northwind and a snow-shower almost hindered me from going; the steward and the gardener have very kindly had a path swept for me to the top of the village.

On the way back I made a short call at the Pastor's. They were all sitting together in the little study; even the cradle stood there; one could scarcely turn round. But they all looked cheerful, — the Pastor himself at the head of them. When it was getting dusk, I started for home. I would not suffer that anyone should go with me. It was dismal outside; the wind swept through the bare trees, and over the desolate white plains, and then again thick eddies of snow drove into my face. At the door Vollberger received me, and almost scolded me that I had gone out; and aunt Julia came very attentively to meet me with warm tea. It grew dark, the wind roared more and more. "If anyone were out he must perish," said I; "the snow covers up the roads, and the wind takes the traveller's breath away." As my imagination busied itself with such pictures, I often seemed as though I could hear the rattling of a carriage.

"Do you expect anyone?" asked aunt Julia play-fully, when she observed my frequent anxious listening. Then a post-horn sounded, and a carriage drove quickly over the bridge, into the castle-yard. We sprang up in astonishment, but I only left the room. I ran to the door. It was he; Herr von Schaffau, hidden by fur and snow, greeted me kindly. I know not whether my joy was greater, or my sympathy in his frozen state. I went before him into the room, but Lucy was already coming to meet me.

It was a great delight! and we did everything to refresh him. Then Lucy sat on a footstool at his feet. "Dear uncle, we are very happy that you are here," said she, tenderly. "*We?*" said Herr von Schaffau, playfully and looked at us. "Yes, *we*, my dear Frederic," said aunt Julia with kindly sincerity, and patted him on the shoulder. It is the first time that I have heard her call him by his Christian name. I am so very glad to see a light again in the little tower. He did not tell us much of the town, but only wished to hear about things here. Aunt Julia informed him.

But Rosalie has written a long letter. Herr von Tülsen has been there for some days. He has made friends with her mamma. Rosalie does not trust him, and warns us against him. I do not know what he has told about us here. Mr. Heber is mixed up in it. I do not understand it, but it is of no consequence to me. The whole household was assembled next morning for prayers. I felt that Herr von Schaffau must now undertake my office. He did so for the first time in such a large company. I thanked the dear gentleman very much for it. I thought of the first Sunday when I sang in the same rooms, — "The Holy Ghost we now implore." I sang it to-day; it was different to then. After breakfast aunt Julia had spoken to me. I do not exactly know what she was aiming at. She begged me to be open; I have nothing to conceal from her. She asked whether I really had the intention of refusing Herr von Tülsen's hand, I replied that the matter was long gone by. She seriously set before me whether I had not trifled away my happiness, whether I should not repent it in time. I was able to set her at rest about it. She hinted to me that he would be my greatest enemy, he would calumniate me, he would seek to injure me; she certainly believed he would try to get me out of the house. Even that cannot make me uneasy. How should he calumniate me? My life lies open to everyone. Aunt Julia reproved my supineness, and indeed, as I would not understand in what way I could be calumniated, she eagerly drew the letter of her sister-in-law from her pocket, and read nearly as follows: "The girl is very sly, more sly than you think. If you will not believe that, dear sister, from me, prove it yourself. Does she not already manage all those around her? I hear that in the house and village, she is already considered as the mistress. I think it very natural as I have observed her character. I call it an all-usurping nature. She naturally does not do it by violence; in that very thing her slyness consists. She does it under the guise of love and humanity. Examine how much you yourself are under her influence. Rosalie evidently speaks of her with longing; even Thekla assures me that I do her injustice. So I am the only one who estimate her with clear sight. I except Frederic who, until now at least, does not appear to be deceived by her; though Herr

von Tülsen tries to hint at it. In one thing I do not
understand her — why she leaves Herr von Tülsen so
long in uncertainty. The foolish old man really believes her pious words about poverty and riches. But
I wish from my heart that her slyness may mislead
her here, and that he may give her up."

"Is it possible?" said I, after she had read to the end.
"Yes, my child, it is possible, and still more," replied
aunt Julia. "I only wanted to shew you that you are
not wiser than old people, so that you might believe
me." When she saw how very much I was cast down,
she tried to comfort me. "Go quietly on your way,
and do not allow yourself to feel embittered," she said.
"Oh no," I said, "certainly not; it shall always be a
warning to me to put off the appearance of love, and
to put on the reality. If Frau von Schlichten only
comes here again, I will seek to convince her of my
sincerity; and surely, with the Lord's help, I shall succeed. And do assure her that I shall never give my
hand to Herr von Tülsen; and that I should like to
shew her by my words how very much in earnest I was,
even if, in my great weakness, I should be behindhand
in deeds." Aunt Julia embraced me tenderly. "My
sister-in-law is wise, but I am wiser: my knowledge of
human nature is not small," said she. She begged me,
at the same time, always to give her my confidence.
"Could you really prefer a life in a confined parsonage
to a splendid position?" asked she. "Certainly," I replied. "And Mr. Heber?" she falteringly interrupted
me. I could not help laughing heartily. "Does Mr.
Heber belong to every parsonage? — the kind Mr.
Heber." Aunt Julia laughed with me. "I have just
been thinking, people do not know what they wish;

but confess, has your heart never felt something peculiar?" I grew quite red, but I was able to say to her,
that I had never cherished foolish thoughts. If they
hover over the soul, I cannot really prevent it, but I
give them no room there.

"Then we are quite agreed," said she, "you remain quietly with us; the tempests will pass over."
We both became very merry, and laughed with each
other over the wonderful doings of people. I cannot
say that the letter made me anxious. I was encouraged
rather to go on my way unconcerned. Herr von
Schaffau wished to go with me on my rounds. I took
him to the most needy cases. As the winter continues
so severe, large families are among them whose fathers
are capable of work; only work fails. Herr von
Schaffau was satisfied with our arrangements; and
especially praised the practical counsels of the Pastor.
On the way back we made a short call at the parsonage. It was very disagreeable to me, to find Herr
von Tülsen there. He had brought plenty of toys for
the children from the town, and acted as if he were
the best friend of the house. Filled with the impres-
sions of the letter, I tried to show him my sentiments
plainly.

I earnestly wish that he would no longer stay in
this part of the country on my account. The Pastor
himself reminded him of the way back: it was growing
dusk, and the wind was already driving scudding
showers of snow before it. Herr von Tülsen took very
friendly leave of the parsonage people, then he turned
to Herr von Schaffau, and said lightly with great irony
and bitterness, "I vacate the field to you." Herr von
Schaffau replied nothing; he looked serious and quiet.

On the way back, he walked silently beside me; the wind often drove the snow so violently against us, that he often placed himself protectingly before me. "Only steer as bravely against all the rough weather that comes to hinder you," said he, half in joke, when we entered the door. "It was not bad," I replied. "Nothing is bad," he continued. "It is all as we look upon it; but often we are weak, and look upon the doings of other weak mortals as sad calamities." I thought of Herr von Tülsen, of Frau von Schlichten's letter, and calumnies, and things like that. I then said aloud, "they cannot hurt me." He appeared to rejoice in this confidence.

Yesterday he had business the whole day; the weather is rather milder. Lucy was able to accompany me on my visits. In the evening we sat very comfortably down-stairs in the drawing-room; the parsonage people were invited. Aunt Julia was very cheerful, and Lucy too in the hope that her uncle will return in a short time. I poured out tea, and handed a cup to Herr von Schaffau, and the sugar-basin as well.

He took three of the largest pieces; and then I turned away with the basin. "I beg for just one more," said he; and added that in past days he had not dared to make his tea sweet, but to-day, he begged for this favour on parting. Aunt Julia laughed very much, warned him not to tell his sister that; who maintained already, that I governed house and village. Herr von Schaffau protested rather earnestly that his sister was not wrong, and the parsonage people also jokingly agreed with him. The Pastor said that he must be very careful that I did not encroach on his spiritual office; — in the house my rule was no longer disputed. They combined with it, indeed, great protestations of friendship, but I felt rather awkward; and will be very much on my guard. And I will really leave helping himself to sugar entirely to Herr von Schaffau! I was very friendly with all on saying good night, because I had resolved never to be angry with anyone at the end of the day. One or another might die during the night. Should we not always be on our guard? This morning he went away; we are again alone. After such pleasant days a certain extreme stillness has intervened. We seem all three to feel it.

Lulu to Trinchen.

15th February.

DEAR TRINCHEN,

I direct the letter to you that you may take out this note beforehand. Tell me openly what causes you anxiety? Your last letter is hard to bear. You say that money for your daily need is not wanting, but I enclose ten thalers. Aunt is not worse than usual in winter. Now what is it? Have you secret enemies? I have many here, but what can they do to you? I do not understand you, and desire to know the truth. Is your courage become weak? Oh, then I will speak to you in all confidence. The mighty Lord God is our dear, dear Father. Lent begins this Sunday. I am always so fond of it; — so rich and quiet; mourning and waiting — bright days in between, — foretastes of the spring — of the great resurrection. We are practising now that beautiful hymn: "A Lamb our guilt has borne." Shall I say the fifth verse quite in to your dear faithful heart?

Throughout life's day, oh Lord above,
My thoughts shall rest on Thee;
Thou hast embraced my soul with love,
And it shall cling to Thee.
Thou art my light which shall not pale;
And when my flesh and heart shall fail,
Still I am ever Thine:
And, Lord, to Thee — my high Renown,
Mine utmost powers, to be Thine own,
I steadfastly assign.

So now we are His: to Him belong our cares. I am very joyful whatever may happen; and when my heart fails, Thou shalt remain the portion of my heart. Now good-bye and may He be with you.

Your faithful
LULU.

Friday, 22nd February.

A mild breeze is blowing, the snow is melting, new hope animates the hearts of the poor people. Sophy almost bewails it, because cooking and providing and caring for them will very much cease. I represented to her to-day, and to myself too, that it is not *doing* alone: there lies indeed no small danger in devoting ourselves too much to outward things: the soul has need now and again of introversion, of quiet contemplation; and Lent is a beautiful time for that. How the Pastor warned us about it at prayers to-day.

To-day, oh Lord, to sin I'll die,
And live to Thee eternally:
Thy death (when death had reigned before)
Brought life to me for evermore,
And opened wide the heavenly door.

Oh Saviour! with Thy strength, be near,
And strengthen me to persevere;

Thy word, oh Lord, Thyself explain,
Help me the conflict to maintain,
That there I may the crown obtain.

So praise I Thee eternally, —
My Saviour, Who hast died for me;
I'll praise Thee till the strife is o'er,
And then, safe landed on the shore,
With joy and bliss for evermore.

Saturday, 23rd February.

The Pastor was lamenting to-day that the steward had some wood moved last Sunday, and to-morrow wishes to have the horses put in again. Aunt Julia called him a foolish old fellow, with whom *she* would not be mixed up. He did not desist at Vollberger's warning. *I* must undertake the matter. Since the severe illness of his wife, he has been very attentive to me, and spares no pains to be agreeable to me. The Pastor reminded me of that; but yet I had no inclination, first on account of my "government," and then the steward is head-strong, and feels besides that he has faithfully served the family for more than thirty years, and was accustomed for many years to rule alone. The matter was very burdensome to me, and I put it off. Towards evening I was walking alone by the quiet hedge, a soft air was lightly blowing from the south, the birds were hopping among the twigs, long stripes of green and brown were rising from the fields of snow, the evening bell was sounding from the church on the hill. My heart grew uneasy. It called me to the steward; and I went too. Dear Lord! Thou wishedst to show, that everything which happens in Thy name, has a wonderful power. Dear, faithful Lord! I am still very weak. I went trembling in. The married pair were sitting together: they had just received the news of the happy arrival of a first grand-child. I rejoiced with them. After some time I asked, "Mr. Schulz, shall you have wood moved again to-morrow?" "There we have it!" he roared out, "I thought that a plot was being fabricated there." His conscience was struck; his vehemence gave me courage. "Do you consider it nothing wrong yourself?" asked I. "If I do not have the wood fetched as long as the road is rather firm, I shall ruin waggon and horses," answered he, rather vehemently. I told him how sorrowful at heart it made me, when I saw him act so; because I was convinced that at heart he reverenced and honoured the dear Lord. "Oh, my husband is honest and god-fearing," said the wife, "even if he is different from what is the fashion now." "The ten commandments must always be the fashion," I replied to them, and did they consider it a greater fault if one of their people steals, with the excuse that his children must starve if he did not, than if they desecrate the holy day, in order to spare the horses? Schulz laughed, but his wife said, "The young lady is right, and you are wrong." "Do not let them go to-morrow," I begged earnestly: "and come to-morrow to church, I so seldom see you there. Do not always oppose the Pastor; he means well towards you and towards all, and do you know that thereby you very much grieve Herr von Schaffau?" "If I may I will come often," said the wife. "And you too, dear Mr. Schulz," I went on imploringly," do not only have the fear of God in your heart; make a sacred profession also before the world." "I have grown so old, and should I begin anything new?" he said, half in earnest, half in joke. "The older one grows, the worthier one is of higher honours," I continued.

"Until now you have served men with fidelity and love, now serve the Lord of all men. Will you come to-morrow?" I asked in conclusion. "Out of love to you," he said. "Out of love to me," I asked in wonder, "why so?" "Because I have so much to thank you for," said he, with kindly sincerity. "If you have so much to thank *me* for," I eagerly interrupted him, "as to go to church from love to me, what then must you do from love to the Lord, Who has done a hundred and thousand times more for you? Oh, Mr. Schulz! consider how foolishly you spoke, and come from love to the Lord. Let your whole life, and every action, every breath, be thankfulness towards Him Who has so faithfully led you day by day, for more than fifty years."

I went away and prayed the Lord that He would begin and finish. Sincere prayers have an influence on other souls: I knew the old man was in the church to-day. If I had not secured him yesterday, I had drawn him there to-day. When I went in he was sitting in the steward's pew. The pastor spoke of what the Lord had done for us, and of what we should do for Him in return. That agreed with yesterday's conversation. In the afternoon the Pastor said playfully to me, "Is there no more need of your personal action, and do your very thoughts rule all around us? Schulz was at church to-day, the first time since the harvest festival." I expressed my joy at it, but said no more, and broke off the conversation. I feel as though I should take strength away from my soul, if I speak about such things without some sacred purpose.

Saturday, 2nd March.

The air is mild, the waters are flowing, a yellow-ammer sings all day under my window — I cannot stay in doors, and run towards the quiet hill, and there I hear the larks singing up high in the air.

Oh, Lord God, wilt Thou soon open Thy world of wonders? Oh glorious and mighty God, Thou art my dear Father in heaven!

Monday, 4th March.

Old Werder seems near his end; he is quiet and joyful. Lucy read to him to-day the 17th chapter of S. John. "Dear Miss," he then said, "we shall see each other again above. *I* am going to sleep, *you* will wander longer; but life is short, eternity is long." Lucy feels it very much. She wishes to see him die; and more than once a day looks into his cottage. Mrs. Grosser is well; her two elder boys are employed at the brick-kiln; they work there now, and will soon dig in the field.

Wednesday, 6th March.

A week ago I spoke in the sewing-school to the children of what we could do from love to the Lord. We would not be satisfied with beautiful hymns and stories only, but would make room for Him in our heart, and would clear it of all that may not be worthy of Him. We will go bravely to the work, and then begin to exchange impatience and quarrelsome feelings and unkind words, for gentleness and patience and humility, and pray for a quiet loving spirit, — the greatest ornament for girls and women; — and so on.

To-day I reminded them of the conversation, and told them they might examine themselves whether they had had opportunity of exercising gentleness and patience. One little girl, the baker's Lizzie, looked at me earnestly with her large blue eyes, and nodded. The poor child has a passionate mother, and I have already heard a good deal about it, and because the children with time grow dearer and dearer to me, I feel as though I must do something for them out of school too. Only to this poor child I do not know how. "Do not pry into what is not thy business," and yet I feel strongly about it.

Sunday, 10th March.

Who wishes to get us out of the Plettenhaus? Who are our secret enemies? what causes the old miller to give notice about his money? It would be insecure because the property would deteriorate every year. It must be either paid, or the place sold, by the 1st of May. It seems so incredible to me, that I can scarcely rest. "No one will lend us the money," says Trinchen, "because the miller has right on his side." Aunt has suffered more for some time, how I long for home. I hope to go at Easter, I said so in my letter to Trinchen. I will speak to the miller myself.

Suppose rugged paths should be in store for me now? I was getting on so well that, perhaps, I have grown confident and proud; therefore, I will take patiently, what the Lord sends me. I have great confidence; — He will help us. He will not cause this sorrow to my poor dear aunt. Now, faithful Lord, give me a strong heart.

20*

Thursday, 12th March.

We have laid a wreath of snow-drops on old Werder's grave. Lucy was not with him when he died. She found he had already fallen asleep. He was a poor man, he has worked a great deal, has had a great deal of care; his wife and children died before him; one son lives at a distance, but he was a *rich* man; he was joyful and full of comfort — happier than many thousands. In the afternoon I took Lucy to our work in the garden, a suitable employment in such beautiful spring days. We first made plans — flower garden, vegetable garden, and plantation, — everything will be laid out. We stayed till it grew very dusk, till the little birds became silent one by one, and the children's voices louder in the village. I might well be cheerful; the spring so beautiful, my heart so full. But then the thought of the dear ones at home distresses me.

Saturday, 16th March.

My heart is heavy again. I do not know exactly why; — the days are so bright and spring-like. I feel an anxious presentiment; I cannot help thinking a great deal of home. I was uncertain whether I could not make aunt Julia a confidante of my anxieties, but she might think I wanted a good deal of money from her, as she was always so kind. How could I desire it? Trinchen is right. Aunt really lives much too expensively; the house is almost unused; it would be an advantage to live in a little hired house, and yet I would gladly see my dear aunt spared the sorrow. I spoke to the Pastor; — he has given me more than one piece of good advice.

To-day I seriously considered why I was not more cheerful. Is *that* my joyful courage, my trust and confidence! I walked, in the warm sunshine, by the borders before the green-house. I picked violets, crocuses, snow-drops, hepaticas, and the delicate green of the spiræa. I held the nosegay up against the blue sky. I looked into the bright shining cups of the flowers, my heart expanded, and tears ran gently on to the flowers. Oh, those were happy tears! Yes, dear Lord, Thou art the dear faithful God, I heartily love Thee; love makes me immeasurably happy, rich, and of good courage. Now come what will! If I had been with Trinchen to-day! Everything, *everything* must be ordered and overruled; my heart is very joyful. I could trip again through the garden with Lucy. We hastened to the parsonage.

We were called in there because our talents in gardening had become rather notorious! They wish to make some alterations; the garden was laid out by the old clergyman unpractically and without regard to beauty. The flower-beds and bushes ought to be near the house. The Pastor asked me, indeed, for my advice, but yet would think his own ideas the prettiest, and act upon them. I gave him his way, in order not to call down upon me the reproach of a wish to rule; although I thought it very tasteless. The vegetable garden was left to us. I laid it out with Mr. Heber.

The Pastor's wife was satisfied with everything. We measured out the beds, and then they were firmly trodden; — that was fun! First I, then Mr. Heber; Lucy and the whole troop of children followed. In the midst of the merriment, the garden-gate opened, and Herr von Schaffau came in.

We welcomed him with great joy. He was so very quiet over it, that I was ashamed of my liveliness, and quickly went to my work again. But I was very sorry about it. Mr. Heber's good humour too seemed at an end; did he feel himself injured?

I tried everything to make him merry again, and I succeeded too. But what did the Pastor mean when in the evening he warned me to be cautious towards Mr. Heber? I do not know what they mean; but can scarcely think that Mr. Heber is deceived by my friendly behaviour.

Thursday, 19th March.

My heart almost stops beating when I think that the words of the Pastor's wife might be the truth! Oh no, she talks too much, and likes talking! Could he really believe that my esteem, and what more could I call it, was anything else? Ought I to cherish such foolish hopes? Is he obliged often to be so proud and cold towards me in order to cure me of such folly? and on that account greeted me so coldly yesterday. Oh no, it is not possible!

I thought a great deal, but could not rest. I was sitting by the open window, a mild breeze was blowing on me, the moon looked golden, everything was still, and yet I could hear the movement and breath of spring.

The spring flowers, in the glass-vase before me, looked wonderingly at me with their bright eyes. It seemed as though I must rejoice with the joy of spring.

Then he came in. I knew not whether to be comforted or afraid; he was grave but kind. Oh, if he could but see into my heart. I have no foolish thoughts there, but I cannot endure such a cold apathetic nature. "Lulu," he said, "I thought you had something to forgive me." I looked quietly at him; I cannot understand him. I should like to have told him what was annoying me then, should like to have begged him not to be anxious about it, but I could not, and he seemed to have guessed my thoughts. He laughed and said, "We make ourselves many unnecessary anxieties." Then I felt as though there were nothing that could trouble me, his expression was bright as the spring flowers before me. "What was it?" I said cheerfully. "Foolish thoughts," he replied. So perhaps he knew. I grew confused. I gave him the flowers which he thought so beautiful, it would all have been well if the Pastor's wife had not said that!

Thursday, 21st March.

To-day was too beautiful! We first worked till we were tired; and then we went — aunt Julia, the pastor, and Herr von Schaffau — for a walk — a long way up to the mountains — to the little pine-forest. Here we seated ourselves on the moss, and looked down into the valleys. The pastor began the hymn,

> "To God alone be glory in the highest,
> And thanks for all His grace."

We all joined in. We walked by the beds of spring flowers for a long time, up and down in the moonlight; only aunt Julia went in. The gentlemen talked of beautiful, serious things, and we listened to them.

To-morrow Herr von Schaffau is going to Plüggen; he wishes to be *here* again, before the arrival of his sister. I am very glad of that; I am afraid of her, and should not like to be alone with her. Oh no! that is wrong! I will not fear her, I will very kindly beg her not to be mistrustful, as I am so very sincere in my intentions. She will not be here on my birth-day; I am really glad of that. I wished to have that day still in repose with my dear friends, — and the spring.

Saturday, 23rd March.

The bells are ringing in Palm-Sunday, the sounds are borne to me on the soft air, the sky is rosy and golden with the setting sun; the rosy light is glowing on my white hyacinth, in the open window. Oh, my heart should be thus white, and tender, and pure, and irradiated by the light of heaven. Such deep peace, such spring-like life, and such a festive peal should be within! I read the 13th chapter of Corinthians, and drank it in with all my soul. "Love is long-suffering and kind, is not puffed up, seeks not her own, is not easily provoked, bears all things, believes all things, hopes all things, endures all things." I no longer fear Frau von Schlichten. Oh no! however much she may be against me, I will hold fast this love in my heart. With this love, I will overcome everything. I am of good courage because Thou, dear Lord, art my faith-ful Lord.

Sunday, 24th March.

Lucy sent me in the afternoon to the parsouage. She has something going on with Sophy. She knows, indeed, about my birthday; aunt Julia too is mysterious. I rejoice in the anticipation of the day! Herr von Schaffau will come to-morrow evening, or Tuesday morning.

Only I will not look forward to it too much, that is not well. But, dear Lord, I am also contented that the day should be as Thou hast appointed.

Monday, 25th March.

I considered the day as the eve of my birthday. Lucy wished to be alone, I was glad of it. I walked by the quiet hedge, I listened to the singing of the birds, and watched the little weeds, so modest, and yet so fresh, and in such lovely flower. Wild geese were passing over far above me on the bright blue sky; it was no melancholy autumnal note, but the cheerful note of spring; they were going to the north. Oh, I should like to soar and fly far, far away! What is going on now?

I am sitting in the quiet room; the moon is shining on the white hyacinth; I am so anxious. We went towards evening to meet Herr von Schaffau, he did not come; the carriage, which was to fetch him from the train, brought Frau von Schlichten unexpectedly. She saw our joyful greeting, and then our disappointed hope; she was very sharp. Since there was only room in the carriage for one person, Lucy was told to get in. Lucy refused. Frau von Schlichten commanded. Rosalie got out to accompany me, although her mother did not seem to wish it. Rosalie is very cordial. She said with a sigh that alas we should not be able to be long together. Must I go? Surely Frau von Schlichten is thinking of it. Why does she hate me?

Frau von Schlichten was downstairs in the blue room. I tried once more to greet her kindly; until now her heart has been closed against me. When we were placing ourselves at table, and wished first to pray in silence, she sat down quickly and whispered something about "intolerable hypocrisy." I was frightened and hesitated, but I thought I ought to do it. Lucy and aunt Julia followed my example. Aunt Julia is very much set against her sister-in-law; but yet not in a desirable way. Frau von Schlichten was out of humour all the evening; even the flowers which we have in the windows gave her cause for vexation.

"*She* had never been able to get such from the gardener,", she said, bitterly. I went upstairs early. How must it be? It will be very hard to me to go from here. I opened upon the verse, "The heart of man strikes out a path, but the Lord alone grants to him to walk on it."

> Lord, as a child I Thee obey,
> And thus my blessings shall increase:
> For, walking in that narrow way,
> My feet shall find the path of peace.

Dear Lord, as Thou wilt: receive my heart!

———

Trinchen to Lulu.

Plottenhaus, 23rd March.

You were right, dear Lulu, I made myself unnecessarily anxious. The Lord has ordered all, even if otherwise than we thought. Your dear aunt lies

without hope, and yet with a great deal of hope.   She
says from her full heart,

> * "Jesus my Redeemer lives,
> Christ my trust is dead no more;
> In the strength this knowledge gives
> Shall not all my fears be o'er?
> Though the night of death be fraught
> Still with many an anxious thought."

So be of good comfort, dear child; the Lord has
redeemed her from many sorrows.   Yes, she has fallen
asleep; I cannot keep it back from you, she has joyfully departed.   Anxiety about you did not trouble
her any more; your letters were a bright fountain of
life and refreshment to her.   Come my child! you
shall lay a wreath of violets on her white forehead,
and put a nosegay into her tender hands.   Travel
post to Wenderburg.   Jacob will be there; you can
then go on foot.   But the Lord be with you.   These
are rough roads — these are trials; but see whether the
Lord can yet help.

TRINCHEN.

Plottenhaus, 29th March, Good-Friday.

Dear Lord, I am still Thine; the deeper Thou
humblest me, the more Thou wilt lift me up; the more
tribulation Thou sendest me, the more shall I be comforted.   I feel myself resting on Thy heart.   The bells
have died away, the hymns have ceased.   I stood
alone by the fresh made grave.   A damp mist came
on, the sky is clouded, everything mourns — a true
day of death.   I could not help weeping very, very

much.　Dear Lord, Thou hast wept still warmer tears; Thou hast been in agony before me; oh, come and comfort me!　Oh Lord, I know well Thou *wilt* come. I feel it already, only I am very weary and ill to-day.

30th March.

Trinchen goes about as if in a dream; I must be her strength.　Because I must be, the Lord will fit me for it.　She thinks of the future; it will be hard to her to leave our dear home, only on my account.　Yes, indeed, it will be mournful when *I* must wander out, to see strange people in my dear rooms, in the garden, up there under the beech-tree, when the door is closed against me.　I cannot help crying, but Trinchen must not know it; — that will make me strong.　But now I am weary, I will rest.　Where was I a week ago?　I was sitting on the grassy ridge by the pine-trees. Spring was in us — around us; we sang,

"To God alone be glory in the highest."

Can I not sing that now?　I have sung it; at first, I could not help crying, but more and more firmly with a full voice.　Trinchen and Jacob were soon standing behind me, and then I got more cheerful.　I wished to comfort them.　Yes, "Well for the servants of the Lord."　"Trinchen," I said, "we will be very cheerful; with the Lord's help, we will celebrate the feast of the resurrection to-morrow."

"The one whom we love has fallen asleep, so we three will hold fast to each other, and love each other dearly, and never part.　If we live no longer in the dear house, we shall take peace with us; and the Lord

Who has enriched us here, will above all be with us."
Trinchen gave me her hand and smiled. "It is well,"
said she; but Jacob went away and I quite believe he
was crying. The few days since I left Braunsdorf
appear like a long life-time to me.

On my birthday I rose early. I went towards the
hedge, I saw the quiet parsonage, the castle dreaming
in the mist of spring; I did not think it was for the
last time. When I came back I had a joyful surprise.
Mr. Schulz himself was standing on the corridor to
bring me his congratulations, and from his wife a tea-
serviette, spun from her own Braunsdorf flax.

Oh, I love her very much! The gardener presented me a little group of dried flowers, — beautiful
and fresh as I had never seen them. But in my room
was a garden of flowers, and lights and cakes and
presents.

The aunt and Lucy and almost all the household
were assembled, and on my entering they sang, "Praise
the Lord, — the mighty King of glory." I joined in
with emotion, then gave my hand to each, and thanked
them with agitated heart. Aunt Julia kissed me tenderly and wished me every happiness; Lucy hung on
my neck. Oh, the abundant love was the most beautiful thing in the festival! Suddenly I saw Frau von
Schlichten standing at the open door.

She had been watching; then she said, in great
excitement, "You are formally receiving homage here."
"The homage of sincere love," said aunt Julia, bitterly.

But I grew sad. I begged Frau von Schlichten
not to be angry with me. She looked angrily at me,
and left the room. Aunt Julia tried to comfort me;
"it cannot continue so," she said. "Then must I go?"

"Either you or she," replied the aunt. I know not how joyfully that thrilled my heart — I repent very much of my pride. We had prayers, we breakfasted together as usual. Scarcely half an hour had passed, I was alone and rejoicing over my beautiful presents, when in came Betty — the far from respectable maid of Frau von Schlichten, and gave me a letter. I read it; I felt how it chilled my heart like ice. I was obliged to hold by the chair. It was written in the utmost anger. She had seen through my plans, I should leave the house this moment, and no sooner leave the room, than get into the carriage; — with a threat of shameful scenes for me. "Shall I help you pack?" asked the maid, scornfully. I was quiet and kind towards her, and also allowed myself to be helped by her, — hard as it was to me. "Betty," said I, "do you know that you make me sorry when you try to injure me?" She looked defiantly at me. "Oh, Betty, you will repent it some day; I have never done any harm to you; and if I have injured you, I beg your pardon to-day when I am going from here. I certainly have never meant any harm." She now looked at me in wonder. "Yes," I continued, "Frau von Schlichten too will repent some day that she has been so violent, but tell her that I am not angry with her, and that I am only very sorry not to have gained her love." Betty was from that moment embarrassed but kinder. "Yes," she said, "her mistress was in a terrible rage. But, perhaps, it will be of no help to her," said she, and then gave similar hints to those of the Pastor's wife. I am very much ashamed that I should have given occasion to such speeches. I broke off the conversation. I only asked for aunt Julia and Lucy. They

are in mistress's boudoir and know nothing of it. My
things were soon packed, the carriage drove up. I
stepped in. Before that, I sealed up the letter of Frau
von Schlichten. I wished to find an opportunity of
sending it to the Pastor; then he would be clear about
it, and my journey explained to him. I had begged
him to break the news carefully to aunt Julia and
Lucy; Betty herself undertook the care of my letter.
She was for the moment very honest in her good intentions towards me. At the door, Betty handed me
another letter from Trinchen with a black seal. I
broke it open. I read it, I cried passionately. I know
not how Betty persuaded me to get into the carriage.
I was as if in a dream. In the yard Vollberger ran
after me. "What is the matter?" He saw me crying.
The coachman did not wish to stop; he was obliged
to. I gave him Trinchen's letter, with the request
that he would give it to aunt Julia. My departure is
now explained, even if Betty does not take any care
about my letter. The coachman did not drive me to
the first station, but to the second. I was sorry for that,
but Frau von Schlichten had seen through me; I was
hoping and wishing to meet her brother at the railway
there. I wished to pour out my heart to him, he must
share my sorrow. I got out, I stood waiting for the
train; then a train came on the other side. It stopped;
suddenly I saw Herr von Schaffau's astonished expression from a window. I involuntarily raised my hands
at him; the train roared away. After a few minutes,
I was flying in the opposite direction. Unwillingly
I got in to the hateful post-chaise. Can I not walk
as well as the bürger-women? But I must overcome
much in life.

In Wenderburg I found Jacob. That was a quiet
mournful walk. We read a great deal together the
first day here, and I often went to my aunt's coffin.
How beautiful and peaceful she looked! I always
thought she would see better days through me, and
now it is well that she has not lived to see my ill-
fortune.

***

Lucy to Lulu.

Braunsdorf, 28th March.

DEAR PRECIOUS LULU,

Will you open this letter? Will you not hate us
too much? How I have boiled over since yesterday!
But uncle also bit his lips and turned away. Dear
Lulu! you *must* come back again! We shall not be
able to make up for the wrong, but if you are only
here! If I had but come by the railway yesterday!
I ran after you, but I had forgotten the money, and
uncle soon came and fetched me back. Lulu, I
must write to you that we are all very sad. Aunt
Julia has been very angry; uncle reproved us. Oh
dear Lulu, I have overcome, — I prayed for my mother
and for myself, that I might have patience and love
in my heart. "What was Fräulein von Plettenhaus
doing at the railway?" asked uncle abruptly when he
arrived. I laughed at him. "Lulu is keeping her
birthday." Oh no, he had seen you too plainly. He
was very earnest and would know the truth. Mother
was gentle and kind, spoke of domestic peace, of
heartfelt love to each other, — I know not what all,
but she said that she was the cause of your hasty departure.

It was then that uncle turned away, and I ran quickly beyond Grauberg. If uncle had not come after me, I should have been with you now. I would comfort you, yes, and love you dearly. If you do not come, I must hate my mother! Oh, forgive me these words. I cannot live without you. Write at once, I am very impatient.

Your dear

LUCY.

Aunt Julia to Lulu.

DEAR LULU,

Do not wonder that I write so quietly. I must tell you that I think it is quite right, that it has come to this. Fire and water do not do together. My sister-in-law is going to Plüggen; I shall stay here with you dear children. The last time pleased me so, that I only wish to live so till my end. Frederic, in my opinion, could not have been more angry; yet he was grave enough. Directly after the festival, his sister is going into banishment;—so it appears to me. Thekla is beside herself. Rosalie hopes to remain with us.

I do not know yet whether I ought to say yes to it. What do you think? It was so delightful alone. My brother-in-law wished at first to write a few words to you himself, but he declares it is not necessary. You know all that he could say, and what he thinks of the matter. I think so too of myself, and so will be brief. The death of your aunt makes your quick departure explicable to people. It is whispered about indeed, but what does that matter? You, dear Lulu, are no doubt very sad at your loss. Hasten as fast as possible to us. We will comfort you. You know that

I am your dear aunt now. Adieu, child of my heart! We will all fetch you from the railway. My child, you surely wish for money; — I send you herewith fifty thalers. Such opportunities do not often occur. Vollberger attends to the flowers in your room. The birthday table is unmoved, but it has become richer; you can guess by whom! There is a sorrowful condition of things here now, you may be glad that you are away.

I press you very tenderly to my heart.

JULIA VON SCHLICHTEN.

Lulu to Aunt Julia and Lucy.

You dear, dear ones! may I open my softened heart to you? I have been crying the whole evening; when I received your dear letters, I believed my happiness was gone for ever; because I never can return to you. Oh, hear me farther. Just because I love you so much, I cannot go: I ought not to separate mother and child. Trinchen has maturely considered it with me. I feel she is right. I give up everything; I stay here. The Lord has already foreseen what will become of me. But hold me dear! You, dear precious aunt! even when far from you, I must yet be near to your heart; and you, my beloved Lucy! will be my companion from morning to evening. I shall love you and will pray for you; will write to you much and often, and you must write again to me. My longing after you is very great. The Lord will help me. Oh, how quiet and lonely it is here, and the spring is coming joyfully on. Many thanks, dear and honoured aunt, for the money. The twenty thalers which were in advance, I send back again. Everything here is in a tangle, but I have not got to business yet; it is all the same, I am not afraid, and the faithful ones here in the house will also be provided for. I will write more next time, I am so weary and tired. The Lord be with us all.

In faithful love

Your

LULU.

.3rd April.

The letters are written and sent off, and so it is settled. I remain here. I was crying: Trinchen came behind me, then I turned round. "Trinchen," I said cheerfully, "I shall soon leave off crying, and shall soon be merry again." Trinchen kissed me on my forehead. But Jacob said to me, when I was standing by him under the chestnut, "It is all right: you are here again." That touched me very much, I told him we should never separate again.

We have made a plan that as Trinchen is not on the full allowance from the foundation, we shall remain together. From this year she gets an annuity of thirty thalers. Jacob wishes some time hence to go to his brother's son, but when that is over, he says, he wishes to enjoy the rest of his years here.

The Bailiff is by Trinchen's advice my guardian. He quite agrees that I should remain here some years. I shall become rather more sensible then. Trinchen always believes that I have been rash and careless. I willingly leave her in that opinion; I would rather stay here than make any new attempts now. The

21*

Bailiff has set before us that it would be much better
to sell the house and garden: and he hopes to get so
much that almost a hundred thalers interest would remain for me.   He wishes us to rent the gardener's
cottage in the plantation.

Jacob shall be employed; and if Trinchen and I
take in sewing we should get on.   But we have all
three resolved rather to live sparingly and to live here.
Trinchen is the bravest, but it would go to her heart
too if she were obliged to go out of the house.   Dear
house! every nook in the garden — my heart stops
beating when I think of the little house in the plantation.   Early to-morrow I am going to the Miller.

Thursday, 4th April.

The morning was lovely and still.   I went through
the meadows along by the little swift brook; up above
on the road ploughs were rattling along, and larks and
black-birds were singing.   I felt as though I could
take hope.   I knew not yet that things go on very
strangely in the world; and that the Lord makes use
of many things to draw our hearts to Him.   I flew
into a passion, and felt deep scorn for the man who
could do such an abominable thing.

Just that has made me strong: he shall not triumph.
I will serve my God also up there in the little house.
Herr von Tülsen is 'our secret enemy; ho has driven
me away there also.   Does he think that he shall win
me more easily when so helpless?   Trinchen thinks
so, but can but little reconcile herself to such conduct.
The old Miller reckons himself and me happy to have
found such a wonderful purchaser, who is so set upon
it, that he would pay beyond the price.

The Bailiff with great wisdom as he wishes to make the best of the property, will drive him higher. At the sale at another time without this opportunity, there would be nothing remaining. The Miller's money is really unsafe: nothing has been done to the house for ten years. But should I like to live by such money? the thought is repugnant to me. I cannot, and I cannot tell the reason to the Bailiff. I have written everything to my dear Pastor — everything! He will advise me. It seems to me as if the Lord would send help through human beings. I told Trinchen much about Braunsdorf. She loves Herr von Schaffau very much; she says to me, she fancies him herself like my late father. I cannot help thinking a great deal of Braunsdorf; it is quite impossible that I should never go there again. I have had a comforting dream, and could not help thinking of it the whole morning.

Tuesday, 9th April.

I walked in the garden; the chestnuts are just bursting into leaf, the gooseberries are green, spring is lovely as it was last year. Jacob is digging, has planted his peas and other things beside; I have not the courage to prevent him; — I do not know what he expects. I went farther down the meadows. Goose-Riekchen was here again with her golden company; she was glad to see me. Dora also came to meet me with her knitting. She looked orderly and so did the little one. I was glad, and resolved as soon as possible to begin the school again. On that account I went again to the plantation-cottage. It was shut up and quite empty. I looked through the windows at the rooms — room enough. Before the door there is a stone bench and two acacias. I seated myself. The sunshine lay so quietly on the lonely garden; only the birds were singing merrily. My dear Plettenhaus with its grey gable is to be seen here. I cried at first, but when I had sat longer and thought and looked more earnestly into the blue sky, a great peace came over me. Dear Lord, I know it well! Thou wilt make me very rich there, in the little house.

I will take care of Trinchen and Jacob, and I will keep a sewing school and will love everybody very much. I came joyfully home and told Trinchen how comfortable the plantation-cottage was; and how cheerfully we should live together there. We sat very industriously at work by the open window.

Trinchen told about the past, of the youth of my dear aunt. It was so full of hope and yet unobserved, — its leaves have dropped off one by one — it is a melancholy picture.

Trinchen warns me to expect nothing from the future. At that she looked so sharply at me. No, I will live in the present, and leave my dear Father in heaven, to care for the future. If my health is good, I can earn money: if I become weak and ill, the Lord can provide. Yet the world is very beautiful and glorious. I rejoice in the splendour of the spring. Shall I soon have some letters?

Tuesday, 16th April.

The will is to be opened on the 1st of May, and the seals will be taken from the things; but we have an inclination to move beforehand. Many people come to look over the house and garden which is very disturbing. It will be sold on the 3rd of May.

Trinchen looks so pale that I am afraid she is taking harm. I also — and must not let it be observed. ,Grey clouds are piled up over the village; single heavy drops are falling; the nightingales are singing.

Jacob is standing under the chestnut-tree with folded arms, and is looking over the garden. He is often lost in thought, and has left off working.

Sunday, 21st April.

We are in the plantation-cottage. Lord, dear God, help us! We were at church. The day was very quiet. Towards evening I sat down to the piano and sang, "Commit thou thy ways." Trinchen and Jacob sang with me, and then we wept together. And yet we are not sad, we felt wonderfully supported.

Tuesday, 23rd April.

Trinchen is lying in bed. The weather is very ungenial; it is well that we have made the necessary move.

If Trinchen lies ill in bed, I might be anxious. Oh no! my soul is still in the Lord, Who will help me, for "He is my refuge, my help and my defence; for that He is great, I shall not be moved. Hope in Him at all times, ye people, pour out your heart before Him; God is a refuge for us."

Wednesday, 24th April.

A bill came from the physician. I did not wish to wake Trinchen; besides I knew that we have not so much money. I wrote to the physician to say that we would pay in May. It was very hard to me, but I asked him to come immediately to Trinchen: she seems to me very ill. Cold showers are driving against the window. It is desolate outside, and no letters from Braunsdorf.

Friday, 26th April.

The physician came: he also prescribed medicine. Jacob went with the last money to the apothecary. I set little Dora as a watcher in the house, and ran quickly to the Bailiff's. I begged to borrow a little money. They were very sympathizing. The wife thought whether I was equal to so many cares, and that I should rather go among other people. "I will first wait upon Trinchen till her death," I said, and could not help crying. When I came home, I made some soup. The wind rushed through the chimney; doors and windows rattled. I lighted a fire in the room, because it was cold. Trinchen sighed, I ought not to do so much. Oh, how gladly I do it! She looked searchingly at me. I repressed my feeling. She did not observe how anxious I am about her.

Jacob came back with the medicine. Towards evening Trinchen fell asleep. I wandered out. The house is too small. I cannot find a place in it to have a good cry. I went along the Herrenstieg — the wind was roaring in the tree tops; it was desolate upon the common; the shepherd was not sitting under the beeches; great rain clouds were passing over the valley. The rain drove me on. I came by the Plettenhaus; it lay so still and grey and desolate. I wished to go in; it was shut up. The wind clattered on the old green-house, a heavy gush of rain drove me in there; I sat and wept — I know not how long.

A wonderful gleam roused me from my thoughts. I went into the garden. The dark clouds were gone towards the east; the sun had found an opening and shone upon the world of spring in wondrous colours. The young green and the dark pines looked purple and golden. The poplars gleamed bright against the deep violet sky; there was a complete rain-bow over the dear Plettenhaus. Not a breath was stirring, it was hushed and cool, and fresh fragrance filled the air: the colours became more and more glowing; earth and sky vied with each other. I breathed deeply, I folded my hands, it was a miracle — a glory. I could have shouted aloud for joy, and awe, and adoration.

Should I still be dismayed or sorrowful? Oh no! I went to the plantation-cottage; it was illumined with the same light. Jacob in his little room was singing,

> "Only be still a little while,
> And draw your comfort from within."

Trinchen was sitting up in bed; the glow of evening was rosy on her face. She was watching with joy the rain-bow over dear Plettenhaus.

She was better; she had had some sleep: her courage too and her confidence were strong again. That is a token of peace, she said, a token of blessing. "Oh yes, the Lord will make up for all Trinchen." My heart is already full of thankfulness beforehand.

> * "Oh would I had a thousand tongues,
> To sound Thy praise o'er land and sea!
> Oh! rich and sweet should be my songs,
> Of all my God has done for me!
> With thankfulness my heart must often swell,
> But mortal lips Thy praises faintly tell.

Ye little leaves, so fresh and green,
That dance for joy in summer air,
Ye slender grasses, bright and keen,
Ye flowers, so wondrous sweet and fair;
Ye only for your Maker's glory live,
Help me, for all His love, meet praise to give.

Father, do Thou in mercy deign
To listen to my earthly lays:
Once shall I learn a nobler strain,
Where angels ever hymn Thy praise,
There in the radiant choir I too shall sing
Loud hallelujahs to my glorious King."

So we sang. Trinchen is up; she is better. We
have made our plans.

Braunsdorf, 26th September.

Oh wondrous King! Ruler of land and seas,
Thee let our feeble praises please.
Thou hast dispensed to us Thy Father's grace;
If through temptation we should flee His face,
          Be Thou, indeed,
          Strength in our need;
          Let our tongue sing,
          Our voice with praises ring.

Praise thy Creator's wonders, glorious sky!
So far beyond man's utmost majesty.
Light of the sun, shoot forth thy golden rays —
The brilliance which earth's utmost round surveys.
          Praise Him afar
          Each moon and star!
          Such a glorious Lord
          Well may be adored!

Sing thou, my soul, sing with a joyful voice,
    Sing hymns of faith and trust!
Let every thing that breathes in Him rejoice
    Cast thyself in the dust.

He is the same,
His praise proclaim;
The Lord of hosts adore,
Here and for evermore!

Bring alleluias ye who know the Lord,
Who hold your Saviour dear;
Sing alleluias ye who keep His word,
Abiding in His fear.
Believe the word from me,
It shall be well with thee:
When sin and death are passed,
Thou wilt rejoice at last!

The Lord blesses us ten-fold. He blesses a hun-dred-fold without our merit; — pure mercy! He has blessed me a thousand-fold. I can do nothing but love Thee! Lord, receive me, with all my weaknesses, just like a weak child! but yet receive me wholly. Trinchen has given me a beautiful wedding-address — "Do not suppose you are at an end now, and can rest securely on your happiness. Life for you is now only beginning. Hitherto it was like a walk on the shore: you rejoiced in the lovely flowers and in the sparkling waves, but now you must go out on to the restless sea, and storm and waves will not fail to rise. Thank the Lord that you have a faithful friend at your side; but hold fast to the true Pilot, Who alone can support you over all the waves, without Whom the love of the truest friend is neither comfort nor help." Amen! so may it be.

Dear Trinchen, your education of me is finished. Some one who loves me as dearly will continue it.

But every spring, with God's help, we shall go for some weeks to the dear Plettenhaus. Jacob is already pleasing himself that, on my birthday, the old greenhouse shall be a real flower garden, and we shall eat ripe cherries! He is very glad that it came to nothing with his brother's son; and smokes his Louisiana again: and Trinchen is taken care of, and eats coffeebread now every morning. I was afraid she would not get on well with aunt Julia; but Lucy writes to me that they are living splendidly together. The dear Pastor's sister is the right person among them, and is a better governess than I was. Although my dear lord and husband said playfully yesterday, that as my education had been so eminently successful in the Plettenhaus, he should like to see there an educational establishment for young ladies! House and situation would be suitable for it.

Vollberger came just now and asked, with what horses I should please to go out.

I could not help smiling. "That is your master's business to decide," replied I, "go and ask him." "Master has just sent me," was his answer. "Then go to him and say, I would rather go with the horses that he has decided on." Vollberger did not like going. "Will you not fix, dear lady; master is in rather an ill temper," said he. I could not help replying to him, "My husband is *never* in an ill temper." Vollberger cannot forget that he has carried his master on his arm.

But I will never decide in matters which are not in my department. I wish to be a very lowly wife —

a noble lady like the one who is kneeling in the effigy by the altar — thus gentle and devoted and pious and faithful.

In that help me, dear Lord!

THE END.